A Trick of Fate

**More from Phase Publishing
by**

Rebecca Connolly

Agents of the Convent

Fortune Favors the Sparrow

The Ears Have It

Of Mist and Mirrors

The Arrangements

An Arrangement of Sorts

Married to the Marquess

Secrets of a Spinster

The London League

The Lady and the Gent

A Rogue About Town

A Tip of the Cap

The Spinster Chronicles

The Merry Lives of Spinsters

The Spinster and I

Spinster and Spice

A Trick of Fate

Agents of the Convent
Book Four

Rebecca Connolly

Phase Publishing, LLC
Seattle

Cover art by Tugboat Design
http://www.tugboatdesign.net

Phase Publishing, LLC first paperback edition
October 2024

ISBN 978-1-952103-73-5
Library of Congress Control Number 2024918746
Cataloging-in-Publication Data on file.

Acknowledgements

To Baroness Orczy, the queen of writing masters of disguises. Thank you for inspiring my very first love of spies, spy romance, and the intricate weaving of the two into historical settings. I bow before your awesomeness.

And to Percy Pigs. Oh, I miss you all the time. Ten points to Marks and Spencer.

Want to hear about future releases and upcoming events for Rebecca Connolly?

Sign up for the monthly Wit and Whimsy at:

www.rebeccaconnolly.com

A Proclamation

By Miss Leonora Masters
Headmistress of Miss Masters's Finishing School

Forasmuch as it has been thus Ordained by the powers that be that the Rearing of gently bred ladies requires some assistance, and in Keeping with traditions long established, It has been decreed that such rearing Needs proper establishment for training purposes, Given the span and scope of such development.

As it pleases the powers that be, Never forgetting the honor due to her subjects, Development and education of young ladies shall be Courteously and courageously given.

Owing to the need for such establishment, Unto the finishing of the female sex, Nobility shall be thus encouraged, Their patronage much desired, to Relinquish the education of such female persons as aforementioned Yet in their youthful and less informed state Into such qualified care.

Nevertheless, with charity and succor, females of a Lesser status shall be generously and Indubitably sponsored in their similar attendance herein For the purpose of gaining appropriate Education as befits needs and station.

Occupied thusly, this establishment shall henceforth Render such superior instruction and care, Defending the virtue and honor of her pupils, Engendering appropriate accomplishment upon all, Avowing to maintain the standards and Traditions of her forebears, and shall Henceforth fulfil all other obligations as so indicated.

Given under my Hand at Miss Masters's Finishing School in Kent, the 1st day of March, 1790, in the Thirtieth year of His Majesty's reign.

God save the King
Leonora Masters

Chapter One
London, 1826

This was not the way to her father's house.

It could not be.

Granted, Lucy Allred had never been to the house, given that her father had only recently retrenched, but this was not in a part of London that any respectable person would choose to reside. Night was falling, and with the natural shadows seemed to be several unnatural ones. Light did not seem to touch any portion of this region, and she wondered if that was also the case in daylight. The discoloration on buildings was evident, the filth of windows plain to see, and the scraps of life itself seemed to merely hang about on the prevailing dampness in the air.

This was certainly not the same neighborhood she had left her father in when she had gone to live and teach at Miss Masters's School for Fine Young Ladies at the start of term. Not even remotely close in location or respectability, which meant her father had been lying when he had assured her that the house he had retrenched to was not far at all from the house she had left him in.

It was no great surprise that her father had lied to her; it was only the magnitude of this lie that was irritating.

Where in the world was the coachman taking her?

She should have known something was wrong when her father had refused to give her the address of the new house. Before today, she'd thought perhaps he had only neglected to do so, but now…

Was it shame that had kept him from sharing that detail with her? It was not as though she had all of London memorized and could place a particular address in a moment. They had been coming to London every Season since she had turned sixteen, but her familiarity with the city had been limited to Mayfair, with few exceptions. And then earlier this year, she'd grown more familiar with Cheapside. Not excessively, though, as her father was rather particular about how and where Lucy spent her time.

Whatever it was, her uneasiness was growing the deeper into London the carriage was taking her. She hadn't expected her father to send a coach to meet her at the Bell at Bromley, but there it had been, the driver unfamiliar, but seeming to be perfectly respectable in all aspects and waiting to take her into London to return to her father. It was even a comfortable coach, which was also unexpected, given her personal history with their family's coaches.

Oh, bother… Had her father changed in location only and chosen to exploit the newfound savings into other amenities? It would be just like him to pride himself on living within his limited means in house only and maintaining the lifestyle he craved in every other regard. The man could land himself in debtor's prison and still expect to be waited on by someone of a lowlier station. Everything was about appearances and standing, regardless of the reality of their finances.

He would have foisted Lucy off on any man of distinction and fortune had she any sort of dowry to tempt them.

But her dowry was limited to the portion of her mother's own dowry that had been designated as such. It had been intended for her father to add to the portion as time went on, but it had sat on its own for her entire life. Five hundred pounds was all she could answer for, and no one wanted so meager a sum. Her father had no idea that Lucy had discovered the paltry amount of her dowry some weeks ago, and she intended to keep it that way.

The rush to get her married off had halted when her mother had died last year, and the mourning period that had followed had granted her a blessed reprieve. Her father had hoped she would make an advantageous match in what remained of the Season when she had been permitted to participate in it, but the interest had been minimal at best.

Lucy was two-and-twenty, which meant she ought to have been

married, or soon to be, according to Society's standards, but here she was, a teacher at a finishing school. A highly respectable one, there was no doubt, but an employed woman would never truly be sought after by those of a station to which her father aspired. He hadn't argued when the position had been offered to her, making some offhand comment about the cost of running a household being decreased for having her gone and the benefits of being associated with an illustrious school, and he had assured her that as soon as his finances were resolved, he would secure her a better dowry so she could make a match.

Lucy had no aims or schemes for any such thing, but she would welcome the opportunity to form a life away from her father's increasingly bad habits and poor taste. They were in such debt, it was a wonder anyone still associated with him. But the name still carried weight somehow, and so they were not cast off yet.

Yet being the operative word.

It was only a matter of time, and Lucy finally had a contingency plan for herself with being at the school. She would never make enough to free her father from eventual prison, and he would call her an ungrateful daughter for doing nothing to get him out, but she would accept the insult. They could sell everything they owned, and it would still not cover what was owed. He was making his own messes and would have to take the consequences when they inevitably came.

If they came.

There seemed to be no haste in ensuring that a gentleman became aware of any such thing in his life. Everyone seemed perfectly content to let the man sink himself deeper and deeper into the chasm of debt, which was an utter farce if she ever saw one. If they never received what they were owed, how could they consider themselves satisfied in any manner? What good could it possibly do to have someone remain indebted to another?

One thing was for certain: there would be no one calling upon the Allreds in this part of town. Perhaps that was something that could assist her father in limiting his spending habits. If no one called upon them, how could he be tempted?

Lucy laughed to herself and rubbed her brow in disbelief at her own naivete. Her father needed no incentive to be tempted. Temptation was the topic of his thoughts at any given moment, and the very air that he breathed. Temptation was his oldest friend and his truest love.

She'd have thought temptation killed her mother if she hadn't known better.

As the coach took another turn onto a somehow even darker, danker street, Lucy sighed to herself, her humorless laughter gone along with her indignation. She would have done better to stay at the school for the winter break. Even spending the Christmas holidays there would have done her more good than coming home to this. The headmistress, Miss Bradford, and her niece, Miss Tess Ridley, would be at the school, after all, and both of them were good company. Tess was only fifteen, but she was wise beyond her years and had a sparkling wit that was remarkably engaging.

Lucy had enjoyed having Tess as a student this last term in her logic and philosophy course, but she could not say how the girl would have responded to social occasions with her teacher as a guest. The same could probably be said of her comportment and elocution students, but she did her best to be relatable as well as respected.

The bigger question in Lucy's mind was what she would teach in the coming term, aside from French. That had been her sole subject initially, but then one of the other teachers had needed to take a holiday for the fall term, and Lucy had leapt at the chance to teach more, particularly with the increased income from it. Now, as she understood it, the teacher she had been covering for would return and take up at least some of her classes again. Miss Bradford had assured Lucy that she would have a place and that it would all work out, but there was no comfort in those words for Lucy. Her father used the phrase regularly and nothing ever worked out.

As evidenced by wherever this coach was taking her.

So long as Miss Bradford did not have Lucy teach composition or art, she could probably manage any of the basic topics of the school. But there was also a penmanship class, and Lucy had been praised for her elegance and neatness of hand. Perhaps…

The coach hit a dip in the road, and Lucy was jostled roughly against the side, smacking her head on the window's edge with surprising sharpness. Wincing and rubbing at the spot that her bonnet had done nothing to protect, Lucy pushed herself farther away from the window and wondered if they were actually going to drive through the Thames at some point.

London was far too large for her comfort, and there was far too much of this rather seedy side of it than she had ever expected.

Where were all the people? London was always bustling—she had experienced it year after year—but she hadn't seen a single person in at least ten minutes.

Surely, there was no corner of London that was actually unpopulated, and yet…

Lucy bit her lip as she looked out of the window, feeling the blow from it still throbbing beneath her bonnet. Where was she? Where was she going? What had her father gotten himself into?

What had he gotten her into?

Oh. goodness. What if the coach hadn't actually come from her father? What if there was some plot against him and she had fallen for it? What if she wasn't actually in London at all? What if she was somewhere else entirely?

"Don't be an idiot, Lucy," she hissed to herself, trying to talk sense before her mind fully ran away with itself. "Who would go through all of that for him?"

Her father thought himself very important and influential, but he really wasn't, and Lucy was certainly not the way to get at his purse strings. Or heart. Sending a carriage for Lucy on the exact date and time she would be at Bromley only to dispatch with her in some way that would provoke a reaction from her father was ridiculous, and thinking so was childish.

She was only fatigued from her journey and uneasy about her present location, and she was letting her imagination run rampant in this state.

She might have been missish once, but recent years had rid her of such mannerisms. Now she had almost coarse hands, irritated knuckles, uneven nails, freckles on her cheeks, and mostly secondhand clothes. She could not afford airs, financially or personally, and saw no need for finery, knowing now how tarnished it could be.

Lucy Allred might have been a beauty if her life had been otherwise; now it was behind her without fully blooming. Had she remained with her father and not found gainful occupation for her time and her intellect, she might have minded. As it was, she was perfectly content to let her looks and her fashions fade.

Well, perhaps not perfectly content, but content enough.

Marriage was not her aim at this time in her life. Her father would find some way to bleed her husband dry, had he any assets to be realized. Far better for her to eventually find a quiet country parson or landowner in Kent, near the school, and leave the elaborate ruse of her father's lifestyle behind.

Someday, perhaps.

Provided she escaped from this holiday in a godforsaken alley of London's undercarriage.

Had her father really sunk this far? He'd never dress like it, eat like it, or spend like it, and he utterly refused to feel shame for anything.

He probably wasn't even ashamed of whichever one of these shoddy homes belonged to him. It would be only temporary, in his eyes, and he was shortly to be on his way back into his proper ranks.

He was always on his way, and the only way he ever went was down.

Perhaps she ought to consider marriage sooner rather than later. It would keep her from having to deal with her father, if she married wisely, and then she might find some hope or consolation in wherever her home was.

But… there was an odd sense of daughterly devotion that she had never quite understood. Her father never treated her poorly, and he was never cruel. He simply took minimal interest in her apart from whatever social currency she might hold. He did his duty as a father in the traditional sense, but she had never known a single moment of affection or concern at his hands. Certainly never respect.

What was roughly between active negligence and fervent care? Blatant indifference? He expected Lucy to maintain the position of dutiful daughter and all that was associated with it, in spite of his own disinterest in her, and she played her part well.

But there was no doubt that she would have been of more worth to him as a son.

A son might have married a massive dowry, after all.

Alas for being an only child and a woman all at once.

Lucy had no spine for standing up to her father, as evidenced by having Miss Bradford send a formal letter to him with an offer of a position for his daughter at the school. It was a strategic move on Lucy's part, as she would never have been able to tell him she had sought out employment. He would never have accepted that. But an offer from the most respected institution for educating and training ladies of Society?

Stars had immediately appeared in his eyes, and he insisted Lucy write a letter of acceptance that instant, which she had done.

But if he was really living in these conditions, Lucy might have to try for a spine. Or stiff knees, at the least.

She was jolted out of her thoughts as the carriage gently came to a halt. Peering out of the window, she felt her stomach plummet through her hips and into the cushioned seat beneath her. There was not a single light on in any of the buildings before her, as far as she could tell, and at least a third of the windows were cracked in some regard. The lamp lighters hadn't been out yet, which made the entire street dark and ominous.

And this was where she was supposed to get out?

Heaven help her.

Though, as she clenched her now chattering teeth, she doubted archangels would swoop down and snatch her away from this imminent danger, no matter how pious she became in the next few seconds. Or how good a Christian she had been up to this point.

And yet, the door of the coach opened, and the kindly driver inclined his head at her, smiling as he folded down the steps. "Your stop, Miss Allred."

"I was dreadfully afraid of that," Lucy murmured, though it was not as if the driver could do anything about the location. She took his proffered hand as she scooted closer, rising from her seat and stepping cautiously down from the coach. "Thank you."

"Of course, Miss Allred. One moment." He shut the door behind her and moved around to the back of the carriage.

Lucy let herself feel the grimace across her face as she looked all the way down the street, as far as her eye could see, and found only a cold expanse of darkness. The sounds were unfamiliar, the scent was distasteful, and something on the air actually tasted of grime. Some sour, salty, plant-like taste that also had a texture that coated her teeth and made her want to clamber back into the coach to hide.

And this was the miserable corner of the earth she now had to endure until she could return to Kent?

Lovely.

A strange crackling sound came from behind her, and Lucy whirled quickly to face it, her gasp more instinctual than impulsive. But impulse took over with a vengeance when she saw the coach rolling away and picking up speed as it moved, without offloading her trunk or pointing her in the direction of the residence she ought to be approaching.

He was leaving her? Like this? What about her things, and what about her safety?

"No!" she cried as the coach disappeared around the first street up ahead, leaving her completely and entirely alone in the dark.

In London. Seedy London. Dangerous London.

Scary London.

Suddenly chilled, Lucy rubbed her arms quickly, looking around to try and find some sort of bearings. She couldn't call out for her father and hope he might appear in one of the doorways, and she most certainly could not wander far if she hoped to survive the night. But neither could she stay here and hope that someone kind might direct her to Cheapside or something.

After all, she didn't even know if that was where her father was.

She didn't know if this was where her father was.

"I refuse to die here," Lucy whispered to herself, wishing the words didn't shake when she said them. "I refuse."

Boldness had never known so pathetic an attempt, and Lucy Allred would not have known courage if it struck her in the face.

Surely, she would get some credit for her efforts anyway.

For pity's sake, she didn't even have a proper coat on. The weather was mild today and she hadn't thought... she hadn't expected...

Biting her lip, Lucy walked to the corner, glancing up and down the street to no avail. Nothing familiar, nothing light, nothing encouraging. That was all it was. Nothing.

"I r-refuse…" Lucy tried again, her legs shaking beneath her. "Ref-fuse…"

"You called, pet?"

The rasping, jeering tone would have made her whirl around but for the fact that her arms were seized, and her feet lifted from the ground.

"What are you doing?" she cried, with desperate attempts at flailing that only succeeded in flapping the fabric of her skirts. "Put me down! Put me down, now!"

"Oh, the lady doth protest a bit much," another voice crooned, his voice sounding the slightest bit strained and muffled.

The blackguard must have been the chief one holding her, which only encouraged Lucy to flail a bit more. Kick her legs. Wriggle however she could move to make containing her bodily that much more difficult.

As it happened, the hold he had on her was rather complete, and moving at all was a trial, which was perfectly maddening, altogether terrifying, and it did not help that he smelled of tobacco and sweat, along with something alcoholic that made her want to gag.

She wasn't going to get free of them, that much was clear. But what did they want? What was this?

"I have no money," Lucy told them, trying not to shout it. "Nothing. Take my reticule, there's nothing in it. My trunk is gone, and…"

"We don't care about the money, gel," the first one scolded impatiently. "We're here for you. Now shut up." He struck Lucy across the face, sending a searing fire across her cheek and startling the breath from her lungs.

She whimpered against the pain, now making her ear tingle. "Please. Please, whatever it is, whoever wants whatever with me… Please, don't do this. Please. I am begging you, please, don't…"

"I will strike you again if you don't shut your mouth!" came the dark retort.

"Oh, that seems a bit harsh," a new, bright, rather crisp voice broke in as though only strolling by. "The lady did say please, after all. Now, why don't you make this all rather tidy and put her down before I am forced to make you bleed?"

Chapter Two

It was always unnerving when an operative failed to call upon their training, but this was something Hunter Mortimer had never seen in all his years of spy craft.

It was like Briar had never done this before, and if he'd understood right, she'd been working in the field almost as long as him.

One would never know it at the moment, which was one of the reasons why he was stepping in before the blokes could move her very far. It was entirely possible she would lash out with beautiful blows in a moment, but he wasn't willing to risk what he was witnessing.

The one holding Briar off of the ground looked startled at Hunter's words, while the scrawny one who seemed to have the biggest mouth was immediately charging toward him.

Hunter sighed, shaking his head. It was so unnecessary, this. But if he insisted, Hunter would engage.

One swift punch to the face and an elbow to the ear, and the little one was down.

Smiling as though to a wayward child, Hunter looked at the other one. "Put her down, please. It would not be good if you dropped her when I fell you."

"Who are you?" he demanded as he set Briar down almost gingerly. "The Gent?"

Hunter barked a loud laugh. "No, my good fellow, but I will give him your regards if I see him in the next few days. And I think it will be better for us both if introductions are avoided. Now, would you like to attack first, or…?"

The answer came as the man barreled toward him in some weak attempt to startle Hunter into forgetting how to defend himself. Instead, Hunter stepped slightly to the side at the last moment and slid his hands into the collar of his attacker as he reached him, gripping hard and forcibly flinging the man away using his own momentum. It was a most satisfying grunt of discomfort and dismay as the fellow landed against the nearby building, and Hunter strolled after him, fighting back the temptation to whistle a particularly jaunty tune as he did so.

He watched the man push to his feet and waited for the bloke to come at him again. He was rather beefy, but he did not look particularly bumbling as he exhaled harshly. "Look, I was only told to snatch the girl and take her to a meeting point. I don't want all the trouble; I don't even know what she's for. So if you'll just club me on the side of the head, I'll drop here until I come to and report the attack to my employer. No more harm done."

Hunter grinned at the suggestion. "A wise choice, my friend. Have you a club you wish me to use?"

There was an eager nod as a club was produced from his waistband, then handed over to him. The man went to his knees and removed his cap, nodding once. "Whenever you're ready."

There was nothing to do but chuckle at the ridiculousness of this situation. "I do hope you will remember that you asked for this, mate."

Before any retort could be made, Hunter struck the club against the man's head, knocking him to the ground. He didn't move once he was down, and Hunter checked that there was still regular breathing taking place before dropping the club beside the now unconscious figure.

He turned to face Briar, who hadn't moved from where she had been dropped. She was dressed in a finer manner than was called for under the circumstances, but he would not pretend to understand the intricacies of feminine dress and did his best not to judge.

He gestured towards the street. "Shall we away?"

"How did you do that?" she demanded, her face shadowed by her bonnet and the relative lack of light in the street.

Hunter gave her a bewildered look. "Do what?"

He couldn't see her face, but he imagined a slow blink. "Knock them out so spectacularly."

"Basic fighting tactics," he told her, doing his best not to sound utterly patronizing. He needed her help, so it would not do to offend her.

Though, if she was this clueless, he couldn't see how much help she would be.

"I am quite certain that was more than the basics," she retorted in a remarkably crisp tone for someone apparently skilled for blending in anywhere. "They never stood a chance, did they?"

"Not really, no," Hunter said with more bluntness than he might have done otherwise. He folded his arms and tried to give her a more thorough look. "Why didn't you get out of that? I know the training regimen, and I know you can get out of worse without breaking a sweat."

The woman actually reared back. "I beg your pardon? Why would I know how to get out of that? It is rather rude to criticize a young lady for not knowing how to avoid abduction, and entirely unfair to presume that I should know how to free myself from capture. What sort of a hero are you, anyway?"

She was rambling, and he hadn't expected that from an experienced operative. The pace of her words was picking up, as was the pitch, and she was speaking absolute nonsense. But there wasn't time to go into all of that, and this was certainly not the place.

"Not a very good one," Hunter admitted. "Come on, we cannot stay here."

Her feet inched towards him but didn't move far at all. "Can I trust you?"

This was getting tiresome, and he only had so much patience. "Considering I literally just knocked two blokes unconscious so you could avoid being snatched, I think you might be safer with me than otherwise."

That seemed to convince her, and she stepped down into the street, now coming towards him. Hunter shook his head and turned to start walking towards the next street, venturing farther into the neighborhood and closer to where their headquarters would be.

Honestly, setting up the mission was supposed to be the easy part. He hadn't been handed this assignment for nothing; one of the largest interdepartmental operations ever mounted had taken place only weeks ago because of the information uncovered in its development. He'd actually been part of it, which was rare enough, given his deep cover, but the finer details of the original assignment…

Those were now his. The investigation into a man who was housing a traitor, the attempt to locate that particular traitor and, if he could manage it, get some kind of a lead on what exactly was going on down here. He didn't like something like this developing under his very nose, but he'd had quite enough to be getting on with from his usual crowd and the information they unwittingly gave him.

He still hadn't figured out how the coves around the Convent had been pegged as useful by the Faction, given the sheer volume of accessible coastline in all of England. It could not be a coincidence, but he couldn't ask too many questions on the subject either. Repeating topics tended to get noticed, and he had to make a habit of being unnoticed. It was how he managed to get anything done down in this world of his.

Working alone had its own challenges, but he had done well without a partner. Better, in fact, as it allowed him to act independently and lowered the risk of betrayal or compromise. He could act on instinct, change his plans on a whim, push the envelope as far as he dared, and compromise his morals and integrity left and right without guilt or shame. It had served him very, very well over the last five years.

Hunter Mortimer was a rascal, a rake, a cheat, and a flagrant sinner, which was why he had disappeared from good society and exiled himself to Europe.

So they said.

The cover of a shamed profligate was rather perfect when a deep-seated operative was needed quickly after the London League operative known as Trace had been killed. It hadn't been the League's favorite decision ever that the underbelly of London was to be taken from them, but it was the best decision for all departments.

Now Trace was, amusingly, not dead, so they were both down here, working independently and staying out of each other's way.

Mostly.

But in order for Hunter, working as Trick, to get a decent start on his new assignment, handed over by Mist and his partner/wife Mirrors, he needed to know what Briar knew, as the leading Convent asset working both sides of the Thames. No one came in or out via the waterways of London without her knowing, and her team of barely loyal bottom dwellers could be vital to his work. The shipment of new operatives—as well as arms—weeks before was unnerving, but others had their assignments there.

Hunter wanted to know how it even got to that point.

There had been an attempt at mass assassination earlier in the year, which was when Blaine had first appeared on their radar. Before then, Blaine had simply been the name most people of the streets knew to avoid, but he had seemed to be a heartless curmudgeon and no more. Now he was housing traitors, meeting with the enemy, and actively working to undermine Britain.

Hunter wanted to know how he and everyone else missed the signs.

The League was an utter mess these days. Trace had been given bad information after years of flawless work. Cap had been compromised. Rook had been compromised. Their assistant was the traitor, for heaven's sake. Their families were being hidden in country houses outside of London for everyone's security. No one knew why or how or if, in many respects, and nobody liked unknowns.

Nobody.

There were bits and pieces to everything that had been taking place recently, and Hunter was collecting them all and assembling the lot.

It was what he did best.

Well, one of the things, anyway.

His instincts were never wrong, and there was something absolutely off about Briar.

He slowed his step, letting that sink in. Something was off, if Briar was who he had heard she was. Briar wouldn't be caught by anyone, let alone someone who was actively sought out by people who didn't know her. And if she had caught wind of being sought out, she would have disappeared. With her network, with each of the networks housed in these parts of London, someone would have known, and she would be gone.

Which meant…

Damn it. He should have seen it sooner. The dress, the accent, the situation…

He rounded another corner quickly and grabbed the faux Briar's arm, forcing her against the wall and covering her mouth so she wouldn't scream. "I am not going to hurt you," he told her immediately, her eyes widening at the sudden change in situation. "Understand?"

She nodded quickly, her impossibly dark eyes fairly distracting this close, particularly when there was minimal light to reflect in them.

She was pretty. He didn't need light to tell him that.

Didn't matter, he reminded himself. He needed answers.

"I think," he went on, "there has been a misunderstanding here. Now, whether that is my part, their part, your part, or all of it, we will hopefully soon know. I was supposed to meet someone in about the same location where I came across you. Were you meeting someone down here tonight?"

She shook her head quickly, her mouth moving against his palm, and muffled sounds met his ears.

Hunter sighed and gave her a warning look. "I'll let you explain, but keep your voice down, all right? This isn't a safe area, as I am sure you have surmised."

She rolled her eyes, which made him smile. He removed his hand, leaning back a little. "My name is Lucy Allred," she whispered, her voice so low he almost missed it. "I'm a teacher."

"And does the word 'Briar' mean anything to you?" Hunter pressed.

Miss Allred shook her head, her brow creasing, and clamped down on her lips hard.

"Means something to me, though," a low female voice said.

Hunter glanced behind him, relieved to see a woman who was likely approaching forty years of age, dressed in the blandest shade of baggy calico, a tattered shawl, and a stained cap, all of which hid a muscular figure that he only knew to look for out of practice. She folded her arms and cocked a brow at him.

"Briar?" he ventured with a nod.

"Trick." She nudged her head towards Miss Allred. "Company?"

"Something like that." He stepped back from Miss Allred and rubbed at his brow. "She was being abducted when I arrived. I thought it was you, so I intervened."

Briar scoffed once. "I'd never be abducted."

Hunter frowned at her. "There wasn't exactly time to wait for her to display the extraordinary talents you possess for me to be certain. I realize now that she isn't dressed appropriately either, but quick thinking and all that."

"So what business do you have down here, pet?" Briar asked Miss Allred, coming towards her with a practiced nonchalance that Hunter also saw as intimidation.

"I don't know," she admitted with a whimper, a laced fist going to her mouth. "I don't know where I am, and I don't know where I am supposed to be. The coach left me without address or luggage, and I'm supposed to be at my father's house, and I don't even know where that is. I don't know why they were abducting me, and I am just so confused."

There was a hint of a sob at the end of that, and Hunter, for one, was not unmoved by it. He'd met a number of actors and actresses in his occupation as a spy, but there was something about Miss Allred that rang perfectly genuine, not to mention innocent. She was likely the most missish of young ladies, as were found in Society, unaware of any danger in her life and only concerned with the names on her dance card.

And now she was here.

Poor thing.

"Oh, pet," Briar whispered, tsking softly. "I can see you trembling from here. I'd tell you my name, but it is safer if I don't. Call me Briar. I fear our friend Trick here thought you were me when he intervened, but I hope he would have done so anyway." She didn't spare him a look as she came to Miss Allred and took her hands. "What is your name?"

"Lucy Allred," came the trembling whisper.

Hunter took a step back and let the women speak more privately, looking about them to make certain they were safe enough to do so.

"And your father? You are supposed to be at his house?" Briar pressed.

"Yes. He consolidated and moved to a cheaper place while I was away. I teach at a finishing school, and he didn't tell me where his new house was. The coach was supposed to…" She gestured towards the street they had come from, and Hunter needed no light to see that her jaw was quivering.

Briar muttered darkly under her breath, and he could only imagine what creativity she was using there. "What is your father's name? Between Trick and I, we could find his address for you."

"James Allred."

Hunter met Briar's eyes and nodded once. It wouldn't take long to get the correct address, though how her father could have relocated to this part of London…

The situation must have been beyond desperate. And why would he want her to join him here? Surely any father worth his salt would keep his fair and respectable daughter far away from this sort of shame.

"And which finishing school do you teach at?" Briar asked gently, rubbing Miss Allred's arms. "It may help us."

"Miss Masters's."

Lightning shot down both of Hunter's legs and seemed to crackle into the ground itself at those words. He did his best not to move or actually react beyond what was taking place inside him, but he looked at Briar anyway, and her eyes were hard on his.

The Convent. This girl taught at the Convent, but was clearly not one of the operatives there, and she had been almost abducted upon returning to London. On a night when operatives were to meet and from a location very close to where they would meet.

That was too many ironies for Hunter to be comfortable with.

And if he was reading Briar's expression correctly, she felt exactly the same way. "Right," she said briskly, returning her attention to Miss Allred as Hunter took a step closer, now readying himself to ward off further impending attacks on any of them. "We need to get you to a safe place. Well, safer than out in the open street, at any rate. Trick? This is your area."

Hunter nodded and stepped off the curb, looking around

quickly. "Stay close," he murmured behind him, more for Miss Allred than for Briar.

He would have given anything for a cloak to hide Miss Allred's comparative finery, if not the brightness of her gown, but if they hit the shadows well enough, and she was tucked against Briar, they could probably get away with it. He glanced over his shoulder and saw, to his relief, that Briar had had the same impulse. Her arm was around Miss Allred's shoulder, the bulk of her fabric and the expansive nature of her shawl doing a great deal to hide the woman beside her without being obvious about it. It wasn't perfect, but it would do for now.

But where was he going to take them? The only place available to him at this hour with guaranteed safety was his own quarters, and the idea of bringing anyone there…

It defied every rule of operatives he had ever been taught. But what choice did he have? Secure lodgings were not easy to come by, and he couldn't risk some of his assets until the danger posed by Miss Allred's presence was assessed. If she was with him, she could be protected, and he could act swiftly. Briar would be with them as well, after all, and they could discuss her possibilities privately.

He had no idea what her personal life entailed, and he wasn't certain how deep her cover was. Some of the Convent operatives lived perfectly respectable, high society lives, others were practically hidden amid the poorer masses, and there were dozens of others in between, scattered all about and in all stations. He'd heard a rumor that there was even a Convent operative in the king's court, but he'd never receive confirmation of that, of course.

It was amusing to imagine, though.

Hunter took them in a roundabout way to his lodgings, more out of habit than protectiveness, but when he had doubled back on himself a second time, he decided enough was enough and took a more direct route. By this point, if someone was following them, he and Briar would simply have to take them out once they were inside. Miss Allred wouldn't have any idea where they were, what they were doing, or why they were going around in circles, if she had even noticed.

But at least she hadn't swooned. There was something to be said for that.

The boarding house was completely dark, just as it always was in the evening, and one might have thought the place abandoned from its appearances. Which was, he would admit, part of the attraction of the place for someone in his position. He didn't even see the cobwebs or the rats anymore; he was only ever focused on getting to his bed and getting whatever sleep he could.

It was certainly not a place that he would use for entertaining or bringing ladies back to.

The stairs creaked ominously, a deep groaning sound that spoke of the need for reinforcement, but Hunter led the women up anyway, ignoring every sound and crawling sensation that hit his hair. At the first landing, he turned left and pushed open the no longer locking door leading to the flats, holding it open for Briar and Miss Allred.

He put a finger to his mouth with a quick look to them both, then moved down the corridor to the last room on the right. He pulled the key from his inner pocket and jammed it into the lock, turning quickly and shoving the heavy door, pushing it open wide enough for the ladies to enter.

Once the door was closed, and all three locks engaged, Hunter exhaled heavily and moved to the fireplace. "Let me get this going. You could probably use some warmth."

"Don't do anything out of the ordinary," Briar urged in a low voice. "We cannot be obvious."

He looked at her almost sardonically. "I have been known to do this a time or two, Briar. And I do occasionally light a fire for myself."

She held up her hands in a sort of sarcastic, faux apology, her eyes widening in a manner he presumed she used on her husband regularly when he said something stupid.

It was very effective.

"Sorry," Hunter mumbled with a quick tilt of his head. "But I live here, and there are no staff. So when I want a fire, I make one. On the occasions when I actually sleep here."

"Wh-where else would you s-sleep?" Miss Allred asked, her teeth chattering audibly as she ran her hands over and over each other in a strange folding pattern.

She looked small and pathetic where she stood, and it wasn't fair that she had been dragged into all of this.

"Briar," Hunter said calmly, returning his attention to the fire he needed to build, "there is a clean blanket on the bed just there. Would you wrap up Miss Allred so she might get warm? I think she might be having a bit of a shock now that we are in here instead of out there."

"Oh, of course!" he heard, followed by some rustling from the bed. "Here, Miss Allred. A chair by the wall, hmm? Trick, do you have something to soothe her nerves? Madeira or port?"

Hunter clicked his tongue a little. "There may be some brandy in the bureau there. Normally, I would use a sideboard, but as you can see, none to be found." He laughed a little, but no one else did.

That never was anything less than awkward, even in these conditions and with strangers.

Shaking his head, he focused on the would-be fire. He picked up the flint and steel from the grate and began striking it together into the kindling. The sparks were quick and the kindling dry, which created the flames in the most rapid and efficient manner he'd ever had in this place. He would try not to take that personally; flint and steel couldn't know when he wanted a fire just for himself, after all.

Now, he did know some operatives named Flint and Steel, who would have made it personal, but they were not here.

For which they should all be grateful.

He added a small log to the now blazing kindling, then a slightly larger one, before rubbing his hands together and rising. He turned towards Miss Allred, shivering in the chair against the wall. Briar was crouched beside her, glass of brandy in hand, smiling gently.

"Perhaps we can move you a bit closer to the fire, Miss Allred?" Hunter suggested. "Then we can sort out what to do for you."

Chapter Three

Lucy wasn't certain what was happening here, and she was definitely not certain who these people were, but she was absolutely certain that this was a nightmare she desperately needed to wake from.

She just wasn't exactly certain how.

She let herself be pulled to an upright position from her chair, watched and heard the chair be pulled closer to the fire, and let herself be sat back into it again. Her fingers were cold, her toes were numb, her legs felt heavy, and her head positively swam. A glass was shoved into her hands, and she sipped from it, immediately despising the perfumed taste and the painful burning she felt in her throat and grimacing at it.

"That's disgusting," she wheezed, pushing the glass into someone else's hands. "I think my chest might explode."

A low rumble of laughter made her grimace fade a touch, but she still couldn't seem to swallow enough to rid herself of the taste or sensation.

"It can have that effect," the voice told her, sounding wry and amused, "but I've yet to meet anyone who has actually had their chest explode. You do get used to it."

"No, thank you." She shuddered, followed by a cold chill down her spine. She inhaled deeply, which burned like the devil, then managed an exhale that felt heavy.

Amazingly, her mind did seem to steady and clear just a touch. Distraction, perhaps, but she was grateful, nevertheless.

The woman rubbing her arm, whose name Lucy hadn't quite

seemed to catch or retain, tutted softly. "Poor chick. Do you feel like telling us your story? I don't have much reassurance to give you that you can trust us other than good faith, but perhaps that will be enough?"

Lucy looked at the woman in confusion, her pale hair, inscrutable eye color, and sharp angles of her jaw making her quite striking in spite of the dirt and oversized, threadbare clothing. And there was no way a woman dressed as she was ought to speak with such a cultured tone.

Especially since she hadn't done so earlier.

"What happened to your speech?" Lucy asked. "You were not so refined earlier."

The woman winked, rubbing her arm once again. "Quite the astute observation, my dear. One I'll thank you not to share with the rest of the world after tonight. This will suffice for now: I am not what I appear, but I am, in my own way, rather respectable."

Lucy bit down on her lip, unsure if she was afraid, cold, or simply fatigued, and lifted a shoulder in a shrug that could be taken in a hundred different ways, even by herself. "I suppose," she whispered.

The man who had saved her arose from his place by the fire. "I can go, Miss Allred, if it will make you more comfortable to speak only with Briar."

Briar, that was what he kept calling her. That could not be her real name, but it would do well enough for now.

"No," Lucy said softly with a quick shake of her head. "It's all right." She tried for a swallow, which was difficult, and cleared her throat instead. "I am a teacher at the Miss Masters's School, and I've just finished my first term. My father, who is dreadful with money and prone to reckless gambling, only agreed because it is a respectable establishment and might put him in higher circles."

Oh heavens, what would her father think when she did not arrive home tonight?

Fighting panic, Lucy went on. "He sent a carriage to meet me at Bromley today, which I had not expected for the journey home for Christmas. I have not received the address of the house to which my father has retrenched since I began teaching in Kent, so I could not direct the carriage even if I wished to. Then the carriage stopped, and

I was let out. I thought the driver was going to retrieve my trunk, but then he left me. He just left me there, and while I was trying to figure out what to do, I was attacked by two men. I have no idea why, and I had nothing of value on me. They were supposed to take me away? And then you… he… I am so sorry, what was your name again, sir?"

He smiled at her, a rather crooked grin that crinkled the corner of his eye. "Trick, Miss Allred. At your service."

Lucy nodded, sniffling back invisible tears and a slight run to her nose. "And why were you…? That is, how did you…?"

"How did I happen to intervene?" he offered helpfully when she continued to struggle for words. At her second nod, he smiled more evenly. "Quite simple, really. I was set to meet with Briar this evening at almost precisely the same spot where I found you. Briar and I have never met in person, so it was not an unjust assumption that she was you, which was why I intervened. I would like to think that I would have intervened anyway, but we'll never know, will we?" He shrugged, not seeming altogether that concerned about the prospect, and the ease with which he dismissed the idea put him squarely in the realm of not-a-gentleman, which his manner of language made her suspect anyway.

Not that it mattered.

He had rescued her and made no attempt to compromise her in any way since doing so. He was making certain she was warm and had Briar taking the lead on most of this.

What was lower than a gentleman but still had proper manners?

Why did a category even matter?

"And then when I showed up, he knew, quite frankly, that you were not me," Briar finished with a laugh in her voice. "But never you mind the pair of us, we're going to keep you safe from whomever was trying to abscond with you."

"We what?" Trick retorted, giving Briar a surprised look.

Lucy avoided moving her gaze between the two of them, not really wanting to know what sort of exchange they would be having with their eyes. She was a problem in the midst of whatever plan they had for themselves and their evening, and she had spent her entire life trying not to be a problem. Her mother had taught her very carefully how to do so, as both of them were inconveniences for her father, and Lucy had always been an excellent student.

Not that it had helped matters.

Some hissing sounds seemed to be coming from both Briar and Trick, and Lucy glanced up just a touch to see Trick exhale with an expression of pure resignation.

That was interesting.

"Right, then," he said in a faintly louder tone. "I have enough contacts to ascertain the whereabouts of your father. Remind me of his name and I will have him found."

It sounded so orderly when he said it like that. As though she ought to have been able to see it done already. It wasn't quite patronizing, but it was something.

He found this task exasperating, she suspected.

Well, he should imagine how she felt sitting here and exasperating people through no fault of her own.

"James Allred," Lucy said softly, wishing she did not sound like a child. "No title, no sir, no distinction. James Allred, Esquire. Well, he says esquire after his name in introductions, but truthfully, I don't believe it has been earned or designated. There is no help in pointing it out to him, however. He declares it is implied, and there is no argument."

Trick seemed to clamp down on his lips at that, but Lucy wouldn't dare call it a laugh. That might be too optimistic, and it was clear that in this neighborhood, at this time of night, optimism did not reside. Perhaps it never did regardless of the time of day.

Optimism. Joy. Good humor. Sunlight.

Perhaps none of those things inhabited this part of London.

Considering Lucy had always done very well with those very things, she needed to get out of this chasm of darkness as soon as possible.

"I don't mean to cause any trouble or inconvenience," she added in a softer voice, her need to accommodate and apologize overwhelming. "If I could have found my father's house straightaway, I would have."

"Nobody is blaming you," Trick said with some force, though the tension in his face eased a bit. "God knows, you'd never show up in this part of London yourself. Not with your quality and good breeding, not to mention taste and refinement. None of this is your fault, Miss Allred, so do please put that out of your head."

"Indeed, do," Briar encouraged, now sounding her most refined yet. "As Trick has said, we will send out help to locate your father and have you delivered home in no time at all, and this will all be some horrid dream you can pretend never happened. I promise you, we have each handled far more complicated circumstances in our time."

That was oddly comforting, but Lucy wasn't certain what Briar meant by it. What exactly did they do? What circumstances were they handling? They were no beggars of the street, and they had no authority that was perceptible. Yet they somehow had power in presence and in spirit, though they had lowliness of character that did not belong to the upper class, and they were both speaking in a manner that would not be out of place in her own drawing room.

Contradictions and curiosities.

What a night this was turning out to be.

Lucy allowed herself a small sigh. "Fine, I will not think of myself as an inconvenience, despite knowing I am one." She paused, clearing her throat. "And I would be most appreciative of any help you could provide so that I might more speedily allow you to return to your own business and affairs."

Briar heaved a much grander sigh. "I suppose that is the best we are going to get out of her, Trick. Go on and send your people about to find Mr. Allred. I will see Miss Allred settled in here. Might she use your bed for sleeping? I fear she is quite done for."

Done for? Lucy rather thought she was going to explode from all of this pent-up energy that was now racing through her. In fact, she was starting to shake from head to toe, but not with the cold. It was just… shaking.

It would be obvious to Briar and Trick in a moment, if she was not mistaken.

"Right you are, Briar. Are you hungry, Miss Allred? I could probably find something resembling a meal from somewhere." Trick put his hands on his hips, looking at her expectantly.

Food? She couldn't even remember when she last ate, and her body was not giving her any indication that it wished to. In fact, she was quite certain that anything that could be procured from this part of London that was claimed to be even remotely edible would have several small and crawling creatures along with it.

She would never be hungry enough to eat something in that condition.

"No, thank you," Lucy told Trick with a hint of a smile. "Please do not trouble yourself."

He nodded, his own smile returning, which seemed naturally crooked now that she saw it again. "It wouldn't be any trouble, but as you say. I'll return shortly, Briar. Then, perhaps, we can talk business?"

"Of course. Why waste the meeting?" Briar shrugged out of her shawl and plucked her linen cap from her head. "I'll be awake."

Trick surprised Lucy by bowing to her, and rather properly so, before heading for the door and leaving, bolting it behind him, if the loud clunking was any indication.

Alone in the room with Briar, Lucy willed herself not to sag against the chair, and instead stooped to remove her shoes. A fatigued groan escaped her as she freed one foot, curling and splaying her toes a few times, and then the other, doing the same. Then she leaned back and stretched her feet towards the fire.

"You must be so tired, pet," Briar said softly. "What a dreadful day for you."

"I am sure I would be tired," Lucy assured her, forcing her teeth to not fully chatter against each other, "if only I would stop shaking."

Briar tutted and brought over her shawl, draping it over Lucy as she shivered. "That can happen with overexerting experiences, my dear. Especially if you aren't prepared for it. It will pass, and you will be well."

Lucy looked at her, a cluster of tension and heat coiling in her chest and prickling at the corners of her eyes. "Will I?"

Her voice broke, and she lowered her gaze, embarrassed by the wash of emotion when she ought to be strong and resilient. She was already a naive Society chit, and now she was actually helpless as well. Crying pitifully in dank rooms on some unnamed street, inconveniencing people of no consequence who were, at this point in time, the only creatures she could trust.

How hopeless could one girl be?

"Oh, pet…" Briar came around the chair and sank down, taking Lucy's hands in her own, her thumbs rubbing over her knuckles. "It is not so bad as all that. I'll not let anything happen to you. I'm not good for many things, but I have fought off henchmen before, and my husband always praises my good company."

Lucy hiccupped a half laugh, half sob as her tears began to come with a greater force, entirely against her will and rather like her trembling. "Y-you're m-married? I th-thought you m-might be a-a-a-a courtesan."

Briar laughed a rough, raspy, rather pleasant laugh. "God love you, pet, that is the most polite term I have ever heard. But no, I am not, despite knowing a great many rather amusing courtesans, to use your phrase. It would be too complicated to explain to you what I am in actuality, but I have been called the godmother of the Thames."

"D-does the T-Thames need a g-godmother?" Lucy asked in confusion, oddly relieved to not be sharing space with a woman of loose morals.

"Some parts do, some parts don't," Briar told her with a quick smile, her eyes sparkling impishly with her evasiveness. "And Trick, bless him, is very, very skilled at his work."

"Which is?"

There was a much more subtle smile from Briar then. "Complicated."

Well, that was even more evasive, but Lucy got the hint.

She wasn't going to know anything about her rescuers apart from what they called each other, and somehow had to trust them anyway. They were kind to her, and that was enough.

"Why would someone want to abduct me, Briar?" Lucy whispered, shaking her head. "Do you think it was a mistake?"

"I think it is entirely possible that it was a mistake," Briar assured her. "Though I cannot account for the carriage doing what it did. But I have seen stranger things. Come, let's get you into bed while we wait for Trick's contacts to find your father. You deserve some decent sleep, and I doubt you received that in the coaches from Kent. Come on, pet."

Lucy let herself be pulled from her chair and led to the bed like a child. "Are you a mother as well, Briar? You've got the right tone for it."

Briar chuckled in a rather warm manner that was answer enough. "I am, indeed. But I am also an older sister, and the tone is nearly the same."

"I'm sorry to be so simpering," Lucy said, wiping her eyes and nose with her sleeve, forgoing a lifetime of training to use a handkerchief. "You must think me a child."

"Leave my thoughts to myself, thank you," Briar quipped as she pulled back the sturdy bedcovers. "I know enough ladies of your station to know what you are equipped with as a group, and the fact that you have not swooned, screamed, simpered, or required a good smack across the face already puts you far above the pack."

Lucy cocked her head in amusement, her exhausted tears still trickling. "How many of us have you had to smack across the face?" she asked as she sank onto the bed.

Briar tapped her legs, waiting until Lucy swung them under the blankets. "Enough to know it works, and not enough to satisfy the urge to do so again. Come on, pet. Questions will not settle your mind for sleep. Take another sip of this brandy."

"Ergh, must I?" Lucy asked with a grimace, taking the glass anyway.

"It will help," Briar assured her. "Small sip, and settle in."

The taste was no better this time than it had been the first, but as the first drink had not killed her, the second would not do so either. If it would help her to rest after all of this, she would take it like laudanum and settle in.

Lucy sighed as she leaned back against the pillows and moved onto her side. "Thank you, Briar. I don't know what I would have done without you and Trick."

"Think nothing of it, pet. Have a good rest, and I'll wake you when there's news."

Chapter Four

Women were utterly maddening creatures, without sense or reason, and without any consideration for their natural inconvenience to the male species.

This was not new information for Hunter; it was simply rather enforced at the moment.

After a night of spreading his contacts around to find the elusive Mr. Allred, he had returned to his rooms not only empty handed, but also to be told that Briar had to return to her home, and they would have to meet again another night to discuss the mission. Not only that, but she was leaving the sleeping Miss Allred in his charge, as she could not risk taking her back across the Thames to her home and family. No argument from Hunter, either on the impropriety or on the danger, would persuade her, so he was left to pacing his rooms and waiting for his charge to wake.

An entire night wasted when he could have gotten started on his mission and spent the day exploring various avenues of investigation.

Now he would be hard-pressed to get anything done while playing nanny to a woman who had no business being in his company or in this part of London.

Lovely.

It was not as though he had other things to do. Things related to the security of the entire British kingdom, the strain that the deceptive faction of French operatives was creating, the danger dozens of British operatives could be in at this very moment, and the possibilities of circumventing almost certain disaster in the way of life for all British citizens. Nothing too grand or of great importance, clearly.

Luckily, Hunter thought well when he paced, and he was laying the foundation for his investigation in his mind at the present. Without knowing Briar's information, he would be missing an aspect, as well as a possible avenue of exploration, but he could certainly work with what he knew at the moment.

If he'd had success in the night, it would be another story. But none of his contacts had recognized the name of James Allred, which meant they'd had to go search their sectors and he'd had to continue on to a different one, and it had taken all night instead of a couple of hours. He was tired, he was hungry, and he could not have wanted anything less than to watch this young woman while he waited to hear back from his people.

But despite the reputations about his real persona, he was not a cad, reformed or otherwise. He did have an understanding of morals and respectability, and he did not abandon people in need if he could help it. After all, it wasn't Miss Allred's fault that she had been dropped on his block last night, and it was certainly not her fault that he did not have contacts of quality with whom he could entrust her care. In fact, he may need to check with his contacts to be sure that none of them had known about the abduction plot the night before. Some of them did odd tasks for a quick bob or two, and abduction was not murder, was it?

It was exactly these sorts of internal arguments and rationalizations that made him entirely unfit to renew his position as a gentleman in the world, and until they started to truly gnaw at his soul, he might as well make use of the time by serving king and country in a way that few others could boast. There were several operatives, male and female, in Britain, but there were not many who could work successfully alone, without supervision or interference, and without the trouble of a true moral compass.

Well, mostly.

What in the world was he supposed to do with a young lady who was actually a young lady and not a spy? Who had no skills that could protect her in the streets and would be of no use to him in his investigation. And worst of all, she did not even know where she was supposed to be, and none of his contacts knew either.

Which meant he would have to tap into the resources of other operatives, and he hated doing that. It took a great deal of coercion, bribery, and exchange of favors.

He hated doing favors.

Dash it, he was not fit company for a young lady! His sister barely tolerated him for more than twenty minutes altogether, and she knew him better than anyone!

What was more awkward, possibly, was that the young lady was still asleep. The respectable education and upbringing of his youth screamed in his mind that he should not even be in this room without some older female relative of the lady present, though a trusted servant or respectable married woman would suffice.

There was also the slight complication that Hunter himself wanted to be asleep in his bed, but that was beside the point. He'd worked successfully on minimal sleep for quite some time, and this would be no different.

It was the lack of working and the lack of sleeping that was irking him at the moment.

"It's not her fault," he muttered under his breath as he paced some more, reminding himself not to take his personal irritation out on the victim of a cruel prank or scheme. "It's not her fault, it's not her fault, it's not her fault…"

His eyes flicked to the bed, and to his utter horror, the young lady's eyes were open and staring right at him.

Devil take it, had she heard his rambling?

Hunter paused, his heart seizing with the sort of panic he rarely experienced. "Erm… good morning."

"Is it?" she asked in a sleep-roughened voice. Her dark eyes blinked, and she sat up, her equally dark hair rumpled and tousled in an almost childlike fashion.

Her appearance was not helping matters. She was a beauty, there was no question, and a beautiful woman in his bed…

Well, his morals weren't that intact.

"I believe so," Hunter said gruffly, forcing his mind elsewhere. "How did you sleep?"

"Apparently well." She ran a hand over her hair and then let it flop into her lap almost immediately after. "I didn't think I would be sleeping here all night, though. Does that mean you didn't find my father?"

The frankness in her voice was matched only by the flatness, and Hunter pitied her instantly. "Correct, madam. None of my contacts knew anything about a man with your father's name. Which, in a way, is good news for you."

Miss Allred scoffed softly before both delicate brows rose. "How is that?"

"This is, without a doubt, one of the seediest sides of the city," Hunter told her. "It means your father is likely in a better situation than you feared."

Miss Allred seemed to consider that, then she pursed her lips, her brows lowering impressively. "Or he is just in a different seedy side."

Hunter debated arguing the point, but he couldn't. After all, she was right. Mr. Allred could be in any number of places in the city that Trick was presently not integrated with. Briar had agreed to use her contacts to fleece out any James Allreds in her area, but that was still only a portion of London.

Miss Allred didn't need to hear that from him, particularly when it seemed that she already had the general idea.

"True," Hunter hedged, "but we have plenty of options for finding him. It won't be difficult."

"You sound fairly certain of yourself." Miss Allred craned her neck from side to side, then looked around the room. "Where's Briar?"

Ah-ha. Right. That.

Hunter leaned against the sideboard and folded his arms. "She went back home to her family. She said to pass on her best and she'll let you know she's thinking of you in her own way." He shrugged, allowing himself to smile. "I have no idea what she means, but I only met her last night."

Miss Allred didn't look nearly as amused. "So we are here alone."

At least she wasn't panicking about the idea.

"Yes, for the moment," Hunter allowed with a nod.

"That isn't good." She swung her legs down from the bed, her feet bobbing just the slightest bit as they hovered above the ground.

"You undoubtedly have things to do, and my being here is hindering that. And I certainly cannot be in your company without someone else. Not that I mean to imply that you would behave badly, but neither of us need the gossip."

It was oddly sweet, her naivete about gossip in this part of town. Inane, but sweet.

"Miss Allred," Hunter said on a heavy sigh, "I can assure you that, in this part of London, a young woman in the company of a man like myself is one of the tamer sights. No reputation is going to be ruined on that score, be it yours or mine, unless we see someone you know."

"Down here?" She made a loud scoffing sound, entirely inappropriate for a lady of her station. "Not bloody likely."

Hunter stared at her in surprise, smiling a little when she clapped a hand over her mouth, her eyes going wide.

"I am so sorry," she mumbled behind her hand. "I never... I mean, I rarely..."

"Are you apologizing for your benefit or mine?" Hunter overrode as he continued to smile. "Rest assured, I've not been offended by such a mild curse on your part, nor do I think less of your quality, breeding, or respectability for saying what is merely an emphasis of truth. And as for yourself, I am quite certain you will hear worse before the day is out, so perhaps we ought to lower your expectations now just to be on the safe side."

Her hand slowly lowered, her lips pressed in a very tight line when they appeared again.

Hunter raised a brow. "If you are currently living under some shroud of shame for that, Miss Allred, I beg you to toss it off. This isn't Mayfair, and I am no gossiping hussy."

Miss Allred's mouth quirked, and a small laugh-like sound escaped, her dark eyes finding a new light in them. "Well, if we're going to remove ourselves from the confines of my upbringing, you might as well call me Lucy. Otherwise, I'll keep curtsying and being mortified, or thinking one of my students needs something, none of which is going to be pleasant for you to endure."

There was no arguing with her on that point, though something in the back of his throat ticked at using her given name.

A byproduct of his upbringing, no doubt.

"Very well, Lucy," he replied with a faint bow from the neck. "Call me Trick. I think I said that before, but it's really for the best if we leave it there. Now, as you said, I have matters to attend to today, and being your nanny, much fun as that sounds, is not one I was prepared for."

Lucy shook her head fervently. "No, indeed. I will just stay here and wait for you to come back and take me wherever my father is."

It was all Hunter could do to avoid laughing uproariously in utter incredulity. Poor chit had no idea just what dangers lurked around them, not only outside of their building, but within it as well. How feeble the locks could be. How determined the local vermin were.

Not to mention the rats.

But it was not Lucy's fault that she could not understand that or comprehend the ugliness with which they were surrounded. She likely only ever understood the finer, more polite way of living, and anything less was unthinkable. Probably unimaginable.

So he did not laugh, and instead shook his head very firmly. "That will not do at all, Lucy. While this place is safe enough for me to stay, it is no place for you."

Her pale brow furrowed, the creases seeming almost crass upon her fair skin. "Then why am I here? Why have I been here at all?"

"Because last night, there was no better place to take you," he explained as patiently as possible. "Briar and I were with you, and because of that, there were the means to protect you, should it be necessary. If I—or, indeed, she—were with you, this place would be safe enough. Alone…" He shook his head again, so there would be no misunderstanding. "Not safe at all."

Lucy folded her arms, shifting her weight slightly on the mattress. "Then what are we going to do? Surely, I won't be accompanying you on your day-to-day activities."

He did not know if she was offended by the idea or simply certain of its ridiculousness, but it was difficult not to laugh in her face about it.

Because that was exactly what they were going to do, though he wasn't sure how it would work out for either of them. It was the only option, unless he wanted to sit here all day.

Which he did not.

Especially with her.

"As it happens," Hunter told her, clasping his hands behind his back, "that is exactly what we will be doing. You will be by my side, so you will be quite safe, and I am not doing anything particularly dangerous today. The school is too far to send you back, and it should be easy enough to find your father."

There was silence for an exceptionally long moment. "What?" She blinked her wide, dark eyes, clearly not comprehending. "Say that again. If you please."

"I don't please, as it happens," Hunter retorted without spite. "But since you seem to require further elucidation, let me enlighten you." He leaned forward, though there was a great deal of distance between them still. "I have things to do today, and as I cannot and will not stay here with you while they need to be done, you are coming with me."

Again, she blinked.

And said nothing else.

So much for the hopes that she was a quick-witted woman. What sort of teacher must she be? What in the world did she teach? But it was the Miss Masters's School, after all, which meant there were spies in training there and active spies on the teaching staff. Clearly, Lucy Allred was not one of them, but she had to be of some value, or Milliner, the spymistress of Great Britain and also the headmistress of the school, would not have hired her on.

Still, it had been some time since Hunter had interacted with a woman who was not common, or an operative or asset. His patience for such tepid conversations was out of practice, and thus, quite thin.

Hunter exhaled and rubbed at his brow. "Where did I lose you, Lucy?"

"Nowhere. I am right where you left me, and simply waiting for some competent explanation as to how I am going to be anything but an obstacle to whatever it is you do."

He looked at her in mild surprise. "You're not affronted by the situation I am putting you in?"

Her expression became rather bland. "I am in no position to be affronted. I was dropped in this part of London without friend or direction, and you are considerate enough to at least keep me from disaster. I'm not about to swoon over dirty streets and foul language. I am more concerned about irritating you to the point of abandonment in a worse part of the city."

That… was not what he had expected.

Hunter found himself smiling, in spite of his surprise and confusion. "Are you in the habit of plaguing someone into such a desperate state of affairs?"

Her lips pulled to one side in a slight smile of her own. "My father despairs of me, but I am not the one driving us into debt and retrenchment. And I cannot say with any certainty why I was left in this part of London, so that ought to be a sign of some concern."

"True, that is worth a thought," he mused, more out of playfulness than real consideration. He shrugged and gestured for her to follow him as he moved to the door. "But we do not have any other option, so you might as well come along. If I leave you somewhere, I'll make it a nice spot, I promise."

Lucy laughed once, a rather pleasant sound, even if it was a little hoarse and raw to be the prim and musical delicacy young ladies were expected to laugh with. "Like this? Was it not you who told me I was too finely dressed to belong here?"

"You are," he replied at once. "But I do not possess a bureau of gowns for your perusal."

"More's the pity."

He folded his arms, curious now at where exactly her mind was going and how it got there. Why was she not terrified and shrieking in some dirty corner of this room? Where was her indignation and her outrage at not having an answer to her father's location? How, precisely, was it that she was teasing him about the lack of feminine clothing for her to choose from to improve her appearance in these seedy depths? And why was he so amused by it, and by her? He was going to be remarkably inconvenienced by toting her around all day, and yet…

"I have so many questions based on that response," Hunter told her, "but no time to ask them. So, will you consent to donning one of my coats over your gown in an attempt to blend in?"

"I will consent," she said simply, pushing to her feet. "More than that, I think it sounds like a fine idea. I have no doubt your coats are dirty enough to hide all sorts of finery."

Hunter had begun to open his mouth to express entertained gratitude for her compliment, only to close it again when the insult as to his clothing followed.

It was true that his clothing was worn, filthy, common, threadbare, and a thousand other descriptors that would have been equally appropriate from her lips, there was no denying that. But she needn't sound so sure of it, or so dismissive of other options.

That was a trifle offensive, even for him.

His smile turned sour. "It will suffice. No one will question you, at any rate." He strode to the bureau and reached behind it, rather than into it, and pulled out his rattiest, most well-used coat in his collection, holes and all. It wouldn't smell—he had the laundry done as often as he could when he was home—but he couldn't vouch for what creatures might have found a home in its folds and pockets.

He might have hopes of a mouse or a cricket or a frog somewhere in there, just to hear her squeal.

Turning, he tossed the coat at her, not particularly caring if it hit her face or her shoulder, or the bed beside her. "Put this on, cinch it tightly across the waist, and hopefully your shoes won't be an obvious issue."

"My shoes?" she retorted with a bit of a screech. "They are your average traveling boots, who could have an issue with that?"

"Anybody who is wearing something less," Hunter said with as minimal a reaction as possible as he reached for the same coat he'd worn earlier. "I've seen people robbed for gloves, Lucy. Desperation breeds crime and calls it life. Come on, I imagine you're hungry."

He unlatched the door and held it open for her, sliding his attitude and his manner into that of an ambivalent gamekeeper tending a particularly attentive puppy. It was safer for both of them if he established as little a connection as possible, keeping her with him just for safety and just until they could find her father. He owed her safe passage and to keep her free from any more trouble than what she'd already had, nothing more and nothing less.

Well, and to make sure she didn't learn anything about the Faction, his mission, and the fact that he was an operative for the

Crown.

Minor details.

"Of course I'm hungry," Lucy grumbled as she moved through the door, her elbow brushing against him as she fastened his coat around her. "Last time I ate anything of substance was at Bromley yesterday. Not sure what will be available around here, or what you normally eat, but you will find I have very limited expectations."

Hunter rolled his eyes heavenward, noting the stained and warped boards in his ceiling and feeling oddly proud of them. Miss Lucy Allred wasn't an unreasonable young woman, but she was sheltered, and a trifle spoiled, as all young ladies of her station tended to be. If she managed to not get him into trouble with his contacts and assets today, he would consider it a victory.

She was not significant enough, or troublesome enough, to get him killed or compromised, but she could certainly get in his way just by being there. So he would rearrange his day by visiting those individuals who held a more minor role in the scope of things but would still further his assignment. Inconvenient, but not impossible.

Making his way down the stairs, it occurred to Hunter that Lucy was still talking, though he couldn't say with any certainty what about. She was just… talking.

A constant stream of sound that seemed to have no relevance, no point, no need, and yet it was still there. Not necessarily unpleasant sounding, but just babbling like a stream and just… there.

Was this a sign of her nerves? Or was she like this once awake and moderately comfortable?

"Right," he said loudly, overriding whatever it was she was saying, or not saying. "You're going to stop talking, or I will find myself obliged to find the nearest hack and send you to Whitehall just to get you away from my ears."

She gasped behind him, her tread on the stairs faltering. "That's not very nice."

"Whatever gives you the impression that I am nice?" he asked over his shoulder. "Now, rules for staying with me today. Number one, don't talk unless I talk to you or tell you to. Number two, stay where I can see you at all times. Number three, don't call me Trick, or call me anything else. Number four…"

"How many rules are there?"
"As many as I deem necessary. Number four…"

Chapter Five

Lucy wasn't enjoying herself. Not one iota.

Not that wandering about London with a strange man ought to be enjoyable, but she would have preferred being stuck in that dingy flat than this.

She wasn't saying a word, as instructed, and there was something about silently walking beside a man she barely knew that was exasperating.

She couldn't admit to having as much control over her face, though. Heaven knew, that was contorting and scowling and eye-rolling more loudly than she had ever done in her entire life.

But Trick, whoever and whatever he was, couldn't hear it, and therefore, had no scolding for her.

It was a delightful game she was playing with herself, if she could manage to keep her giggles contained.

So far, she had succeeded.

Perhaps she was enjoying herself, then. Just in that respect.

Her stomach rumbled loudly with hunger, reminding her yet again that they hadn't encountered anything remotely resembling food, and yet Trick had spoken with at least three people. She'd lost count during the second person, as a stray dog had yapped across her path, pawing at her skirts with his front legs and following her for a time. With her focus so completely distracted by a far more attractive, and attentive, creature, it was entirely possible that he had managed another person or two before this one.

And still, there was no food in her belly.

But she wasn't supposed to talk. She was just supposed to stand here silently, stomach rumbling indelicately, and wait for Trick to decide where they went and what they did.

If anyone was doing anything to find her father, she wasn't aware of it, which made her wonder why she was even here with Trick.

All she knew, besides her hunger, were the idiotic rules he had given her as they had left his lodgings. She had listened for a while, but once he hit number nine, she had completely tuned him out. The day was fine, and this was London, and this was a portion of the city she had never seen. She was going to look at it, and she was going to allow herself to indulge her curiosity while it was safe to do so. She could not wander, and she could not speak, but by heaven, she could observe.

It was an interesting thing, these poorer streets of London. Children laughed more freely than they did in Mayfair or Cheapside. The streets bustled more, for certain, and with far less attention to detail or politeness. She had seen plenty of women out and about, most of them carrying baskets or children or animals, but some of them simply striding out on their daily business, whatever that happened to be.

Lucy was desperate to ask one of them what their business was. What did they do all day? What occupied their waking hours? Were they free to simply raise their children or did they have employment as well? How did they manage both? What dangers did they face in their lives here?

And what of the younger women? She saw fewer of them. She presumed they were more likely occupied as servants in households or the like.

But a few quick glances around proved that Trick had been quite right—her gown had been too fine for the setting and the coat was certainly needed. She would have been gawked at, if not robbed, had she gone out as she was, or in any of the clothes that had been in her trunk.

One must give credit where credit was due, she supposed.

She glanced over at him, still talking with a small man with beady eyes and crooked teeth, and sighed, putting a hand to her stomach as it growled furiously.

Trick glanced over his shoulder at her, and she blanched, hoping she looked apologetic. He couldn't possibly get angry with her for something her stomach did. It was entirely outside of her control and unintentional. Surely, he had to know that.

He looked back to his companion, said a few words more, then stepped away and gestured for Lucy to come with him.

"I'm so sorry," she whispered, still clutching at her stomach. "I didn't mean—"

"I am well aware that you are hungry, Lucy," Trick overrode without concern. "I have heard your stomach's complaints all morning."

Her face flushed in embarrassment, much as she hated to be mortified in front of him. "I did apologize."

Trick scoffed softly, his long strides taking some effort to keep pace with. "I'm not scolding you, for pity's sake. I've been gathering information on that topic as well as the others. I am not entirely selfish. I've just been given the name of a bakery a few blocks away where hand pies can be got for cheap."

Lucy's stomach roared in approval, and she forced her feet to keep up with him. "I really hope I don't get in your way today," she murmured.

"Rule ten, Lucy."

She scowled. "I won't do this all day, but I can tell you have things to do, and I feel as though I am a ball and chain at your ankle."

He barely glanced at her. "I am more than capable of adapting my tasks to your presence. If I weren't, I wouldn't have taken you on."

"Oh no?" Lucy asked, more irked by the complete superiority in his tone than anything else. "What would you have done, then? After feeling that you had to intervene last night for my sake, even if you did think I was someone useful to you at first, what would you have done if I were in the way?"

"Left you with someone else who could tend you. Simple."

The urge to bite his ankles like an angry lapdog suddenly raged through her veins, and she clasped her hands together to keep from dropping to the ground in an attempt to begin. "How magnanimous. You are such a gentleman."

Something about that made Trick snort a hint of laughter.

"Actually, I am a gentleman."

Lucy almost tripped on the perfectly level street. "You cannot be."

"Cannot," he repeated, nodding to himself. "Well, that settles that. I'll let the world know."

Shaking her head, Lucy folded her arms. "That is not… No gentleman would be like this."

"Like what? Am I rude? Am I disrespectful? Am I so ungallant?"

He was baiting her, and what was worse, it was working. "You live like this!" she insisted, flinging one arm out to indicate the way he was dressed. "Your lodgings are what they are, and you… a gentleman would never."

"Oh, and a gentleman has never lived below his privileges, has he?" Trick asked with a voice full of derision. "I see. You'll have to forgive me. I haven't properly behaved for a woman in some time. Haven't had to."

"That is not at all surprising." Lucy ground her teeth together, focusing her attention on a slow-driving hack up ahead.

There wasn't anything fascinating about it, nor anything particularly strange. It was simply a moving object in her line of sight and did not answer to the name of Trick. If she had any way of actually avoiding him for the rest of the day, she would have done so, but she needed him to get anywhere safely and to find her father.

Besides, as irritated as she was, Lucy had to admit that she was not brave. Not in the least. She could never be so bold as to stride out on her own and trust her instincts. She didn't even have instincts in that regard. She was as utterly useless in the real world as any other Society miss, no matter how she might hope to be different.

She was not better informed, better prepared, or in any way aware of what actual dangers could present themselves at any time, which meant she was in no way equipped to cope with them.

What sort of a life and education had she even had?

"Surely, I haven't offended you with my frankness," Trick suddenly said, and Lucy could feel his eyes on her face.

She shook her head. "No, I am simply irked that I even have to be here with you. That I cannot go off and find my father on my own. That, however inconvenient it might be for either of us, I am a young lady of breeding and, as such, completely helpless right now. I feel like a blossom on a tree."

Trick grunted once. "You'll have to explain that one to me."

Lucy sighed and lowered her arms to her side, letting them swing in a natural pattern as she walked. "Tree blossoms are only there early in the spring, aren't they? Pretty to look at, but ultimately useless and short lived. Because trees have leaves when they are in bloom, not blossoms. I would much rather be a leaf right now."

The man beside her said nothing for a moment, his footsteps more scraping than clipped against the hard stone beneath their feet. "Eh," he eventually murmured, "leaves are overrated."

There was something oddly amusing in that response, and Lucy found herself smiling in spite of herself. "No, they aren't."

Trick nodded quickly. "Yes, they are. Once the leaves come out, they're all the same. Sure, each tree has leaves that are shaped a little differently, and maybe a shade or two off another, but they're just leaves. And then in the autumn, the leaves die, and they fall and make an awful mess of things. Blossoms on trees, on the other hand. That makes people smile and hope and look forward. We forget that leaves are all the same, and we're just excited to see anything on the tree branches. Blossoms are only there for a short time, and if you miss them..." He made a quick sweeping gesture with his hand. "They're gone. And you won't see them again until the next year, if you're lucky."

"Don't be ridiculous," Lucy scolded, though it was difficult to not feel a little touched and a little playful. "You know what I am trying to say, and I don't actually care about leaves or blossoms."

"It's your analogy," he pointed out. "I'm only trying to support it."

She rolled her eyes. "I mean ladies. Of my station."

He looked at her, his eyes wide with exasperation. "I know. I told you, I'm a gentleman, remember?"

"You are not."

"I am," he insisted with a quick lift of his chin. "Believe it or not, I'm in line to be a viscount. Once my uncle dies, that is. Not looking forward to it. I've always found the House of Lords an abysmal prospect."

It was even more preposterous than before, and Lucy barked a laugh. "You're just teasing me."

"I never tease about politics or inheritance," came his all-too-sage reply.

Lucy sputtered in mockery. "Why have we never met, then?" she asked pointedly.

He shrugged. "Probably because your parents, guardian, or chaperone know full well to keep you clear away from me. That and it's been five years or so since I've been in any respectable gathering. Don't worry, though. I'm not half as horrible as they say."

"That is exactly what a villain would say."

"I know," Trick said without hesitation. "I fed the gossips the stories about me. Did I say half as horrible? Three quarters. I'm no saint, but I'd not have much to confess in church."

Lucy gave him a disparaging look. "You go to church?"

"Every Sunday," he quipped. "Best nap of the week."

Lucy couldn't help it, she began to laugh merrily and heartily, her irritation with the man beside her not necessarily gone, but certainly falling into the background of everything else for the time being. The idea of Trick being a gentleman was amusing enough, but to hear him claim he went to church only to sleep there…

Well, that she could certainly see.

She had no idea if Trick was laughing along with her, and quite frankly, she didn't care. It felt so good to be able to laugh without fear or worry, and to forget, for just a moment, that she was an inconvenience and lost in a lower part of London than she had ever seen, that she had been nearly abducted last night, and that she had no idea what was going on or where the day would lead. She was just laughing in London, and that was almost like being home.

Almost.

"You have a nice laugh," Trick told her as she began to settle. "Not too high-pitched or giddy sounding, and not braying or wheezing. It's very natural."

"Thank you?" Lucy shook her head at the ridiculousness of the statement. "I'd say that I try, but I really don't. This is just how I laugh."

Trick grinned at that and turned at the corner. "I suspect, Lucy, that most things you do are just the way you do them.”

“What is that supposed to mean?” she asked with some interest, hurrying to catch up to him.

He held up a finger and entered the bakery, waving her behind him. “Two of your morning pies, please. Freshest you've got.”

“Cost 'ee extra, 'ansum,” came the reply from the portly woman with flour on her cheek.

“'Course it will, and I'll pay.” His accent became perfectly common in the conversation, and Lucy obediently kept her mouth shut, marveling at his ability to blend in so well. He certainly looked the part, there was no question, but to go from a middling accent that could float upper class to one that squarely put him far, far beneath without taking so much as a breath for the change was extraordinary.

He certainly hadn't sounded fine and prim in his conversation with her, no matter how he claimed to be a gentleman, but she had heard accents like his in drawing rooms and at suppers before. Climbers, her father called them as he steered her away from any using such tones. The distaste was always evident, which was rich, considering her father was the most desperate climber she knew.

But he came by his status honestly, he was always saying, no matter how he lived as though it were being taken from him.

Two hand pies were passed to Trick, and he slid several coins across the counter with a wink. “For your fine service.”

“Come back anytime,” the woman said with meaning.

Trick dipped his chin and turned to Lucy, nudging his head towards the door. She hurried out and then turned to him expectantly.

He handed her a still-warm pie and sighed. “There you go. That should keep your stomach quiet for now.”

“Does it always work like that for you?” she asked as she cradled the pastry in her hands.

“Like what?” He bit into his pie, exhaling slowly from the heat.

She pointed behind them at the bakery. “That. Flirtation and bribery.”

He laughed once, swallowing. “That's just the way things are down here. She doesn't mean anything by it, and I don't either. I paid a little extra because they did us a favor, and maybe the next time I come by, they'll be even more useful.” He gave her a quick look. “Are you judging?"

Lucy shook her head, taking a small bite of her pie. "No, just curious."

"You don't see much of the world, do you, Lucy?"

There was no judgment in that question either, nor pity. Just a simple statement.

And unfortunately, it was true.

"No, I don't," she admitted around her bite. "More than some girls of my station, thanks to my father's habits, but I'm not well traveled or well rounded. I've learned more in one term of teaching than any of my students, and it has nothing to do with the topics I've been assigned. The girls I teach… Some of them are part of a program run at the Miss Masters's School called the Rothchild Academy."

"I've heard of it," Trick said simply, though he added nothing else.

Lucy acknowledged that with a nod. "They take poor girls, usually foundlings, and educate them. When they have reached a certain degree of accomplishment, they are then placed in the main classes on the Miss Masters's side with the finer students. It is an extraordinary thing to see their progress, and especially to know that, unlike a great deal of the typical students, they will actually put it to use as businesswomen or governesses or housekeepers—some sort of occupation—whereas the upper-class students will simply be considered accomplished and might even forget it all, depending on what kind of husband she has and how she wants her children to be brought up."

Trick hummed softly. "Seems like a waste of information for those who won't use it."

"I agree," Lucy admitted, taking another bite. "I shouldn't even be allowed to be a teacher, with my father's opinions. But he cannot deny that we need money, and the institution is so well respected that he couldn't refuse when the letter requesting me came."

"Requesting you?" Trick swallowed his bite quickly, shaking his head with a whistle. "I've never heard of a finishing school recruiting teachers who had not applied."

"Well…" Lucy hedged, grimacing for herself alone.

Now Trick nearly choked, this time with laughter. "You didn't."

She nodded, still wincing. "I did. My friend Emmeline was a teacher there and encouraged me to apply, and when the headmistress agreed, she also agreed to write to my father personally and request that I join her staff in a teaching capacity to, and I quote," she paused to formalize her tone, "'help mold the minds and behaviors of the finest young ladies in England.'"

"Nicely done," Trick praised, still laughing. "And I suppose your father could not refuse such an honor?"

"Precisely." Lucy shook her head as she bit into her pie. "I had to appear shocked and a little dismayed at taking up an occupation for his sake, but once I allowed him to convince me of how it would help our station, I was quite amenable to the idea."

"I should say so!" He smiled at her, something almost like pride mingling with his mischief. "Perhaps you don't always do things just the way you should. You've a bit of the actress about you, in your own way."

Lucy peered up at him, confused. "There you go again. What are you talking about?"

He pressed his tongue to his teeth, his lips puckering just the slightest. "Lucy, in my line of work, nobody tells the truth. Not the whole truth, anyway. Nobody behaves naturally, nobody speaks as they truly do, nobody does anything in their own way. It is all pretense and hiding something or other. It's not a problem, since I do it too, for my reasons, but that's the way of it. And it has been so long since I've met somebody who doesn't behave that way, think that way, talk that way, that I'm finding myself a trifle refreshed by it."

"Is that supposed to be a compliment?" she asked, even more confused now. "I don't know if refreshed is a good thing or a bad thing."

"Quite honestly, I don't either," he admitted. "I don't know what to make of it. Or you. I suppose I could make a case for your personal, if natural, integrity, but we haven't known each other long enough for that word to come into it."

She shook her head at once. "Definitely not. And it's a little patronizing."

He wrinkled up his nose. "It is, isn't it? I could say you have no artifice? Is that applicable?"

"I suppose, but it still doesn't sound like a compliment."

"Do you need it to be a compliment?"

Lucy thought about that as she chewed on another bite of pie. "I suppose not. I've never liked artifice, and I don't need it in my life. But in yours, it probably serves well."

"Yes, it does. So artifice is what it is, depending on who you are, I suppose." He took her arm gently and pulled her a little closer as they neared a cluster of people. "Bit of a serious topic for gadding about London, isn't it?"

"A little, yes," she admitted, chuckling easily. "Why don't you show me your favorite thing about this part of London while we're out and about? If there's time, I mean."

"My favorite thing?" he repeated in disbelief. "You think I have favorite things about this part of town?"

Lucy gave him a bewildered look. "Of course! Why else would you stay?"

"Because I have to. It's… it's not as simple as wanting or liking." He seemed a trifle uncomfortable with the line of questioning, but he wasn't shutting her up, so that was something.

"If we haven't found my father right away," Lucy ventured, finding a hint of bravery within her, "then you have to show me something you like about this part of town. Something I wouldn't know, in my experience."

"Oh, I have to?"

"Yes," she insisted. "If it inconveniences you, drop me off somewhere else. Otherwise, you have to."

Chapter Six

Strange creature, did she not realize that they'd just passed a gang of thieves two moments ago?

She thought he liked this part of London and had favorite things?

As though he had a mind for enjoying anything in his life.

His life was satisfying. It was rewarding and made him proud. He never felt more alive than when he was on the hunt and in pursuit of his quarry. He worked hard, every minute of every day, and it invigorated him. He was damned good at what he did, but he hardly took a leisurely moment to himself to think about what he enjoyed or what aspects of his life were his favorites.

Sleep was his favorite thing at the moment because it was what he most wished for, but that wasn't exactly going to be appropriate conversation for them.

His favorite thing about this part of London? The part where he didn't get shot, shanked, or stolen from. The part where he could go about his tasks unencumbered by a complete innocent. The part where every hour of every day was his own to deal with as he saw fit. The part where he didn't have to bother with politeness every five minutes.

He loved being away from Society and the like. Hadn't missed it for a moment, apart from the lack of quality time with his sister. He'd never enjoyed balls or parties or the theatre, and he had certainly never enjoyed the rigamarole that was courtship. It was a relief to be written off as a wastrel and suspected to be somewhere in Austria or wherever the rumors claimed him to be.

Until his uncle died and he became the viscount in truth, he wouldn't have to do anything but what he was engaged in now. When he did come to inherit, that would be another story, but hopefully the Shopkeepers would not force him into retirement. He'd heard horror stories about good operatives being taken out of the field because of obligations to the peerage and such.

Hunter could not have cared less about his impending peerage. He didn't even know much about it, other than the name and the county of the country seat. There was probably some horrific marriage clause and some duty to try for an heir, which hadn't worked out well for his uncle, and Hunter had no interest in marriage or children, so if that could be avoided…

He could always see if his sister's son could inherit. Once she had one, anyway.

He didn't think Hal was with child at the moment, but he hadn't spoken with her in some time. It wasn't the sort of thing one put in a letter, so he'd had no word of it.

"What's that?"

He shook himself from his thoughts and frowned at the man with his wagon up ahead. "That is a hawker, and he is trying to sell things that have been pawned or stolen. The streets will be crawling with them in a few hours, but he is perhaps more ambitious than the rest."

The man saw Hunter and tapped his nose, which was exactly what he had been afraid of. This information, whatever it was, wouldn't come cheap and would likely be weak, but he was a trifle restricted at the moment.

"And it seems I need to talk to him," Hunter said on an irritated exhale. "Pretend to be interested in something in the cart. Anything. Don't leave the cart, do you understand me?"

Lucy gave him a sharp look. "Yes… why?"

Hunter only shook his head once. "Later." He gave her a warning look and stepped closer to the cart. "What do you have for me, Gus?"

"Scrawny ginger spotted down St. Giles way with a couple of frogs," the burly man said as he rifled through a basket of tarnished jewelry. "Real interested in empty buildings and storage."

Hunter's ears began to burn, but in truth, it wasn't anything he hadn't heard before. He knew that the man he wanted was somewhere in his seedy network, and he knew the man was interested in buildings. Why and how and where hadn't become evident yet, but it likely had something to do with the shipment that had come in a few weeks ago, which would probably be followed by more.

People and weapons. That's what the Faction was sending into England at the moment, almost as though an invasion was planned. But none of the information coming across the Channel from their operatives spoke of any specific events or occasions in the near future. And they were deep in the ranks of the Faction, in some cases, so they would know.

And yet…

"Anything specific about the buildings or the frogs?" Hunter asked, picking up a tankard and glancing at Lucy to make sure she was still close. "Or a more precise location?"

Gus scratched at the scruff on his jowls, looking up at the sky in speculation. "Nope. But I did hear that he bets a good game."

Ah-ha, now that was interesting. Not that it would necessarily assist him in his investigation, as the gaming establishments in St. Giles and the surrounding areas were more numerous than the brothels or orphans, but it was a direction, which he always appreciated.

"All right," Hunter muttered, reaching into his pocket and pulling out some coins. "Here's for your troubles."

Gus frowned at it. "Ah, Trick…"

Hunter held up a silencing finger. "If it pans out according to your word, I'll bring you more. Especially if you find your memory able to narrow things down."

The eager light that entered the man's eye had nothing to do with honor or country and everything to do with greed and opportunity. "I shall see what my ears can pick up, Trick. You can count on me." He lifted the filthy cap on his head in a sort of bow.

Hunter nodded and started around the cart, taking Lucy by the arm and walking away with her. "I can count on him, all right. Count on him to give me just enough to be useful and not enough to be acted upon."

"Then why talk to him at all?" Lucy whispered.

"Because I need to maintain contacts everywhere." Hunter shrugged easily and nudged her across the street so they might turn the corner and move uptown. "You never know when one of them will actually say something that helps."

Lucy made no move to shake her arm free of his hold as she looked up at him. "Help with what? What is it you do?"

Hunter exhaled a short laugh. "That is a much longer conversation. Suffice it to say, I work in information. Investigation, if you like, for this party and that. It's not clear cut, and it is not particularly honorable most of the time, but there it is."

"Do people die working for you? Or with you?"

"Not lately."

If he shocked her with that statement, she gave no indication of it. In fact, she only dipped her chin in a nod.

Hunter watched her out of the corner of his eye, curious about this pretty stranger who taught future spies without knowing it and could talk of death without paling, yet flushed at the use of a mild expletive on her part and saw herself as a tree blossom.

"Were you talking about my father?" she asked in a small voice. "With him, I mean."

"No," he said in a rush, hoping she hadn't heard their conversation. It would take a great deal of explaining to make any sense of it if she had, and he would have to keep track of whatever story he told her. "I have several people looking for your father and seeking out information. They will find me when they have something."

She nodded again, and this time, gently pulled her arm from his hold. "I don't understand why I was taken to the wrong place. You examined that entire street, did you not? To see if he lived there?"

"I did," Hunter assured her. "None of the homes were his, and none of the inhabitants had heard of him."

Lucy bit down on her full bottom lip, which made her appear very young and childlike as her brow creased with it. "We used to live on Leadenhall Street, if it would help to know that."

It wouldn't, but Hunter wasn't about to tell her such things. "I'll see if my finer contacts can suss out any information from former neighbors of yours."

"I doubt they'd know," Lucy admitted on a sigh. "Father hated being in Cheapside. It is a wonder he agreed to cut costs at all. I had hoped it meant he was finally gaining some sense about the situation, but I can only think it was by force. But if he was still being social before he left Cheapside, it is possible that Mrs. Kirby might know. She was very considerate of us."

She trailed off, looking, ironically, in the correct direction for Mayfair with a whimsical, almost lost expression.

"Lucy?" Hunter prodded hesitantly, nudging her side.

She shook her head, dark tresses bouncing wildly. "Sorry, just remembering. You won't have any idea who Mrs. Kirby is, but her niece Emmeline used to teach at Miss Masters's as well. She's a countess now, of all things."

That detail meant he knew exactly who she was talking about, though he could never admit it. Not that he knew Mrs. Kirby, but he knew her niece, who was indeed a countess, but also an operative known as Ears. She was just as talented in the lower levels of London as Hunter, though in different ways. He'd heard about her for years, never knowing she was a woman, but one of these days, he really hoped to work with her.

And Briar, if they could ever really team up.

"I will see what I can do with this new information," Hunter told her, biting the inside of his cheek at the falsehood. "Don't distress yourself; we will find him."

Lucy seemed to laugh without actually doing more than sigh. "I might find myself more distressed when we do find him, Trick. I have no idea where he is or how he is living, no idea if anything I have been told in his letters is true. I have no idea if we even have any money at all. I haven't known a moment's peace since my mother passed, when it comes to my father and my home. It would be a relief to marry and no longer be under his control, but then I would be under someone else's control, and if my father has a hand in the match, it will likely be someone in his pocket. Or my father would be in theirs. So my teaching is my freedom for now. My peace of mind. My sanity. What should be considered falling from my station is the most reassuring thing I have in my life. What does that say about my personal state of affairs, hmm?"

He had no idea how to respond to that, but it hurt something inside of him to hear it. Something in the center of his chest that connected to the base of his spine. What a morose prospect she had for her life, even if all was well with her father and this had all been some error of fate.

Not quite the delicate life of a short-lived tree blossom, was it?

"Sorry," Lucy muttered, folding her arms and looking away. "I broke a few rules. Rambling, for one. And I said your name. Probably means we'll be attacked momentarily, right?"

He hadn't even thought of the rules, as it happened. He was far too busy growing fascinated by her commentary, rambling though it might have been.

He cleared his throat and made a point of looking around them. "Well, perhaps not imminently, but I shall keep my eye out. One never knows from which direction danger may spring."

His attempt to make her laugh failed, unless he counted the quirk of her top lip as a sign of amusement.

"What should I call you, then?" Lucy asked. "I hardly think you'll appreciate my picking random names throughout the day, if I cannot address you by the only name I know…"

"Call me Hunter," he said before he could stop himself, every single fiber of his body shrieking in outrage when he did so. Half of the toes on his left foot were instantly tingling, and his stomach resided somewhere behind his throat.

What in all of the devil's circles of hell had he done that for?

Ironically, this did make Lucy smile, and a wry arching of one brow was turned in his direction. "Another code name? You are an interesting character, are you not, Hunter?"

His throat dried at hearing his name from her lips, and it had nothing to do with her beauty or loveliness, nor the way her voice roughened as she said it.

Nobody called him Hunter. Even his sister called him Hunt or Idiot or Trouble more often than not.

But he, in a moment of sheer insanity, had given this young woman his real name. She could think it was another code or occupation or the like, but it was his name. The most intimate secret he had.

And he'd just blurted that out without thinking.

What sort of operative was he? All of these years and he made an idiotic move like this.

Time to retire. That was all there was to it. No other explanation was possible. No excuses.

"I try to be interesting," he managed to say, attempting an offhand manner of speaking to try and calm himself without looking like he had just betrayed himself like an amateur. "Whether or not I succeed is surely fodder for others to discuss."

"Which is another way of saying you are but you're too polite to say so." Lucy laughed through her nose alone, her lips twisting in a bemused smile. "Perhaps you are a gentleman in wolf's clothing after all."

Hunter shook his head. "If you think I'm the wolf around here, Lucy, you really do lead a sheltered life. But I will spare you nightmares and keep things at that."

"Villains exist in every dimension of life, high and low, Hunter. I am not about to dissolve into tears because the monsters here are scarier than the ones I know." She shrugged and rubbed her hands together, inhaling deeply. "London smells so different here."

"Do you want me to tell you why that is?" he offered playfully. "I would be happy to tell you exactly what you are smelling, if you're that curious."

Her head fell back on a throaty laugh that made the back of his right knee itch. "No, thank you. I only mean that it's different from last night, and even from leaving your lodgings this morning. It's just a little different, but it is."

"You're making a note of how London smells in various places?" he asked dubiously. "Are you part bloodhound?"

She slapped his arm with surprising sharpness. "No! Do you mean to tell me you never notice these things?"

He shook his head without shame. "I am so accustomed to life down here in the slums that things like smell no longer register as part of the experience. I can tell you when suppertime is coming based on how the smells change, but I couldn't tell you much more than that unless I really focus on it. But by the same token, I couldn't tell you what Whitehall smells like, or Mayfair, it has been so long since I've ventured in that direction."

"Mayfair smells like flowers and perfume," Lucy told him without reservation. "And money."

Hunter snorted, biting the inside of his lip. "Seems appropriate."

"Cheapside smells like ambition, rain, and horses," she went on. "Bloomsbury smells of paper, tobacco, and bread."

"My word," he said, truthfully impressed. "You are part bloodhound."

Lucy rolled her eyes, her smile turning rueful. "When your father does not like to hear you speak but insists on dragging you about for this venture or that, you find other ways to occupy yourself. I seemed to focus on how certain places smelled, and it is one of those memories that never really leaves."

The more he heard about the life Lucy led away from here, the less Hunter seemed to like it. But this was not the time to grow sentimental or attached, and there were all sorts of families in England who behaved all sorts of ways that weren't villainous, even if they were distasteful.

"And what does it smell like at Miss Masters's?" Hunter pressed, choosing to redirect the conversation back to fragrances rather than grow more invested in her relationship with her father.

"Have you ever been?" Lucy inquired with a suddenly eager light in her dark eyes. Before he could reply, she shook her head firmly. "Of course you haven't. Why would you have? It is a finishing school for young ladies in Kent. Have you even been out of London in your entire life?"

Hunter paused a step, folding his arms. "Why do you sound so dismissive of me?"

She seemed surprised by the question. "What cause would you have to leave London?"

Oh, if she only knew just how far he had been and the causes that had taken him there…

"I've been to Kent," he informed her with as dismissive a sniff as he could permit given their surroundings. "Not to that school, but still. It was very green and very pretty."

"I apologize," Lucy replied with a surrendering gesture. "I am happy you know just how pretty Kent is."

He tilted his head just a touch. "Well, part of it, anyway. I certainly don't recollect how it smelled."

"Green."

He found himself chuckling without any effort at all. "That is nonsense. How can a color have a fragrance?"

"It simply does!" Lucy insisted, her tone almost childlike, but so filled with certainty and enthusiasm that there would be no arguing with her. "The air is something like grass and the sea and wildflowers and moss, as well as pine and firewood and mint. And if you are at the seaside, there is also salt and jasmine. I don't know how all of that means green, but that is what Kent smells like."

There was something strangely poetic about her description, and he suddenly wanted to go out to the Convent just to see if he could catch all of those scents on the air. He knew he wouldn't get them all, but if he could capture one or two, he might feel more enlightened than he presently did.

What had he smelled in London these last few years? Horse dung and soot and damp fabric, the tang of dirt at almost every turn, the occasional whiff of tobacco or opium depending on where he was, and his own sweat, most of the time. Nothing pleasant or memorable in any of it, and certainly nothing profound or poetic.

But he did feel that all of his senses became more attuned and enhanced when he was on a particularly dangerous mission, especially when he was closest to the end or to the danger itself. He had sworn that he could smell the sweat of another person in such moments, could tell just how alight someone's cigar was, could have written out the menu of the last meal had in a certain room… But he'd also seen more, heard more, felt more against his skin, even tasted more on the air. It was not just smells that he recognized then.

Never in his daily life did he think on these things, though. Ought he to have done? Or was this a distinctly feminine fascination?

"Hunter?"

He shook himself, looking down at her in confusion, wondering when he had drifted away from the conversation and so wholly into his own thoughts.

Lucy's eyes were wide and questioning. "Do you know them? They seem to have some interest in you."

He glanced up the road, where five men stood at a corner, not quite huddled, but certainly clustered together. And as he expected, they were looking at him.

It would have been nice if they had done so surreptitiously, but they had never been particularly subtle in his work with them in the past.

"Yes, I know them," Hunter admitted on a sigh. "You'll be safe so long as I am with you. They work for me. Or with me."

"Which is it?" Lucy whispered, her voice wavering on a fear that was already etched all over her face. "For or with?"

He twisted his mouth rather wryly as they headed for them. "Depends on the day, really. So let's find out which it is today."

Chapter Seven

They weren't the most frightening men Lucy had ever seen, but they were certainly intimidating. Filthy, strong, scruffy, and intimidating. There was a darkness to their expressions, individually and combined, and she wasn't sure what to make of their interest in Trick.

Or Hunter. Or whoever.

She didn't care what she called him as long as he kept her safe.

She was completely out of her admittedly shallow depth in this world of his, and when she was reminded of that fact, she became afraid of her situation. When she was just with Hunter, she could have been anywhere in England and fairly at ease. She wouldn't have necessarily said that the night before, but once she had met him, she had felt she had a decent measure of the man. Whoever he was, whatever he did, however he chose to live his life, he had a sort of honor that could not be denied or ignored.

He might not be a gentleman, no matter what he said, but honor might be more important than anything else, especially in this situation.

But she did not know these men that he knew. She did not know if they lived with the same honor he did, if they would have protected her the way he had, if they would be indulging her the way he was. Would they have been some of the men hired to abduct her for the right price?

What else might they be capable of for the right inducements?

And this was the world that Hunter inhabited?

Perhaps she ought to be more afraid.

Lucy felt her practiced submissiveness rise in defense as they approached, just as it would when she was around her father. She was not naturally willful, and not especially independent, and the diminished version of herself was how her father demanded she act in his presence, so that was her habit. Even when her mother was alive, her father hadn't liked much interaction or communication with her, but since her death…

There was no point in pitying herself for her life, nor for turning into this meek little mouse of a creature. Nearly all of Society preferred their ladies to be like this, not just her father.

She did not know how to be anything else unless she was at the school.

There, she was simply Miss Allred, teacher of French, philosophy, comportment, and whatever other subject Miss Bradford settled on for the coming term. She had some authority, but not enough to go to her head, and she had freedom, but not enough to make her independent. She had contentment there and companionship with the other teachers, but more than that, she had a purpose greater than standing around waiting to be chosen by a man to wed.

When she was anywhere else…

"Something you blokes need?" Hunter asked of the men when they reached them, his accent going as common as common could be.

"Something you might need," the largest one said, using a cigar to point at him. "Happy to patrol tonight, Trick, if you like."

Patrol? What in the world would a patrol be for? Were they soldiers of some sort?

Lucy did her best to not look curious or even interested, but her ears had grown particularly attentive.

Hunter looked up at the sky, squinting at something or other. "Would I like? Why?"

"The weed has a penchant for gaming," one of the others said, clearing his throat. "And tonight is rumored to be a good night in all the local haunts."

"And none of you would be opposed to spending an evening on patrol of gaming hells, would you?" Hunter chuckled in a dark, knowing way that Lucy was intrigued by. "Provided you are not expending your own funds, of course."

The rest of them laughed in the same way that Hunter just had, which made Lucy even more intrigued.

Was he really in charge of these men? Or were they like him and simply offering assistance? Did they do what he did? He seemed to have more authority than the rest, but in what capacity did any of them act? And how?

And what sort of patrols went on in gaming hells? Whatever those were…

Oh heavens, were they going to search for her father in there? They'd likely find him, if these places were what she suspected. Perhaps losing whatever money they had left and the maintenance funds that had supposedly been set aside in his retrenchment.

Lucy bit down softly on the inside of her cheek to keep from asking any of these questions out loud and focused on keeping her eyes lowered.

"Fine," Hunter finally said. "Patrol tonight. We'll meet at The Black Dolphin, usual time."

"And the chick? She yours?"

The growl that came from Hunter's chest startled Lucy and she looked at him in surprise.

He was glaring at them all. "She is no chick. She is not mine, nor is she anyone else's, but she is under my protection. Understand that?"

"Yes, sir, Trick," they all said, more or less, in a mumbling murmur rather like a stream over rocks.

Lucy felt her cheeks heat and wondered if she ought to look somewhere specific while the awkward moment passed.

"This is Miss Lucy," Hunter went on, only slightly calmer, "and should you see her unaccompanied, you will take her under your protection until she is safely at the Garden. I'll be having your word on that as well."

The men gave it, each of them avoiding looking at Lucy and finding unanimity in their acknowledgement. It was oddly comforting to have their words, but it would all mean nothing if they did not have honor.

Clearly Hunter thought they did, or he would not have insisted upon it.

Honor among thieves? Rogues? Dock workers? There was no telling what they were or who, but it was something.

One of them looked fairly young, perhaps not even twenty, and he glanced at Lucy with a small smile. Not one of interest or the sort of leering inspection she had seen in some of her father's acquaintances, but one of almost… friendly reassurance?

That wasn't something in place in this group, as far as she could tell.

She managed a faint smile back, wondering if that was a mistake Hunter was going to chide her for as soon as they were away.

But if he noticed, he said nothing. Didn't even nudge her.

Perhaps the prospect of a patrol was enough to distract him? She was going to have to ask him for details when she could. If he were distracted enough thinking about the patrol for a few minutes after they left, he might answer her questions instinctively.

Freely.

Without secrets.

The possibilities were rather tantalizing, if she considered them for too long.

She gave Hunter a quiet, sidelong look, realizing he was in conversation with the others again.

"Nah, Trick, the pulse is more thready," a short, scrawny one said. "More Irish in the neighborhood than French, and the Irish are a prickly bunch for French secrets. At least right now."

"East India has some French," said a man with a jagged scar down his brow and onto his cheek. "Lots of loading on and off. Need me to check?"

Hunter shrugged. "Tomorrow, if you don't have anything better to do. Briar or Trace might have the pulse there, so don't tread on toes. And Blythe, look at the Irish anyway, eh? I don't want someone getting there before me. Just get some ears there."

"Got it, Trick."

Irish? French? East India? What in the world were any of them talking about? Briar, she knew, if they were talking about the woman from last night, and if they were, then Trace might be someone else who worked in their world. But how did anybody follow these conversations without a list of references?

It was an entirely new language they were speaking, and while the majority of the words might have been English, they certainly did not have the same meanings.

So much for her curiosity being sated.

"Any of you know the name Allred?"

She did her best not to jerk in response to hearing her surname, but knew she failed at once when Hunter's hand came to her arm in a surprisingly gentle hold.

But alas, every one of the men shook their heads.

Of course they did.

"If you hear it tonight, you tell me at once," Hunter told them. "I'll see you at the rendezvous." With a quick nod, he strode away with Lucy secure beside him, not giving any of them a chance to ask further questions or provide any insight on any other detail they had been discussing.

Were all of his conversations so abruptly ended? She glanced over her shoulder to see the men breaking up and apparently going about their day. Like a class when dismissed.

What sort of world had she been dropped into, and what in the world was happening tonight?

She looked up at Hunter, but he shook his head quickly. "Don't speak yet," he said in a low voice, as though he could hear her questions brewing. "Give it another block at least."

"But I—"

"Shh!"

What for? Lucy was practically screaming at him in her mind, wondering what the point would be of waiting another block to talk to him when she didn't even understand what they had been talking about until he'd mentioned her surname. The entire area was filled with people just like those men, according to Hunter himself, so if anybody heard her talking to him, would it not carry the exact same risk no matter where she was? And they had been speaking freely enough before this without his shushing her.

Back to irritation, then, and may the day thrive in it.

She began to grind her teeth together, which she almost never did, but some impulses were too strong to ignore.

Must not punch him, must not punch him, must not punch him…

She would not punch him, of course. Ladies did not punch those who were trying to help them.

Imagining punching him, however, was perfectly acceptable, and quite a pleasurable pastime. She had no idea if she would be any good at punching. Growing up without siblings, she had never thrown a punch or taken one, but she had observed the occasional fight a time or two in her life, so she had a general idea of how to go about the thing.

With her luck, she would probably break her hand on his chiseled face while he laughed at her. He'd probably feel tickled by whatever blow she struck, if she managed to land one at all. And then he'd never answer her questions and probably leave her somewhere else for someone else to deal with, and while that might give her a more sympathetic nanny, it would require her to start the entire process over again.

She wasn't willing to do that.

Acting in one's own interests long-term when the short-term ones were so very enticing was surely the most righteous form of self-control, if not the most rigorous.

When they had reached the apparently perfect block of streets away from the men, Hunter exhaled. "Right, now you can talk."

For the sake of spite and every woman who had ever been properly irked by a man, Lucy said nothing on that particular cue, and simply lifted a shoulder in a half shrug of nonchalance.

Just to see what happened.

It took all of three paces for him to react. "What?" he grunted darkly. "Where did your insatiable curiosity go?"

"I'm not at all certain I know what you are talking about," Lucy replied with a prim sniff that any of her great-aunts would have been proud of.

Hunter released a knowing, exasperated sigh. "I have a sister, Lucy. I know how this works. What have I done to irk you so?"

She folded her arms tightly. "You shushed me."

"Oh, for pity's sake—"

"No," she insisted, cutting him off with a quick finger. "No, don't do that. I know what you're going to say."

He lifted an imperious brow. "Which is?"

She cleared her throat before attempting to deepen it in an impersonation. "'There's going to be more than shushing today.' 'It'll happen again.' 'Are you going to be miffed every time you need to be quiet?' 'It was for your own good.'" She made a face and looked up at him. "How did I do?"

He wore a lopsided smile that did interesting things to her stomach. "Not bad. You forgot about the part where I know the sort of people around here and you don't, but all in all, fairly accurate. I don't sound like that, though."

"It's not my fault that my voice won't go as low as yours!" she protested with a laugh.

"That wasn't the part I was talking about." He rubbed a hand over his face, sighing again, but this time it sounded more fatigued than anything else. "I apologize for shushing you. I didn't mean to treat you like a child, or however it came across. But in this part of town, no matter the time of day, certain corners and blocks are simply not safe, and I wouldn't have put it past any of those men to follow us for a bit just to find out more about you. I wasn't going to risk that, and there wasn't exactly time to explain myself fully."

It was sobering to hear the reasoning, but also hard to fathom in broad daylight.

"Me?" Lucy snorted in a rather unladylike fashion. "Please."

"I am quite serious," came his calm, unamused retort.

She shook her head. "What, any new face in a street will do? Surely even this part of London has some sort of standard."

"You greatly underestimate this part of London, and you are hardly just a new face. Objectively speaking, Lucy, you are quite pretty, and that makes you a target for all sorts."

Objectively speaking? A target? Only this man could bracket a compliment with two rather unflattering statements, which kept her stomach fluttering to a brief twitch that could have been an internal sneeze for all she knew.

"Allow me to roll in some dirt to make myself less appealing, then," she grumbled, sandwiching her hands beneath her arms as though cold. "Anyone robbing me would come away disappointed, so no need for hiding anything there."

"Dirt wouldn't help," Hunter told her, unmoved. "Not down here." He yawned and didn't bother to hide it. "Everybody has dirt. You'd just be prettier than most."

Again, the lack of actual compliment in the compliment.

"Is this boring for you?" Lucy asked him, allowing her irked state to remain fairly evident. "Am I inconvenient and boring?"

He looked at her, his eyes practically doleful. "I'm tired, Lucy. I was up all night trying to find your father, and I'm going to be up most of the night again due to the patrol I now have to do, so forgive me if yawning in your presence is offensive."

The sting of embarrassment was swift and sharp, and Lucy actually hissed as it lashed across her chest. "Sorry. Is there somewhere you can take me so you can rest before your patrol? What is a patrol anyway? I mean, I know what a patrol is, but what is your patrol? Are you looking for my father in the gaming hells? I know you mentioned him, but it didn't seem like the point of the patrol. Do you need to do a lot of preparing for that? What kind of a place is The Black Dolphin?"

"Bloody hell, woman, would you take a breath?"

Lucy did so, without realizing what he was saying, then released a breath on laughter. "Sorry, I was doing it again, wasn't I?"

Hunter was shaking his head, his eyes wide. "I have never met anyone who rambles like you. Ever. It's like your mind and your mouth are skipping along in some country green and ignoring the fact that questions generally require a response."

"I doubt either my mind or my mouth would be capable of skipping," she admitted with a wrinkle of her nose. "I am really not very coordinated."

"So you don't teach dancing at Miss Masters's. Duly noted."

Lucy managed a giggle and lowered her arms to her sides, letting them swing naturally with the motion of her walking. "If you can remember any of those questions I asked, feel free to answer them."

"Why, don't you remember them?" He grinned down at her, and again, her stomach did that fluttery, twitchy thing, only this time it seemed to shift three ribs or so.

"Not really. They just kind of fly out of me, but I'm sure they'd come back."

He scoffed softly. "Homing pigeons. Nice."

She jabbed him in the side with her elbow before stepping around a puddle in her path. "It's not my fault! This is just the way I am!"

"All right, all right," he protested, playfully rubbing at his side, though there was no possibility she had actually injured him. "Yes, there is a place we can go where you'll be safe and I can rest, and we might as well head there now. I was going to have you there during the patrol anyway."

Lucy squealed in an oddly girlish manner for being told they were going somewhere new. "What kind of a place is it? Darker than your flat? Safer neighborhood? Worse neighborhood? More colorful people for me to meet? Do I need a false name?"

"Lucy…"

"Sorry!" She did her best not to cover her mouth with both hands. "I'm just excited to go somewhere I've never been that is going to be safe for me."

"I can tell. You have a very odd sense of what is exciting." He chuckled, glancing in her direction. "I'd say you need to experience more of the world, but here we are."

"Only if it's going to be useful to you," Lucy said in as calm a voice as she could manage. "I'm already in your way, and I know it."

Hunter mumbled something under his breath, then turned to her. "Stop apologizing. I know, you didn't, but you are every time you use your breath to say something about being inconvenient or in my way or whatever. Stop doing that. It's unnecessary, and it's getting annoying. And I wouldn't be taking you to this place if it weren't also in my best interest. I can rest, but I can also get information that I need, both for my patrol interests and for finding your father. I am capable of acting in my own self-interest while also acting in yours."

Lucy clamped down on her lips hard, finding something incredibly amusing about his speech, in light of how he had just mocked her for rambling.

His eyes flicked to that motion, and his shoulders slumped. "And now you're laughing at me. What?"

"Nothing," she said, squeaking in a rather betraying manner. "That was just a lot for you to say at once. Either you are really tired, or I am rubbing off on you."

He groaned and pinched at the bridge of his nose. "Probably both, honestly. But going to see Tilda will be helpful for both of us. You'll have plenty of company, we can get you some different clothing, and I can rest after checking in where I need to."

"Who is Tilda?" Lucy asked brightly.

He peered up at the sky, almost wincing as he did so. "She's a costumer for several of the London theatres. One of the most eccentric people I have ever met, and I think she may have murdered someone in Austria in her youth, but no one has ever been able to confirm that for me, or prove it, come to think. She's very frank, very creative, and very protective of her girls."

Lucy frowned a little. "She's a mother?"

Now Hunter barked a loud, hard laugh. "No, my dear Lucy, she is not. Wait and see."

Chapter Eight

The look on Lucy's face was utterly priceless.

It was to be expected, given that the girls Hunter mentioned were actresses. But also…

Well, courtesans, for lack of a better word, but also some of the finest unofficial operatives England had.

This place of Tilda's, this compound of back rooms of theatres, was no brothel, and there was nothing untoward happening in any of the rooms they were seeing.

None of the girls gave Hunter and Lucy a second look as they walked through, which ought to signal to her well enough that this was not that sort of establishment, but it was also simply a place of business. The girls were used to random comings and goings of men and women, and everyone had something to do, so why should there be distractions?

"We just walked in through the most unobtrusive side door of the most boring building I have ever seen anywhere, and now there are corridors upon corridors of rooms and costumes and chaises and boxes…" Lucy was muttering, her nerves clearly getting the better of her.

They had found her in the middle of a dark London street in the middle of the night after a foiled abduction, and this was what she was nervous about?

Curious creature.

Hunter could feel her hand at his sleeve, and he suppose he ought to be grateful that she was not clutching his hand in her own like a child.

He was not at all nervous and moved freely and confidently along the corridors of ladies, costumes, and doors. He was here at least every other week, usually, and was far more focused on finding a place to sleep for a few hours than anything else.

Including Lucy's rambling.

"At least it's clean," she whispered as they walked.

Hunter found himself looking around to see what she was seeing, or not seeing, as it were. No cobwebs, no gaping holes in the walls or floors, no mysterious stains on wallpaper. It was tidy and orderly and, although lacking decoration, seemed a rather well-tended place.

Through her eyes, this must be bewildering.

She would have no idea where they were.

"Trick?"

Lucy jumped beside him and fully clutched his arm, while he simply looked around and broke out into a grin as a familiar face came towards them.

He started laughing. "Callie? What in the world are you doing here?"

A tall and remarkably pretty woman with pale golden hair was suddenly flinging her arms around him and laughing in sheer and natural delight. "I knew it was you! Nobody strides around with that kind of determination and pride except you!"

"Pride?" Hunter retorted, setting her down. "I am incredibly humble. Praised for it, in some circles."

Callie, one of his oldest friends from the underbelly of London, slapped his chest. "Oh, stuff it, you know exactly what you are."

He chuckled and put a hand on her shoulder. "I'll ask again—what are you doing here, Callie?"

She beamed. "I finished my training, and my first official assignment is to work under Tilda. Not as one of her girls, but as her apprentice."

"That's bloody marvelous, Cal!" Hunter all but gushed. "I'd heard, of course, that you went into the service after Gent's house, but nobody tells me anything."

"Perhaps if you took yourself out of the slums every now and again," she suggested in a rather drawling tone. She winked then and looked at Lucy, sobering. "Ah, and who's this?"

Hunter turned slightly, placing his hand on Lucy's back. "This is Lucy. She happened upon Briar and me last night when someone tried to abduct her. So she's in my care until we find her father's new home and return her to safety."

Callie's eyes widened and she looked at Hunter quickly. "Have you told the League? You know how they keep tabs on everything."

"One of my runners went to them first thing this morning," he assured her with a nod. "Haven't heard anything yet."

She returned his nod and cast her eyes back to Lucy. "My name is Callie, since Trick isn't going to do proper introductions. We've been friends for ages and ages. Don't worry, you're safe here."

Lucy cleared her throat very softly. "Why don't you have a code name like Trick and Briar?"

Callie's smile was swift and wide. "I do have one, Trick just doesn't know it. My name is Willow."

Hunter hissed, forgetting belatedly that, thanks to her now completed training, Callie would have a new name. She was right, he really did need to emerge from the darkness of his assignment every now and then, if for no other reason than to keep abreast of such information.

He knew what he needed to know when he needed to know it, but this was something he really wouldn't need to know for an assignment. It was just something that he would want to know for future reference, really. And no one gave him anything for the future in the life he led.

He would be lucky if he had a future, with the life he led.

"I'll call you Willow, then," Lucy replied with a brief bob of her head. "Just in case. I don't know what any of you do or what any of this means, but I'm learning that you cannot be too careful with whatever it is."

Callie's smile turned slightly rueful. "Very true." She looked at Hunter quickly. "Are you both here to see Tilda?"

"Yes, but also because I need a safe place for Lucy while I sleep." He shrugged a little sheepishly, knowing that Callie would have nothing to say on the subject, but Tilda most certainly would.

She would have a great deal to say, in fact.

And from the look Callie was now giving him, he could tell she knew that as well.

"You'd better follow me, then," she told them both with a quick wave. "We're between fittings for the opera, so it's a good time."

"I trust that Tilda would tell us directly if it weren't a good time," Hunter said on a laugh. "Or me, at least. She might like Lucy."

"Does she not like you?" Lucy asked him, keeping her voice down. "Why are we here if she doesn't like you?"

Callie laughed merrily. "Tilda likes almost everyone. It just depends on the day and the given circumstances if she likes you at the time. And she adores those who are in awe of her, which is almost everyone, and those who flatter her, which is almost everyone who actually knows her and what she is capable of."

"She sounds terrifying," Lucy murmured.

"She is," Hunter and Callie said together, both without much concern.

Lucy made a soft sound of acknowledgement, which only made Hunter smile. He could understand her concern, in a way. They were likely confusing her with the way they spoke about Tilda and the way they described her, but she was one of the most unique and eccentric people Hunter had ever met. Any attempt at a true description would be lacking and incomplete, as Tilda surpassed what was able to be described. She had to be seen and experienced to be believed.

All would become clear soon enough.

As clear as any encounter with Tilda could ever be, at any rate.

Callie led them down the main corridor, then down the final side corridor to the left, passing racks of dresses bearing the sort of elaborate finery one usually saw on the opera stage. They passed two ajar doors, the rooms clearly used for fittings, and then stopped at the third door, which was only cracked.

She knocked three times in quick succession, then waited.

There was a dramatic sigh from within the room. "Come."

Callie pushed the door open and strode into the room with a confidence that Hunter had never quite seen in his friend, and it made him smile. "We have visitors, Tilda."

The dark-haired woman turned in the chair at her desk, the light in the room illuminating the slightest sheen of silver dotted throughout her tresses. Her eyes narrowed as she gazed at the door.

"Come in, whoever you are."

Hunter moved farther into the room so he could be seen clearly and plastered the most apologetic expression on his face he could. "Good day, Tilda."

A light of recognition lit her features for a moment, then she frowned. "Trick, what have I told you about coming here in the middle of the day? I am far too busy to accommodate whatever it is you need this time."

"If it were for that, I would know better, Tilda, dear. I do apologize." He gestured for Lucy to join him. "But alas, this is for another sort of matter entirely."

Lucy came to his side, biting her lip and looking at Tilda with the sort of terror and helplessness that usually revealed itself in the woman's presence.

Tilda pushed up from her chair slowly, a small smile on her lips. "My, my, my, what have we here, Trick?"

"This is Miss Lucy Allred," Hunter said softly, nodding in encouragement, though Lucy wasn't looking at him. "She is lost. Well, not precisely, but she was—"

"She can tell me," Tilda overrode, cutting him off with a quick hand in the direction of his face. "Tell me your story, Miss Allred."

Lucy bobbed her head in a nod that was practically a curtsy. "I was coming back to London between terms. I'm a teacher at Miss Masters's. My father sent a coach for me, and it was to take me to his new house, which I did not have an address for. And suddenly I was dropped off in a dark and unfamiliar part of London, the coach left me without unloading, and two men tried to abduct me. Trick intervened and saved me, thinking I was Briar, and then Briar showed up. Both of them took me to Trick's flat for the night while he looked for my father, and we still don't know where my father is or lives, and I'm stuck."

She had started to speak more quickly by the end, rambling again, and she ended with a shrug.

"Oh my," Tilda murmured, folding her arms and tapping her upper arm with a finger repeatedly. "So much to digest in one little story. I'll have questions of more detail in a minute, once I've finished processing it all. But firstly, Trick, why are you here? You know I have no messenger contacts, and I am hardly in a position to know someone's respectable father."

"He's not that respectable," Lucy said quickly, surprising Hunter enough that he snorted softly.

Tilda's lips quirked in a slight smile, but she only looked at Hunter pointedly.

Oh right. His reasons.

He cleared his throat. "I don't think it would be a good idea for her to stay in my flat again tonight, given the neighborhood. And I have a patrol, so I wouldn't be there to watch her. Would she be able to stay with you?"

"Of course, there is plenty of space and we could ensure she has a change of clothing, as it sounds as though her belongings departed in the runaway coach." Tilda looked Lucy up and down with her usual calculating expression, then returned her attention to Trick. "But that is hours away, so why now? What do you need at this very moment? And do not tell me it is nothing, because I know you, and it is never nothing with you. You are a 'four steps ahead' sort of creature, and I do not like not knowing a plan when it involves me."

Hunter shook his head, grinning helplessly. "I adore you, Tilda."

"Yes, I know," she quipped without much reaction.

He rubbed the back of his head, feeling as though he were about to tell his mother or his most terrifying aunt something he was embarrassed about. "I did not sleep last night, which wouldn't be a problem, except now I'm going on patrol tonight. So I need sleep, at least two hours, if I can manage it. And Lucy needs to be safe while some of the League's people and mine try to locate her father. So… would you mind?"

Tilda blinked once, then again. "You want me to be a glorified nanny to a Society chit who doesn't know London's left from its right? Whose only trip to the arse-end of this city was an accident of fate? Who is so proper and polite that she'll call me madam and do whatever I ask out of an innate desire to please a slightly older woman in authority?"

Hunter clamped down on his lips for a moment, then nodded. "Yes, actually."

There was a long, slow beat before Tilda all-out beamed at him.

"Why, of course! I would be delighted! I do have some additional fittings to do today, but that shouldn't get in anybody's way. Have you been to the opera recently, Lucy? You don't mind if I call you Lucy, do you? Formality is such a waste of breath. The rehearsing opera will be stunning, simply stunning, so you must make an effort to see it when the shows start. But I've also just finished the costume for Love's Labor Lost at the Theatre Royal, and they have decided not to do modern dress for this one, which delighted me, of course. And if you're quite accommodating, Lucy, I shall fit you up with a few ensembles before you're off in the morning. But what to do with an entire day of you? Have you fed her, Trick? Willow, would you be a dear and make sure we have a hefty meal for supper? Luncheon will be as planned, but we should have a proper supper."

"What is she doing?" Lucy asked Hunter in a slow undertone.

"Rambling," he told her with some satisfaction, setting his hands at his hips and trying not to laugh. "She's clearly very excited about you being here."

"Why?" Lucy shook her head, exhaling shortly. "I'm just a lost high society chit, like she said."

Hunter gave her a bemused look. "Do you know how often she gets to be with normal people? And you're pretty, so she'll be perfectly delighted to dress you up however she likes. She does have impeccable taste, so you will look lovely, and I trust she'll find something you can walk around London with me in as well."

Tilda was pacing the room now, talking to herself rapidly. "Green would be glorious, but red… Oh, she would slay a man in red. Gold, even. Ooh, with spun gold throughout… Is it worth the funds for such extravagance? I'll make it worth the while…"

"Need anything from me, Tilda?" Hunter called out playfully. "Or shall I just…?"

She immediately waved him off. "No, no, go find a quiet corner and nap, you naughty chump. I'll talk with you later. I am sure we'll have something to discuss once I've got all my ideas for Miss Lucy out of my head and am clear once more. Better yet, take one of the empty rooms along the route. But if I catch you sleeping on my costumes again, so help me, Trick…"

He held up his hands in surrender as he backed out of the room.

"I did that once, and I learned my lesson. Never again. Just a few hours of rest and I'll be back for a cup of tea. Two sugars for you?"

She dismissed him with flicks of her fingers, her frown pursing as though she were fighting a smile.

"Wait," Lucy said hastily, taking quick steps towards him. "Where are you going?"

Hunter jerked a thumb over his shoulder. "To sleep, remember? Very tired, patrol later… You'll be fine."

"Don't you dare leave me here with her alone," Lucy hissed, her eyes widening.

"You aren't alone with her," Hunter said. "You also have Callie. Sorry, Willow."

She shook her head rapidly. "You said she killed someone."

"She isn't going to kill you," he assured her with a laugh. "Neither is Willow. You're about to have a wonderful time."

"Do not patronize me, Hunter," Lucy ground out almost viciously. "She is terrifying, and you need to stay here."

He slowly shook his head, still smiling. "I need to sleep. And you need me to sleep. So take a breath, smile, and have fun. I'll see you in a little while." He waved and backed all the way out of the room before turning and strolling down the corridor away from her.

"Trick!" Lucy called in a fairly restrained voice, considering the reverberation in the place. "Trick! Come back here!"

He ignored her and began whistling to himself, knowing exactly which room he was going to use for his nap, if it was available. He knew, from experience, that the chaise in there was plush and comfortable, and that it was not a room used for anything he might find unappetizing for his sleep. He'd been here enough times to test out all of the acceptable furniture, and when he needed a decent sleep…

Well, he didn't usually get decent sleep when he was here because somebody he knew needed something from him and/or a new clue turned up and he wound up lying on whatever furniture, thinking too much. So he needed to hurry to the room before he was found and that happened again.

Sleep was crucial if he wanted to have a decent patrol tonight. He had functioned for longer on less sleep, but tonight was too important. He needed to explore those gaming hells with his assets and try to uncover the traitor among them, if he could. Or find a path to him. Find a link somewhere. Get some insight into this murky mess of factions and guns and betrayal. His assets only knew that he would pay well if they got intelligence that led somewhere, and that he would look the other way on their minor crimes, if not help them get away with it, as the case might have been at times. Nothing where someone was hurt, of course. But he had allowed the occasional robbery from time to time.

His eyes began to ache, a telltale sign that he would sleep very hard when he permitted himself to, and he was more thrilled about that than he was of the idea of Lucy getting fussed over by someone who loved nothing more than fussing over pretty people.

Despite her fears, Lucy would be safer than she knew in Tilda's company and in this place, and she would enjoy herself more than she believed as well. He would wind up hearing all about it when he woke, and it would undoubtedly be entertaining, but nothing would surprise him. He had seen and heard it all with Tilda over the years, and the best course, he had learned, was to expect nothing and be prepared for anything.

She had seen him suitably trussed for every single assignment of his entire career, thinking of details he would never have considered that had proven to make all of the difference in one way or another. She had kept secrets that could have gotten her killed. She had hidden people whom the entire city was on the hunt for. She had met royalty and dressed those of the highest ranks as well as those of the lowest, and somehow, she treated everyone in exactly the same fashion.

He was slightly in love with Tilda, if he were to be honest with himself, but only in the sense that one might love a goddess who had bestowed kindness and favor. She was old enough to be his mother, though he would never tell her so, and admitting any sort of feelings for her would earn him a slap in the face and a stabbing in the back.

Literally. He'd met someone who'd experienced it.

No, Tilda was one of the secret marvels of the world, and he would have need of her later. His patrol tonight, for one.

Exploring gaming hells for the elusive Mr. Martin, formerly of the London League office, while also sniffing out any potential

Faction sympathizers, if not actual operatives on English soil.

Wouldn't that be something? To tie up all of these issues in one neat little patrol…

Realistically, he would find nothing. It would be an evening of information gathering, very little of which would be useful, and he would have to figure out how to keep the men happy and attentive to his interests when he couldn't pay them for a success.

But he'd sleep for a while and see what ideas occurred to him after he woke.

With a deep yawn, he pushed into his chosen room, which was blessedly empty, and collapsed onto the settee, already close to sleep before he could exhale a deep, relaxing breath.

Chapter Nine

Lucy had never met a more terrifying woman in her entire life.

She'd also never met anyone with such talent, genius, and taste.

How her mouth was not fully gaping like some unfortunate fish was astonishing.

She hadn't done anything useful while she sat and observed Tilda work, but she wasn't supposed to do anything, so she was doing exactly as she should. Still, she felt that she should be useful if she was in the room for these fittings. No one wanted an observer in these things who was not an assistant or in possession of a trained eye, and Lucy could boast neither. She was supposed to stay with Tilda while she was here, and so she had done, and this was the third fitting of opera actors since Trick had abandoned her. Each one of them a different stature, of different characters and needs, and differing opinions. But each and every one of them was delighted with what Tilda had done.

This one was positively beaming, and Tilda was almost impervious to the praise. She just continued working with the sort of steadiness and skill that spoke of decades of experience and a certainty of her abilities and taste. She knew she was doing magnificent work and did not need anyone else to confirm it. One might have considered that arrogance, but with Tilda, it instead had all the bearings of confidence without the narcissism and pride of arrogance.

She was a curious sort of person, but Lucy liked her.

At least, she thought she liked her. It was difficult to say when their personal interaction had been limited to their first meeting, but she was fairly certain.

She would know more when the fittings were done.

Willow came and went from the room at Tilda's beck and call, fetching this fabric or that particular thread, pins and ribbons in her hands at any given time. She always offered Lucy a smile or a wink, apparently contented as could be in her work and delighted to be scurrying about for Tilda. It wasn't the sort of occupation that Lucy would have enjoyed, but she could not pretend to understand how Willow would feel about the opportunity.

What she truly did not comprehend was what in the world either of these women had to do with Hunter. He was not a professional actor nor, as far as she could tell, did he have any need for costumes. But she had not even known him for a full day, and he had been wearing the same clothes from the first moment until the present, so what could she really know? Whatever it was he really did, when he was not minding her, could require costumes of some sort.

Perhaps he would require something of the sort for his patrol tonight, whatever that would entail.

"So many questions," Willow murmured as she folded some fabric near Lucy.

Lucy looked at her in shock. "Did I say something aloud without meaning to?"

Willow laughed warmly. "No, love. I can simply see the questions all over your face. Is it Tilda that raises them? Or Trick?"

"Both," Lucy admitted with a tiny smile. "I confess, I have no idea what is going on and am still attempting to catch my breath from last night. Trick is so confusing, and I cannot figure him out in the slightest. I mean, I know I can trust him. He has kept me so wonderfully safe, considering, and he did intervene on my behalf last night, but as to who he is… the sort of man he actually is…" She bit down on her lip hard, more to stop herself from rambling than anything else.

Willow raised a brow, her lips quirking.

"Sorry," Lucy said quickly. "I ramble. Trick has brought it to my attention more than once."

"Ramble away," she replied. "I don't mind. And it only makes sense that you should wonder about him, given your station and being in his protection for the time being."

Lucy's teeth pressed into her lip again. "Yes, of course."

Her station and his protection hadn't exactly been what caused her curiosity about him, but she would let the woman think so. It was certainly more polite and logical than what had caused her questions and mental wanderings on the subject.

She cleared her throat as the image of his crooked smile made her stomach twirl uncomfortably within her.

"And Tilda," she went on hastily, shoving the rather tasty image aside, "is simply extraordinary. I struggle to formulate the questions I have about her. It is more like an existence of questioning in her presence."

"Oddly enough, I understand you perfectly there." Willow chuckled and set the fabric aside, lowering her voice. "I doubt any person alive knows everything about Tilda. She dresses royalty, actresses, members of Society looking to impress at a masquerade…"

Lucy scoffed softly, shaking her head. "Next you're going to tell me she dresses spies for the Crown."

Willow did not laugh. "It would not surprise me," she told her simply. "I ask as few questions as possible. For my own protection. But Tilda is the most loyal person I have ever known. When she likes you, she will protect you to the death. And she's a remarkable amount of fun."

It was not so difficult to see how that could be, given what she had already witnessed in Tilda, but she was still far too intimidated to let herself believe it fully. There was nothing amusing about a woman who could kill you as soon as adorn you in finery and seemed to know everyone and everything.

One did not irritate or irk Tilda, of that much Lucy was absolutely certain.

At that moment, Tilda tsked loudly and flicked her fingers towards the door. "Very well, Signore Conti, away with you. Willow, see him divested of the ensemble without disrupting the setting. It will need to be ready for his performance on Thursday."

"Of course, Tilda," Willow returned with a quick nod, gesturing the actor towards the door and following him out of the room.

Leaving Lucy alone with Tilda.

She met the woman's eyes and tried not to swallow.

"No more appointments for the theatre, darling," Tilda told her, setting her hands at her hips and looking the most relaxed Lucy had seen her yet. "What would you like to do?"

"Do?" she repeated, her voice rasping in surprise. "I don't..." She shook her head. "I don't expect to be entertained, Madame Tilda. I am quite content to sit quietly while you go about your business, or pay calls, or... take a rest, if you... erm..."

"Pay calls." Tilda grinned wryly, her eyes twinkling. "Do you think me so very fine that I pay calls in my spare moments? Use your imagination, dear."

"I'm one of the young ladies of higher society," Lucy said bluntly. "I'm not permitted an imagination."

Tilda's brows rose in unison, and then she burst out laughing. "What a delightfully frank yet apt description!" She clapped her hands and dropped herself into a nearby chair, crossing her legs inelegantly and revealing at least half of her lower legs and the tidy stockings encasing each. "You've a very clear sight of yourself, don't you, Lucy?"

There was not much to do but lift a shoulder in what was hopefully a dainty shrug. "What else can I have? My upbringing doesn't allow me much, and when I have seen as an adult that my father wastes everything we have, I have realized how utterly useless I am to changing my life or my situation."

"Careful, darling," Tilda warned, drumming her fingers on the arm of her chair. "That smacks of cynicism."

"Which I am also not permitted to have," Lucy retorted, her fingers rubbing together as though in response to what Tilda's were doing. "Is it dreadful to not be overly concerned that I am not spending this time with my father? All I have that I can be proud of is my teaching position, and being away from it to visit him is mere politeness. I would gladly have remained behind and felt useful and valued instead of being reminded of the reality of my life."

Tilda waved her hand dismissively. "Your reality is what you make of it, and you are doing so by teaching. It may feel slow to you, but one of these days, you will find that there is a path you've been walking that is leading exactly the way you wish it would."

That was rather patronizing, in Lucy's mind. Far too simple an idea for someone she had just met, and someone who clearly had the means and motivation to be as independent as she chose. That told Lucy that Tilda had not grown up in high society, where ambition was only focused in improving station by marriage, and had been raised to climb instead, so to speak.

Lucy had been raised to sit.

Sit and wait.

Do as she was told.

Be accomplished and appealing.

So far, Lucy had failed there.

But arguing with Tilda wouldn't serve anything, as far as she could tell, so she only dipped her chin. "Still, I find I'm enjoying myself far more than I should, considering I was nearly abducted and, for all intents and purposes, am lost in London."

"Trick does have that effect on people." Tilda nodded rather sympathetically, not at all shocked or perturbed by the revelation. Nor did she seem to find it amusing. Rather a simple statement that she could verify.

What a bewildering world Lucy had stumbled upon.

"I don't know about it being him, specifically," she began slowly, twisting her lips in thought. "Do not misunderstand me, there are certainly some fascinating qualities about him."

"Fascinating ones, yes," Tilda murmured with a sage nod that might have been mocking.

Lucy chose to ignore the possible mockery. "But it is more than that. Life is… well, it is so different like this. Less structured and more exciting. More dangerous, certainly, but I haven't been particularly afraid. Perhaps I do not know enough to be afraid, but Trick has certainly warned me enough that I should be. I have yet to feel much concern about my father's whereabouts, not because I do not care, but because I know him. I have no doubt that his new house is in a part of London that is far more dangerous and unfortunate than where we were previously, and I have no doubt that he continues to lose whatever we have at gaming tables and other gambling avenues. You will notice there are no Bow Street Runners scouring London for me, or if they are, they are dreadful at doing so."

Tilda made a soft snorting sound, tilting her head on a sort of laugh, but said nothing.

Curious.

"He is not concerned about me," Lucy went on, wondering what had loosened her tongue before this woman so easily. "And I am not concerned about him. So what sort of family does that make us? Why should I not prefer seeing a new side of London under good protection instead of wasting hours of my life with him?"

The room was silent, but not uncomfortably so. Rather like Tilda might be truly considering the questions and wondering how to answer, and Lucy had no issue with waiting patiently for those answers, whatever they might be.

"You prove a valid point," Tilda eventually said, "and provide valuable insight."

"For what?" Lucy asked, blinking in confusion.

Tilda's mouth stretched into a smile. "For how I should dress you, of course. You'll need a couple of days' worth of common wear, and I think I may work up a fancy or two."

"A fancy?" Lucy shook her head. "What in the world do you mean?"

"I have a fancy to fully adorn you in finery, despite the present circumstances we're putting you in." She shrugged, resting her chin in her hands and batting her lashes.

Lucy stared at the insane woman for longer than was polite. "Whatever for? As you said, it will not suit the present circumstances."

"When has that ever stopped a woman from getting her way in fashion?" Tilda retorted. "I'll think of some reason and keep the fancy things here, but I simply must do it or the ideas will not leave my head. Dreadful things happen when ideas do not leave my head. I almost ruined one of the Mozart operas once due to the issue." She shuddered dramatically, making Lucy smile in spite of herself.

"Surely, you have better things to do," she murmured, scratching behind her ear awkwardly.

Tilda set both feet on the floor firmly, leaning closer to Lucy with a mischievous smile. "Better things than to make a pretty girl who has been through hell feel a little bit better by putting her in lovely gowns and costumes to make her feel more like herself while she explores this new side of London she's been dropped in? I think not."

Lucy giggled at the idea. "I thought you said this was the arse-end of London."

"I thought high society misses did not use such language." She winked and pushed herself up to her feet. "Come on, dear. We'll do the initial fittings, and then I think you deserve a lovely, hot bath. I never offer Trick a bath here because I don't want him to start getting spoiled, so if he knows that is something I can offer…"

"I won't say a word," Lucy swore earnestly, suddenly yearning for a hot bath with lovely-smelling soaps and a warm fire. She hadn't enjoyed anything so elegant since her mother had decided to treat her on one of her birthdays, but living in this particular part of London even for a few hours left her feeling perpetually filthy, and she wondered if her hair was crawling with nits or the like.

Her scalp itched as though the creatures were indeed there, and she barely avoided scratching out of instinct.

"Come with me, and we'll find one of the other fitting rooms that is not in use," Tilda told her, offering a hand. "Willow and a few of my other girls will help and advise, and I think you'll enjoy their input. Particularly for your common wear. Now, is there anything you actually need besides the present requirements?"

"I'm not sure," Lucy admitted as she took the woman's hand and allowed herself to be led from the room. "My trunks did not get abducted with me, so I have nothing."

"Pah!" Tilda exclaimed, pressing a hand to her chest as though distressed. "I forgot! Never mind, I will tress you up like a modiste for a bride."

"I cannot possibly take a whole trousseau!" Lucy protested. "I cannot afford it! And however would I transport the things? I have no lodgings!"

Tilda gave her a scolding look. "We'll store some things here, and I will give you a lovely carpetbag that will perfectly blend in with your disguise, and you will appear as nothing more than an average woman possibly seeking employment or lodgings in London, and no one will be the wiser. Besides, you are sleeping here tonight, so we do not have to worry about transporting anything until tomorrow!" Tilda began laughing uproariously, sounding a bit too much like a villain of novels or stage for Lucy's taste.

"You are enjoying this far too much," she told the older woman as they moved down the corridor.

"I love what I do," Tilda admitted without shame. "I enjoy almost every moment. Now, given that tomorrow you will be back on the streets with Trick, at least for part of the day, I am going to also fit you for some defensive objects that you will find useful." Lucy stared at her. "Don't look so startled. They do not require skill or training, and I know several fine women who carry the same on their person."

Visions of booted daggers and tiny pistols sprang into Lucy's mind, and she shook her head to clear the ideas, knowing Tilda would never give her such dangerous items when she was just as inept as a fern when it came to such things. Surely, she only meant some stays with additional boning in them to protect her from attack, or secret pockets for coins or the like.

A bonnet with excessive hair pins to become weapons under extreme need? Boots that bore metal in the toe to injure any future abductors? There was no telling where the woman's mind might go or what other women in London secretly carried on them for protection or defense, and Lucy did not want to know for certain.

The more her eyes were opened, the more she wanted them closed. Not entirely, not completely, and not until her curiosity was sated, but she did understand a little more how ignorance could be bliss.

Well, maybe not bliss, but comfortable.

Then again, she also completely understood how it was confining. How it narrowed one's view of the world. How it birthed naivete and encouraged aloofness.

Perhaps she could keep one eye open in the future. It would be better than going back entirely. Besides, she was already having to open her eyes further than other girls, given her situation. What was wrong with seeing a bit more of the world as it really was?

She might need to know such things one day. Might need to live in such a world, if her father could not mind himself. Perhaps Tilda's faux trousseau might become necessary after all.

"Nancy, Amy," Tilda called out, flagging down some women ahead. "Bring the fabrics and patterns from the Wicker Room to Algernon Three and see if Polly and Agnes can join us as well. We're going for a full set with Lucy here, and I will need several hands and even more notes. See that a note is sent to Cobb for any footwear he can spare and send one of the lads to Martinique to call in what she owes me. I finally have a use for it."

The girls nodded and dashed off, and Lucy felt more confused than ever before, but as had been the form of the day, kept her mouth shut and let the one with insight do the talking. And the leading. And everything, really.

Lucy was about to become a doll, it seemed, and it was time to play dress-up.

"Now, you just smile and pretend this is part of your plan for the day," Tilda told her in an undertone. "Nothing amiss, nothing strange, and it is all just a bit of fun. Then we will see you bathed and clothed in something you have not worn for two days, and that fine dinner we spoke of earlier will be brought in. And I promise you that tonight you will sleep like a goddess, as I never keep bedding fit for any other on the premises."

All of it sounded delightful, and Lucy bit back a sigh of anticipation. "And Trick?"

Tilda scoffed loudly. "He's going on patrol later. He does not need to know that we will be enjoying Belgian drinking chocolate and expensive Parisian biscuits in our dressing gowns in his absence, does he?"

Lucy grinned without any reservation whatsoever. "No, he most certainly does not."

Chapter Ten

Hunter sat bolt upright with a gasp that completely racked his chest, beads of perspiration at his hairline, and his lungs seizing at any and all air in their vicinity.

It took him a moment to recognize his surroundings, as they were a far cry from the dark and dank alleys he had just been exploring, but once he did so, he fell back against the chaise with a relieved exhale, putting a hand to his brow.

He didn't normally dream so dramatically. In fact, he rarely remembered his dreams at all, when he had them. But he hadn't expected to find his sister in the dangerous places he investigated, and certainly not with the focus of his current investigation, the elusive Mr. Martin, holding a knife to her throat. Of course, Mr. Martin was, by all accounts, such a scrawny and limply build chap that Hal could have set the man flat on his back and had the knife in her possession before Hunter would have had to even move for his own weapon, but rationality rarely made itself a part of dreams.

Rubbing at his face, Hunter blinked hard, trying to force the remnants of sleep from his eyes and his countenance. How long had he managed to rest for? If he was dreaming so intensely, and of his sister, he either had slept for a very long time, or had simply been in far greater need of that sleep than he'd anticipated.

Why had he dreamed of his sister anyway? He rarely worried about her. She was a capable operative and asset in her own right, and was married to one as well. Not to mention, their home was filled with more operatives posing as servants than they likely even knew, so they were quite well protected. But better spies had died with less, and he was well aware of it. He ought to visit Hal and John one of these days, just to get whatever inkling of worry that was inhabiting his deeper mind out of his system. Assuring himself of their mutual safety and protection of each other would do him good.

Hal would mock him incessantly if she knew he was dreaming about her safety. And then she would scold him for getting distracted from his work, which was going to risk his safety.

She understood him and the world he inhabited too well, and their relationship was only stronger for it.

Her last letter hadn't indicated any trouble in her life, but she was very careful not to tell him anything that could cause worry. He had learned very early on that he needed to have his own set of eyes and ears involved in his twin's life in order to know the truth, and the reports he received lately matched her letters.

There was no cause to worry. None whatsoever.

But the panic still hovered right above his chest, and he knew it would not go away until he had seen Hal for himself and talked with her.

Hunter allowed himself several long, slow breaths that settled his lungs and calmed his still-rattled pulse. He fumbled about his pockets for his watch and glanced at it lazily, then started and jolted back to a sitting position. He would need to leave within the hour for his patrol if he did not want to rush things. How in the world had Tilda let him sleep so long? She was typically rather exacting with her allowance of his use of her comforts, but he had been in here hours taking his rest. He hadn't needed all that much, especially for tonight's functionality.

And yet…

He craned his neck from side to side, feeling an invigorating crack or two there, then swung his legs from the divan and set his feet solidly on the floor. He took a minute to inhale a slow breath again, then pushed himself up on the exhale and moved to the door of the room, yanking it open and striding out in the direction of Tilda's office.

Or drawing room, parlor, workshop, or whatever she was calling her private room these days.

The place was far less bustling now than it had been earlier, but that was how things went around here. The ladies had work to do, in one sense or another, and the later in the day it got, the more varied their places for that work became. Tilda, on the other hand, he knew would be here, given she had begun living on the premises in the last year or two. Whether that was for her own comfort or safety, or it was something that financial demands required, Hunter couldn't say, but nobody, not even the Shopkeepers—those in charge of all operative assignments and tasks in England—could tell Tilda what she could or could not do with her personal life.

He was fairly certain that was how Weaver had gotten the scar over his left eye.

Hunter gripped the back of his neck absently as he rounded the corner, his step slowing as he heard a chorus of loud giggles in at least three different tones come from one of the rooms up ahead. Laughter wasn't uncommon here, but people were usually too busy for so many of them to laugh at once. And given the time of day, he couldn't imagine who would be gathered around to do so.

Ah, Tilda had mentioned something about a supper. Perhaps she and Lucy had recruited some others to eat with them.

Perhaps he could grab a few of the foodstuffs for himself to devour as he headed to his patrol. His stomach rumbled hopefully.

The closer he drew to the room, the louder the voices within became, though there were no repeated peals of laughter during his progress. Still, he was curious, and he wasn't certain if he was going to need to apologize to Tilda, encourage Lucy, or beg a favor of Callie after missing so much of the day. Knowing better than to just push a door open in this place, Hunter knocked lightly.

"Come!" Tilda called out, laughter rampant in her voice.

Nudging the door with his foot, Hunter fixed a polite smile on his face, his eyes scanning about in instinctual observation.

He froze when he saw the large screen drawn about a section of the room and only saw Tilda and Callie on this side of it, both of them in thick dressing gowns over the dresses he had seen them in earlier, their hair half-down but by no means unkempt.

Lucy was nowhere to be seen.

"Did you have a nice nap, Trick?" Tilda asked him as she ran her fingers through her hair, her other hand cradling a glass of something or other, which could account for the slight looseness of her tongue.

"Quite satisfactory," he replied without much effort, looking at Callie questioningly.

But Callie, it would seem, was spending too much time with Tilda and only grinned mischievously at him. She held no beverage, but there was an empty glass nearby.

Marvelous. Inebriated women were watching his charge for him while he engaged in dangerous work.

His charge who was missing from this space.

"It ought to have been," Callie said bluntly. "You were at it long enough. We've gotten so much done in that time."

"Congratulations," Hunter told her, looking at Tilda again. "Where is Lucy?"

"Here!"

To his immense internal horror, Lucy stepped out from behind the screen in a dressing gown that matched that of the other two, but her hair was completely down, soaking wet, and her bare feet and ankles exposed as she walked into view.

She was the most beautiful, tempting, distracting sight he had ever seen. Ever.

His throat clenched painfully, and his eyes were instructed to move to the floor, but all they did was move to Lucy's feet, focusing on her toes as though he had never seen such a thing in his entire life.

"Sorry," she continued in a low voice just for him, unmoved by or unaware of Hunter's present state of torture. "Tilda offered a hot bath after we finished our fittings, and I just could not resist. You are not supposed to know about that, so pretend I said nothing. Your flat is very nice for where it is, but I couldn't shake the feeling that I might have nits or something, and I just felt coated in a state of dirt in some way. Perhaps from the carriage travel? Who can say? And Tilda does have some marvelous soaps and oils, but don't worry, none of it will set me aside from anyone when we have to be out and about tomorrow. And the water was perfectly hot…"

Bloody actual hell. The woman needed to stop talking about the bath, the water, the soap, and anything else regarding pretty much anything at the moment, rambling or not.

He lacked the power to tell her so, but his thoughts raced back and forth between scolding and imagery with such furious speed, his head was beginning to ache.

"…and you should see the gowns that Tilda has being made for me! Whenever we get me to where I need to go, I am going to have to send for them because there is no possibility of my wearing anything of the sort while I'm with you."

Hellfire. That was what was currently licking at his ankles, the inside of his left knee, the pit of his stomach, and his right ear. It burned like the devil and the smell of brimstone was definitely infiltrating his nostrils.

What he had done to incur such eternal torment, he couldn't say. Nothing recent, certainly, but perhaps some of his older assignments…

"You'll be very pleased with what we're dressing her in tomorrow, Trick." Tilda's voice pushed into his non-burning ear, reminding him of his present place and situation. "She'll be a perfect little street urchin."

Now that was an image he could dwell upon without any problem, and a blissful cooling sensation began to settle on him, starting inside his own mind, ironically enough.

"Good," he heard himself say, his eyes shifting over to her without traveling over any other part of Lucy's person. "Does this mean I can have my coat back?"

"That is your concern?" Lucy demanded with a laugh. "Utterly ridiculous, that thing is so tattered and torn."

"Shh," Tilda soothed. "They have been through a lot together, my lamb. He's very attached to it."

The women giggled again, and Hunter couldn't find it within himself to even smile. The cooling bliss hadn't gone that far to settling him.

He didn't give a damn about his coat. He was simply trying to get through the conversation so he could get out of there and get to work. Actual work. Focusing work.

Non-distracting work.

But it was a nice coat, all things considered. Tilda had made it for him.

Where had it gone, anyway?

Tilda tilted her head at him, her knowing eyes seeing far too much. "Trick? Still with us?"

Hunter blinked. "Yes, of course. I trust you will all be quite well here while I am gone on patrol?"

One of her trim brows rose. "Yes…"

He nodded once. "Good." He made himself look at Lucy, just her face, and forced a smile. "I will see you in the morning. Hopefully, I will have news of your father."

Her forehead furrowed amidst the damp tendrils currently dancing against the skin. "I thought you were not focused on him tonight."

"I'm not. But my contacts are still looking, so information could come while on patrol." He cleared his throat and took a step back, though no one had come anywhere near him. "Tilda, might I avail myself of whatever is ready to wear?"

"Yes, yes," she said with a wave. "You know where to go. Bring it all back in a timely manner. The laundress gets most fussy when things are out of proportion."

"Supper is in the Skye Room," Callie told Hunter, reaching out to take his arm quickly. "It's very good. Take something for on the way out. You know they don't have good food in those places."

Actually, the food was improving in the gaming hells, so Callie would be wrong there, but he would let her think she was doing him a kindness.

"I will do that, thank you," he replied with a nod in her direction, backing up farther. Taking in a quick breath, he met Lucy's eyes once more. "Enjoy your evening. But don't let these two take you out of the building. I don't trust them that far."

"I beg your pardon?" Tilda protested in a shrill voice, while Callie cackled with glee.

Lucy grinned, looking between the two of them with the sort of air that told Hunter she was already too fond of them. "I don't know, I think it could be rather fun."

"Ha!" Tilda pointed at him with a victorious finger. "Get out. Go patrol. Collect my winnings, if you don't mind."

He snorted softly and bowed with all politeness, not in the least surprised that Tilda had standing bets with the clubs he would be frequenting. She probably had understandings with owners all across

London. That could even be where the steadiness of her income came from, if the costuming returns were down.

One never knew with Tilda.

"Is it wrong to wish you a good night when you are going on patrol?" Lucy asked, innocently following him to the door.

He tried not to back up more quickly. "No, not wrong. I hope it is good. There's a lot to do and wasting time has never been enjoyable for me. I wish you a good night as well."

"You said that."

Did he? Time to go, it seemed.

Lucy smiled, beginning to plait her damp hair, which had the unfortunate effect of drawing his eyes to her fingers, which made his fingers itch to feel her hair, which made him picture plaiting her hair himself, even if he didn't know how to do it. "Will you bring me a souvenir? I've never been where you're going."

He cleared his throat again and stepped out of the room. "If I remember it and find something suitable, perhaps. Good evening." Before he could say or do anything else stupid, he turned on his heel and walked pointedly down the corridor as fast as he could without looking suspicious.

He barely remembered to go to the ready racks, as Tilda called them, and pick up a new shirt and coat as well as a hat, and it was fortunate that he remembered the Skye Room and the food within, let alone that he stuffed his new pockets with things.

It was fortunate that he remembered which way to turn when he left the building, and it was fortunate that the scent of whatever soaps or oils Tilda had given Lucy had faded from his nostrils by the time he was four blocks away.

Now he would forever think of Lucy fresh from the bath when he smelled that.

He prayed it was some foreign scent he would never encounter again. He could not afford to.

The sun was close to setting now, and he was grateful for the increased darkness of the winter months. It was much easier to accomplish his tasks in the dark, and when night fell earlier, the men he needed to associate with appeared earlier as well. Of course, he was farther away from his usual haunts today than on other days, but there was still plenty of time.

He needed any and all information he could garner from this patrol. If Martin liked gaming and was keeping his nose to the dirtier London ground than he had been before, it was entirely possible that he might find the man himself tonight. There were far too many dens and clubs to inspect in one night, even with his eager bunch, but he could get to the most likely locations and find out what others were saying. He had contacts in all of them anyway, and they knew enough to report key words to him.

It needed to be a useful night after a fairly useless day. How could he have let himself sleep so much? He could have been making himself useful somehow, and instead…

Well, there wasn't much to be done about it now.

He would just have to make the most use of the time he had. He wouldn't hear a thing about Lucy's father tonight, no matter what he had told her. Not unless her father was in one of these places, but that wasn't likely. Even the worst Mayfair folk never set foot down there, preferring what they thought were the filthy haunts over in St. James.

The gentlemen were never as dark and villainous as they liked to think. Those qualities belonged to an entirely different breed of men, and it was Hunter's job to know those ones particularly well. After all these years, he could think like them, track them, and even smell them, and anticipate their next actions.

It was what made him so good that he had stayed in his deep-cover position for this long.

Adjusting the cap on his head to sit lower and tugging his collar to look a little unkempt, Hunter turned down a block that would allow him a more direct route to the Thames, preferring the darker river walk towards the clubs than the street level. People were more likely to avoid him and more likely to behave naturally, which made his observations more accurate.

He needed his thoughts to be as clear as possible for the night ahead. And if he could practice his observational skills while he walked, even better.

The smell of the river soon wafted around and through him, and though it wasn't a classically pleasant scent, he inhaled it deeply. This was a smell as familiar to him as that of home, and there was an odd comfort to it that he might never be able to explain. Some of his finest as well as most dangerous times had taken place with this smell pervading his senses. In some ways, he wouldn't know how to do this if that smell were gone.

He found himself smiling as he strode along the darkening river walk, the comfortable mantle of his position and cover falling across his shoulders perfectly and sinking deep into his chest. Becoming part of him, and soon encasing the entirety of him.

This was the beauty of his persona as Trick. It was so much him that the lines between truth and alias were impossible to fully distinguish. He could have lived his entire life as one or the other without anyone knowing the difference, and as far as he knew, he would be doing so. Not because he was that good and anticipated working as Trick until he was old and grey, but because he would probably die while he was doing it, and he had become perfectly accustomed to the idea.

But he would take growing old and grey as Trick too. If the option was possible.

He walked a while more, finally finding a good side street to turn up, and settled into his stride, winding his way through various blocks until he was to the Black Dolphin. One of his men was already outside of it, cigar in place, the glow of its tip one of the few lights in the street.

"Anyone inside?" Hunter inquired as he reached him.

He nodded once. "Two. Still early, though." He puffed out a long breath of smoke. "Drink before we go?"

Hunter snorted once. "You buying?"

His man shrugged. "I'll buy you one. Any more, and the others will have to do."

"You must be confident we'll find something, if you're willing to buy even one." Hunter laughed and clamped a hand on his shoulder. "I'll take the one and pray that you're right."

The cigar was tapped against the wall, glowing ash tumbling to the ground. "Don't pretend you have religion, Trick. Just trust me."

"I don't," Hunter replied. "But I trust your instincts, so that will have to do."

Chapter Eleven

"We already did fittings, Tilda. I don't understand why we're doing more."

"Because I have more ideas, Lucy, and I will not be able to sleep until they are out of my head."

Lucy sighed and submitted to the endeavor again, though she was quite certain there was only so much that could be done now that had not been done hours before.

She had been to the modiste plenty of times in her life. Had been fitted for several gowns for various occasions. Had been pinned and pricked and prodded and measured from head to toe again and again, as her position in Society dictated.

But never in her entire life had she experienced what being worked at by Tilda and her assistants was like.

There were only two assistants now, but there had been five earlier. They all bustled about Lucy while she stood on an actual pedestal in various states of undress. She was measured in places she had never been measured before and had endured at least twenty-seven fabrics being draped over her, though it seemed only a portion of those fabrics were actually selected. She was certain that the women were speaking English among themselves, but there had to be some sort of code to their words because Lucy wasn't understanding any of it.

Now, she had one of the previous fabrics wrapped around her upper half and one of the assistants—Polly, perhaps?—was busy ruching the bodice into delicate folds and pinning them into place. Long swaths of the same fabric were tucked into a ribbon at her waist and dangled at her toes, but parted into an almost curtain-like pattern in her front that presently revealed her petticoats in their full. The skin of her shins and ankles was beginning to tingle, gooseflesh raising on their surfaces in the exposed air of the room.

Not that her shins could be seen. Her petticoats, she flattered herself, were long enough to be polite and appropriate, but without her stockings to shield her skin from contact with the thin cotton of them, everything was more sensitive.

What was going to go in this gap of the sprigged fabric? It was a lovely golden primrose shade, with the sprigged details in black thread, but what was Tilda envisioning to accompany it? And more to the point, where did she imagine Lucy was going to wear this? The fabric wasn't silk, but it was similar in texture and sturdier than muslin. It seemed very fine, and Hunter had wanted Lucy to have a more common set of gowns for their wanderings.

She was not likely to wander into a ballroom or card party, which was the only place she felt this dress would be appropriate for.

Still, Tilda got her way, and even at this late hour of the night, she would be obeyed.

Lucy hid a yawn behind a hand, but apparently not well enough, for Tilda gave her a shrewd look, her lips forming a tight, thin line.

"Sorry," Lucy murmured, her cheeks heating.

Tilda waved it off. "No matter. I plied you with warm beverages after a luxurious bath and then expected you to be able to stand still and be alert. My own fault, entirely. But this is the last one, I promise."

Lucy felt her more outspoken side arise. "You said that two gowns ago."

"No, I said 'one more' after those," Tilda corrected with a flash of a grin. "I never said it would be only one more."

Eyes had never rolled as hard as Lucy's did at that moment. "We are going to have too much for the simple carpet bag you said I would carry."

Tilda shrugged without any concern whatsoever. "We'll pack what makes sense for your present situation and keep the rest here until you are home."

"Would it not be prudent to only create what makes sense for my present situation?" Lucy posed, trying not to sound derisive in her tone. After all, the woman was doing all of this without the prospect of payment, and Lucy was very much enjoying the time she was spending with her, in spite of feeling rather like a pin cushion.

"I cannot be bothered with only thinking in terms of sense when fashion is my calling," Tilda scoffed as she stretched out a measuring tape and came to mark the distance between the hollow of Lucy's throat and the dip in her bodice that Polly had pinned.

Lucy did her best not to shake her head, particularly when an intimidating and potentially dangerous woman had her hands near her throat. "You are such a contradiction, Tilda."

"Hush, darling, we're trying to work." But Tilda's lips twitched in a hint of laughter, and Lucy struggled to hide a smile as well.

Polly stepped back from the bodice and cocked her head as she surveyed her work. "Madame, I think some black lace or ribbon might help the neckline. And flowers, if we're doing the beading."

"Oh, we will certainly do the beading," Tilda assured her as she now measured the circumference of Lucy's throat. "Beaded flowers among the sprigged details. It's a lovely fabric, but I intend to see it enhanced. Yes, a trio of black rosettes at the apex of the neckline… I quite agree, Polly."

Lucy clamped down on her lips to keep from speaking, imagining great feathery rosettes hiding pretty much all of the ruching work Polly had just done, given the lack of substance to her bodice region. It wasn't flat, exactly, but no one had claimed her figure to be ample.

Still, they were the fashion experts, and she was the one who simply had to wear the items. And they could see her size in all aspects, so they must believe something good could come from the design.

One could only hope it was the best of imaginings instead of the worst.

Lucy shifted her focus as Willow brought a shimmering ivory fabric into the room, sighing heavily as she did so. "I found it, Madame. Aberdeen Suite."

Tilda groaned and shook her head, stepping back from Lucy and taking a corner of the fabric between her fingers. "Who the devil put this in the Aberdeen Suite? As though I would ever… Well, never mind. It is here now." She turned to Lucy with a satisfied smirk. "This is the perfect touch to the gown. It catches the hint of gold in the outer fabric and reflects it beautifully. We'll layer this beneath, and you will be amazed at how this style elongates your figure."

"Do I need elongating?" Lucy quipped to the laughter of everyone in the room.

Tilda narrowed her eyes, a small smile pinching at her mouth. "Elongation adds majesty and grace to any woman. You have plenty of both, but who wouldn't love more?" She nodded to Willow and released the fabric, wiping a hand at her brow before setting her hands at her hips and looking Lucy over.

And frowning.

And looking her over.

And frowning.

Lucy was not normally a self-conscious woman, but even she had her limits. "What?" she eventually asked with more than a hint of strife to her tone.

Tilda shook her head in a surprisingly firm manner. "I adore this gown. But something is telling me to change it."

"Change it?" Lucy cried, looking down at herself and all of the work that had been done already. "It's more than half-pinned now!"

"You're right," Tilda murmured slowly, tilting her head and pursing her lips. "This should stay. I think we may need one more gown, then."

Lucy groaned, letting her head fall back. "Tilda!"

"Don't argue, darling. I need to put you in something red." She nodded once, then again, and snapped her fingers. "Agnes, I need the burgundy silks. Aspen Room. I don't know which yet, so bring me your three favorite bolts."

"Yes, madam." Agnes rose from her position at the hem behind Lucy and hurried from the room. Willow took up her place to finish whatever needed to be done, humming to herself.

Lucy shook her head in disbelief. "Tilda… All of this is just too much. I don't need—"

"It's not about need, Lucy," Tilda overrode at once, coming over to pin sheer primrose fabric as sleeves to the present gown. "It's about celebration. We only have our bloom once, and then spend our entire lives making the best of its fading. Allow me to highlight your bloom for you while it is still here. Not for the purpose of securing a match or the like, but to celebrate being a woman in her bloom."

It was a powerful, poignant, beautiful sentiment, and one that Lucy had never considered before. Perhaps she had been too quick to discount the value of a bloom. A woman was fortunate to have beauty, but it was simply another accomplishment to make her attractive to a suitor. No one had ever led her to believe one could enjoy their appearance for their own sake.

What would it be like to live in a world where there was freedom to think and feel that way? To dress in such a way? To experience breathing and living just with the joy of being herself?

"Red," Lucy finally said, her voice slightly choked with unexpected emotion. "Do you think red will suit my bloom, as you call it?"

Tilda paused in her action, her eyes widening as she looked Lucy directly in the face. "Suit? Dear girl, if I were you, I would only wear shades of red. Not only while you have your bloom, but for the rest of your days. You have the most perfect coloring for wearing red I have ever seen. It will highlight your complexion into something glorious and enhance the dark depths of your eyes into mystic pools. You will look exotic yet classic; ethereal yet tangible; natural yet supernal. And it will be all for yourself, my dear. I don't care if there is a single eligible man in the room when you wear red. You will wear red for yourself."

How could she have tears forming in her eyes at that? How could it move her to such an extent that she was actually near to full-on weeping? She had been complimented before, and occasionally with some sincerity, but this? This was a woman who had nothing to gain from making Lucy feel good about her appearance and her apparel. There was no benefit to anyone by doing so; Lucy had no money to spend on Tilda as a modiste, and she knew it.

Which meant she must be telling the truth, even if it was only the truth as Tilda saw it.

Lucy wished with all her might that she had discussed Tilda with Hunter further before he had left. She believed she could trust her and what she said; that the woman would not say things unnecessarily or in flattery. And she further believed that the woman was not inclined to be kind for the sake of kindness, however good her heart might be in secret, but she'd only known her a few hours. If Hunter were here, or if they had discussed Tilda in a bit more detail, she might have a better understanding of the woman, and therefore could tell with more certainty if the woman was being sincere.

People said all sorts of things to each other that weren't strictly true. Lucy's father had proven that to her time and time again, which had the unfortunate effect of making her prone to disbelieving anyone's words of praise. But Tilda seemed too genuine an individual to follow in the same path as her father. If she felt a certain way, she would express it, for good or for ill.

Lucy had to believe her. There was no other option.

Somehow, her neck and head began to move in sync, nodding at Tilda's words, and her lips curved upwards. "All right. Red it is."

Tilda winked at her, smiling widely. "Marvelous. Not that I am giving you a choice. The red ensembles that I will array you in will speak to my genius as well as your beauty, and I intend to be quite the artist with you as my canvas. Prepare yourself for being the object of fashionable envy, Miss Lucy, for it is coming, and it will come in hordes."

That was a trifle intimidating to fully comprehend and gave Lucy the sudden sensation that she'd bitten into a lemon, but she avoided any external reaction that might bring further comment from Tilda. After all, she did not wish to imply that she did not trust the woman's skill and vision. If she wanted Lucy to be some sort of sculpture of her lifetime's artwork, then Lucy would do her best to accommodate her, even if she were never brave enough to wear the exquisite creations in public.

It would become a beautiful fantasy that Lucy would keep to herself and cling to when she could not sleep at night. The idea of walking into a ballroom in a stunning, unique gown of wine red, the fabric practically liquid across her form as she moved. Shimmering like a living ruby in the candlelight, as beautiful as Tilda envisioned her to be, and not at all the awkward chit that Lucy had always been socially. She would dance as much as she liked and with whomever she liked, gliding across the floor like a goddess of grace among the partners, not giving any of them particular attention, but dancing for her own amusement. Wearing red for her own amusement. Looking beautiful for her own amusement.

Not paying any attention to where her father was, if he was, or what he was.

Just her.

She could almost feel that freedom now, standing here as the ladies finished with the yellow dress and then stripped it from her. She could almost feel the tingles of her skin shedding its demureness, its shield, its reserve that she had practiced so intently. She could almost sense the confidence rising in her chest, changing the way she breathed and the way she carried herself. She nearly felt the permanent smile fixed upon her lips, which would be as brilliantly red as the gown she'd wear. She was so close to the brilliance in that fantasy.

So close. But not quite.

Just almost.

A burst of sadness hit her stomach as though she had been stabbed, sending ice into her lungs where only moments ago there had been a hint of warm independence. Her fingers became cold as they hung by her side, as Agnes returned with the red silks and the quartet of women began to hold each against her skin and debate their merits. She was barely aware of Tilda's selection and of the design details she was suddenly instructing to her capable assistants.

It was not that Lucy was now uninterested in this process, or not invested in the gown and its creation. It was not that she wished to resist or be reluctant. It was not even that she had never worn a bold red before.

It was simply that she knew it would only ever be a fantasy. She might be able to wear the dress if her father were not attending an event with her and she could convince someone else to escort her, but she would never have the poise necessary to make Tilda's vision—and now her own—a reality. She would never be so confident and so beautiful as she wished, which meant the gown would never perfectly suit, no matter what Tilda thought.

None of this was real.

She was going to end up married to a moderately incomed clergyman who would probably have no taste for finery, so the gown would hang in her bureau like some forbidden fruit. Unable to wear it yet unable to let it go. A life she could have had but wouldn't.

A woman she could have been but wasn't.

She closed her eyes while the women worked, no tears at hand, but a deeper ache as she longed for a different life. A different father. A different home. A different version of herself.

A different anything, at this point.

But she would take this gown anyway, and with it, she would dream.

"How do you feel about black gauze overlay?" Tilda asked with a quick glance up at Lucy.

She tried to shrug without moving for fear of disrupting the pinning process. "Fine, I suppose."

Tilda was either distracted or not as intuitive as she had been earlier, since she didn't press Lucy on her tone or hesitation. "Perfect. I think these reds would have more power on you if we darkened them further. And if we go for the thinnest gauze we can, it will shimmer between shades beautifully. Very rich and bold without being particularly daring, if you will. We don't want people to simply gawk at you. We want them to be envious and in awe."

Lucy managed a smile but could not let herself imagine that anyone would ever look at her that way. It was simply not possible for the life she led and the way she was, no matter how splendidly she was arrayed. Tilda had beautiful visions and dreams, there was no question, but she was not the person to bestow them on.

She couldn't be.

She watched as Tilda pulled the red fabric tightly around her torso, clearly taking the present fashion of a lower waist to heart. Lucy did have a small waist, she could say that, so perhaps something would work in her favor in that regard. Then came the painstaking process of ruching the bodice again, but this time, it was not just the bodice. They ruched careful and delicate folds into the entire top half, creating a bow-like shape that centered at the dip in her neckline.

It was not a deep dip, thankfully, but the tension they held in the dress itself improved her décolletage into a rather flattering form without being distracting to anyone or embarrassing for Lucy. The dress itself would not be much in that regard without better stays, but she knew Tilda would take care of that as well. She never did anything halfway.

"I want scalloped flounces in the skirts," Tilda told Agnes as she started draping material into the skirt area. "Particularly in the gauze, but in the red as well. Black bows holding them. Two rows of them. And black ribbons lining the hem. Give her a slight train in the skirts. We are aiming for majesty."

"Lovely," Agnes breathed as she nodded.

Lucy only understood half of what was said, but she was trying to envision the details all the same. It sounded pretty enough, but what did she know? The modistes she had been to before hadn't expressed their thoughts on details and accoutrements aloud while she was being fitted. She didn't know many of the names of such things, but she wasn't completely ignorant either. Enough of Society's gossip was fashion related to give anyone some sort of education.

"Willow," Tilda continued, turning to her with bright eyes. "Fetch me some silver thread. The best we have. I have an idea."

She left the room at once, and Lucy looked at Tilda curiously. "What idea?"

Tilda jerked a little and gave her a quick smile. "Forgive me, I am not used to being questioned."

"Oh, sorry," Lucy murmured, ducking her chin.

"No, no, not at all," Tilda told her in a rush. "You do not work for me, darling. You can ask me anything at any time."

That was sweet, though Lucy wondered if it would be quite the same way if Tilda had known her for longer than a few hours. Still, Lucy would take advantage of her kindness as long as she could.

"What are you thinking with the silver thread?" she asked, looking down at the beautiful red silk that was being pinned together.

"I am thinking," Tilda said, leaning forward to run her hand under the silk and let it drape over her palm, "that with the silver thread, I could add some detailing to the silks. I am not sure what yet. Perhaps a series of lines from waist to hem. Perhaps some floral motif, or vines. I don't use metal thread often, because the costumes are never worth the effort and my regular clientele has no need for it.

But for this gown, I do believe it would serve well. Beneath the gauze overlay, it will glint occasionally in the light and add a beautiful lightness and aura to your appearance. And as it will be under another fabric, it will not be so ostentatious. A subtle extravagance that will elevate the garment into another realm."

Lucy shook her head very slowly. "How does your mind work in such a way, Tilda?"

She shrugged and dropped the silk, turning her attention to Lucy's arms. "I haven't the foggiest. It's always been full of art and elaborate things, and my imagination always runs rampant."

"Do limits mean anything to you?" Lucy inquired as she held her arm out for Tilda to fiddle with pieces of red silk to create sleeves.

"I leave limits for those with lesser imaginations," she replied without any hint of humor. "I cannot be bothered with them."

And that, it seemed, was that.

Tilda adjusted herself to peek at Lucy's face and snorted to herself. "Just a bit longer, darling. Then we will sit down in my rooms and have some more drinking chocolate, and this time, you can have some of the whiskey in yours, too, if you wish it."

Lucy shook her head, grinning widely. "I doubt I'm ready for that."

"We shall see, dear girl," Tilda said slyly, laughing to herself. "We shall see. By the by, did you know that red is Trick's favorite color?"

The pedestal beneath Lucy's feet seemed to shift slightly, giving her the distinct impression that she was going to stumble and crash into the ground, though her feet never left their position. Her knees shook, her right one buckling ever so slightly, but her balance managed to keep her upright in spite of the shock.

Tilda's quiet laughter continued, a low, humming melody of amusement that made Lucy's cheeks heat until they would likely match the silk she was being arrayed in.

She couldn't make herself appear unaffected, and she could not—would not—look Tilda in the eye for fear of seeing more of her amused understanding. She would simply stand here and endure the pinning of her new gown, waiting for it to be over so she could relax with her new friends once more.

And perhaps she might be drinking whiskey tonight after all.

Chapter Twelve

Second gaming hell of the night, and Hunter was already tired of the patrol.

His fellow players at the tables were not nearly as shrewd or alert as he needed them to be in order to be in any way useful to his investigation.

The first club had been a complete waste of time, which was why he had moved on to the second. His men were scattered all about this corner of London in the various gambling institutions, officially sanctioned or not, and he could only hope that they were having a better night than he was.

For information, that is.

He was doing quite well at the gambling. He always did.

Years of training and practice had enabled him to win and lose in an unsuspicious pattern based on what he needed to accomplish for any given night. Whatever would serve the mission or assignment and the character he was playing. He never lost enough to ruin his reputation or his night, and he never won enough to attract unwanted attention.

He'd have to lose again shortly. He'd won several hands in a row by now, but never blatantly.

The player to his left, an unshaven, burly man who reeked of tobacco and seaweed and kept his cap down low over his eyes, sniffled noisily before making a coughing, choking sound in his throat and spitting upon the ground beside him. Then he tossed out a card and picked up another, shuffling through his cards with pursed, stained lips.

The dealer sighed and turned the discarded one over.

The man to Hunter's right groaned. "Ye ain't returned me trump lead, man. What are ye playin' at?"

His partner belched. "Shut it. I know what I'm about."

Hunter looked across the table to his own partner, who only widened his eyes and shook his head very slightly in disbelief before returning his attention to his own cards.

It was destined to be a poor night at cards for many if the inconsiderate player continued to be so. He'd have to content himself with other card games that did not require four players when word spread that he did not play well with others.

Hunter played his card to end the hand and cleared his throat. "Just in, mate?"

The man to his left nodded once.

"Where from?"

"Calais."

Hunter already knew that, as he had been tipped off by his contact in this particular club, but he was still pleased to have the man admit it. "Been there several times. Bringing in brandy?"

"What's it to you?" came the snappish retort, along with a quantity of snorted snot.

Hunter chuckled to himself. "Just someone who prefers to purchase his liquor from the source rather than bother with legalities. It always tastes purer, and paying those who bring it in seems better than putting more coin into the pockets of fat and silly merchants."

Hunter could see the man's eyes shift in his direction, though they were shielded by his cap. "What makes you think I'd be the sort of man to engage in private purchase?"

"I've a contact who keeps an interest in the shipyards, and particularly anything coming out of France," Hunter mused as he pretended to look through his cards. "Lanky fellow with a deceptive air of authority. He hinted I might find a man at the tables tonight. But if that man isn't you, I'll take my investigation and investment elsewhere."

The man was silent while another hand was played, ending the game in triumph for Hunter and his partner. Then he turned to Hunter only slightly. "We can talk at the hazard table."

Hunter nodded graciously and rose from the table, collecting his winnings and following his new comrade over to the hazard tables. He signaled to the barman to bring them a few drinks, which was acknowledged with a wave.

There were a dozen or so men already at the table, and the caster was currently throwing after a chance.

"How much brandy might a body be interested in purchasing from a private source?" Hunter's companion asked in a low voice.

Hunter kept his smile slight and smug. "How much might a body be able to spare without suspicions rising?"

The man grumbled. "Martin is putting me in a great pickle with this, sir. The risks…"

"Of course," Hunter said when the man trailed off, "additional funds would be paid for the trouble. And if there were, say, other items that might have come across the Channel in the same ship that weren't strictly listed on the ship's manifest…"

He could almost feel the man's intake of breath. "I am not aware of what you speak."

Was he not?

"If Martin told me about such things," Hunter went on in a much lower voice, "do you not think I know very well of what I speak? As should you?"

There was a dark cursing while the gathered men groaned as the caster rolled the chance, thereby winning his stake. Further bets were placed before his next throw, but Hunter and his new friend offered none themselves.

"Well?" Hunter pressed, holding his breath that he was not pushing too hard.

The burly man shook his head. "Martin hasn't indicated those were for private sale. Seemed to think everything was spoken for and desperately needed with each shipment. They might have already been unloaded."

"So take me to the warehouse and let me haggle with the manager," Hunter suggested with a shrug. "Brandy is my main interest, but if I find the chance to protect my next branch of investments without having to venture further afield, all the better."

"As though Martin would have any of the ship's crew know

where the warehouse is," he scoffed with another hacking spit on the ground. "You should have asked him more questions, mate."

Damn. Hunter had been afraid of that, but he had to try.

"No matter," he hedged, clearing his throat and looking over the shoulder of the man in front of him to see the result of the second throw and place his bet for the third. "I'll be content with the brandy, and you can check as to the other items remaining on board. With some additional payment for your investigation."

The man heaved a noisy sigh. "Fine. But only because of your connection to Martin. I really should check with him first."

"If you must. He might lie, though, to keep others from doing what I am." Hunter took his drink from the wench who approached with them on a tray, and took a long swig, hoping the distraction of a drink would lure his new contact into some semblance of comfort.

He reluctantly accepted his drink, but only sipped. "He does change his mind and moods…"

Hunter scoffed, nodding with a sage firmness. "That he does. You should have seen him ten years ago, mate. Bleeding nightmare to get any straight answer."

That earned him a wry smirk. "I can only imagine. How much will you give me to check?"

Cheers rose from the gathering as the bets on a third throw were successful, and Hunter took his amount from both whist and that round and tucked it into the man's pocket. "How's that for a start?"

A cough and a series of nods were the reply, and Hunter clapped him on the back before downing the rest of his drink. "I'll see you back here in two nights. Will that be enough time?"

"Yes."

"Good." He patted his back once more and slipped away from the hazard table, knowing he wasn't going to get anything else out of the man without raising suspicions.

He didn't like the idea of coming back so soon, especially if Lucy were still in his custody, but he could not miss the chance to confirm with this bloke if his shipment still contained weapons. After the mass mission a few weeks ago to find out where weapons were going and who in the city might be sympathetic to the Faction, the warehouse where such goods were occasionally kept had changed, and it was only a careful investigation that would uncover it. The homes of sympathizers were watched closely, and an entire shipment never went to one location, but it was not exactly the weapons Hunter was after.

It was Martin.

And with more frequent shipments of weapons and operatives coming across the Channel and directly into London, he was certain Martin was going to take a more vested interest in the delivery of each. The man had once worked in the London League, after all. He knew how capable they were and how quickly information could be discovered and dispersed among the other operatives.

He could only pray that the idiot wouldn't check with Martin on his story. It might wind up with the fellow being killed, not to mention it might make the rest of the shipments shift to another docking place.

It wouldn't be that big of a deal if that did happen, though. Briar's team had their thumbs on the pulse of the docks themselves, and it wouldn't take much for them to discover which dock was used.

He'd touch base with her before tomorrow night to see about the warehouses. With her capable assets, they might already know and have eyes on them.

If they'd been able to properly discuss matters last night, he might already have that information.

But there had been Lucy…

Hunter smiled to himself as he made his way down the stairs of the club and out the door, heading to his next one.

Lucy. What a character she was, considering her station and situation. What a beauty she was, without any effort or finery. What a lovely creature, fascinating companion, comforting presence…

He'd never met anyone like her in any of his assignments, or even before he was an operative. She was truly unique, and finding someone like her was such a rarity that he felt himself drawn to her to such an extent that…

That…

Well, he wanted to know more. Wanted to know her better. Wanted to understand the way her mind worked and the way she saw the world. Wanted to see her features change with every emotion and during every time of day.

What would the glow of sunrise to do her exquisite countenance? Would sunset look the same across her skin or would the shades alter? Were her lips always that tempting shade and shape or were her nerves making her bite them more often and giving them that appearance?

His stomach clenched as he strode down the street, and he began counting to twenty in Latin silently, needing the image of Lucy and her lips in the rosy light of sunset to be far away from his mind. He couldn't be thinking of her right now. He needed to be thinking about that traitor, Martin. Needed to be making connections that would help him find the man. Needed to find some idea of where he was and whom he trusted enough to confide in.

There had been the house that Ears had infiltrated last year, but no one was living there at present, as far as his contacts could tell. That was the trouble with this lot—everything was always shifting and moving whenever progress was made. It was one of the main reasons why Hunter was given this assignment alone. One person could make less of a fuss than a team of operatives, and he would not be arranging any great mission based on what he found. He worked alone and only passed on information to those who could act and order others to do so.

Martin. The skinny, ginger-haired former member of the Foreign Office and clerk of the London League. The one who had fooled all of them and worked his way into the most secret, most trusted ranks in England, and then disappeared from the face of the earth, leaving them all to wonder if they had lost another operative. And then to discover that there was no rescue that need to be mounted, but a hunt to secure him and keep him from bringing the Faction into the highest powers of the land.

Hunter had to find him.

How could he forget about that when he was with Lucy? How could he care so much about finding Lucy's father when England was at stake? When hundreds of operatives on both sides of the Channel had been working against the Faction for so long?

He didn't care about Lucy's father; he cared about Lucy. Her happiness and her security. Which meant finding the creature that was her father.

The fact that they couldn't find him easily was almost as irksome as his assignment with Martin. The average gentleman of London ought to be the simplest find in the world, especially one with the penchant for gaming that he seemed to have. And yet…

He didn't want to believe that Lucy's life could be professionally intertwined with his in any way. He wanted Lucy to be completely and wholly personal for him.

And personal to him as well.

Whatever that might mean.

But when someone was as suspicious and elusive as her father, he had his doubts and concerns.

Not about her, exactly. But him. Imagine if Hunter had to have her father arrested for treason or something. She'd not thank him or think kindly of him for that.

Not many things made him question how he would act in certain situations, but the prospect of that did.

Could he do it? Probably. Should he? Absolutely. Would he?

He honestly did not know.

And that was terrifying.

Hunter stopped outside the third club of the night and shook his head, more like a dog trying to get dry than a human doing anything. It didn't push Lucy from his mind, but it did give him a little clarity and reset his thoughts. This club was more renowned for cheating than the last one, which meant he was going to have to be more aware. He was skilled enough to spot even the most talented of cheaters and to decide in a split second if he would let himself be one of their victims, but it did require him to watch.

If he was distracted enough to dull his senses…

He'd never been that far gone. Surely one woman and his present curiosity about her weren't enough to make him lose his focus so much.

He inhaled deeply, letting the pungent smells of the street seep into his very bones, to fill his very veins, and exhaled slowly, almost able to taste the nastiness of his surroundings. He needed that taste in his mouth. He would have picked up a stick to chew on it, if he'd had one, just to make him feel the grit of his character more perfectly.

He hated tobacco, but he'd have put some in if any had been available.

Anything to fit in better. Anything to make Trick blend in. Anything to center himself in his current situation.

Dank and tepid Thames air would have to do.

With a quick nod to himself, Hunter entered the club, slouching pointedly and shortening his stride to more of a shuffle. He tapped a finger to the brim of his cap at the doorman, a light-fingered fellow named Skips who did some excellent work for many of the operatives based in this part of the world. Skips clicked his tongue against his teeth and spat to his far side, which Hunter took as the best acknowledgement he was going to receive.

Skips would make himself available later now that he knew Hunter was present. He was good about taking advantage of his breaks, and he heard absolutely everything that went on in the club. Once, he'd helped Rogue find a man who had taken advantage of a butcher's daughter, a girl of fifteen, just from how the man boasted after his fourth gin and a good night at commerce.

Hunter didn't dare hope that he would have as much success with the current location of Martin or any of his more friendly contacts, but he'd take hints towards anything of the sort. A hint of a hint. A speculation he could look into. A rumor he could verify.

He'd even take a lie he could seek to disprove. Anything would do, really.

"Jones," greeted the proprietor when he saw Hunter, using the name Hunter had given him last time. "What do you fancy tonight?"

He looked around without much interest. "Dunno. What's good?"

"Eh, macao seems hot, and my eyes tell me the cheating isn't bankrupting me. You could disrupt some of that, if you like." He pointed to another corner of the room. "Faro has been cold for an hour or so. Means you'd breathe life into it, which I'd appreciate. Give you a pint of ale and a snifter of whiskey for your trouble there."

"Add in a five-pound lead on my bet, and I'll do it," Hunter shot back, pushing his sleeves back above his elbows.

The proprietor whistled low. "Come on, Jones. It's only Thursday."

"Three, then."

He grumbled incoherently. "Fine. But then I'm capping you at fifty."

Hunter barked a hard laugh. "If you think I'll sweep anything near fifty at your faro table, you've had too much to drink already."

"We all have our limits," came the stiff but wry response. "After last week, I'm taking no chances."

Now that was interesting. This man, St. John, wasn't usually one to exert such control over his proprietors, though his dealers all could cheat enough to stop the overt winners neatly. But he usually left that to their discretion and did not get involved himself.

"What happened last week?" Hunter asked with a slow, sidelong look.

St. John sputtered darkly, shaking his head. "One of the regulars hit a lucky streak. Too lucky. Cheating so well my dealer couldn't keep up. Swept us of one hundred before he could be stopped, and one of the other players had demanded triple the call early in the round without any objection from the others, so it was three hundred when he cashed out."

"Bleeding hell," Hunter muttered, running a hand over his face for effect. "Three hundred? Did he move to any other games?"

St. John shook his head. "Left like a bleeding thief in the night. And since others were cheating, too, I couldn't call him out. Took me four nights to recoup the losses."

Hunter folded his arms. "Need me to find him for you? Intervene unofficially?"

"My thanks, but no. The skinny blighter brings in some good meat for us when his ships come in. Poor sots who are too eager and too slow. I can't afford to irk him, even if he is Irish."

"Irish?" Hunter frowned at that. "Recently over?"

St. John shook his head. "Not that recent, he has no accent. Just the ginger hair. Beady eyes, though. Sees everything. I'd hire him if he didn't look like a lad."

Hunter's chest all but burst in anticipation, adrenaline now pumping into his legs. "Has he been in since?"

"Nay, he said he'd be away a bit, but I expect him next week. He's pretty regular." St. John nodded towards the faro table. "You'd best get started, Jones. The table will be ice soon." He left before Hunter could ask him any further questions.

That was well enough, he supposed. Martin frequented this club, and that was decent information.

Of course, he could frequent a number of these clubs, but that was neither here nor there.

Hunter wandered over to the faro table and made his call as he took a seat. Three hundred pounds. Martin could do a great deal with three hundred pounds. The Faction could do a lot with three hundred pounds as well, though they would likely let him use it as he wished. Martin had proved himself to be their man, and perhaps even sat at the top, at least on these shores.

If Martin could cheat like that, how much money was he fleecing out of the other clubs and hells in the area? And what was all that money going towards?

What if he had contacts and assets who were also able to raise that much so easily? The amount of money they could regularly bring in could be astounding. There were plenty of wealthy supporters in Paris and in London, as the Shopkeepers were well aware, and for the most part, they didn't intervene for fear of letting the Faction know how much they were actually aware of. If they had information as to what the money was going for, or it posted an imminent threat to England's shores, they might do something, but the bigger picture was often their aim.

He'd need information from the other clubs about large amounts being won by a single individual. It might be too obvious, and this might be the only club where it had happened recently, but he had to check. Martin wouldn't want to raise any suspicions about himself, so he might have kept his amounts more reasonable in the other locales.

What Hunter wouldn't give for a list of known associates so he could examine each and compare them all.

He shook his head when the dealer asked if he wished to change his bet and took a drink of the ale that had just arrived near his elbow. Then, for good measure, he belched.

Imagine if Lucy could see him now.

He smiled to himself as he imagined the distaste that would wash across her lovely features. It would then be replaced by curiosity, knowing how he had looked before, and she would begin to ask question after question without giving him a chance to answer any of them. She would begin to speculate on who he was and what he was doing, likely getting closer to the truth than was strictly good for her, but only because she was cleverer than she ought to be.

She'd ask about the stains on his shirt and try to guess the different fragrances emanating from him. She'd want to know what games he'd played at the clubs and how he'd fared in the bets. She wouldn't judge him for his bets, once she knew his stakes and his spread, but she would be a little disapproving of gambling in general, given the history of her father's habits and waste. She'd ask what he wanted to know from gaming hells that he couldn't get from other places and want to know the sort of characters he'd want to connect with.

He imagined himself being practically interrogated in some drawing room before a fire as he took his shoes off and simply wanted to rest and recover, but she would be incessant in her questioning, canting forward in her chair with her eagerness. He would wear a tired smile, his eyes closed, and answer what he could when he could, keeping things purposefully vague, which would irritate her. She'd grow cross when he wouldn't budge on the details, and when he reminded her of the conditions, she'd sulk moodily and tell him how much she hated them, which he'd already know.

It was a comfortable, content sort of scene, and he had no idea where it had come from.

He had no such drawing room, and neither did Tilda. And even if he did, Lucy certainly wouldn't be in it upon his arrival in the morning. She didn't know about any conditions that would allow him to answer her questions with a certain vagueness, though she certainly would hate them if she did. And he'd never answered anybody's questions about his missions or patrols with such a smile as he'd worn in his imagination.

What the devil was going on here?

With a growl from the back of his throat, Hunter turned to the gin and downed the entire thing, barely cognizant of the burn to his throat and chest. He looked over at the wench and tapped the rim of his glass, then chased the burn with a deep drink of his ale.

Then he doubled his bet and kept his eyes on the cards, his brow furrowing as darkly as any other man in the room.

And it had nothing to do with maintaining any sort of character for the night.

Chapter Thirteen

Lucy woke blissfully, if almost languorously, from sleep, stretching to her heart's content on the softest mattress she had ever lay on in her entire life. It certainly took a long time to pry her eyes open, when she was ready to do so. Faint images of her dreams flashed through her mind while her eyes tried to adjust to the dimness of the room and make sense of the shapes they saw.

She hadn't felt this luxurious upon waking… ever. Not once in her life before this.

And she wasn't living in any sort of luxury at the moment.

She smiled to herself as she recollected the night before—spending the entire evening with Tilda and Willow, laughing and learning card games, particularly ones with gambling, though they taught her how to cheat at them. They had indulged in the Belgian drinking chocolate and Parisian biscuits that Tilda had promised, and she had heard all sorts of stories from them both, none of which she was certain she could believe. They were simply too extraordinary, and yet there was an air of easiness and familiarity as they told the stories that made her wonder.

What time they had managed to decide it was time for bed, she could not have said. There were no clocks in the rooms that she had seen, and windows were minimal. The room she was in had very small windows just at the tops of the walls, and the morning light was streaming in quite brightly, even if the gaps weren't large enough for much effect.

Still, they allowed enough light for her to attest that it, indeed, was morning.

Which meant she ought to get out of bed.

But, oh, she could stay here forever. She wanted to stay here forever. Right here in this bed, knowing she was safe, in spite of her situation. Being this comfortable, this cozy, this delightfully snug and cuddled up in a way she might never be or feel again, without anyone or anything making demands on her time, was utter perfection, beyond even her most wild fantasies, and she had never been more loathe to leave any place in her life.

There was one little thing that could provoke her out of this cloud of heaven she had been sleeping in.

Breakfast.

She knew full well that Tilda would have decided on something marvelous for her breakfast. Not that Lucy was anything special, really, but because having a guest meant that Tilda herself could rationalize a marvelous breakfast. And she had promised Lucy something of the sort the night before, so she knew she was not thinking of it in vain.

Lucy yawned and forced herself to sit up, tousling her hair a little and sighing. "All good things must come to an end, I suppose."

On cue, there was a knock on the door.

"Come on, old girl," Willow called from the other side. "No trays here. Breakfast down the hall. Do you need help with your dress?"

"No, thank you!" Lucy replied, grinning. Once, she might have found dressing impossible by herself, but her time at Miss Masters's had made her quite comfortable in doing just about everything without a maid.

One of the benefits of a diminished style of living, she supposed.

Patting the soft bedding beneath her, Lucy sighed and pushed out of the bed, padding over to the corner of the room where her new clothing items were neatly set out. She shrugged out of her night shirt and picked up the pristine chemise, grinning again as she slipped into it. Stays and petticoat next, though both were a trifle awkward to fasten without another set of hands. Her dress was a simple, unimpressive green version of grey, and she secretly adored the color. She'd admitted as much to Tilda when she'd been pinned up for it, and Tilda promised to make her an evening gown in a similar shade to wear someday.

Then came the grey pinafore, which Tilda thought would help with Lucy's need for a more common appearance, and a simple blue redingote that looked secondhand for her outerwear. How in the world had Tilda managed to make a brand-new coat and have it look so used and worn by the time it was finished? Lucy shook her head as she tucked her arms into the sleeves, and then went to work on the simple stockings and boots for her feet.

When all that was done, she began the now habitual practice of plaiting her hair and twisting it into a low chignon of sorts, taking the few pins left for her and securing the mass of tendrils into place. It was how she always wore her hair to teach, and it had not failed her yet. There was no looking glass in the room, but she could tell by the way it felt against her scalp that it was properly affixed and wouldn't fall or slide without significant effort on her part, which was not anticipated.

But she hadn't talked to Hunter about the day's activities, so it was a possibility, she supposed.

She gasped a little as she thought of him. He had been gone all night, and she had forgotten about him until just now. She dashed to the door of the room, grabbing the redingote from the bed and hurrying out.

Had he found out anything about her father? Had any of his contacts reported in positively for them? Had anything of use actually come of the evening? Had he been in any danger?

Her step slowed as she considered that, her mouth going dry.

Had he been in danger? Was there any chance that he had been wounded? Was he even back?

Her feet began to scramble forward, her heart in her throat, and moved down the corridor as fast as she could go. No exact room had been given for breakfast, but perhaps it would be the same place as supper the night before? Food was the last thing on her mind right now, though. She needed to see Hunter and assure herself that he was safe and well, and perhaps then she would find her hunger again.

Lucy's eyes darted along each of the doors she passed, and her feet skidded on the floor when she finally found the breakfast room, as it were. Willow was seated there, sipping something steaming in a teacup, her plate laden with pork, eggs, and toast with marmalade.

She saw Lucy and smiled, setting her teacup down. "Come in!" she called. "There's plenty!"

She did so, looking around the room, but only finding Tilda and two other women.

Lucy bit her lip as she moved to fetch her plate of breakfast. "Has anyone seen or heard from Hunter? I mean, Trick. Has anyone heard from Trick this morning?"

Tilda's brows rose, and she folded her silk shawl around her more tightly as she cradled a steaming cup at the head of the table. "I have. The man smelled dreadfully, even for me, and I sent him off for a wash and a shave. Amazing to think he could walk back here at all, given the stench of such alcohol. And I will not tell you what else he smelled of, but it is not something to be experienced again." Her eyes widened meaningfully, and she shook her head, exhaling in a huff. "He will be along shortly, I have no doubt. Men always are when there is food."

The offhand, almost short, manner in which this report was given did little to assuage Lucy's concerns, but it did lower her panic and allow her hunger to push through. Surely, if Hunter had been injured, Tilda would have mentioned it.

Blood would have to come before a poor smell, would it not?

But Tilda was watching her carefully, and Lucy did not dare make her think more of the question than she already would. So she returned her attention to the food and carefully filled her plate enough to be appropriate, but not enough to draw comment.

It reminded her of being at home with her father.

"Coffee, tea, or chocolate?" one of the other women asked her kindly, gesturing to the three teapots nearby.

Lucy's stomach lurched left at the idea of anything. "Tea," she said in a rush, though she would probably kick herself later for not indulging in chocolate once more when she could have tea anytime she wished in her life. But she needed something simple to drink at this moment, if she wished to drink anything at all. Or to appear to drink anything, as it were. She had to keep herself above suspicion until she could get the answers that would return her sanity and calm, if not control.

He was here. She let herself be consoled in that. The plan would still go forward with her staying in his protection until they had enough information to return her home, wherever that was. He would undoubtedly check on her as soon as he could, and if Tilda hadn't made him clean himself up, he would probably be doing so now.

Odd that she should feel so concerned and protective over her protector, considering how little she had thought of or about him the night before while they had been having a lovely and enjoyable evening. She hadn't dreamed of him or anything, hadn't grown fonder of or fanciful about him, and certainly hadn't been thinking whimsically about any sort of a future with him, but suddenly she couldn't—wouldn't—feel right or whole until she saw him for herself.

It was an unnerving feeling, to say the least.

"How did you sleep, my dear?" Tilda asked Lucy as she set her plate on the table and began to sit.

Lucy managed a smile and a swallow as she scooted in her chair. "Like heaven, as it happens. I was more than willing to stay there forever, but the prospect of breakfast was very appealing."

Tilda chuckled in her warm, natural way. "Let it never be said that the wealthy and influential in Society have everything better than the rest of us."

"Hear, hear," one of the women said with a wry, scratchy laugh as she raised a piece of toast in salute.

Lucy didn't have to work so hard for her smile at that. She knew all too well that there was plenty lacking in the lives of the wealthy and influential, or those who could appear wealthy and influential, and she had never seen any person so content and satisfied as Tilda was. Whatever life Tilda led, she adored it, and there was a natural enviousness beginning to bud in Lucy's heart about that.

Freedom was difficult for a woman in her station, unless one were born independently wealthy or widowed from someone wealthy. Lucy had neither, and thus was susceptible to the plans and whims of others to guide her life.

Perhaps if her father continued to lower them in station and standing, Lucy could be more independent as a teacher and distance herself from him. She would need to speak to some kind of solicitor about that. What power her father held over her was unclear, and if she was permitted to go her own way at her age…

She would need to find her father in order to find his solicitor, and at the present, she was perfectly content to remain where she was.

Carefully cutting into her pork, Lucy focused on keeping her expression vacant and on looking like she was enjoying her breakfast. After all, once she was with Hunter out and about in London, there was no guarantee that she would enjoy a decent meal.

"Your new clothing suits you, Lucy," Willow said with a quick grin. "How do you like it?"

Lucy took a bite of her breakfast and swallowed with a smile. "It is remarkably comfortable. You are quite gifted, Tilda."

Tilda inclined her head as though the compliment was simply her due. "Thank you. It is functional as well. You will find pockets in the skirts. A woman should always have pockets at her disposal, regardless of the garment."

"What am I supposed to put in the pockets?" Lucy asked, thinking the idea one of the more ridiculous ones she'd ever heard.

"Whatever you like, my dear," came the laughing reply. "A handkerchief, some spare coins, a knife." Tilda shrugged and sipped her drink. "That fan with a blade hidden in its spine would fit nicely in such a pocket, if I do say so myself."

"I keep toffees in my pockets," one of the other women offered helpfully.

"I knew a woman who kept a spare pair of stockings in her pockets," someone else said. "She was always finding holes in hers."

"My sister likes to keep a bit of charcoal pencil in her pockets. And some paper, just in case she wants to draw."

"My neighbor's pockets are filled with whatever she can pick from the pockets of others."

The room went silent as they all looked at the young woman.

She met all of their eyes without shame. "I've told her to stop, but she refuses. What else can I do?"

Lucy shook her head, marveling at the differences in something so simple as pockets between the classes of women. What was not obvious to her was clearly a staple of the wardrobe of these women, and nothing could have illustrated the differences between them in such a blatant fashion. Pockets, for heaven's sake. She could see the use of them, of course, but pockets were for coats or aprons in her world. And rarely used when they were in coats, given she always had a reticule.

Dresses with pockets. What a new world she was going to inhabit now.

"I'd stuff scones and cakes in the pockets of my gowns. Just saying."

The rumbling, bemused voice made Lucy's heart leap, and she looked at the entrance to the room with a bright smile.

Hunter stood there, hair dark with dampness, surveying the room with the sort of ease and comfort one might have done with one's own family. His eyes caught Lucy's, and his smile spread as he nodded briefly.

"Ugh," Tilda scoffed. "Men." She waved her hand towards the food. "Get yourself some breakfast, for heaven's sake. You're so ridiculous on an empty stomach."

Hunter's eyes flicked to the woman in response, and he moved obediently to the food without another word.

Lucy watched him as though her life depended on it. Her eyes traced over every single aspect of him without shame, looking for injury or dishevelment, any hint of trouble that he might portray. The slightest limp or guarding motion, halting movements, winces, grimaces, bruising… She looked for absolutely anything that was out of place in, on, or around him.

As though he could feel her eyes on him, Hunter glanced over his shoulder directly at her. He raised a brow, no doubt curious about her blatant staring and lack of embarrassment over doing so.

She only continued to stare, waiting for him to give some indication one way or another as to his condition or his night. Any bit of information would do, and she was certainly entitled to that.

Surely, he ought to know that.

He seemed to be fighting a smile as he resumed fixing his plate, and Lucy did not understand that. What could possibly be so amusing about this situation? How could he be laughing at her right now? It was not only rude, but remarkably inconsiderate.

She could feel the tension in her brow as she continued to watch him, wondering if one could injure the brow by excessive force.

As though determined to test her question about her fiercely furrowed brow, Hunter took a seat at the table far enough away from her to make private conversation impossible and where her continued focus would be noticed by anyone around them with the power of observation.

His tiny smile as he did so told Lucy he knew exactly what he was doing and was taking great pleasure in it.

Perhaps Tilda would take on a murder plot on Lucy's behalf today. She had no money to give her for the crime, but she was sure she could come up with something.

Despite her focused glare and concentrated fury at him, Hunter did not so much as glance in her direction even once as he pointedly ate his breakfast.

Death was going to reach this man rather quickly once they were separated from witnesses.

Moodily, Lucy returned her attention to her own meal, deciding that the infuriating man was clearly well enough to not be deserving of her care and consideration, let alone her attention. If he were unwell, he would have looked it, and been less of a devil in his behavior towards her. If he had learned anything that would be useful to her in the course of his evening, he would surely have said something right away, as he claimed to be a gentleman.

But then, it was entirely possible that he was no such thing, and thus could hold any information that might concern her to only release when he felt like it. He could tell her tomorrow, if he liked. He could tell her never, if he liked.

And apparently, he did like, and wouldn't tell her anything one way or another until his mood persuaded him to.

She might as well enjoy her food, then. He certainly wasn't going to give her anything to enjoy for the rest of the day. Would it be dreadfully improper to ask Tilda if she could stay here instead? After all, being alone with a man wasn't proper for a woman of any station. It was a far better option for her reputation, as well as her sanity, to remain where she was while Hunter figured out where her father was.

Surely, no one would mind that.

"What is your plan for the day, Trick?" Tilda asked from the head of the table. "Where will you and Lucy go?"

Lucy blinked at being mentioned, then again when she realized Tilda's insinuation that she would be leaving at some point.

So much for remaining here, then. Blast.

Lucy stabbed at a piece of pork and shoved it into her mouth, clearly not needed for this conversation, and not entirely caring what answer Hunter gave on the subject. In fact, she concentrated hard on the sounds of her own chewing rather than the sound of his voice, and it was working. His words were only a faint murmuring at the moment, like the babble of a brook she didn't quite care about.

Wherever he decided to take her, she would simply go, making whatever noises she pleased regardless of how he felt on the subject, and only smiling when she reached her father's house.

Of course, even in her present ire, she knew that was wrong. She wouldn't enjoy returning to her father's house. Her personal belongings had escaped with the carriage, and whatever her father had of hers at his new residence could hardly be sentimental to her. She had learned long ago not to leave valuables unattended, which was why most of them were at the school and not anywhere her father could reach.

But at the moment, she found the prospect of returning to his house less irksome than spending the day with the maddening man intentionally sitting apart from her and avoiding giving her any information when it was clear she wished for it. How could a person as perceptive, quick, and handsome as he also be the most irritating creature she had ever met?

Ridiculous man.

"They're talking about you, Lucy, you know," the woman next to her whispered with a nudge of her elbow.

Lucy raised a brow, keeping her eyes on her plate. "Well aware. But if I give them attention, they will only get worse."

"Dunno about that, I think Hyde Park sounds lovely."

Lucy jerked and looked at the woman in surprise, ignoring the pox scars and scanning her features for any sign of jest instead.

She found none.

Reluctantly, but with some curiosity, Lucy slid her attention down the other end of the table to Hunter, forcing her ears to tune in.

"Hyde Park," Tilda was saying, snorting loudly. "And be mistaken for street hawkers who have lost their way? Who in the world would think you both belong in Mayfair dressed as you are?"

"Other people go to Hyde Park than just the ton, Tilda," Hunter told her. "We'll just be deferential."

The older woman waved her hand at him in the most patronizing manner possible. "Idiot. Don't blame me if you both get insulted. What else?"

"Well, since the evening was a loss for information on her father, I thought we might try another tactic and go see Hal." He shrugged his broad shoulders, apparently feeling he'd said enough, as no other explanation followed.

Now, Tilda looked outright alarmed. "You don't think that's taking a terrible risk?"

"What's risky about it?" he shot back. "We need a picture of the man at this point to get Lucy home, and there's nothing dangerous at Hal's for her."

"Risky for you, Trick. Honestly, you can be so dense." Tilda shook her head rather pointedly and sipped her beverage, brow creasing so deeply Lucy was a little taken aback. "Risking your neck, going there, if you ask me. If you need Lucy to see Hal, have someone else take her."

"No, it has to be me," he said simply. "And it will be fine. And if it's not fine, I'll have Lucy brought back here to you. She can hide among your fabrics until the coast is clear." He chuckled to himself, though the joke seemed to be lost on the rest of them.

Lucy looked back and forth between them, the real concern in Tilda's face raising all sorts of questions in her mind, and the utter disregard for that concern in Hunter's face creating even more havoc in her mind.

Tilda huffed loudly. "At least tell me that risking yourself in such a way will also benefit your own tasks? I'll not have you sacrifice yourself for something else."

Something else being Lucy and her father? Was she really so small in comparison to whatever it was Hunter was doing? She felt no self-pity at the idea; it was rather more awestruck than that.

Hunter's smile for Tilda was rather warm, all things considered. "It will. I have several questions that need answers, and between Hal and Sphinx, I will have the resources I need to get them."

"At least send a note to Weaver that you're going," Tilda suggested, her tone turning almost pleading. "For my peace of mind."

Hunter's eyes rolled heavenward. "You may send him a note, Tilda, if you wish. Tell him whatever you please. I'm still taking Lucy there later."

Still not addressed by either of the parties involved, and still not having an explanation that seemed to make sense to anyone else at the table, there wasn't much else to do but drink her tea, wishing she had opted for chocolate, and wait for her opinion to be requested.

If it ever was.

"Do you feel a little like one of those small dogs that ladies carry around when they gad about London?" the woman to Lucy's left asked her with a small giggle. "No say in anything, but still forced to endure whatever excursions their mistress has in mind?"

Lucy choked a laugh on her tea, swallowed, then very carefully said, "Woof."

Their snickering earned them a stern look from Tilda, but thankfully, nothing further.

"I'll find you a lovely collar before you go," her new friend whispered. "Our little secret."

Feeling a little brighter, loving nothing so well as a good private joke, Lucy nodded and resumed her breakfast with a smile she did not have to force.

Chapter Fourteen

Visiting his twin sister in the light of day was usually a bad idea, and something he almost never did, but there really wasn't another course of action.

Hunter needed some better way to identify Lucy's father, given there hadn't been a shred of evidence the man even existed, according to his sources and assets, and his sister's artistic ability was the only way he could think to proceed.

He also desperately needed to talk to Hal, and the sooner he did so, the better.

Lucy wasn't speaking to him at the moment, but that was entirely Hunter's own fault. He had been intentionally provocative in his behavior that morning, knowing she would be perishing with curiosity and unable to pepper him with questions in the presence of Tilda's ladies. Was it gentlemanly? Not at all. Was it kind? Not in the least.

Was it enjoyable?

Abso-bleeding-lutely.

Her expression of fury was utterly irresistible as a temptation, and the rewards of seeing it so beautifully on display were full and rich indeed.

It had been a very long night on patrol, and he had needed the satisfaction of such a sight to give him some relief. Little additional information had come of his efforts, which was always disheartening, but little was better than nothing, he had reminded himself. Especially in his particular line of work and realms of investigation. Sometimes, it was the little information that proved the opening he needed for true answers.

Time would tell if the hints and whispers his team had collected among the clubs and gaming hells during the night would amount to anything. Under normal circumstances, the time would have been that day or that evening, but with Lucy in his protection, he didn't dare. He needed her safety to be secure before he could risk himself in any way. It was only fair.

It had nothing to do with feelings; his life couldn't be given up when someone relied on him. He couldn't trust anybody to take care of Lucy except him. Until she was deposited in her father's house, he had to proceed carefully. It was irritating, it was irksome, it was deuced inconvenient, but it was the truth.

It was also, he would admit, not the worst thing he'd ever had to deal with.

Which was why he needed to talk to Hal.

Nothing had ever distracted Hunter like Lucy. Nothing. And it was a pleasant distraction, to boot. One he smiled about and felt right engaging in, not to mention the sensation of warmth it elicited in his chest.

Indigestion, surely, but it was the best sort of indigestion he'd ever experienced.

Very strange.

And it had made attempting to eat his breakfast in her presence this morning a tad more difficult. Engaging with Tilda in conversation, especially conversation that would irk Lucy, had been a useful avenue of distracting him from her beauty and her presence— as well as the sensations she produced in him. It was all self-defense, but it was all harmless. Of course he planned on telling Lucy what he could and answering what questions he was able to. Of course he wouldn't be intentionally infuriating all day with her. Of course he would continue to do what he could to locate her father without personally knocking on doors and possibly risking his identity.

But he might play with Lucy a little more before he did so.

Walking away from Tilda's, well-fed and far cleaner than he'd been when he arrived, Hunter glanced over at the silent and clearly brooding Lucy. A small muscle below her ear twitched visibly in consistent intervals, and he wondered if her teeth ached from being clenched so tightly. If she huffed, she could not have displayed her ire more blatantly.

He took great pleasure in picturing her eyes, a rich, warm, deep chocolate shade of brown at all other times, but surely some cold and furious blackness with the ominous nature of a well in this mood. Would he feel the effects of seeing such a change in their depths directly? Would a chill race up his jaded and unflappable spine in spite of his exposure to more dangerous things? Did she hold that much power over him already?

Why did that idea make him want to laugh instead of scare him into some evasive action? He was actually forcing his face to remain fixed in serenity instead of bursting into laughter, and it had nothing to do with his success in bringing her to this point. It had everything to do with being with her.

Oh, all right, it had a little to do with his success. He was a competitive man, after all, and if she was going to plague him, he might as well plague her back.

They had been walking, and away from the ears of others, for some time now and yet Lucy had said nothing to him. He must truly have aggravated her to a new degree if she was fighting her own natural tendencies and curiosity so successfully. He was impressed, he would not deny it. His sister would have attempted to pummel him by now, and Lucy was keeping her hands to herself as well as remaining silent. She wasn't glaring or sniffing dismissively, wasn't trying to push him in front of a moving coach, hadn't muttered a single insult or obscenity…

Perhaps she was simply better behaved or more well-trained than his sister.

Then again, why would Lucy attack him the way Hal might have? Siblings had the familiarity that enabled frequent assassination attempts without losing the innate fondness lying in their foundations. He'd known Lucy for less than two days.

Even he had to admit it was too short an acquaintance to act upon injurious inclinations.

Well, most of the time. He was a covert operative, after all.

What would it take on his part to get her to talk? If talking was too much to ask, what would it take to get her expression to twitch or flinch or shift in the slightest? What would provoke her enough to shove him into the street?

He didn't want to make her even angrier, did he?

It was a tempting idea, but it occurred to him that going to his sister's house with an angry woman might be a dreadful thing. Hal was going to side with Lucy, there was no question, which meant Hunter would take a great deal of abuse from his twin, possibly in Lucy's presence, and arguing with his sister in front of Lucy would make him look worse in her eyes. But worse and more unforgiveable than that, it could make Hal look like a right harridan or shrew to Lucy if they fought in front of her the way they usually did.

No one would see Hal like that while Hunter could help it. Those were grounds for a duel, and he could not exactly duel with Lucy. Nor would he ever want to. Particularly when the fault would lay squarely with him for Hal's appearing in such a way.

Hell and the devil. He needed to mend this relationship between them with great expediency, and probably take the long way to Hal's home to ensure things were healed and happy before they arrived.

For a covert operative of the Crown with a record as impressive and impeccable as his, he could be remarkably short-sighted in his personal life.

Which sounded like something his sister would tell him, but that was beside the point.

He cleared his throat in what was probably the most awkward manner possible. "I suspect you would like to know where I am taking you."

Lucy said nothing, her steps even and sedate beside him.

"As you may have suspected," he went on, doing his best to be undeterred while actually feeling quite deterred, "I learned nothing about your father or his whereabouts last night. I did my best to inquire about him while engaging in my other tasks, but to no avail. I did check with my sources this morning before returning to Tilda's, and there is still nothing to report. I can only presume that he lives in farther areas than my contacts go, or that his name is not well known in his neighborhood as yet."

If Lucy heard a single word he had said, she gave no indication. They reached the intersection of two streets, and she stopped, clearly waiting for instruction or direction from him, with her gloved fingers folding neatly within each other and gracefully draped across her midsection. The posture alone would belie her station, let alone the pose, but he wasn't about to correct that detail now.

He had other issues at present.

"Given all of that," he went on, doing nothing to direct her, "and how quickly I can usually procure requisite information around here, I thought we would pursue another avenue of inquiry."

Now he waited for her to react or respond in some way. Some indication that her ears were functioning, at least.

He watched as she blinked, then felt an absurd jolt of delight when her chin dipped in the briefest nod known to man. He set his hand at her elbow and directed her across the street.

"Which is why I am taking you to an artist." He bit back a grin, thinking it best that he hide his personal relationship with the particular person for the time being. "This artist works with all sorts of investigators and people from high to low. If you can describe the person, they can draw them. It is the most accurate likeness I have ever seen in most instances and has solved many more complicated cases from the drawings alone."

Other than a faint exhale, Lucy did not react or respond.

So much for the earlier delight, fleeting as it had been.

Losing much of his energy, Hunter looked away. "Once the drawing is done, the artist can make a few copies for us to have shown about the area, and that should give us some sort of information for you. It shouldn't take all that long, if you've made other plans for the day. I don't intend to drag you along from this place to that. Lord knows, we both have better ways of spending our time."

He might have imagined it—though his well-trained ears were usually particularly skilled at such things—but he thought he heard Lucy scoff with some derision.

He glanced back at her and found traces of the same emotion on her face.

Signs of life had never been so encouraging.

"We're not headed into Mayfair or anything so exciting," Hunter told her, keeping his voice controlled and aiming for nonchalance. "But perhaps the neighborhood will be familiar to you anyway. If you see anything you recognize, let me know. Which brings to mind the question: Did you recognize anything in the vicinity of Covent Garden when you were there?"

A direct question that was intricately related to the search for her father. She couldn't ignore or deflect it without being blatant, and if she was as eager to get away from him as he suspected she presently was, she would have no excuse to prolong his investigation.

He had her sufficiently trapped.

Lucy wet her lips, then said, "No."

And that was it.

It was Hunter's turn to blink and stare, and he almost missed the turn of the square they needed to make to head towards his sister's house. Taking Lucy's elbow very gently, so she would not feel abused by the action, he steered her the right way, trying not to feel stupid for his momentary smugness.

He should have known she would best him somehow. A woman in her ire was the most dangerous of creatures.

He would need to tread very carefully.

"Right," Hunter said slowly, scrambling for a new avenue of approach on the topic. "I suppose we were in a sort of underside, and you were not likely to have seen it before. And I don't suppose Tilda or her ladies took you on any sort of tour out of doors, did they?"

"No," came her clear response, her lips barely moving to form the word.

He nodded as though she had replied in any normal way. "Of course not. I should have considered. If we have time, and you wish to do so, we could venture back that way later and see if you do recognize anything from the public side. But I don't think we should have you stay there again tonight, if a place is needed. Lovely as she is, Tilda's hospitality has its limits, and I would much prefer her to be a safe resource for you if you need her in future. That may not happen if we continue as a charity case, in her eyes."

"She likes me," Lucy said simply, her voice so matter-of-fact that he was inclined to think she forgot that she was not speaking to him.

"Of course she does," he immediately answered, wincing at the potential for patronization in his words. "You're exactly the type of opinionated, independent woman she adores, and when she also has the opportunity to dress you? It's better than a birthday. She did a brilliant job, by the way. You look perfectly ordinary in the loveliest way, and the color and style suit you well."

Lucy folded her arms, the carpet bag she held in one hand clapping against her side with the motion. "Do you always compliment with an insult in tow? Or just with me?"

"Do I what?" He stared at her in shock, though she never looked his way. "Say that again. Or explain. Something. I'm feeling affronted, and I am not sure that's appropriate for the situation."

"You're affronted?" Lucy barked a laugh, tossing her head.

Hunter fought the impulse to swallow with dread. "I did say I wasn't sure it was appropriate."

"Believe me, it is not." Lucy cleared her throat, her eyes widening. "You just said I looked perfectly ordinary."

Hunter frowned. "But you're supposed to look ordinary," he protested, something hot and sharp uncoiling in his stomach. "And I did say lovely."

"Compliment and insult," she said firmly, as though he had just proved her point. "No one wants to be told they look ordinary. Ever. Looking ordinary in a lovely way is rather like being told you are clever for a woman, as though being a woman limits your wits. Or that you dance well for a man, because men cannot have grace. Or that this pastry is good for a beginner, implying it is not good for any other sort."

"Then what should I have said? I didn't mean to imply that you look ordinary. The new clothing is ordinary in appearance, as it was supposed to be, and you wear it well. That's all I meant."

"And yesterday," Lucy went on, ignoring him, "you said I was pretty, objectively speaking, and that it would make me a target."

Oh dear, he had, hadn't he?

She shook her head. "That has to be the most insulting way to be called pretty I have ever heard, Hunter. As though it is somehow my fault that I look the way I do, pretty or not, and that it is a problem for you. Objectively speaking? What are you, a scholar studying a fascinating specimen of insect? The distance you put between yourself and whatever nice thing you think you are saying is so gaping, it would need a full naval ship and crew to get from one side to the other. And even then, it would take months to get there! Just say it straight out, whatever you really mean!"

"Isn't it considered bad form to call a woman pretty if you have no designs on her?" Hunter dared to venture. "Or, more specifically, isn't it considered rather familiar to call a woman pretty? And might make a situation awkward?"

"We are not in a ballroom here," she all but spat. "What sort of scandal is it going to cause?"

Hunter sputtered very softly. "Lucy, I cannot call you pretty, though you blatantly are, if I am trying to be respectful, which I am, and retain some semblance of decency, which I actually do have. I don't engage with women of your station anymore, and I am woefully out of practice, though I am trying. Clearly, I have been bungling up what I thought were… well, decent statements of praise that did not indicate anything untoward on my part. My sister taught me from a very early age that what men say and women hear do not always correlate, and are often at odds, and I have done my best to heed her warnings in my life. I apologize that I failed with you."

He all but held his breath as he waited for her response, his speech having gone on a little longer than he had intended, quite against his natural inclination.

Did she like speeches? Had he rambled? Or had he said what was necessary and right and just might save his hide?

Or had he just done an unnecessary explanation of himself that would only make him look more like a heel and sink him lower into this hole of his?

He heard her slow exhale and watched her expression carefully. That muscle by her ear ticked again, and somehow he smiled at that. And felt the impulse to laugh.

Damned nuisance, impulses.

"Fine," Lucy grumbled with a quick nod. "I will do better to give you the benefit of the doubt, but really, stop trying for so much respect or politeness or whatever you think I deserve. Just say it, will you? I do not care about decency, in that regard. Not with you. I realize you are not a villain or a rake, and that you might be the only person on this side of town that I am perfectly safe to be alone with."

"Not that safe," he muttered before he could stop himself.

If she heard him, she gave no indication. "Which means it's safe for you to speak absolutely freely in my presence. If you want to compliment me, do so. If you simply want to say something, do so without attempting whatever respectful flattery you believe I am accustomed to hearing. It is so tiresome."

"I do believe I have been called tiresome before," he allowed as he carefully released his breath, the relief hitting his chest in subsequent waves as the tension abated.

He felt as though he'd just been shot at by about seven pistols, all of which missed him by a hair.

That was too close.

"Of that, I have no doubt," Lucy quipped, her tone only mildly warmer. She looked down at herself, then unfolded her arms, finally. "I will admit, this clothing is far more comfortable than what I am expected to wear in my father's house or out and about in Society. Much more like what I wear at the school, and what I would rather wear all the time. Do you know how delicate and thin the dresses of ladies can be these days? It is utterly ridiculous!"

Hunter made a face. "Lucy, don't tell any man things like that. It's just not something any of us need to know, no matter how respectable we are."

"You don't have concerns over the quality and durability of women's fabric?" she asked, quirking her brow and giving him a very slight smile.

"I am certain I do," he told her with an exhale. "But, as I've tried to establish, you are a beautiful woman, and the idea of flimsy fabric and you makes me afraid."

Lucy reared back, all traces of humor gone. "Afraid? Why?"

Hunter clicked his tongue against his teeth. "Because if anyone else knew and tried to take advantage of that fact, I would probably tear them limb from limb, and it would be a trifle difficult to continue to do my job if I'm in prison."

Her dark eyes widened, and her lips parted in shock. Shades of pink began to dance in her cheeks, dawning across her face like the sunrise, and it was one of the most intoxicating, tempting sights he had ever seen. Thankfully, his frankness on the topic was rather refreshing and allowed him the clarity to remember he had done so on purpose, which further allowed him to shrug and look away without shame.

He did feel the need to clear his throat, however. He was only human, and her blush was stunning.

"Right, then," he said, taking in a breath that he hoped would serve to change the topic. "Just a few streets more. I think you'll like Hal. Actually, I'm rather afraid you'll like Hal too much. Most people like Hal more than me, and I cannot say I blame them. Hal has always been the more affable of the pair of us. Well, that's not true. Hal simply knows how to sway people, and always sways them away from me."

"Hal is the artist?" Lucy asked in a small, somewhat wavering voice.

He nodded, feeling a trifle smug that he had rattled her with his words. "Don't let the butler scare you. He's just as dangerous as he appears, but he is there to protect Hal, and so long as you are friend and not foe, he won't do a thing. In fact, if you are a true friend, Thad will probably defend you, should the need arise."

"Why does the world seem to be at war in your circle?" Lucy wondered aloud, her words still fairly quiet.

He smiled at that, but it wasn't particularly a smile of amusement. "The world is always at war, Lucy. Those in my circle simply try to keep the rest of you from realizing it."

Chapter Fifteen

Why had she told the man to be frank and speak his mind? Lucy was absolutely rattling about his calling her beautiful and admitting he would attack anyone who tried to take advantage of her, which made walking beside him quite the challenge.

Tingling knees did nothing for steadiness of gait.

Miss Corrigan would have been appalled by her loss of comportment, given how many hours they had worked on it when Lucy was young. Not that such fine comportment was needed in her current setting and disguise, but all the same…

What was it about a man calling a woman beautiful that suddenly made noticing his attractiveness quite simple? It was like a bombardment of handsome traits, and she felt like a silly, stupid creature for being so susceptible to flattery.

Idiot girl. One compliment did not a dashing fellow make. Even if she'd found him dashing before the compliment.

But no! She would not turn that way. She would be unmoved by his angled features and charming smile and becoming stature and amusing ways and would cling to the maddening torment he had put her through that morning of his free will and choice. He could be as appealing as he liked, and she would not budge. She would be just as frank and free with her words, as an equal, and avoid becoming dependent on him while they looked for her father. She would be as forgettable as possible so that their departure from each other would be the most natural thing in the world, and she could go back to her life with fond memories of a brief adventure and nothing more.

Apart from suddenly fearing she would be attacked around any corner because of some secret war nobody knew about, that should be quite simple.

This Hal person Hunter kept talking about seemed an interesting fellow, and the fondness he felt for him was evident, even to her. He must really trust this man, if he was bringing Lucy to him for help. And to be moving into a nicer part of London than any they had been in yet was a relief, but also a strange sort of feeling that made her tone crisp and her spine straight.

A lifetime of training to be something among those of a certain station that did not exist in other places.

Even at Miss Masters's, Lucy felt that she could slump in a chair at times. Did not have to be so perfect or so accomplished. Did not have to impress anyone. Did not have to be anything other than what she was.

In the lower parts of London, she could be who she was as well, even if who she was might be a trifle naive and helpless. She did not have to think so much or remember her years of tutoring. But even here, a few scant blocks above that, her manners would be something she noted, and she would go over events in her mind later to see how she performed.

What a ridiculous lot of nonsense in all of that tutelage. In the expectations of her station. In nearly every young woman considered to be of breeding. Good manners were one thing, but this?

If she ever had daughters, they would be taught good manners and some skills, but they would be encouraged to be themselves, whether that were a bluestocking, a musician, or a hoyden. So long as they were not shaming the family or creating scandal, what harm could there be in that? And they would not be valued for whatever dowry could be attached to them, of that, she was certain.

Considering Lucy would probably not marry a man who could provide daughters with a dowry worth mentioning, the point might be moot anyway.

Even so, it would be her intention to parent them in such a way.

Provided she parented anyone at all. There was no certainty she would.

Hunter was still jabbering on about something or other when she started noticing the cleanliness of the streets and the shift in local aroma. She couldn't smell the dankness of the river anymore, nor was there a pervasive heaviness to the air. She wouldn't exactly say the air was fresh or fragrant or floral, but it was less oppressive. Less of any smell at all. Quieter, too, with fewer hawkers and street animals and the like. There were more people, but it wasn't bustling either.

She had the feeling it was a forgotten portion of the middling sector of London, which might make it an ideal living space for those who neatly fit in that station.

Or those who wished to disappear.

Perhaps her father had taken up residence in this area as well. It was certainly a step down from where they had been, but not exactly low enough to be cast out.

Even if no one in their former circles would know the name of this street.

The best part about being here, however, was that Lucy did not feel out of place in her attire. And if the manners of their company were better than she predicted, she could rise to their level. Perhaps it would force their host to think more kindly of her and he would do more to help them find her father.

Lucy frowned slightly and looked at Hunter, barely hearing a word he said. "Hunter?"

He stopped whatever he was saying, looking at her in surprise. "Yes?"

"Why does it seem as though my father is not looking for me with quite the same fervor that we are seeking him?" She gestured to the streets around them. "This is the sort of neighborhood where we might hope he has retrenched to, and I don't see a single Bow Street Runner out here. Your contacts haven't heard whispers of my name, have they?"

He wasn't surprised by the question; she could see it in his eyes. He had probably already considered the point hours earlier, but she had not. Being in the lower streets of London, it had been easy to think that her father would not seek her there. But even in Covent Garden, she might have been discovered. And here, rather like Cheapside, she should have been discovered.

And yet…

"I honestly do not know," Hunter admitted with a slight crease to his brow and nose. "There could be a number of reasons, but I don't like that we aren't crossing paths with mutual searches. Something doesn't sit right about it. Yours might not be the most attentive of fathers, but surely he expected you at an appointed time and would be concerned when you did not arrive within it?" He gave her a questioning look.

Lucy could not answer it. "I don't know anymore." She shook her head, sighing. "Perhaps it was all a plot, and he never actually wanted me home. It would be easier to believe that than the alternative."

"Which is?"

She smiled with more than a hint of bitterness. "That he simply does not care."

Hunter's soft hiss of breath told Lucy that he was a better man than her father, which she already knew, and that the idea was just as horrible as she thought.

Which meant it could be true.

"I don't know your father," Hunter said in a low, rumbling voice. "Nor do I know anything of him but what you have told me. My own father died when I was a young man, but I saw how he was with my sister even then. And any father worth claiming would be tearing London apart to find his daughter. If yours is not, and all is well with him, then don't tell me. I'll never be able to leave you with him if he's managing to sleep soundly right now."

Lucy's heart lurched from right to left in sharp, swift, forceful motions that left her slightly dizzy before a cascade of warmth washed over her from head to toe. She smiled up at Hunter with genuine affection. "That may be the nicest thing anyone has ever said to me."

"Then you really ought to start associating with better people in your life." He cleared his throat and started looking up and down the street. "Right. Two blocks, and we'll be there. Up this one, take a right, down three houses."

His diversionary tactics were blatant, but she would let him change topics if he was more comfortable that way. She might smile to herself about it, but at least he had said what he felt, and she had said what she felt.

Perhaps there was more gentleman to him than she had

previously allowed for.

Or perhaps he was just a pastry of a man, with a crunchy exterior and the softest, sweetest interior that existed.

Oh heavens, she could not think of him as food. What a horrifying comparison! Whoever wanted to be a baked good?

Even if it did make her mouth water slightly. Pastry sounded delightful. Actual pastry, not… not Hunter as a pastry.

Oh dear.

Her cheeks heated at the implication, and now she was looking around the streets as well. "Two blocks, did you say?"

Moments later, they were turning on the street he had indicated, and Lucy was taking slow, careful breaths as silently as possible in an attempt to cool her cheeks before they met this Hal person. It would not do to ask for help from anyone when she was flushed and tongue-tied. She needed to be composed, well-spoken, and somehow look like a damsel in distress without too much emphasis on the distress.

A woman in need would always receive help from those with certain standards of morality.

A hysterical woman would only receive pity.

Lucy had never been hysterical, but one did tend to assume things when meeting someone for the first time. And there was no telling what Hunter might say in secret.

"I will let you do the talking," she mumbled around the tingling, frozen feeling in her lips. "Hal is your contact, and this is your idea. I will speak when spoken to."

Hunter gave her a wry look, his mouth curving. "You're not a child. Speak when you like, especially with Hal. You can trust every person in this house to keep any secret, so be as free as you like. I don't say that often, but here… Well, I trust Hal more than any person alive. I'd suggest you stay here tonight if I thought there was room."

Lucy frowned at that. "Why wouldn't there be room?"

Hunter only laughed. "You'll see." With a surprisingly light step, he strode forward and rapped sharply on the door before coming back to Lucy's side.

She stared at the bronze-colored knocker on the door, studying the shining surface as though a face might appear from it.

Why was she suddenly incredibly nervous?

The door opened and a hulking, burly man with a stubble-laden jaw and a scar-riddled face appeared, dark eyes surveying both of them without interest or warmth. "What?"

"Trick and guest to see Hal," Hunter said simply.

The man grunted once. "Is Hal aware of this?"

"Not at all. Sorry for the inconvenience." Hunter grinned widely, and Lucy almost elbowed him in the side. Couldn't he see that the man was in no mood for any sort of shenanigans?

To her surprise, the pseudo-butler stepped back and nodded them in with his head.

Hunter gestured for Lucy to go ahead of him, and she did so, startled to find the house neat and tidy, without a single speck of dust to be seen, and with remarkably comfortable furnishings for even someone of her station. There was nothing from the exterior of the building that would indicate finery, and even inside, nothing was elaborate or expensive, but it would also not be out of place in some portions of Mayfair.

Curious.

Once the door was closed and bolted—with two bolts, she noted—the burly fellow turned to face them and gave Hunter a hint of a smile. "Didn't recognize you without a beard, Trick."

"Ah, right," he mused, rubbing his jaw as though in memory. "I miss those whiskers. They were fantastic. You should try it, Thad. A beard would suit you, and probably hide you better from the authorities."

Lucy said nothing, taking in the red tinge to the whites of the man's eyes, and thought two bottles of whiskey might suit him better than a beard. Then again, the whiskers would hide some of the scars.

Thad snorted and pointed up the stairs. "She's in her office." He looked at Lucy then. "Tea for the guest?"

She wouldn't trust the man to make her toast, let alone tea, and was minded to kindly refuse when Hunter answered for her. "Please. And scones, if you've got any to hand."

Lucy stared at Hunter with wide eyes, though he didn't look at her.

Was he trying to get her killed? Or intoxicated? Or ill?

If the apparent criminal-turned-butler named Thad could make a decent cup of tea and produce edible scones, she would eat one of Tilda's French silks with mint sauce.

But Thad was unruffled and nodded, moving past them and leaving them to fend for themselves with Hal, apparently upstairs.

Except…

Lucy squinted up at Hunter, who now looked at her. "Did he just say 'she' was upstairs?"

Hunter's smile was incorrigible. "Didn't I mention? Hal is a woman. Come on, up you go."

Now this was a bunch of nonsense, and Lucy was ready to demand he explain himself when there was a great crashing sound from above them.

"Oh, lord," Hunter muttered, shaking his head.

"I'm fine!" a woman's voice bellowed. "Nobody rush in! Just the new easel collapsing! It's all fine!"

The snort Hunter produced was nearly thunderous. "Idiot woman. She always blames the easels." Without waiting for Lucy another second, he started up the stairs at a normal pace, still shaking his head.

She took a moment to blink her confusion to a corner of her mind instead of etched all over her face, and followed him, now completely clueless as to what they were about to encounter up there.

"Hal!" Hunter bellowed when he reached the next floor. "That had better be an easel the size of an elephant, or so help me…"

A tall man with sandy-colored hair and a somber expression came out of a room, his eyes wide. "Trick?"

Hunter chortled and went over to him, shaking his hand and thumping his back hard. "Sphinx! I didn't expect you to be home at this time of day."

Sphinx pulled back and smiled at Hunter with surprising ease, his face creasing as though unused to smiles. "I don't always have to be at Bow Street, you know. They let me do as I please. But what are you doing here? Is everything all right?"

The way his voice dipped with that second question told Lucy there was something deeper and darker at work in Hunter's life than he let on. Some real concern for him that meant his appearance here put them all on alert.

Hunter shook his head and indicated Lucy. "Just helping Miss Allred here. She was nearly abducted while being delivered to her father's house, which the carriage driver was apparently in on, as it was not her father's house at all that she had been delivered to. At any rate, we've been looking for said house, but as Miss Allred was never given the address, we are struggling to locate it. I thought Hal might do a drawing of Mr. Allred to assist us."

Sphinx looked from Lucy to Hunter with calculating eyes, and she knew at once that this man was one of those brilliant minds who lived a life that was not what it appeared for ignorant eyes. The sort who always knew more than they let on and saw what most would wish unseen. Of course he worked for Bow Street. He probably solved crimes in mere minutes and knew London like a small neighborhood.

But he was a fairly wiry figure, so physical strength was clearly not something he required for his tasks.

"Welcome to our home, Miss Allred," Sphinx greeted with a belated bow of his head. "If anyone can help with a drawing, it's Hal." His smile spoke of genuine affection, whatever his relationship, and there was a kindness to his eyes that set Lucy at ease.

"Thank you," she replied in a soft voice, buckling her knee for a hint of curtsy to match his bow. "Trick spoke of Hal with such confidence, I am certain you are right."

Sphinx gave Hunter a sidelong look. "Careful going in there. She always blames the easels, but you know…"

Hunter was already nodding. "Your wife far more likely fell off the ladder because she couldn't reach something."

"Or was adjusting the curtains for lighting," Sphinx offered. He looked back at Lucy, winking. "I am sure I appear a bit of a heel of a husband for not racing in to check for her safety, but believe me, after the first few months of marriage, I learned it is better to listen to her when she bellows that she is fine."

Husband and wife? This was the most peculiar place, and these people…

"TRICK?" screeched the feminine voice from before. "Bloody actual hell, what are you doing in my house?"

Sphinx hissed softly. "Apologies, Miss Allred. She only speaks like that to him, if it helps."

Hunter, still at ease despite the imminent arrival of the voice of indignation, scowled at Sphinx. "Don't lie to her, man. The only person she isn't like this with is you."

Sphinx did not argue the point, shrugging a trim shoulder and looking down the corridor in anticipation.

A blonde woman soon appeared, her hair mostly pulled back in a loose chignon with straight tendrils streaming out in places. A pair of spectacles sat atop her head, strands of hair curled and tangled in them, and her bright blue eyes flashed dangerously as she marched to Hunter.

Lucy started backing up, though the woman hadn't seen her yet and was not coming her direction. This was a woman in full ire, raging and furious, which made her fit to trample anyone in her path. She was more formidable than Tilda at this moment, and Lucy felt she would do well to remove herself from the line of fire.

Just in case.

"You know better than to show up here!" the woman—presumably Hal—bellowed, despite being close enough to jab Hunter in the chest with a finger. "Especially unannounced! Did you even think about what a risk it was? What if I had people here that you shouldn't see? What if John were working on something you shouldn't know about? What if we had been compromised and you were walking into a trap?"

Hunter sighed and gripped Hal's hand, twisting her wrist slightly so her finger now pointed up at the ceiling. Hal seemed to almost buckle with that motion and grimaced at it, grunting very softly.

Sphinx did not move or seem in the least concerned about his wife's predicament, nor about the argument brewing.

What sort of home had she been brought to?

"First of all," Hunter said calmly, "I am here because I have need of the skills that I only trust you with. Secondly, I did think about the risk, and the benefits outweigh them. Thirdly, if you had people here that I should not see, Thad would have used the code. Fourth, John wouldn't show me his work if I had a weapon at his throat, and I probably wouldn't understand it anyway."

Sphinx snorted very softly at this, but if there was laughter involved, Lucy couldn't tell, as the man covered his mouth at once.

He must be John, then.

Hunter batted his lashes in an almost playful manner, though there was a tension to his frame and face that spoke of true irritation. "Finally, Henrietta, if you had been compromised—again, Thad would have used the code so I would know there was danger, and I would probably have come in anyway because no one compromises you without dealing with me as a result. Now, would you like to stop screaming like a banshee and let me explain myself?"

Hal glared at Hunter, her jaw jutting out as short bursts of air expelled from her nose a few times. Then she seemed to slump without her posture shifting, nodding once.

He dropped Hal's hand and pointed his own finger at Lucy without looking at her. "I'm not alone. So you've just made a fool of yourself and exposed your husband's name, all of which will be fun for me to explain later. Sphinx was doing a marvelous job of keeping things superficial, but now..." He shrugged dramatically, pressing his mouth in a tight line.

Hal glanced at Lucy, her lips pursing and twisting to one side.

Lucy did her best not to react to that, smiling in the smallest manner possible to show that she should not feel too bad about any of this. It was not as though Lucy had anyone to tell, and she wouldn't do so anyway.

"All that aside," he went on, "we need you. This is Miss Lucy Allred. Teacher at Miss Masters's."

Hal looked at Hunter sharply, eyes wide. He gave her a shake of the head.

What in the world was that about?

"We need to find her father. Can you please spare some time to do a drawing of him that we can show around to people?" He looked at Lucy then, and she felt a jolt at being suddenly acknowledged.

Was she supposed to say something? Do something? Explain herself?

He gave her no indication as to what part she was meant to play here.

"Please?" Lucy found herself laughing very softly, awkwardly, and trying to force a hopeful smile at Hal.

Hal looked between Hunter and Lucy, then nodded a few times, her expression clearing as she smiled at Lucy with what seemed to be genuine warmth. "Of course. My apologies, Miss Allred. Allow me to begin again. Good day, my name is Hal. Shall we get to drawing?"

Chapter Sixteen

Hunter wasn't usually uneasy in his sister's house or company, but today, all he felt was discomfort.

Not about his sister or her husband, nor about the situation all of them were in at the moment.

It was entirely about the fact that Lucy was sitting in a room with his sister, and Hal had forbidden Hunter from being present while they worked.

She hadn't explained why he couldn't be present for the drawing of Mr. Allred, only insisted that it would be better if Lucy spoke with her privately while they worked, and that no one else was present to influence her thoughts or images of her father.

Hunter didn't understand how him being in the room would affect how Lucy pictured the father she'd known her entire life, but his sister would brook no opposition.

So he was out in the corridor pacing instead. Not directly in front of the door, but along the entire length of the corridor. He might slow his steps in front of the door to Hal's studio to try and hear what was being said, but Hal knew better and had set up their drawing far enough away to avoid eavesdropping.

He cursed himself for allowing her studio to be such a large space. It had technically been the house's expansive library when they'd set her up, which had been an exciting prospect for them both. So much space and references to hand in the same room—perfect for the way her mind worked and the sort of art she loved best.

Why hadn't he seen then that it would work against him someday?

Most things involving his sister usually came back to haunt him.

By his calculations, they had been in there for twenty minutes so far. It took Hal roughly thirty minutes to accomplish a passable likeness unless the person's memory was poor or affected. If she followed her usual pattern, she would then ask Lucy to take a break and read a book or take a walk, something to shift her mindset and her thoughts, before having her back into the room at least an hour later. For those with more complicated schedules, she'd have them return another day at their convenience.

Hunter couldn't risk bringing Lucy back here on another day, more for his sake than her own, so they'd remain here as long as Hal needed for an accurate likeness to be completed, both to her satisfaction and Lucy's. It would probably give Lucy some comfort to be in a stable, clean environment with people of a certain quality for a time. Tilda's was all well and good, but it was a world unto itself. Hal and John at least lived in some semblance of the real world, as well as a world that Lucy would recognize.

And Hunter wanted to stay a while as well. He missed his sister from time to time, and there was no one who understood him in quite the same way.

He'd met other sets of twins who felt the same way about their sibling, and some of whom had a truly deep connection that could not be explained. A sense of knowing what the other was thinking or experiencing without being in their vicinity, or feeling an echo of the same themselves. Hunter couldn't go that far with Hal, but they were each able to see beneath the surface of the other with surprising accuracy.

Which shouldn't surprise him, given how his twin did everything with accuracy.

He should be perfectly comfortable with Lucy being in his sister's company. Who could he trust more? And he did not for one second believe that Lucy was in danger or would compromise him. He did worry that Hal might tell Lucy too much about himself, particularly about the childhood and youth they had passed, which would mean she would tell him about their relationship, which would allow Lucy to know him on a personal level.

But mostly, he was just uncomfortable with Lucy being out of his sight.

He'd been dealing with this the entire night during his patrol, leaving him more distracted than he ought to have been in a potentially dangerous situation, but there had been nothing he could do about it. He'd tried every single mental trick he'd ever built up for himself, but not one of them had managed to keep Lucy out of his mind for more than ten minutes. It wasn't always that he was dwelling on her for pleasure either.

It was fear. Worry. Concern. Anticipation made of agitation and dread. A gnawing edge to every other emotion, as though he were already feeling guilty for something happening to her while she was in his care. There was no proof that anything would go wrong, nothing to hint that those who'd abducted her would try again, and he had taken necessary precautions to protect her. But still, he feared whatever would happen to her next.

Only when she was in his sight did he feel that panic ease. Did that edge disappear. Did his thoughts run smoothly.

Perhaps it was the nature of having someone in his custody when he had never been so saddled. Perhaps it was that he knew how shocking his world could be to someone as sheltered as Lucy. Perhaps it was that she had already been the victim of an abduction attempt, and without his intervention, she could have suffered untold injuries and indignities. Perhaps it was that she was a teacher at the Convent—one of the few who had no idea of its true purpose as an operative training facility.

It could have been any number of things that provoked this response in him, but there was something else nagging at him. Something difficult to define and intimidating to explore. Something that was all of those reasons and yet none of them entirely.

He was the one responsible for Lucy, and he didn't know what had prompted the abduction attempt. He didn't know what danger lurked for Lucy without him. And the more time he spent with her, the more dreadful that unknown danger became.

He did not like that they could not find Lucy's father, and he very much did not like that there was no one looking for her. Good manners and common sense told him there was a chance that her father was in danger as well, but real-world experience told him that greed and dismissiveness were easy bedfellows. Mr. Allred had never been a doting father, as far as Lucy had described, but surely, he could see her as a valuable asset for himself in Society, if nothing else.

Yet here they were, hunting him when he ought to be hunting them.

Something was wrong. Until he knew what, Hunter could not—and would not—be comfortable with Lucy out of his sight.

"I have never seen you like this."

Hunter looked over at his brother-in-law, leaning with surprising casualness against the wall near the stairs. "You've known me a year. That isn't surprising. I could be like this often."

John raised a brow. "Are you?"

He could lie, but what was the point in that? John was a genius and an operative of sorts. Besides, he'd be asking Hal later, and she would tell her husband everything she could.

Hunter shook his head, clasping his hands behind his back and continuing to pace. "All of this is a puzzle, Sphinx. And puzzles have never been my thing."

"Is it the sort of puzzle that might be my thing?" came the soft response.

Again, Hunter shook his head. "It is more like a game of chess, only the rest of the board is hidden from me. I must make moves without knowing where anyone else is or what danger lies before me."

"Are we talking about your assignment or your guest?"

"Don't ask stupid questions," Hunter replied without animation or energy. "I'd never be this confused about an assignment. I get all the information I need to proceed for those. No, this…" He gestured to his well-paced path. "This is all about Lucy."

John grunted a half laugh of sorts. "That raises so many questions for me."

Hunter scowled in his general direction. "You've been spending too much time with my sister. The tone says it all." He waved it off, sputtering to himself. "You don't understand."

"And your sister is somehow going to understand better?" John folded his arms and leaned forward a little, his smile too knowing. "Not bloody likely, and you know it."

Hunter did know it, but Hal was his only hope for making sense of it all.

"I don't understand," he admitted to his brother-in-law, his pacing slowing to more of a meandering speed. "I don't understand how we're in this situation, I don't understand what lies ahead of us, I don't understand why this is eating at me…"

"I may be able to help with that last one," John offered, raising his hand like an eager schoolboy.

Hunter shot him a look. "No. Not what you're thinking."

John smirked a little. "I was going to say because you're a skilled operative trained to see inconsistencies in the ordinary. What were you thinking I was thinking?"

His brother-in-law was a bare-faced liar, that's what he was thinking. But there was no point continuing to argue. Perhaps he did need to speak with John about this. It certainly couldn't hurt, and John had a very straightforward way of looking at the world and the people in it. Clarity was never his problem.

Hunter desperately needed clarity.

"I foiled an abduction attempt on Lucy," he admitted, lowering his voice, though the entire house was filled with trusted operatives who could keep a secret under the worst duress. "That's how we met and how she came into my protection. I thought she was a contact, but it turned out she was just a teacher. From you-know-where, but she is truly just a teacher."

John nodded, straightening and settling against the wall, his brow furrowed as he apparently listened.

Hunter turned on his heel, proceeding with his pacing once more. "She had no idea who would want to abduct her, nor who had been trying to. Her father had sent a carriage to bring her home for the holidays, and it was to take her to his new residence. He has retrenched, and she does not know the address, so did not realize the carriage was not going where it ought. I sent scouts throughout the area and spent the entire night looking for her father, and we came up empty. Entirely empty. Suspiciously empty."

"No one even knew the name?" John pressed, his voice filled with doubt.

"Exactly," Hunter replied, both to the question and the tone. "Not a whisper. We spent yesterday with Tilda, and I left Lucy there for the night while I saw to details of my assignment, but I kept my ears open for any sign of her father. My scouts would continue to look around, but I cannot have them too far out of their usual scope, considering…" He shrugged, dismissing the explanation with a flick of two fingers. John didn't need to know everything Hunter was involved in right now. And in fact, it would be dangerous for him to know too much of what his assignment entailed.

He ought to be used to a lack of explanation in some areas.

Hunter exhaled shortly. "Nothing last night either. Nothing this morning when I checked in with them. It's like the man doesn't exist, Sphinx. Except he must, because Lucy was going to stay with him. And I don't know why someone would go to the trouble of taking a young woman to a remote part of London to abduct her if she isn't… Well, her father is in debt and such, so there cannot be too much money to hand for a ransom."

"And clearly he isn't doing much to find her," John pointed out.

That brought Hunter to a screeching halt in his pacing. "How the devil could you know that?"

John smiled a tight, humorless smile. "I work for Bow Street. No one has put in a search for a Miss Allred. And you'd have crossed paths with someone by now if they were looking for her."

Well, that made Hunter feel a little stupid, but he supposed, in that sense, it ought to have been obvious. John was exceptionally intelligent, and puzzles of any sort were simple when he looked at them. He would have been able to see the maze of Lucy's situation for what it was with just as much ease.

Hunter heaved an exhale, feeling a remarkable amount of relief. "Right. So I'm concerned about the information that I might find, should we discover anything about her father. And what sort of situation I would be leaving her in, once I deposit her back into her usual life."

"It is not your place to protect every young woman whose family situation is less than ideal," John murmured.

A wry laugh escaped Hunter. "No, we know in the streets to leave that to Gent. And I don't want to save everyone. But Lucy…" He hissed and glanced at the still closed door. "I don't like it, Sphinx. And what I don't like sticks with me."

John made a face of consideration, staying silent for a long moment. "Well, Trick, your instincts are important and have a history of being in tune. Perhaps you should stop thinking Lucy is a distraction and listen to the instincts instead. They might tell you something."

The door to the studio opened then, silencing any further conversation between them. Lucy led the way out while Hal followed, both of them smiling in a fairly natural way. Hal's eyes darted to Hunter, and he caught the knowing flash in them that meant he would have a lot of explaining to do in a short while.

"How did it go?" John asked, saving Hunter the trouble of asking for himself. Much to the man's credit, he asked Lucy and not his wife.

Lucy shrugged very lightly. "I think well. It's interesting how much you can both remember and forget when you are intentionally focused on a person's face from memory."

John grinned, cocking his head. "How so?"

"I could remember the jowls that sag about his mouth and jaw, but it took me ten minutes to remember the color of his eyes." Lucy shook her head, laughing at herself. "It will be even more interesting to see what I can recall on the second sitting."

"Well, my wife does have amazing skills, so I have no doubt the drawing will be perfect." He shifted his attention to his wife. "*Ange*, would you like to take a break yourself? I can have Thad bring out luncheon. When would you like her back for the second sitting?"

Hal smiled for her husband, and the shades of adoration Hunter could see in his sister's face were something that warmed his heart. He'd always hoped to see her that happy in a marriage but hadn't dreamed she would find it. Here was the proof, and for this moment, he was perfectly content.

But it soon passed.

"Give it an hour or so," Hal suggested. "And yes, let us do luncheon. But I do require a few moments with Trick before I do that. Thad will need time to arrange it all anyway."

Hunter eyed his sister suspiciously. "Why?"

She only looped her arm through his, continuing to smile at her husband, though the smile tightened. "Go ahead and take Miss Allred down. Or give her a tour of the house. We'll only be a moment."

With surprising force, Hal yanked on Hunter's arm, hauling him out of the corridor and into her studio. She flung him into the room and shut the door behind them, not giving her husband or Lucy a chance to respond or react very much at all.

Ah, so his twin's ire was still in full force, was it? Marvelous. She was much more fun when she was like this. And she was more inclined to speak her mind, which was what he needed at this moment.

Hal's hair was far more disheveled now than it had been when she'd marched at him, and the glare she was currently spearing him with matched the frazzled state of her, charcoal on her fingers and all. Her bright blue eyes were narrowed as she stared at him and folded her arms tightly.

Then said nothing.

Hunter knew what she wanted, but he'd be damned if he gave it to her so easily. He set his hands on his hips and raised a brow at her.

She widened her eyes, leaning forward a little and using her head to gesture some sort of circle.

It did not take being a twin to understand what she was indicating, and in fact did not take much intellect either. But still, he wasn't interested in taking the silent hints. If his sister wanted to know something, she was going to have to ask him very clearly.

Now Hal used one of her hands to accompany her silent beckoning, rolling it in a circle for a moment and then holding it out palm up.

Hunter chose that moment to yawn loudly.

"You are insufferable," his sister ground out through clenched teeth, "and I hate you."

"You bloody adore me," Hunter reassured her with a bold wink. "But I am insufferable."

"As long as you're aware of it." She sniffed and closed the distance between them, wrapping her arms around him and hugging him close. "It is so good to see you."

Chuckling, Hunter put his arms around her as well, affection and warmth filling every part of him. "It's good to see you too. You look well."

"I ought to look well," Hal grumbled. "I'm unwell every

morning, so there is no chance of me putting on unfashionable weight anytime soon."

Hunter pulled back in shock, looking her over. "Are you expecting, Hank?"

Hal nodded quickly, averting her eyes even as a small smile played at her lips. "Don't tell anyone, you're the only one who knows. We haven't even told Jeremy and Helen yet."

"I won't say a word." He hugged her quickly but fiercely. "Hank, that's marvelous! John must be thrilled. Are you pleased?"

"I suppose so," she mused as she pulled back and started towards a pair of chairs in the room. "I've never really thought about having children or being a mother. But with John, I want everything and anything. Whatever comes in life with him, I want. And the idea of having his children is intriguing and appealing. I don't know that I'll feel much about it until I can start feeling the child within me. It still feels… hypothetical, in a way. Aside from the illness in the morning, but that improves with breakfast." She huffed and sat down in a chair, flopping inelegantly and giving him a hard look.

"What?" Hunter asked her as he also moved in that direction.

Hal rolled her eyes. "You're obtuse as well as insufferable. Tell me about Lucy. From the beginning, first of all, and in great detail, secondly."

Hunter chuckled, sitting and crossing one leg over the other. "Anything else?"

"Yes, I also need to know what your plan is going forward because clearly you cannot parade up and down my street with my sketches or walk into Mayfair to do so. Not in your condition." She gestured to his plain but clean ensemble.

"I'm very clean and presentable, thank you very much," Hunter retorted with a faux offended scoff. But she did have a point, and he wouldn't pretend otherwise.

So he recounted everything for her, in more detail than he had for John, and including Briar by her code name, knowing Hal had dealings with her before. He told her about the panic of the abduction and his confusion that the woman he thought was Briar was not fighting back against her foes. About the night he had spent scouring his part of London to find Lucy's father while Briar watched her at his flat. About finding no success and having to figure out what to do with Lucy himself. Spending time with Tilda and the ladies.

He barely touched on his patrol, since Hal shouldn't know much about his assignment, but he took the story up to where they were at this moment in Hal and John's home, needing a picture of Mr. Allred in order to have any hope of finding the man. At least without recruiting finer society to ask around.

And he was not going to risk Lucy's reputation by bringing her into finer society, with all of their judgments and speculation.

Hal sat fairly quietly through the telling, her brow creasing from time to time, but making no comment or noise. When Hunter finished, she just began slowly shaking her head.

"What?" he asked with a nudge of his foot against hers.

"I should be hearing her name called up and down the streets," Hal said softly. "John should have recognized her name immediately from Bow Street so we could take her home. But you still have her, which means she was brought to your side of London purposefully and it has nothing to do with her father's location. You're never going to find him in your corner, and that might have been the point."

"My scouts are going everywhere," he pointed out. "Anywhere that a Society gentleman might relocate."

Still, Hal shook her head. "In talking with Lucy, her father is ashamed of his diminished position in Society, and he won't make his address public knowledge. He won't go somewhere that others of his station might see. You're far better off looking where you are and such." She tsked loudly and wiped at one eye. "Why isn't he looking for her? That's cruel."

"I know," Hunter answered in a low voice. "I don't know why he isn't looking for her, and I don't like it. Part of me wants to leave Lucy here with you until I figure this out."

"I am not watching her like she's some kind of dog, Hunter," Hal protested hotly, swiping at the lone tear on her cheek. "Be serious."

Hunter gave her a quelling look. "I am serious. You think she's better with me? Safer with me? Where am I supposed to take her tonight? Tilda cannot host her, and she cannot stay in my flat with me. Briar is across the river, and her family is in no position to host anyone."

"She's safer with you than with anyone else," Hal shot back. "Most likely including her own father, should you ever happen to find him. You need a place for her to stay tonight where you can be as well and keep an eye on her without ruining anyone's reputation? What about that pub and inn we have connections to in Poplar? Isn't that supposed to be some sort of safe destination?"

Hunter stared at his sister with wide eyes, unsure how to respond, and when his chest would loosen from the shock of her suggestion.

She blinked at him briefly. "What? What's wrong with it?"

"Nothing," he said slowly, feeling every ounce of air coming in and out of his lungs. "You're just not supposed to know we have connections there."

Hal's smile was slow and sly. "I know. But know it I do, so let's not pretend that I don't."

"It's not the safest place I could take her," Hunter told her, sitting back and rubbing his palms together in thought. "I mean, operatives meet there, and we take targets there, good and bad. We know that we won't be compromised there, but others use the place as well, and we cannot account for the sort of people that might—"

"She's already met some of your crew," Hal overrode with impatience. "And you can sleep outside her door." She nodded to herself as though the matter were decided. "Sailors and smugglers might be there, but you will too. She'll be fine, and you can likely still do something related to your assignment in that neighborhood."

Hunter cocked his head in interest. "That's true…" He speared his sister with a suspicious look. "You don't know what I'm looking into, do you?"

Hal barked a laugh, tossing her wild hair. "Of course not. I have speculation, but no certainties. I enjoy making up scenarios for you, so kindly do not disillusion me." She cleared her throat. "Now, shall we talk about how remarkably pretty Lucy is and how that's perturbing you? Or are you roaming about the Kingdom of Denial at present?"

Ah, there it was.

Hunter pulled out his watch and examined the time, nodding in thought. "Goodness, you've been practicing your restraint. I expected that question a good seven minutes ago."

His twin ignored his quip and kept her gaze steady on him, now waiting for him to stop pretending they were not going to speak on this topic.

He supposed he had ignored it long enough.

Sitting back in his chair slowly and slumping lazily, Hunter relaxed his face and let his lips sputter. "She's utterly beautiful, Hal. I've felt like an idiot is living in my head from the moment I met her."

"Well…" Hal drawled in her way, gesturing faintly with her fingers.

Hunter gave her a scolding look. "Thank you. Anyway… I find myself slower to think and stupid in conversation. I am acutely aware of my kneecaps in her presence and can feel every inch of space between my body and hers. I've met beautiful women before and never been entirely affected like this. I hate excessive chatter, and yet I find her rambling to be charming. I hate not having my privacy, and yet I want her to be in my presence all the time. I hate not being able to do exactly as I please at any given moment, and yet I am delighted to do whatever it is she needs me to do. I've known her for two days, Hank. Two bloody days, and my entire life is in shambles."

"Aww," his sister sighed with a whimper.

"That is not a helpful response!" Hunter cried in outrage.

"I'm sorry!" She covered her face momentarily, exhaling a slow breath before lowering her hands and assuming a more somber facade. "I'm sorry. How can I help?"

He glared her, then grumbled, "I don't know."

Hal clamped down on her lips hard, and he suspected she was fighting laughter.

Also not helpful.

He exhaled heavily. "It's not even the fact that she's among the most beautiful women I've ever seen that's the problem. Not really. It's the fact that I notice that every single time I see her. It's that I dwell on the three damn freckles by her left ear, and that I even know she has them. It's that I don't even know if I want to find her father, because that means…" He bit his tongue to stop himself from finishing the statement, though the thought continued quite easily in his mind.

Finding her father would mean he would have to let Lucy go, and he would likely never see her again.

And that made him feel absolutely ill in a way he did not care for at all.

"When did you last spend any time in a woman's company that was not for your assignments?" Hal asked him in a quiet tone that was now devoid of all mockery.

Hunter shook his head. "I couldn't say. I honestly have no idea."

She hummed very softly. "That makes it rather difficult to tell if what you are feeling is for Lucy herself or the idea of a woman in your personal life."

He winced at the suggestion and shook his head even more firmly. "I'm not feeling like I'm losing my mind to a blissful delirium because I'm lonely and need a woman's company, Hank. I concede that my personal life is singularly lacking in every respect, but I was fairly perturbed when I realized how much work would be going into helping Lucy. She was irksome. She is irksome, depending on her mood, which changes with a fluidity that feels like walking on ice."

"I like her already," Hal mused with a hint of a laugh.

"You would," Hunter assured her, patting her knee. "She's direct and frank and hasn't panicked or simpered about anything since being rescued from the abduction. She'd likely make a good operative, if Milliner is interested in training her. She doesn't long for the love and affection of her distant father and sees him clearly, yet she has no pity for herself or her situation. I… I like her, Hank. Very much."

"Yes, I believe we've already established that." She punched his shoulder lightly, chuckling to herself. "You're not used to feeling anything, and now you're feeling some of the most intense feelings that exist. Poor Hunt, are you drowning?"

He nodded without hesitation. "Drowning, flailing, sputtering, choking… It's as though no one taught me how to swim and now I'm meant to cross the Channel."

"The man has a way with words, but he ain't no poet," Hal teased, throwing a poor attempt at a common accent into her voice. Sobering, she pushed a lock of her hair behind an ear. "Take it from me, Hunter: If you are falling in love, take a breath and see if it might be worth the madness. Fighting against it out of fear or anxiety just makes everything worse. If you truly do not want it, remind yourself that you will find her father soon and she will be gone. Then you can claim it as a good experience for yourself and a lesson to be learned."

Hunter swallowed with some difficulty against his tightening throat. "And if I find that I do?"

His sister smiled and reached out a hand for his, which he took and held tightly. "Then you hold on to it with all your might, and we find a more creative way for you to fulfill your operative assignments."

Chapter Seventeen

The second sitting for the portrait of Lucy's father was far more comfortable than the first.

Not that the first sitting had been uncomfortable, per se. On the contrary, Hal had been quite skilled at setting Lucy at ease and was remarkably amiable, given the fury with which she had greeted Hunter. To Lucy's surprise, they hadn't started immediately with a description of her father's physical appearance. Instead, Hal asked Lucy about teaching at Miss Masters's and how she enjoyed doing so.

Apparently, Hal had attended that school herself, and their conversation had immediately deviated to the current teachers on staff, the grounds, the corridors and classrooms, the furnishings of the bed chambers, the number of students she currently taught who had graduated from the neighboring Rothchild Academy…

It had felt like chatting with an old friend and reminiscing about a forgotten past, and it made Lucy ache for her life at the school.

Only when they had both sat quietly in their memories of that place had Hal sighed and suggested they start with the drawing, and Lucy found herself talking more about her father than she had in a long time. She found herself talking about more than just his appearance, but his nature. How he had changed when her mother had died, though he had never given her much attention or care before that. How she had come to realize that she would never please him and tried to make peace with it. How she truly did not know what her life would be from one year to the next with him directing affairs.

It had been draining, but healing, in a way. Lucy had been very grateful for the break and the hearty lunch that had been provided, even if Hal and Hunter had arrived well after Lucy and John had begun to eat.

John had no concerns about Hal and Hunter being alone, nor about their being late, which made Lucy wonder what sort of lives the couple lived in their home and just how they were connected to Hunter's world, but she sensed these were not the sort of questions she ought to ask. Were Hal and Hunter related somehow? Was that even possible?

Before they had sat down to luncheon, John had taken Lucy on a tour of their house, which was remarkably comfortable and surprisingly simple in its furnishings. No fuss or frills, and almost every room was filled with books or drawing supplies, which she found particularly amusing. No wonder Hunter had said there was no room for Lucy to stay here. Each of the rooms that were likely designated as bedchambers were being used for other things, and it would be a massive inconvenience for any guest to arrive unannounced here.

Such an active embracing of their life without having to make any consideration for anyone else. What an unusual, independent, yet endearing couple!

Back in the studio with Hal now, Lucy found herself falling back into the easy cadence of describing her father. Hal had told her from the beginning that it was fine if she repeated things from the first sitting, as it would only serve as reinforcement.

Whatever that meant where drawing a portrait was concerned.

Lucy had never been a particularly skilled artist, despite the training she had received in her adolescence. Something about proper shading had never made sense to her fingers, and dimension was simply beyond her ability to convey. But as she was always told, she had other talents and gifts that could make up for the utter lack of artistic ability, and not all gentlemen wanted a wife gifted in the arts. Her tutors had been the ones most sincere in that belief, no doubt terrified of her father and his opinion of their failure to make Lucy into an accomplished lady.

Her mother, on the other hand, had usually made that statement, but with an edge of sarcasm and a wink. She had never been concerned with Lucy's level of accomplishment.

Or lack thereof.

"Lucy?"

Shaking herself and forcing the image of her mother out of her mind, Lucy looked back at Hal. "Yes?"

Hal smiled rather kindly behind her spectacles, perched low on her nose. "You were far away for a moment there. Everything all right?"

Lucy nodded quickly, flashing a smile. "I was thinking about my lack of artistic ability, actually. I am positively dreadful, and my tutors and governess despaired of my marital prospects but tried to encourage me that not all gentlemen cared about such things."

Hal laughed once, her eyes crinkling. "That's true, I suppose. It's never gotten me anywhere with men."

"Says the married woman," Lucy pointed out, her smile going crooked.

Hal opened her mouth, clearly about to argue a point, then closed it, her mouth curving in apparent bemusement. "I suppose my art did have some part in my marriage to John. Not in the conventional sense, but…" She sighed, shaking her head. "Suffice it to say, I would not have married him had I not been particularly gifted the way that I happen to be. But John is no great appreciator of art. Apart from mine." She winked and looked back at her drawing.

Lucy wanted to ask so many questions, but it was quite clear that the topic was closed. "My mother did not care that I was unable to draw or paint. I am not certain anything was flawed in me, through her eyes. Granted, I did not share all my thoughts with her, or she would know how I felt about the way my father treated her, but she ought to have seen me clearly enough."

"I think mothers have selective vision, in that regard," Hal murmured, her eyes fixed on her drawing. "They see everything but choose what to keep in their mind about us. And I have no doubt she would not be surprised by your thoughts about your father."

"How can you possibly suspect that?" Lucy asked without heat. "We've known each other a scant few hours, and you certainly never met my mother."

Hal glanced up, one brow quirking higher than the other. "Your expression is not as blank as you might think, Lucy. It was written across your face."

Lucy put a hand to her cheek in response, knowing her complexion was growing pink from the accusation. "Truly?"

Nodding, Hal sat back, adjusting her spectacles closer to her face. "Truly. But I like that. Now, tell me about your father's hair."

Closing her eyes, Lucy thought back to the last time she had seen her father. "It's dark but gets more grey in it by the year. It's especially greying by his ears. He has almost no hair on the top of his head and his brow, but there are a few longer strands he brushes across the top to try and hide the baldness. It doesn't work, since it's only a handful of strands, but he tries. He wears his sideburns long, and they get thick and more greying the longer they are."

"Straight or curly?"

"Straight. But thick where he isn't bald, if that makes sense. His brow is very high, even before he was balding there. Thick eyebrows, barely any grey in them, and they touch when he frowns." Lucy felt as though she was squinting as she thought, but her eyes were closed, so there was nothing to see. "He has never grown a beard or the sort, but you can tell it would also be thick and dark if he did."

Hal nodded as her hand flew across the page with the charcoal. "Keep going. Tell me anything about his face and features."

Lucy twisted her lips, hoping her descriptions would give Hal something good to work with, something specific that would set her father apart from other men. But in her mind, he was just… her father. His face was just his face, and there was nothing extraordinary or noteworthy in it. What was more useful: the slight cleft to his chin or the mole by his right eyebrow?

"Whatever you are considering," Hal mused without looking up, "tell me both. Nothing is too small a detail, anything can be useful."

Lucy laughed in surprise. "How in the world did you know?"

Hal shook her head very slightly, sighing. "I have been at this for a very long time, and I do this frequently for all sorts of people and reasons. You learn what certain silences mean and how to get people talking about the right things."

"Hmm," Lucy said softly. "I envy your certainty about your skills and your occupation. Your life, perhaps. I know appearances aren't always what they seem, believe me, but you seem fairly independent, even within your marriage. That tells me you married out of love, which I envy greatly. To be yourself—to know yourself well enough to be yourself—and to attain all that you hope for as well. How often are we ladies told to be a certain way and to behave just so in order to find a good match? And no one ever speaks of love, and rarely of affection. I don't know how you've managed it, Hal, but I am truly envious, God help me."

The sounds of Hal's drawing slowed, then stopped. She looked at Lucy closely, then pushed her spectacles on top of her head and set the drawing aside. "Lucy… No life is perfect, as you know. My husband and I married for convenience, and we managed to find real love for each other after the fact. Yes, that does make me quite fortunate, but my husband would have had no interest in who I was had we not been forced into a life together. We could not stand each other, which was probably due to our misguided impressions of one another and a belief that we knew best. As it happens, we're both terribly stubborn, which does not bode well for future children."

Lucy giggled at the idea, and Hal laughed as well. "You seem so happy together. So comfortable."

"We are," Hal assured her, "but it did not start out as so. All we knew was that we could trust each other, and our love flowered through that trust. If you seek love in your life, find it. That sounds simple from the already married woman who did not need a marriage at all to be secure in her life, but I cannot put it any other way. From what I can tell, your father uses you as a tool for his own means. Well, don't let him. You are of age, and you are now gainfully employed at a well-respected institution. No one worth having will look down on you for that, even in Society. You are on a path to claiming your life for yourself, and I think you are determined enough to see it through."

"Am I?" Lucy whispered before she could stop herself. "I feel so uncertain about everything."

Hal grunted once. "That is because we are not taught to think for ourselves, let alone to act for ourselves. We have to discover the beauty and madness of such things all on our own, and usually when it is far too late to do us any good."

Lucy found herself snorting in bemused agreement. "Very true.

Even so, I don't know that I could ever be like you, or like Miss Bradford."

"Miss Bradford," Hal told her firmly as she sat back and took up the drawing again, "is a rare creature that cannot possibly be imitated, but she would certainly be a skilled enough mentor for any young woman. You might confide in her, should you desire a match for yourself with affection at its center, particularly if you do not wish to anger your father with your choice. I have no doubt she would be a great help in that regard. Trust me, people have gone to her for lesser concerns and come away successful."

Lucy did her best not to blanch at the idea, even while her mind seemed to leap with excitement at it. She could never confide in her employer and headmistress in such a way, even if she would be useful in it. The matter was simply far too personal to share with a woman she respected so greatly, particularly when their relationship was so new. In a few years, perhaps, if Lucy was still employed at the school and had formed a closer bond…

Perhaps then, they could talk of potential husbands.

The image of Hunter and his crooked smile came to mind, warming her heart, and sending that warmth into the pit of her stomach with an unsettling splash of sorts.

She inhaled sharply, then cleared her throat to cover the sound. "My… my father has a slight cleft to his chin and a mole by his right eyebrow. It is not particularly large, smaller than the thickness of the brow itself, but it is there all the same. His nose has a faint crease that runs across it, as though it comes from one nostril to the other, if that makes sense…"

She continued to describe whatever she could think of, from the age spots visible beneath the strands atop his head to the faint lines that were now permanently etched between his brows and at the corners of his mouth. It felt strange, isolating particular details of her father's face and head like some bizarre dissection of what created his image. She half expected the picture of him in her mind to yell at her for not behaving like a lady or to tell her to wear a more secure hairstyle if she was going to ride.

Lucy felt herself sit taller and speak more softly the more she described him. Felt the familiar tension in her chest and the strain in her neck. The odd awareness of the hairs on her head, as though they knew they had to be perfect. The ache in her low back as her posture became unnatural, even for a woman of her station. The pressure of her feet against the floor.

Was her breathing too loud? Too obvious? Did her features appear composed and sedate? Was her smile too bold or too easy? Were her hands folded in a graceful way? Was she blinking too much or too little due to staring?

It took her several moments to realize she wasn't speaking anymore. Her eyes flicked over to Hal, who was also silent and staring back at her, expression soft, eyes knowing. Her hands were still, nothing moving against the paper to work on the drawing.

It was a strange, vulnerable feeling to have Hal's eyes on her in such a way. As though she could see every thought Lucy had written out above her head. Could understand every impulse that Lucy had just gone through. Sensed the sort of treatment Lucy received from her father.

Lucy had to look away, finding her throat tightening and trying to swallow. She might have been mistreated by her father, and he might have been particularly stern, but she had not been truly injured by him. He had never come close to striking her or the like. She had heard several horrid stories from the girls she taught who had come to her from the Rothchild Academy, which had been set up for poor girls to attend for free and thereby receive an education that would allow them to better their situation. Some of those poor things hadn't even known a kind moment from their father in the short time of their lives, and some had received tremendous beatings that had prompted them to run away.

No, Lucy's father wasn't like that. He simply destroyed Lucy's confidence by finding flaw in everything, reduced her opportunities in life by his own actions, and somehow expected her to still manage a successful marriage that would benefit him for the rest of his life. He expected her to be the catch of any social Season, though he had given her nothing to tempt the sort of men he wanted for her husband. Her dowry was nonexistent, and she was now at an age to be looked at with speculation as a marriage prospect, all of which he somehow made her fault.

When he was bothered to notice her, of course.

She loved when he did not.

But still, she ought to have been describing her father's appearance, not dwelling on his manner. It was not as though Hal could put his manner into the drawing.

Could she?

"Everything all right?" Hal inquired in the softest voice Lucy had heard from her yet.

Lucy managed the swallow she had been struggling with and nodded once. "Yes. It's only… well, it isn't particularly relevant to our present task."

"That doesn't mean you can't tell me. I won't share, but I won't press. If it would help you to express more, do so. If you would prefer me to focus on my work, I will do so." She cleared her throat and shifted in her seat, drawing Lucy's gaze back. "Trick is always telling me I see too much and say too much, but he's one to talk."

The wry tone Hal had taken on made Lucy giggle, and she nodded in agreement. "He certainly is. He shouldn't say anything of the sort to you."

Hal's mouth tightened as though she would laugh, but she only shook her head, the corners of her eyes crinkling.

Exactly like Hunter's did.

Lucy tilted her head to one side, wondering if she dared ask…

"I don't want to go to my father's house," she found herself admitting instead. "I hate life with him. But he refused to let me remain at the school for the holidays. I ought to have some authority over my life, as I have clearly reached my majority, but he has not made any provisions for me, so there is nothing to claim. I would be perfectly content to continue roaming London with Hunter until the holidays have passed and then return to the school for next term."

Hal's eyes widened very slightly, and it took the space of a few heartbeats before Lucy realized why.

She had said Hunter instead of Trick. Based on that reaction, Hunter might be his actual given name and not just some additional code. Was it really so shocking a thing? Did it signify? Or was it just something that was rarely used and Hal had not heard it in some time?

"I know that's not possible," Lucy added quickly, trying to flash a smile to offset the shock. "But it would be preferable."

"I can understand that," Hal eventually said, her eyes darting to her drawing. "You do realize that the life that Hunter—Trick—leads is not particularly sedate, don't you? He's been taking care of you since your foiled abduction, but usually, there is far more risk, and even depravity, involved in what he deals with."

Lucy felt herself grow defensive at the suggestion. "Yes, of course I know that. I saw the men who know him, and he said they were going on patrol, whatever that means. I had a perfectly good idea of the sort of men they were and how they behave. Hunter is not like them."

"I know that better than you do," Hal shot back without venom, but plenty of authority, her eyes flashing, "but they are the sort of people who fill his life and his days out of necessity. And worse. Wandering with Hunter is not a reality, Lucy. It is simple protection on his part. For you. From his reality. Because his reality is not fit for you, for me, and sometimes, not even for him. But he deals with it out of duty."

Duty? Lucy hadn't heard that word out of anybody's mouth yet. She'd wondered what exactly Hunter did with his life, but nobody had ever indicated that it was somehow a duty. She thought he might be some sort of investigator for the lower classes or a vigilante, if she were to be dramatic about it, but duty?

What sort of duty was involved in the things he was doing?

She wanted to argue with Hal further on that fact, as well as the fact that she knew Hunter led a dangerous life, but what good would it do? It was clear that Hal was filled with concern and regard for Hunter, and probably worried about him a great deal. With the likeness between the two, Lucy suspected they might be siblings, or cousins, perhaps. Family, almost certainly.

And she would not argue with Hunter's family about her desire to be with him no matter what danger he lived with.

They wouldn't understand. How could they? She didn't understand herself.

"I only wish it were possible," Lucy murmured, losing the defensiveness as soon as the words were out of her mouth. "I've never met anyone like him, and being with him… Reality or not, it is liberating, Hal. Maddening, too, considering… Well, he is just maddening."

Hal snorted rather indelicately, making Lucy grin. "That's one way to put it. The polite way, if you will."

There was no irritation in her voice, which meant either Lucy was forgiven or there was nothing to forgive. Hal was an opinionated woman, and especially loquacious in those opinions, but she did not seem to be irrational, either in her moods or emotions. Her fury at Hunter when they had arrived had been all concern and panic over the risk of his coming here, that much was clear at this point.

Which meant they were on the same side in this.

Lucy's grin spread even further. She was feeling rather affectionate towards this potential relative of Hunter's. "I am nothing if not polite."

"I can tell." Hal returned her grin and heaved a sigh. "I wish it were possible for you too. I think you'd be good for Hunter. But the future is so uncertain… Still, when you find your father and are returned to him, let me know. We can be friends. I'm still enough in those circles to be respectable and admitted, even if I've become reclusive. And you can be yourself here." She gestured towards Lucy with two fingers. "Sit back, for heaven's sake. Slouch, if you like. You're making my back ache with that too-perfect posture."

Lucy laughed in surprise and pointedly leaned back until she was all but lounging in her comfortable chair. "Yes, ma'am. If you insist."

"I do." Hal sniffed, rather like Tilda did when she was being authoritarian. "Now, shall we continue describing the unfortunate figure that is your father? I think we're making some good progress on his likeness."

Chapter Eighteen

It was time for them to leave Hal and John's home, and Hal was currently gushing with Lucy over the gooseberry pie at Miss Masters's School like the two of them had attended together or something.

Hunter groaned in faux agony and looked at John with the most longsuffering expression he could manage, making his brother-in-law chuckle.

Truth be told, it was one of the most heartwarming things he had ever seen for his sister to connect with Lucy in this way. It meant more than he knew how to express for them to be friends, to genuinely like one another, to not require him as a buffer or their mutual connection.

Why it meant so much was hard to explain. Lucy could never be in his personal life, in truth. He could not have a personal life, in truth. But it didn't stop him from feeling this way, and it did not stop him from enjoying whatever time he had with her. Perhaps Hal was right, and he should stop fighting everything he felt for Lucy, if for no other reason than to see where it would lead.

And how it might end.

He snorted to himself softly as Lucy went to bid John farewell with a polite curtsy and a few words. How it would end. He knew how it would end. With her entering her father's house and him standing outside of it for far too long, wondering what had become of his life and what he was meant to do now.

Idiot.

"Now, should you wish to practice," John was saying, pulling a folded paper out of his waistcoat, "I've composed a few more for you. Do you remember the key from earlier?”

Lucy smiled brightly and nodded like a child, taking the paper from him. “Yes, sir. Same rules?”

“Yes, same rules. I think you'll enjoy it.” He bowed, smiling in a way that John rarely did.

Hunter looked between them in confusion, taking in the phrases and words on the paper in Lucy's hand, then glared at his brother-in-law swiftly as the realization hit him. “You taught her about ciphers?”

John and Lucy turned to him in surprise, Lucy with wide eyes and John with smugness. “I did,” he confirmed with a lift of his chin. “The tour of our house did not take very long, and luncheon was not prepared, so she asked me what I did for work. A curious and quick mind is a dreadful thing to waste.”

Hunter rolled his eyes. “Save the sermon, Socrates. I can't believe you did that. You know better!” He turned to Hal and took the copies of her drawings with a quick snatch before planting a perfunctory kiss on her cheek. “I'll send you a note when there's something to tell. The usual way. And congratulations again. Truly, I'm delighted for you. Let me know how you get on.”

“I will,” Hal murmured, her brow furrowing as she scowled defensively on behalf of her husband.

Hunter wouldn't explain himself, nor would he ask for forgiveness. John should know the problems with doing what he had done, and it wasn't down to Hunter to spell it out. Still, he shook the man's hand anyway and nodded to Thad as he and Lucy left the house, her carpetbag now in Hunter's hand instead of her own.

The least he could do was carry her bag while they were together.

“Where are we going now?” Lucy asked in a small voice as they reached the end of the block.

Deuce take it. He didn't mean to upset her with his yelling at John. It wasn't her fault that he had a fascinating career, and she had a curious mind. Honestly, if Hunter's skills had been something less dangerous, he might have done exactly the same as John if she'd asked him. He'd have had a completely different motivation, but he would have done it. Lucy was just not someone to refuse, no matter who you were.

“Hunter?”

He smiled down at her, hoping she'd believe it was genuine. That he was genuine. "I was thinking about St. James's Park."

"I thought you said Hyde Park at breakfast," she ventured slowly.

"I did," he affirmed, amused that she had heard that while she had been so focused on ignoring him. "But I think Tilda is right, and that would be a bit of a risk, considering your station. St. James's Park, on the other hand, is less popular as a location for promenades. Would that put you in circles with people who know you well enough to embarrass you?"

Lucy wrinkled up her nose a little. "I don't think so. My father and I aren't particularly social creatures, in that respect. And dressed like this, no one would give me a second look anyway. But isn't St. James's Park out of the way?"

Hunter shrugged. "It's been some time since you've seen anything green. Well, anything that's meant to be green, anyway. What's a stroll through the park on our way to Poplar?"

"Poplar? What's in Poplar?" Her tone was brighter already, and he loved it. Loved the sound of it, love the melody of it, loved the tone of it…

"Our accommodations for the night," he said hastily, clearing his throat. "Supper included. Good beds and all." He managed a quick grin. "Perhaps not as good as Tilda's, but nevertheless…"

"I've never had beds as good as Tilda's," Lucy gushed in a way that made him laugh. "She's full of secrets and finery she shouldn't be able to afford. Not to mention the airs she likes to pretend she has. She could fit in anywhere she might please, and no one would be any the wiser, or give her any bother."

Hunter considered that with a crooked smile. "I think she has done that, actually. Probably a number of times. It wouldn't surprise me in the least if she were to flit among the classes for her own amusement. It could actually explain at least half of her stories if she did that."

They both laughed and continued to amble their way towards St. James's Park. Hunter thought about showing their drawings to those they saw, but he wasn't certain anymore. Oh, if they saw people who wouldn't compromise him or give rise to gossip for Lucy, he would certainly do so, but he wouldn't be displaying it for all to see. That would only call attention to them, and likely not serve them in any way.

It was out of their way, admittedly, and quite blatantly in the wrong direction. But he wanted to go for a stroll in a beautiful part of the city with her while he still had the chance. Who knew what tomorrow would bring? Hal's drawings were just as skilled as he'd expected and hoped, so he had no doubt they would begin to get answers tomorrow. Tonight, if he tried hard enough.

But he wasn't going to.

Did that make him a villain?

Heaven help him, but he did not care.

For the first time in their short but intense association, Hunter chose to engage Lucy in random conversation. Personal conversation, even. Chatting like he might have done with a friend, if not a girl he was courting. He'd never actually gotten around to courtship during his years in Society, so he had little enough experience to call upon, but his years as an operative had him play the courtier or suitor often enough. The only difference was that he was not seeking any particular information with her. He was not attempting to steer the conversation in any direction. He had no ulterior motives.

All he wanted was to know more about her and to spend more time with her.

And he wanted to know everything.

Anything.

And walking towards the park in her company might have been as good as walking the actual park, in his eye. It forced them to spend that length of time in either silence or conversation, and so long as he avoided provoking her into silence again, Lucy clearly preferred conversation. Hunter had heard enough about her father on their walks, and he now considered that topic practically professional, so he'd do everything he could to avoid it.

He wanted to know about her mother and her childhood. Her passions and her fears. Her extended family and her happier home. Her hopes and dreams and wishes, her favorite foods, her least favorite books, her thoughts on flowers…

He'd have listened to her talk about the care and upkeep of half-lame horses, if that were something she liked.

This walk didn't have anything to do with substance or aims or duty; it was entirely about being.

And being with her.

Hunter almost never talked about himself, given his occupation and the hazards therein, but he found himself answering Lucy's questions as freely as she was answering his. Things he'd nearly forgotten about himself were suddenly forefront in his mind; rose-colored memories faint with age now restored to their former brilliance, and his tastes and preferences, so often pushed aside for a cause, now spoken aloud for her ears alone. It ought to have given him pause or at least given him some sense of vulnerability, but instead, he only felt renewed and invigorated.

He might not need a great deal of time to know how he felt about her. At this rate, he'd be stealing a handkerchief and keeping it next to his heart before they had supper, and he couldn't even laugh at the ridiculousness of the prospect.

Because it wasn't ridiculous. He was well and truly on his way to…

To becoming…

Something.

The lack of insight into his own feelings and the words to describe them was as frustrating as the feelings themselves. He was too jaded, too callous, too worldly to be as sentimental as he was beginning to feel, and his suspicions over the confusion were simply his natural reaction as an operative. It was probably heading towards love, if he were to look at it from a rational point of view, but was love simply a shade of obsession? And was obsession nothing more than a passionate, insatiable curiosity? What was the wholesome, soul-filling version of love that his sister was clearly living in with her husband? What was it that made love matches that were sustainable and not simply a lusty whim?

Should he ever decide to make a love match, of course.

Which was unlikely, given his profession and his nature.

But he wished to know anyway. Just in case.

The park was quiet and calm when they reached it, as he

suspected it would be, given how the hour approached the evening. Those in Society would be preparing for their various evening outings and activities, and the middle and lower classes, if they were in the area, would need to begin making preparations for their supper. Which made it the perfect time for a couple to meander at their leisure if they did not wish to be particularly observed or interrupted.

Not that he and Lucy were a couple, of course. It was simply a phrase. A description of their numbers, as it were. Nothing to indicate any sort of intimacy or intent.

Blimey, he was tripping over himself in his own mind. Was that a normal thing for a man befuddled by a woman to do?

This was where years of working alone and sticking to strictly professional associations became a hindrance. He literally had no one he could turn to with questions such as these, seeing as they were particularly personal, embarrassing, and had the potential to leave one feeling especially stupid. Was there anyone in the world with whom he had ever been willing to lower himself in such a way?

His twin did not count; she was a woman, after all. It was different for a man.

He thought.

Couldn't be sure, which was why he needed to ask a man. A happily married one.

Which limited the numbers considerably.

But what was he doing wasting this precious time in his own head? He could overthink every aspect of this outing later tonight, likely when he was trying to sleep. He really should be paying more attention to what Lucy was saying now and how she was enjoying this walk in the park.

He forced himself to step out of his own thoughts and look at Lucy with the barest turn of his head, needing to make it appear as though he was not looking at her. She wasn't actually saying anything at the present, which was a relief, as he would have had to beat himself up if he had missed something she had been confiding. She was looking at the trees to her left, devoid of any leaves in this winter weather, but not yet frost-tipped or covered with ice. They were rather barren, but in her eyes, it would appear there was something of beauty.

What was she seeing that made her lips curve in that very faint smile, her full lips spreading just enough to be more tempting? What could an arid park, with faintly green grass but no flowers, have to be smiled at? He ought to have remembered the season when he suggested the park, but seasons were a trifle lost on him in the underbelly of the city. It was warm or it was cold, it was raining or it was fair, but the state of plants and such were irrelevant to his life. And now, when he wanted some beautiful piece of the world to share with Lucy, he only had this winter-wasted space.

It was simply not fair.

"I suppose we should be grateful it is not snowing," Hunter said without need, glancing around them with a bit of a frown. "I was hoping it would not look so dead for us."

"It isn't dead," Lucy murmured gently. Far more gently than he would have expected, given the usual manner in which she expressed herself. "It's going dormant. Just sleeping while the world cannot support its natural strength and beauty. Haven't you had times when you've kept silent because you could not speak? When you weren't seen because you were not at your best? When you were supposed to be blooming but felt frozen by frost?"

Hunter stared at Lucy without any hint of shame now, blatant and curious and marveling. "I don't know," he heard himself say, his voice sounding distant somehow. "I've never really thought about it. But you have, I see."

Lucy nodded slowly, but no sign of pain or distress flicked across her features. There was only serenity and acceptance. "I've felt dormant and asleep for ages now. So long that I began to be unsure of who I was. What I was. What I wanted, what I was allowed to want. And I only wanted to be seen in spite of being dormant."

"I see you," Hunter whispered, the words ripped from his chest with shocking force.

Her eyes slid to him, not quite meeting his. "I know. That is what has been confusing me all this time. How could you possibly see me when we have only had two days together? When we lead such different lives? When we only met because of some random attempted crime? But you've seen me from the first, and it's the most peculiar thing."

"Yes, it is," Hunter agreed with a smile, delighted that she was aware of his attention, even if she might not know the whole of it. "You should try feeling it, seeing you. Most bizarre."

She jabbed him in the side with her elbow, surprisingly swift and sharp, and he wheezed a laugh at it. "The point is," she went on firmly, "that I have made a point of finding the beauty in the dormant and sleeping for myself. Perhaps one day, I may actually see it in myself, if I practice well enough."

Hunter's amusement faded, and he now stared at Lucy as though she had actually lost her senses. He knew better than to speak of such a thing, given his history of saying things that irked her when he did not think, but the urge to cut her off and correct her was overwhelming.

Could she really not see herself? She was one of the most beautiful women he had ever seen, if not the most. The fact that she was intelligent and quick-witted only made her that much more attractive, and her refreshing way of speaking and looking at the world? She was an exquisite creature, and the only other ways to describe her would be artistic and flowery, poetic and abstract, which were probably not ways she would wish to be described.

Lucy glanced at him, and something in his expression made her eyes dart to the ground. "What?"

Hunter cleared his throat. "What? I'm just… I just…"

"You disapprove of something. I can see it." She exhaled shortly and folded her arms. "You can tell me."

"I disapprove," Hunter said slowly, "of the way you see yourself now. But I understand our tendency to believe what we are consistently told, and further than that, to believe the worst that we hear instead of the best that we hear. That is human nature. And I am trying very hard to not give you a compliment paired with an insult. Again."

Lucy snickered a laugh, which relieved some of the tension he was feeling at the base of his spine and in the center of his chest. "I appreciate such effort."

He smiled at her quip, hoping he was at least walking in the right path with his words so far. "Allow me to say, at least… that I hope you continue practicing. Because it would be for the best if you could see yourself with all of the beauty that the rest of us already see."

There. That ought to be succinct enough.

Lucy said nothing as they continued to walk, and with her attention facing forward, Hunter could not know what emotions were playing across her features.

There was no angry tick of a muscle in her jaw. The color in her cheek was not rising. Her lips were pressed together, but they were not turning white or causing any strain. If there was any angst or distress in her face, he was not catching it from his view. Her breathing had not changed, and there were no tears at hand.

For someone whose emotions were as much a part of her face as they were a part of her soul, the complete lack of insight into her present state was actually maddening for Hunter.

Had he upset her even more by saying something sincere? Had he put too much distance between himself and the statement? Had he said too much?

"I don't know what to say to that," she finally said, her voice barely above a whisper. "But my heart is beating so fast, I cannot even swallow."

Right, he'd forgotten about her frankness.

Now his cheeks were the ones destined to be turning red. He could feel the heat of them stretching into his ears.

He had made her pulse race by what he had said.

He was tempted to pick up her wrist to feel for the thundering she described there. Why, he couldn't say. But something in him wanted to have that frantic pacing against his skin. His own pulse was skittering like a colt over the hills now, and the more he thought about hers, the worse it got.

This could not last. They could not do this, whatever it was. If they were doing anything. Perhaps it was just him, and Lucy was reacting with discomfort to his honesty. It was entirely possible that all of this was only on his part, and he was seeing what wasn't there. Or what he wished to be there.

He could not afford to do that.

Clearing his throat, he looked above them at the sky, pretending to only now notice the shift in position of the sun. "Perhaps we should catch a hack to Poplar. We want to get there before they stop serving supper, after all."

"That's a good idea." Lucy's voice was clipped and careful, rather like his had been. "Will you… will you have something to do for your assignment tonight?"

That was almost too careful, and it was that particular tone that made him determined to be as honest as possible.

"Yes," he confessed as they left the park and moved towards the street. "But it won't take long. In fact, I'll be seeing Briar again, I think."

Lucy's lips curved a little. "Give her my regards and my thanks. Perhaps you'll actually get to discuss what you were supposed to the night you met me."

"Perhaps." He watched up and down the street for a hack, waving one down eventually with two fingers.

"Do you regret your intervention that night?" Lucy asked him as the hack slowed. "It kept you from whatever your business was, after all."

Hunter looked at her in sheer disbelief, stunned when her face showed complete sincerity and a touch of insecurity. "How can you even ask me that? No, I don't regret it." He walked her over to the hack and helped her in before turning to the driver. "Ye Olde Wharf, Poplar."

"Aye, sir," the driver called back as Hunter climbed in. He snapped the reins, and the hack started off again with a jolt.

"I don't mean you wouldn't have done a good deed anyway," Lucy said over the sound of the rollicking wheels. "I mean… I just…"

Hunter exhaled a short breath. "I don't care what you mean, quite honestly. Was it an inconvenience? No. Did it ruin my assignment? No. Have you been an inconvenience to have constantly around? Sure, a little, given what I could have gotten done for my assignment, but if I were to regret that, I would have to regret my own sister, and that would mean regretting my life itself. I don't regret having you in my life, Lucy, nor almost constantly in my presence. My only regret is that your father doesn't deserve to have you back, but I cannot do anything about that, can I?"

Lucy's eyes widened and she looked out of the window, her

throat tightening visibly. "I'm sorry."

"What the hell are you sorry for?" Hunter demanded, already frustrated with what the future held for her, and consequently, for him. "You haven't done anything to apologize for."

"I don't know," she whispered, her voice sounding stretched and thin, making him want to take her in his arms, for some bizarre reason. "For asking. For making you think about it. For whatever has made you so irritated."

"I am not—damn it." He plucked his hat off and ran a hand over his hair, forcing his breath to steady and willing his temper to subside. "Lucy… I cannot get into the details and reasons as to why I am reacting the way that I am. I just can't. It is probably uncalled for, and being with Hal and John today already set me on edge, even though I enjoyed myself. I cannot explain that either. You deserve explanations, and I cannot give them. So for that, I am apologizing. But nothing—and I'll repeat for your silly ears, nothing—of my present mood is due to action or fault of yours. In fact, any recent good mood of mine has been due to you."

Those impossibly dark eyes of hers, darker now than ever before, returned to him with a light of hope that almost stripped him bare of defenses. "Really?"

A lump formed in Hunter's throat, preventing him from an eager answer, so he only nodded. Several times.

Lucy cocked her head, her expression turning almost scolding but still playful. "You're just saying that to make me feel better."

Only the playful aspect saved her from his frustration, and that seemed to clear his throat enough to speak. "I rarely say things just to make people feel better, and I'm also not that pleasant of a person, usually. I'd invite you to speak to people who've known me, but that wouldn't be wise."

"I know Hal and Tilda," she pointed out.

Hunter snorted a very soft laugh. "They don't count."

"Tilda would have said if you were cantankerous."

"Not when she likes cantankerous," he countered.

"Hal is your sister."

He ought to have been taken aback, but he supposed he had left enough unintentional hints, and Hal had behaved in enough of a way to make it clear. He felt himself smiling.

"How long have you known?"

Lucy shrugged her narrow shoulders, her smile sweet. "I suspected before we ever left the house. Your eyes crinkle in exactly the same manner, and the way she was so angry with you for risking yourself… It was very protective. And the way she spoke about you when we were alone…"

"Oh, hell," he grumped, "what did she say now?"

"Ha!" Lucy cackled, falling back against her seat slightly as she clapped her hands, giggling almost uncontrollably. "Nothing! It was all lovely and very sweet."

"Then you were not speaking with my sister," he assured her, grinning crookedly.

"Sweet and honest," Lucy went on, shaking her head, still giggling a little. "So I knew. But still, she didn't say you were always grumpy, or anything like that."

It was his turn to give her a derisive look, though his smile remained. "You really expect my sister to tell you about my nature upon your first meeting? And besides, she doesn't see me that often. My mood almost never comes out in letters, and those are in code anyway."

She brightened at that and sat up, leaning forward. "Does John help decipher them?"

Hunter groaned. "No, and I'm not talking about codes and ciphers with you. I'm still irritated about that."

"Why?" she demanded. "What's wrong with learning that skill?"

He launched into an unnecessary and longwinded explanation about his reasons that served absolutely no purpose but to make time pass in a way that wouldn't make either of their pulses pound. He even claimed that ciphers were positively useless for those who did not work in some sort of criminal field, while Lucy countered that it could be a bit of amusement for those writing letters to each other, and possibly even romantic, if one were so inclined.

It was a good argument, he would concede, but he wasn't about to let that stop him from the debate. And there was some great delight in debating with Lucy, who held her own with firmness and calm, a composure that some of his fellow operatives would have envied. If she could tell he was intentionally wasting time, she made no sign of it, for which he was grateful.

All in all, upon reflection, it probably wasn't dreadful that she had learned something about ciphers. The only thing Hunter truly minded was John being the one to teach her, given it was John's specialty in the covert world. Not that Lucy would necessarily recognize that, but still.

Protecting her from the dangers of their world was of the utmost importance now, which meant protecting their own identities and assignments as much as possible.

He should have denied that Hal was his sister, but it was too late for that now. He would simply have to keep a sharper focus on what else was revealed so Lucy's keen eyes and quick mind had nothing more to snatch up.

Easier said than done.

Chapter Nineteen

Ye Olde Wharf was exactly the sort of delipidated brick building that Lucy had always imagined seeing in the dockyards, given the descriptions her father had always given of that part of London. Shutters hung ever so slightly askew, the windows held an almost crystalized layer of water stains, the roof looked as though cheap laborers had tried to mend it, and the wooden planks of the floor creaked and groaned like the timbers of an ancient ship. The place smelled of stale beer, tobacco, and damp, and the taproom was filled with the sort of people who looked as though they would rather not be noticed.

Lucy loved the place instantly.

She couldn't see enough of it, her eyes darting here and there and catching every little detail. She wished it were earlier in the day so she could explore more freely, but she supposed that would be frowned upon by a guest in an establishment. The proprietor was unsettling enough, with his scars and his scruff and looking as though he was at least partially blind, given the cloudiness in one eye. The addition of a tooth made of gold made Thad seem like a cuddly puppy by comparison.

But the man greeted Hunter with familiarity and smiled normally enough at Lucy, warning Hunter that he did not have any fine rooms for her, but he would offer the best room available. At Hunter's agreement, a teenaged lad came out from around the counter and took Lucy's carpetbag from him, heading up a narrow and rickety set of stairs to the right.

Sitting at one of the large, thick wooden tables now, a bowl of steaming and delicious stew before her, Lucy tried her hardest to remember her very best manners without looking particularly fine about any of it. She also did her best not to examine the spoon too carefully, as it was clearly tarnished in some spots.

What an excursion into yet another world within London this was!

"And here is some warm bread for you, miss," the proprietor said, appearing with a full loaf of bread on a wooden slab, a small crock of butter balanced beside. He set it down on the table without so much as jostling a thing. "Would you be wanting any preserves? I believe we have a few kinds of berry jams."

Lucy stared at the perfect loaf of bread for a moment, then smiled up at him as though he were her own mother. "No, thank you very much. I am very fond of warm bread with simply butter. It smells intoxicating."

He grinned and put a hand to his heart, bowing slightly. "I will tell Cook, miss. He will be most pleased."

Hunter cleared his throat. "I'll take some preserves, if you're serious, Meyer."

Mr. Meyer barely glanced at him. "I'll see what we have, Trick." With another incline of his head at Lucy, Mr. Meyer removed himself back to the desk and made no move to return to the kitchens.

Hunter watched him stand there for a long moment, then shook his head, grumbling as he took the knife and began slicing the loaf for them. "Isn't that kindness itself? After all the years I've been coming here and paying extra for good service…"

Lucy could only laugh and wait eagerly for her slice of bread. "One would think people don't actually like you."

The sawing into the bread slowed as Hunter gave her a speculative look. "Would one, indeed?"

"Not me," she said hastily, playing along with an innocent smile. "I certainly know better than to assume such a falsehood."

"Hmm." He continued his cutting of the bread, and when the slice was cut, pushed the slab towards her.

Grinning, Lucy picked up the crock of butter and small knife, slathering her slice with butter before setting the butter back down and pushing the slab back towards Hunter. "Thank you." She cradled the slice in her hands, sighing in delight. "This might be the freshest bread I've ever eaten in my life." She took a large bite, then found herself sighing again. "Oh my days…"

Hunter chuckled as he cut his own slice. "I told you this place had good food. You wouldn't think so by looking at it, but…"

Lucy shook her head, swallowing quickly. "I'm never leaving. In fact, I'm going to ask for bread with honey around midnight, and I will bet it comes with the same sort of Belgian drinking chocolate Tilda had."

"Not when I've asked, but perhaps for you." He took a bite of his bread, then nodded quickly. "Best bread they've ever given me, no question. That's down to you."

Lucy shrugged. "Feel free to come visit me here whenever you'd like to get better food."

"Thank you, I will." He winked and picked up his stew spoon, taking another bite there.

Why did that wink make the inside of her left foot tingle?

He kept doing things like that to her, saying things that made her blush, looking at her in a way that buckled a knee, breathing in a way that made her fully aware of every corner of her lungs…

It was a maddening, glorious delirium that she hated, but somehow also never wanted to stop.

How could something so irritating also be delicious fun?

Lucy felt her cheeks begin to burn and returned her attention to finishing her own stew, probably losing her manners in the process.

She didn't even look up again until a loud creaking came from Hunter's side of the table, and she caught sight of him rising, his bowl empty, his soup spoon neatly lying beside. "I'll be right back," he assured her, resting his palm on the table. "I see someone I know whom I must greet. You'll be able to see me the entire time."

"I'm not afraid," Lucy murmured around her present bite of stew.

But he didn't seem to hear her as he left, moving to a table by the window where a dark-haired man in a cap sat hunched over his stew.

She watched as Hunter shook the man's hand but did not sit with him, shoving his hands into his pockets and seeming to chat as though they were simply passing the time of day. The man at the table barely looked at him, his eyes hooded by a pageboy cap on his head. He didn't seem particularly irritated, only content with being left alone, which made Hunter's desire to greet him all the more confusing to her.

The conversation didn't last long, and then Hunter, instead of returning to Lucy immediately, went over to Mr. Meyer at the desk, leaning on it while speaking with him. Mr. Meyer's expression did not change, and he handed over a small slip of paper that Hunter put into his coat pocket. With a rap of his knuckles on the desktop, he turned and came back to the table.

Lucy watched him sit, making no secret of her observation. "Can I ask what Mr. Meyer gave you?"

"Sure," Hunter said easily as he pulled the slip of paper out, waving it a little so she could see it, but not read it.

He said nothing further.

Lucy slumped in annoyance. "What did Mr. Meyer give you, Hunter?" she asked in a would-be patient voice.

His smile was slight and damnably attractive. "A note from my friend Briton. Haven't heard from him in a while, and I can only get my notes through Meyer."

"Is Briton his real name?" Lucy asked, fidgeting her spoon against the remnants of her stew.

"Doubt it." He read the lines, his brow creasing slightly. "Never asked. Never do, actually."

Lucy tried to read the words through the back, hoping there was enough light to allow something to shine through.

There was not.

"It's not very long for someone you haven't heard from in a while," she pointed out, popping the last bit of her bread into her mouth.

"He writes in an exceptionally small hand," came the automatic response.

Lucy blinked. "You're focusing with great effort on it."

"He also writes in code. It amuses him."

Given their almost heated debate in the carriage about ciphers and code, Lucy found this to be an irony worth commenting on, even if Hunter was not paying her any attention at the moment.

"Would you like me to decipher it for you?" she drawled pointedly, folding her arms upon the tabletop and staring at him with just as much intensity.

Now his eyes flicked up from the paper, and eventually, one corner of his mouth ticked up. "Point taken." He folded the note up and tucked it back into his coat pocket, keeping his eyes on Lucy for a long moment. "I need to go and meet Briar. Would you prefer to be up in the room or remain down here among the clientele?"

Lucy's brows rose of their own accord. "You're giving me a choice?"

Hunter's smile turned a trifle sheepish, his nose wrinkling in a faint grimace. "That makes me sound like a jailer. But yes. This is a protected establishment, so you will be fine. Besides, Mr. Meyer is just there, and he knows I must leave. In this instance, yes, this choice is yours. I have it on good authority that there is a hot berry pie that will soon be offered, and should that tempt you, feel free to indulge."

"That sounds incredible," Lucy murmured, her stomach somehow rumbling even though her hunger was quite sated by the meal. "I was always under the impression that foods at inns and the like were substandard, but this is some of the best food I've had outside of fine houses."

"Oh, believe me, most inns and pubs have mediocre food at best and will charge you a fortune for the experience," Hunter assured her with a very sage nod. "They'll charge you for using their utensils instead of bringing your own at times. I've seen it done."

Lucy believed him, oddly enough, and looked around the taproom, aware that she felt fairly comfortable when she ought to have been quite the reverse. "What makes this place such an outlier of its kind?"

Hunter took his hat off, smoothed his hair, and replaced his hat. "Probably Meyer, honestly. Takes more pride in the place and his service than others I've seen. And he wants to make sure he gets as many of the sailors coming into port as he can. Word travels fast, and there is nothing like a personal recommendation to encourage others to visit." Hunter pushed to his feet, straightened his coat, and gave Lucy a serious look. "Are you sure you want to stay down here? As I said, it will be safe. I just want to be sure you are comfortable before I go."

It was a sweet thing for him to say, and she would be lying if she did not admit that her heart flipped a few times in her chest at hearing it, but she shook her head, smiling. "I will be fine, I can assure you. Go meet Briar and give her my best."

Still looking slightly uncertain, Hunter hesitated, his eyes searching hers in a way that made her warm all over. Then he nodded and turned away, striding for the door and tapping the front of his hat at Mr. Meyer as he exited.

Lucy almost expected some sort of gasp or change in the atmosphere of the taproom when Hunter departed, but of course, nothing happened. The room remained exactly the same, and no one noticed that anything had changed, aside from Mr. Meyer, who had saluted him on his exit. And now she was alone in this room.

Which was full of men.

A sudden coldness wrapped around her, as though a fire had just been doused, and she became exceptionally aware of the position of every man in the taproom.

This was a precise illustration of her naivete if she had ever seen one. Because she had felt comfortable in a room with Hunter by her side—the man who had been protecting her and keeping her safe and secure since her foiled abduction—and a kind proprietor plying her with good food, she had presumed it was suitable for her. Now that her protector was gone, there was nothing to stop any man in this room from behaving in the worst possible manner towards her. This was practically inviting her own ruination with open arms.

Safe, had Hunter said? Perhaps if she were him, she would be safe alone here. A protected establishment? What in the world did that mean? Protected how? Protected for whom and by whom? Would knives shoot up out of the floorboards if a man came near her? Would Mr. Meyer bring out a rifle if Lucy became frightened? Would lightning crackle across the ceiling and strike down any villains in her vicinity?

Or was she going to sit here, speculating on evil deeds and the possible but unlikely punishments for them, and scare herself into fleeing for her room?

There was no protection from that but her own willpower.

She wasn't certain how that stood at the moment.

Mr. Meyer was at her side scant moments later, bowing slightly. "Might I tempt you with a slice of warm berry pie, miss?"

Lucy smiled as much as she could, afraid that it wavered. "Yes, please. It sounds delightful."

"Right away, miss." He disappeared from her table, evidently giving the instructions to one of the lads who stood ready to handle trunks for guests.

She was grateful he remained in the room and where she could see him. He was well within his rights to go where he pleased in his own establishment, but having him stay close was reassuring for her. There was her one hope of safety and protection. Mr. Meyer was not an old man, but neither was he in his prime. He was a burly sort and of an above average height, but there was the evidence of overindulgence in some degree around his middle. His visage was frightening, so he would certainly be an intimidating figure when in a rage. He might be kindness itself upon closer acquaintance, but she was quite positive he was capable of a dangerous shift in nature when called upon.

Again, that was strangely comforting.

The pie was brought to her straightaway, and the distraction was a welcome thing. The pie itself was divine, as she had suspected, given the stew and bread from earlier. It reminded her of the meals she used to enjoy at home before their fortunes had changed, and the desserts that had been showered upon them due to an excellent French chef who had been given a lenient budget. She had fond childhood memories of tarts and biscuits being available upon any request, and pies were there for special occasions.

This was no special occasion, but the pie did provide her with a hint of the comfort that Hunter had, due to its pure nostalgia.

She might end up eating four slices to maintain it, but who would judge her for that?

Voices began to rise from the table to her right, but not in an angry manner. It was more likely an intoxication-induced increase in volume, which must be expected in a place like this. She did her best to remain unaffected and keep her attention polite, genteel, and reserved, ignoring their behavior for her sake more than their own.

Her eyes tracked to the man Hunter had recognized, and his posture and position remained the same. He paid no attention to anyone or anything.

"How much, do ee reckon? One hour wif 'er."

"More'n ee 'ave, and t'would be worth ev'ry farthing."

Their laughter was dark and raucous, and Lucy focused on eating the crust of her pie, drenched in the juices of the berries it had once contained.

"She be an 'igh class one, t'ain't no mistake. Clean an' all."

"Her sir left her alone here. Practically begging for a new picker."

"I'd pick 'er, eh? I'd sure pick 'er 'til dawn an' beyond."

"Go fer it, then. Let's see ee proposition 'er."

There was no mistaking the figure of their conversation nor their meaning, and somehow Lucy was going hot with embarrassment as well as cold with fear at the same time. She couldn't move, and yet she was desperate to run for her room, lock the door, and burrow beneath the blankets on whatever bed set for her.

Their volume might have been affected by their drinks, but she suspected it was also increased so she might hear them. Had she been the sort of woman they suspected, she might have had a reaction they would enjoy or find amusing. But as she wasn't…

They could have no idea who she really was, and if they did, they might find it even more entertaining. And they might be more encouraged, depending on their persuasion for morality. She could only continue to ignore them, especially while she was eating, but once her pie was finished, then what? Did she ask Mr. Meyer if she could have some tea so she might prolong her occupation? Did she try to get to her room and hope the men did not pursue her?

Were they even in a position to be capable of pursuing her?

"Ee couldna take 'er like tha', ee'd fall flat on yer face."

"I be more stable than ee!"

Why were their thoughts in such concert with hers? The men began rising from their table and testing their relative abilities to walk and balance, and if her peripheral vision was not mistaken, running from one table to the other. The laughter and cheers were only growing more intense, as was their desire for drink.

They were clearly more capable under the influence than she thought, which was only more frightening.

Her pie was gone, and there was no hiding it. She could not wait here for Hunter; he'd given no indication of how long he would be. Mr. Meyer was here, but was he paying as much attention to them as she was? Did he know what danger was presently looming?

How far would he go to keep her safe until Hunter returned?

"One at a time, eh? So who'll be first?"

"Cole has small cards. Cut cards, an' then we'll know."

Oh heavens, she was running out of time, and running for her life would clearly encourage them to act irrationally.

She jumped as a figure approached the table, then froze as the dark man Hunter had spoken with stood before her.

"I believe now would be a good time to see you safely to your room, don't you, Miss Allred?"

His voice was dark and low, so no one had a hope of hearing him but her, and he held a firm and steady hand out to her.

How did he know who she was? How did…?

"Trick told you?" Lucy whispered, her voice wavering weakly.

He nodded once. "I'm keeping an eye on you. My name is Trace. Now, shall we?"

She put her hand in his and tried to return his nod, only managing a quiver of her chin. He helped her up from the table and started towards the stairs with her, his free hand going protectively to her back, his pace swift, but without evidence of panic.

"Room eleven, Trace," Mr. Meyer murmured as they passed him, and Lucy caught sight of a pistol on the counter, hidden from the view of the others.

So Hunter had been right; this place was protected, and she was safe. She was being saved and protected now. It didn't keep her from fear, but at least she would be all right. No matter what choice she made when he'd offered, someone would have been watching over her.

She wanted nothing more than to hug Hunter at this moment.

Trace led her up the stairs, and she heard the racket of the men below, bellowing practically incoherently about her being gone. There were thundering steps that made her want to bolt, but Trace kept his hand pressed to her back, as though he could feel the way her heart was racing.

"Steady," he murmured. "Meyer will keep them from coming up. We'll get you into your room, and I'll sit outside of it until Trick returns. I promise, no one will get to you."

"Thank you," Lucy managed to squeak out, almost sagging with her relief and gratitude.

The pressure at the small of her back increased just a little, and then they were at the top of the stairs and moving down the corridor, passing the other rooms. Her eyes traced each number, seeking for eleven eagerly. Then it was there, and Trace thrust the door open, releasing her hand and remaining obediently outside of the room.

Her carpetbag was within, and it might as well have been a childhood memento reminding her that she was home for the delight she felt in seeing it.

Lucy turned and looked at Trace, biting her lip as words failed her.

He smiled, and she saw, for the first time, the handsomeness beneath the dark visage he had worn, and the kindness in his eyes. "Not at all, Miss Allred. Rest easy. I've got you." He inclined his head and closed the door behind him. "Bolt it, please," he called through the door.

Lucy stepped forward to do so, nodding even though he would not see it. She slid the bolt over and found herself exhaling with far less tension in her chest once she heard it click. There would be no way she would sleep until Hunter was back, just for her own peace of mind, but she needed some comfort and ease until he returned. She walked to her carpetbag and opened it up, retrieving the shawl that was Briar's, grateful she had forgotten to have Hunter return it this evening. She wrapped it around her shoulders and climbed up onto the bed, settling against the pillows and trying to ignore everything else, knowing Trace was outside the door and wouldn't abandon her.

With the thick and cozy shawl around her, even if it smelled like the darker sides of London along with the hint of floral notes that had surrounded Briar, she felt her heart settling and her legs steadying. Her breathing eased and her trembling faded, her entire body returning to a kinder, more calming state of existence. She unfolded the blanket at the foot of the bed and put it over her legs, her shoes still on, and just curled into herself while she waited for Hunter.

What would he say when Trace told him what had happened? Would he blame himself? Would he blame Lucy? He'd said repeatedly that she was attractive and that men of a certain class would be untoward, but she hadn't thought… she hadn't seen…

She'd been an idiot, that's what it was. Naive and an idiot, which was worse.

But he had left her, hadn't he? Knowing the sort of men they could be, he'd let her think it would be fine for her to remain down there in the taproom. He'd recruited Mr. Meyer and Trace to look after her, she reminded herself. He had been content to let her make her own choice and done his best to reassure her without telling her what he had put into place should the worst happen…

Which meant he had known it was possible, and he'd still let her choose. Protected her even from her choice. He couldn't be mad at himself. And he hadn't been mad at her when he'd left, but there had been concern.

She did not deserve the freedom he had attempted to give her. She needed to be returned to her father, much as she hated the idea, if for no other reason than to save herself from her own idiocy. Tomorrow, she would help Hunter to ask others about her father, showing the drawings and giving descriptions to whomever they encountered. It was the least she could do, and Hunter had done enough to protect her from this world in which she did not—and could not—belong. It was time she participated actively rather than waiting for results.

Tears began to leak from the corners of her eyes, and she hadn't even been aware that they had been forming. She hadn't felt the burn of them, hadn't felt anything welling in her eyes or her face or her nose. The tears had just appeared, rather like her realizations. But what were they for? Shame of her ignorance? Fear of her situation? Sadness for returning to her father? Agony for the impending separation from Hunter?

Oh gads, how would she bear it?

She rested her chin on her shawl and blanket-covered knees,

letting the tears trickle down her cheeks and lose themselves in the fabric. Tears were healing, her mother had once told her, and she wondered if she might actually come to believe that in the next few days. So long as she didn't cry in front of Hunter. He couldn't know the emotion that would come with their parting on her side. He was too good and would feel some guilt or pain at bringing on tears for her.

He couldn't know. She would not let him know.

How much time passed, she could not be sure, but there were voices outside her door. Low and unhurried, while the raucous sounds of the taproom had continued throughout the evening and into the night. She had never heard Mr. Meyer's gun, but what might have been threatened or said…

A gentle knock sounded on her door. "Lucy? Lucy, it's me. If you're awake, can you please unbolt the door?"

Hunter.

She released a gasping exhale and all but scrambled from the bed, her legs aching enough to tell her she had been on that bed for hours, just sitting and thinking, as well as crying.

Oh blast, crying…

She immediately wiped her face with the shawl and sniffed as softly as possible. Then she reached up and unbolted the door, pulling it open until she could see him.

He was leaning one arm against the door frame, his blue eyes intense and immediately locked on hers. Trace was now standing a little behind him, awaiting his instruction a few doors down, watching them.

Lucy managed a faint smile for Hunter. "How was Briar?"

"Fine," he replied softly, his mouth barely moving. "She sends her best. How are you?"

He said those last three words in a softer, more emphatic manner, and she felt each one like a thundering beat of her own heart.

She managed a swallow. "Fine," she managed. At his quirked brow, she nodded. "I mean it. I was afraid at first, but Trace was there, and I was fine. You made certain that I was fine. Thank you."

Hunter inhaled and exhaled slowly and softly, his mouth pressed in a thin line. Then he reached out a pair of fingers and tracked them down her right cheek. "You've been crying."

Her skin ignited where he touched it, and it took all of her strength not to rub the shawl over the remnants of her tears again. She didn't want to rid her skin of the feeling of his as long as she lived, but her tears…

"You weren't supposed to see that," she tried to scold, though it came out in a whisper.

"Did they hurt you?" he growled, seeming to lean closer, his fingers still at her cheek and moving to her jaw.

She shook her head. "Only in words. They never touched me. What they implied… what they… I should have listened to your warnings about men in this part of London. I'm sorry."

"No, I am sorry," he told her, his fingers moving to cradle her jaw just a little. "I shouldn't have left you here alone. Even with Trace and Meyer, I should have…" He sighed and his jaw tightened. "Don't worry, love. I'll take care of it."

She didn't like the sound of that, much as his use of the word love set her heart aflame like a love letter cast on a fire. "Don't avenge me or whatever you're thinking," she warned. "It's over and done."

His dark and sly smile told her she was exactly right in her prediction. "It is far from over and nothing is done. There is a certain way things are done down here, and the point must needs be made. So unless you require anything else for the evening, I'll go take care of those things and end it properly."

It was a dangerous tone that he had taken, but also one of pure relish that perplexed her. "No, I am fine, thank you."

Hunter nodded, then dropped his hand from her jaw, leaving her skin cold. "Then bolt the door behind me, Lucy, and go to bed. Everything will be better in the morning." He pushed off the frame, winked at her, and turned back down the corridor, clamping Trace on the shoulder. "Feel like a bit of fun, my friend?"

"I thought you'd never ask," Trace replied, rolling up his sleeves. "I hope you know, I only waited to give you the honors."

"Ah, you're a gentleman, truly." Hunter curled his hands into fists, his knuckles cracking. "Let's get to it."

The two of them started down the rest of the corridor and the stairs, and Lucy shook her head in dread as she closed and bolted the door behind them, waiting for the sounds of a brawl or invasion of sorts in the taproom. It wasn't long before she could hear breaking glass and possibly overturned tables, resembling the sound of thunder in a storm, and she wondered as she clambered back onto her bed, removing her shoes this time, if any storm would have been a match for Trace and Hunter and their furious fists in the taproom below.

Chapter Twenty

It was a good thing Meyer knew full well who Trace and Hunter worked for and why, or he might have demanded an excessive amount of payment for the damage they had caused the night before. Though, to be fair, Meyer had thrown a few punches himself. Still, between the two of them, there was enough to give him a decent enough donation to cover the damage.

There were zero regrets over their actions. It was only fitting to defend Lucy's honor and leave a message that she would be under the protection of several power people in the lower levels of London, should they ever see her again. She ought not to be a tempting prospect anymore, but one that made them run in fear.

He didn't blame them for the attraction to her, for that was only natural. It was the manner in which they had chosen to direct that attraction and the complete lack of respect in it. If he had not spotted Trace in the taproom, Hunter wouldn't have suggested that Lucy could remain there as well. He'd have insisted she go upstairs before he'd left. But Trace was one of his oldest contacts, and the fact that the man had been even more driven in his work since his surprise return from death made him a perfect stand-in protector for Lucy in Hunter's absence.

Sleeping outside of Lucy's door hadn't been the most comfortable night Hunter had ever spent, but it held such a grand satisfaction after the brawl that he had slept like a baby and needed no additional comforts to help him there.

Lucy hadn't been surprised to see him outside of her door in the morning and had only expressed concern for the state of his back from the lack of padding beneath him.

If only she had known some of the places and conditions under which he had slept in the past, she would hazard a guess that his back was likely the most accommodating and resilient part of him. He'd slept standing up against a wall once in Austria and had suffered no ill effects from it. He'd been younger then, but he could probably still do it.

Probably.

They were out walking in the streets now, using their copy of the drawing of Mr. Allred to inquire after him in some of the neighborhoods a step or two above where Hunter himself lived. The other two copies had been given to contacts of his to do the same in their own areas of London, and he had yet to hear from them. But Lucy was an eager and apt pupil in the art of approaching strangers without bringing any personal touches into the conversation.

They had thought it best that she not reveal her connection to Mr. Allred during their attempts, as it could bring out the unsavory creatures who would pretend at information for money, then put forth lies that would not serve their purpose. But if they were simply asking around for recognition and were calm and collected about the matter, there was usually a minimal amount of them to deal with.

They'd been at this the whole morning now, and no one had so much as found their drawing familiar in any way.

If Lucy was particularly concerned about finding her father, she wasn't showing it openly. Her features were a complete mask of indifference and placidity, engaged in a chore as it were rather than a matter of her own safety and security. They had now reached the point at which she was doing most of the approaching and conversing while Hunter strode behind and kept a weather eye out for any trouble, occasionally asking people if they knew the name of James Allred.

It helped that Tilda had given Lucy clothing that allowed her to belong to a middling class of ladies, one that could flit upwards for brief interludes and descend lower as needed without blatantly offending either. And she bore such pleasing features and such a kind countenance that it was rare for anyone to dismiss or ignore her upon approach. He should have thought of using her from the beginning;

she was getting so much conversation out of the exercise.

But he'd been so concerned about protecting her and shielding her from everything and everyone that was beneath her that the opportunity had not even occurred to him. He'd seen her as every other gentleman in the world was meant to see her: a decorative, delicate object that would shatter with the slightest rough touch. He'd not seen her as a woman with wit and strength and untapped potential, one who might have even been trusted with some of the national secrets that assets and operatives bore every day.

She was not there yet, of course, but in time, she could be.

Hunter found himself smiling rather proudly as Lucy bid farewell to yet another couple wandering through Farringdon towards Bloomsbury. She was smiling as well after her conversation with them, and he could not tell if it was a smile of politeness for a decent exchange or if they had actually been useful in their purposes. Lucy was a mystery of sorts today, and there was something especially intriguing about that.

He'd always loved a good mystery. His entire professional life was spent untangling and uncovering them, for heaven's sake. Surely a little mingling between his personal and professional life wouldn't go entirely amiss.

"Well?" he inquired when she reached him.

Her smile tightened and she sighed. "They said he looked familiar but couldn't quite place him, which seems to be the recurring theme of today." She handed over the picture and set her hands at her hips, arching her back a little in stretching form. "I don't know how your friends do this day after day, Hunter. I'm exhausted already."

He chuckled and gestured towards a nearby bench. "Come, sit. And they don't always run around with pictures and the like. Sometimes it is watching places or behaving a certain way. And they are much used to it, so it is not as tiresome."

"I suppose they must have the endurance for it the way young ladies have for a ball," Lucy mused as she sat. "One must allow for differences in situation for activities engaged in as well." She twisted her lips to one side, a faint crease appearing in her brow. "Do you know Lady Vickers, Hunter? I mentioned her before, she is my friend

Emmeline. She was once a teacher at Miss Masters's before she married her dashing half-Spanish earl."

Hunter smiled very slightly, wondering how Lucy would react if she knew that Lady Vickers was also an operative known as Ears. "I've heard the name, I think."

Lucy's brow cleared as she shook her head. "I wish she were in London at present. She and her aunt know my father a little, and she might have heard something about where he has gone."

That sent Hunter's ears burning a touch. "Didn't you say she had an aunt in London, Lucy? She might be someone with information."

"Mrs. Kirby," Lucy replied easily. "She lives in Mayfair, but her attitudes were very kind towards us in spite of our diminishing circumstances. I believe her Christian name is Hermione."

Hunter nodded once. "I will have one of my contacts seek her out and determine what can be done. Perhaps we might gain some answers more swiftly."

"And how will you do that?" Lucy asked, turning towards him slightly, her eyes bright. "Is one of your contacts following us as we go? Do you have them floating about this part of London with us? Do we need to wander into a different neighborhood to cross paths with one? Or can you simply have a message sent via runner like some peer to another?"

Her tone was a little strange, not quite dismissive and not touching superior, but it bore a sharpness that did not suit her. An almost mocking, caustic, sarcastic pulse to her words that set him on edge and put him full on alert. Anticipation of an attack of sorts.

What had he done to earn this ire? Or was it situational? Was she at last tired of this life and ready to be returned to Society and finery? Or was she irked about something in particular?

"I'll have word sent," Hunter told her carefully, wondering if he was being lured into some sort of trap. "Rather like how my friend Briton had word sent to me last night."

"Secrets and more secrets," Lucy mused, looking away and off to the distance. "What a complicated life you lead, Hunter."

He watched her with suspicion, his eyes narrowing as his mind whirled. Had the events of the night before soured her to this extent? He hadn't seen these shades in her last night, nor even this morning at breakfast, but he could not deny that she was entitled to disgruntlement after the third day of being away from the security she had previously enjoyed.

He should have been working harder at this. She did not belong in this life of his, and he'd known it from the first. It wasn't fair to her for him to continue being selfish and sedate about her father's location and situation. He owed it to her to put his full effort into this, even at the expense of his official assignment.

"I do have Briar using her contacts on the other side of the river to try and find your father as well," Hunter pointed out, hoping it would be helpful. "I gave her a copy of his likeness. Do you believe he could have ventured there?"

Lucy exhaled in irritation, her hands slapping her lap. "I have no idea what my father would or would not do anymore. I don't know where he could be or why he would send a carriage for me, only for that carriage to never arrive there, and somehow for him to not care about the fact. I don't know why he was suddenly rational about retrenching and suddenly growing fond enough to want me to visit for holidays. There is so much that I do not know that suddenly seems relevant, if not significant, and yet I am as ignorant as any other girl of my station, which ought to be criminal." She brushed at her knees, huffing. "I only want all of this to be over so I may return to the school, where I at least appear to have some control over my life. Reality is tiresome, and I am sick of it."

He could not argue with any of those points, and he did not intend to. Lucy's life was a complicated one for any person, male or female, but the fact that she was female and therefore had no rights or independence, or dignity, in some cases…

He offered her a sympathetic smile. "What would you like to do for the rest of the day? I can take you anywhere. We can continue taking the picture around, or we can do something else. Or you can do something without me, if you wish to visit Tilda or Hal or—"

"Now what would I want to do without you?" Lucy overrode, raising a brow at him, her smile easing into a beautiful and crooked grin. She chuckled and tilted her head back to catch a few of the sun's rays, though the day held a particularly cold note to it. "It would be lovely to see one of Tilda's operas. My father never cared for the theatre or anything of the sort, so I was only able to attend when invited by those he approved of. Of course, we could not possibly attend with the general public, given the risk of my being recognized and attending unchaperoned with a stranger, but even so. It would be lovely."

Hunter stared at her for a moment, then tilted his head as an idea struck him and began to bounce around his mind like an agitated bee in a hive. "I may have a way to accomplish that, actually."

Lucy gave him a startled look, her dark eyes round and cavernous. "What, we'll go in disguise?"

"No, we won't need to," he replied slowly, his smile spreading as the idea continued to form and develop. "We'll have a very particular view of the stage that might not be appreciated by most people of your station but would allow us to see and hear everything. And all we need to do is go and see Tilda."

"Really?" Lucy's bright smile, so filled with an eager hope, would have driven him to do unspeakable things, should it have been her wish or for her benefit.

As it was, he was now entirely convinced that he would get her to the opera that night, in legal ways or otherwise.

He nodded slowly, everything within his chest softening as he looked at her. "Yes. Really." Sensing he was dangerously close to saying or doing too much, he cleared his throat and stood from the bench. "It is too early to go directly to Tilda's now, especially if we hope to curry favor for tonight. Would it be acceptable to you if we were to visit Green Park and St. James's Park again? They are not out of our way, and perhaps we might find some people who recognize the drawing of your father."

"That sounds lovely," Lucy agreed, rising and brushing at her skirts. "St. James's Park was beautiful yesterday, but seeing people there and taking advantage of their presence would be very wise. And perhaps we might then enjoy the opera without worrying about my father at all."

"I would enjoy not thinking of your father at the opera," Hunter told her with a sage nod, fighting a smile.

Lucy clamped down on her lips hard, a few giggles escaping. "Then let us hurry and see our task done so we might forget all about him for a while."

It was entirely possible that she had never said anything so appealing to his ears, and he made no attempt to hide his smile now, nor to adjust it into something resembling polite warmth. He let his full admiration, bordering on adoration, shine through, and to hell with the consequences.

Her cheeks turned a stunning shade of pink, just as he wanted, and he gestured for her to lead the way. "To the parks, then, Miss Allred," he murmured.

"Yes," she replied in a similar tone, averting her eyes and turning away. "To the parks."

Hunter followed as she started to walk, not bothering to make haste to reach her side quite yet. He rather enjoyed smiling at her from behind, marveling at the way her bonnet could not completely hide the wealth of her hair with how she was presently wearing it. The lower part of the style was visible against the base of her neck, and he was studying the way there were a dozen different shades of rich brown just in that portion of her hair alone.

He also took note of the brilliant way that Lucy's gown and coat nipped in at the waist with an efficiency that left nothing to the imagination of her true size there, while not revealing anything that could be considered inappropriate or scandalous. She was dressed in an unremarkable gown of green and a simple coat of grey, both in sturdy fabrics that likely had never been fashionable, and yet she elevated both to something flattering. She was beautiful even in clothing that was supposed to be plain and boring, and though she presently had a stride that might not be particularly refined, there was a natural grace to her demeanor that could not be hidden.

There was no one like Lucy in the world, of that he was certain. And he was going to take her to the opera tonight. It was an impossible idea, and yet it was going to take place. They were going to spend an evening together with proper entertainment like any courting couple in Society, something they could have done if he were living the life he was born to and not the life that he had chosen.

It would be the most authentic experience either of them had endured since being thrown together.

And it might be the last they experienced together, if their contacts were successful today.

But he couldn't think about that now. They had an afternoon of parks first, and then they could prepare for the opera. Forgetting about her father. Just the two of them together.

Hunter shook his head, willing the impending melancholy away, and moved to catch up with Lucy as they neared the parks.

Hours later, he felt it pressing upon him once more, his heart aching as though he would have to return her home the moment the opera was over.

As though this were the end.

He was trussed in finer attire than he'd worn in weeks, but it was still not enough to be seen in Society. Tilda had insisted upon dressing him as well as Lucy for the evening, and also insisted that neither of them should be wearing something that would put them in the ton. Their seats were well out of eyesight of anyone but, as Tilda insisted, she had a reputation to uphold, and they would not embarrass her by dressing beneath her dignity for an outing such as this.

He would owe Tilda several grand favors for this. It was her secret box that they were using this evening, and she really ought to have been up at the stage overseeing the costumes before the opening. But she demanded to dress Lucy herself rather than have one of her assistants do so, and no one would argue with her.

For whatever reason, Hunter's stomach bore a great knot within it, something that told him someone was spiriting Lucy away from him and returning her to her father, whose location Hunter would never know. It was an entirely ridiculous notion, but there it was. And until he saw Lucy for himself, he could not be at ease.

"Message for you, Trick."

Hunter jumped and looked around the corridor where he waited, his eyes falling on Willow, dressed in dark clothing suited for working at the stage level as Tilda's assistant. "Here?"

She nodded and handed the note to him. "Came from a boy of about fifteen. Said Armstrong gave it to him." She shrugged before turning away, hurrying towards the corridor that led to the theatre itself.

Armstrong. One of his contacts who had been strictly charged with finding James Allred.

Heart pounding, Hunter unfolded the paper, his eyes scanning the brief line and rough scrawl:

Allred. 9 Greenland Street. Camden Town.

"No," Hunter breathed as his eyes dashed across the words again and again, his heart seeming to vanish from his chest completely. "No, not yet…"

Camden Town. Why hadn't he heard of the man if he was in Camden Town? That wasn't far from his haunts, and he certainly had people who had checked through there. Allred must have been keeping his head down, given the shame of retrenching to such a poor corner of London, but even so…

He crumpled up the note and held it in his fist tightly. Lucy wanted to spend the evening at the opera. Telling her that he finally had her father's address would put her in the awkward position of deciding between her duty as a daughter and something she wanted to do in direct opposition to that. He refused to do that to her. She deserved to have one evening of enjoying herself for her own sake before her life was once more consumed with a disappointing father and employment that she enjoyed but could be snatched from her the moment her father determined it.

Tomorrow. He would tell her about their success tomorrow and leave tonight for her wishes. Yes, it was also going to suit his wishes, but it wouldn't be as selfish as it sounded. He did not have the heart to crush her when she had been so excited about the prospect of the evening.

One more night. That was it. Then it would be over.

He heard a rustling from up ahead in the corridor and shoved the note into his weskit pocket, turning to face whomever was approaching. As he'd hoped, Tilda was heading for him, with Lucy just behind. At his look, Tilda quirked her brows precisely twice before stepping aside and revealing her project in full.

Hunter's vanished heart reappeared before plummeting through his stomach and beneath the floor. Lucy was arrayed in a rich shade of blue that was uninterrupted from shoulder to toe, identically matching silk ribbons crisscrossing her torso into a deep V at her hips, emphasizing the purity of her figure. The same sort of ribbons formed a series of wavelike folds at the hem and created thick lines across the sheer white fabric puffing at her shoulders for sleeves. They also seemed to be woven throughout her plaited and curled hair, white flowers glimmering between the dark locks. Her throat bore strands of pearls, and her ears were adorned with the same, but most striking of all was her smile.

Small and demure, but there among full lips that seemed the most tempting shape and shade of pink he had ever seen. She was a vision, and he had never seen anything to compare. He didn't even have the words to describe her loveliness, and he was entirely uncertain how they were meant to blend in this evening when Lucy was better suited for the finest ballrooms in Society like this.

"Ah, I love when the silence outstrips any words," Tilda sighed as she fell into step behind Lucy and they reached Hunter. "I take it you approve of my little project."

He nodded, his throat tightening as he swallowed. "But how are we meant to attract no notice when my lady bears such beauty?"

Lucy's cheeks brightened into a sunset red he immediately adored. "It's only crepe, Hunter. Anyone who knows fashionable fabrics will be able to tell. And there is very little adornment."

"You don't need it," he said, holding out his hand for some unknown reason. "You don't need anything."

"Exactly what I was going to say," Tilda chimed in as Lucy shyly put her hand in his. "What an amusing thing. Now, if you will both excuse me, I am due at the stage. Trick, you know the way?"

Hunter nodded slowly, keeping his eyes on Lucy. "I do," he murmured, running his thumb over her gloved knuckles.

Cursed fabric. If they weren't expected for all in attendance, he might have enjoyed the feeling of her skin upon his fingertips, but politeness must be preserved in some instances, he supposed.

Unfortunately.

"Tilda says we will love our seats," Lucy said, her lips barely moving for her smile. "Have you been in them before?"

"Only for a meeting," Hunter told her as his thumb moved over her knuckles again. "Never for pleasure." He turned and began leading her towards the stage, following in the path that Willow and Tilda had taken. The stairs were wide and shallow, which was a pleasant change from most stairs he encountered these days. Then the corridor was there that only actors and staff of the theatre would use, though the sounds of theatre patrons could be heard quite clearly.

Hunter moved to the farthest door in the corridor before a large stack of chairs—barely visible as it was painted the same color as the walls. He pulled it open and led Lucy into the space, keeping a hold on her hand so she would not venture too far.

The sounds of the crowd were almost deafening from here, and he ushered Lucy into one of the two seats placed nearby. Their view at present was only of curtains and a long corridor between them, which was, of course, the front of the stage itself.

Lucy sat, blinking at their view, then looked at Hunter in bewilderment. "Are we on the stage?" she whispered loudly.

Hunter grinned as he took his own seat, nodding. "In a way, yes. We are behind the main curtain, which separates the audience from the stage, and in front of the draw curtains, which separates the actors from the view of the audience. I daresay one of the actors or directors will come through the draw curtains before the main curtain is lifted to welcome everyone and greet them. But we will know before anyone else, so are we not the fortunate ones?"

Lucy gaped openly at him, then back at the stage. "But we will see everything! Absolutely everything!"

"Unless the curtains get in the way, yes," Hunter replied with some satisfaction, feeling rather smug with the idea of attending the opera in the first place.

Technically, these weren't even seats, and certainly had no reservations. It was a portion of typically unused stage area that Tilda had decided to make use of for those she was connected to. She never sat here herself, given her work behind the scenes, but for those who needed a place to meet and discuss covert things while among others, her private box was perfect.

"Thank you for arranging this," Lucy told him softly, taking his hand in hers and squeezing it gently. "It is so perfect, there simply aren't words."

She was quite right; there were no words.

It was perfect.

"I was glad to do so," Hunter murmured, captivated by her impossibly dark eyes and the way her lips moved when she spoke.

The way her smile appeared in her eyes no matter how slight. The way her throat moved when she breathed.

Captivated by everything she was and every tiny aspect of her.

It wasn't just beauty; it was her.

And it was love.

A curling, coiling fire started somewhere between his stomach and his chest, slowly yet defiantly igniting him in places that had never existed before this moment. Burning him with the building heat, searing him deep into his core, leaving marks that could never be removed. It would consume him, and God help him, he would let it.

He would allow himself to fall prey to this inferno, and he would be grateful for the chance.

"I am glad to be here with you," Hunter told Lucy, fighting the urge to tell her something else entirely.

Lucy's smile made his heart stop. "So am I, Hunter. There is no one else…"

The musicians struck up then, and with their proximity to them, there was no finishing that sentence, nor the conversation.

Hunter was going to be left in torment over those words.

There is no one else…

There was no one else what? No one else she would rather be here with? No one else she trusted? No one else she knew at the moment? No one else… ever?

Because there was certainly no one else for him. Ever.

Only Lucy.

Which meant his doom would come in the morning, and his heart could only live for the next few hours.

He intended to make the most of it.

Chapter Twenty-One

Lucy had seen an opera before, but never like this. Tilda's seats were perfectly arranged for them, leaving them free from the obligation of having to talk with anyone else or mingle, as others were usually expected to. And the intermission left them free to talk without fear of being overheard. They were not disrupted by the curtains at all, and in fact never saw a single person who was not on the stage in front of them.

And the opera itself was positively ethereal. Lucy was transfixed by every aria and duet, probably staring like an idiot and looking as though she'd been clunked on the head with a baton, but only Hunter would see that. And if she did appear that way, he either was not noticing or simply was not mocking her for it.

He certainly was smiling a great deal, though it was difficult to say if that was because of the loveliness of the opera, the amusement of her antics, or some private thoughts that pleased him.

She would never forget the way he looked at her when she'd appeared with Tilda. Not if she lived to be a hundred and three and forgot her own name. She had never felt so beautiful in all her life, even with the imaginations of the red gown. There had been no mistaking his interest and admiration there, and there was a dangerous headiness in witnessing it. All of his previous compliments mingled with insults were erased with that single look, and her toes curled in her slippers at the mere memory of it.

They were well into the second act of the opera now, and Hunter was leaning forward in his seat just enough to make her curious. She tried to get a better look at his face and saw that his smile had vanished and was replaced with a hard look, his eyes slightly narrowed.

"Hunter?" she pressed gently, touching his arm.

"I think we need to go," he said in a low, tight voice.

Her throat clenched. "Why?"

He gestured faintly towards the other side of the stage. Two people were leaning through that portion of the draw curtain, hidden from the view of the audience, as they were, and were pointing towards them and talking.

"Oh dear," she murmured, feeling a little relieved, considering what the danger had been for her the night before.

"Indeed." He cleared his throat and glanced towards her. "Feel like running a little? I think we may have to."

For whatever reason, Lucy snorted a laugh, and clamped down hard on her lips to keep from furthering her laughter. With a swallow, she nodded. "Suppose we'd better. Let's go."

He nodded curtly and rose, moving for the door and opening it, looking quickly before ushering her out. Instead of going out the way they had come, Hunter led her farther down the corridor, their steps quick and somehow echoing in spite of the sounds of the opera wafting in from the theatre itself. He turned down an alcove to the left sooner than she anticipated, and to a door tucked in there. A narrow set of stairs led downwards, and he released her hand to allow her to go first. Gathering her skirts in one hand, Lucy did her best to make haste down them.

They were reaching the bottom when the alcove door opened above them, making Lucy gasp.

"Oy!" a harsh voice bellowed. "Come back here!"

"Go!" Hunter urged with a wild grin, pushing her towards the door in front of them.

Lucy wrenched the door open and started out into the street, running wildly. Hunter was soon at her side, laughing and glancing behind them. "Tilda never told me those seats were problematic!"

"Her idea of a prank?" Lucy panted as they ran.

"Who knows? This way!" He took her hand and pulled her to the left, the pair of them barreling down a small side street almost entirely devoid of people. He was in his element here, weaving along streets and blocks like he had been raised in them, finding narrow passageways that Lucy would not have found even if she had looked for something of the sort.

And he laughed the entire time, which gave her the impression that he was either insane or had a peculiar sense of humor, both of which were amusing ideas. But considering the life he lived, being chased by members of a theatre's staff must have been the least threatening prospect of all. The most innocent of diversions. An irony to a moment of polite entertainment.

Whatever it was, Lucy was laughing as well, and couldn't stop. She'd wanted to go to the opera after being practically nomadic in London for a few days, wearing a dress designed by and borrowed from an eccentric costumer—without having to pay for it—and accompanied by a man who had rescued her from abduction and had been forced to look after her ever since. And now they were running away from theatre staff who had discovered them in seats that they had not paid for, which did not exist.

What was this life she had been dropped into that now had her running around London in the middle of the night? And why was she enjoying every second of it?

Hunter took them around another block and slowed his running, a hand going to his chest as he panted and laughed. "Oh, I think we've lost them."

Lucy released her hold on her skirts, her lungs burning with exertion and humor. "They won't pursue us farther?"

"I don't think so. Not for unpaid seats. Besides…" He gestured around them, the buildings dark and decrepit. "We're in St. Giles. Who comes here to try and find someone for theatre fees?"

St. Giles… Lucy had heard of this place, but never by polite society in decent terms, and never in any flattering terms. Lives were destroyed in St. Giles, and reputations obliterated. She had never thought she'd find herself here, and as she glanced around now, she wondered how she'd never been aware of its proximity to the Covent Garden theatres before. How easy it would be to wander to ruination after an innocent evening. How quickly one could be led astray and find their downfall at hand.

But she hadn't been living the traditional version of her life these last few days. No one knew she was here, and there was no downfall to be feared. Not with Hunter here, and not so long as he cared for her.

The apprehension was immediately replaced with anticipation as she returned her attention to him, wondering what his plan would be now, and where they would go from here.

Hunter was smiling at her now, her hand still in his. "Do you trust me, Lucy?"

Oh, did she ever! She trusted him so much she'd have given him her heart, if he'd asked for it. But of course, he wouldn't do so. Surely, he had to know how impossible it would be as much as she did. And no matter how pretty he thought she was at times, surely he wouldn't seek her heart as well.

Even if she secretly wanted him to.

"Yes," Lucy told him, squeezing his hand. "Of course I trust you."

She might have imagined it, but she thought his smile altered somehow in that moment. Became tender and warm, proud and delighted, disbelieving and breathless, all without shifting more than putting a bit of a delightful crinkle in the corners of his eyes. In that moment, she'd have gone with him to the ends of the earth if he'd asked.

He nodded at her slowly, then started to walk, his eyes eventually leaving hers and looking at the road ahead, though his smile never wavered.

Lucy's eyes began to burn as much as her cheeks already were, and she prayed any forming tears would not fall. What would she even be crying for? This was a magical night of unexpected adventures and unexplored possibilities, and she would never have such a night again in her life. She was determined to embrace and enjoy every single moment, store each of them up in her mind, and call upon them whenever her boring, respectable, financially diminishing life tore pleasure and happiness from her.

She would always have this night with Hunter, and no one could rid her of it.

And it was the prospect of being without it—without him—that was making her cry.

They had only gone the space of a few blocks when the sounds of music met her ears. Jaunty, merry, spirited music of a few fiddles and some drum, perhaps a sort of flute as well, and the unmistakable sound of dancing and cheering to accompany it. It bore hints of the sound of intoxicated masses, but not only of men. There were distinctly feminine voices as well, and every sound was jubilant. What in the world was happening in this dank corner of London that was so delightful at this time of night?

Hunter's step slowed slightly, and he grinned like a young boy at Lucy. "Shall we investigate?"

She practically danced in place with eagerness. "Can we?"

"Of course!" He shook the hand he held a little and turned towards the sounds. Lucy hurried alongside it, covering their joined hands with her free one.

Two blocks later, there was a large group of people in what appeared to be a blind alley, or possibly a space that had once been a mews, but now served as an open space perfect for dancing. Three fiddlers and two men playing flat drums sat on crates, while another stood nearby with a large flute. There were at least a dozen dancers and a dozen other people standing around, encouraging them. Tankards of beverages were all around, and a jolly man in a dirty apron brought another tray of them out from a building, setting the lot down on an empty crate.

He caught side of Hunter and Lucy's approach and smiled, wiping his hands on his apron. "Good evening, friends," he called in a thick Irish accent. "Come to join our *cèilidh*, are ye?"

"We'd love to!" Hunter answered for them both. "What are we celebrating?"

Their host pointed to the tall, dark-haired young man in the midst of the dancing. "My son James secured the hand of his sweetheart Nancy today, and we're celebrating the engagement. Nancy's the fair-haired lass opposite."

"My felicitations to them both," Hunter said as he shook hands with the man.

"Thank ye, sir. There are details to see to, o'course, but first, we intend to celebrate like we're back home in Ireland." He winked at them and nodded towards the dancing with his head. "Join in, why don't ye? If ye don't mind we're not so fine o'dress. We're a welcoming bunch."

Lucy found herself caught up in the energy of the dancing and the merriment of the gathering itself, smiling without any particular intention of doing so. "I can see that," she told him. "Although I don't think I'll know any of the steps."

"Ah, sure, when has that ever stopped us?" he laughed. "We just dance, lass. Ye'll fit in, right enough. And yer man here won't lead ye awry."

Lucy looked at Hunter, beaming at him. "I know he won't."

Hunter quirked his brows and began loosening his cravat, pulling it completely off and undoing his top button before shrugging out of his coat. "We'd better get to it, Lucy. They'll dance all night no matter what."

Nodding, she yanked her long opera gloves off and tossed them on top of his discarded items, brushing at her gown and looking at herself carefully. "Should I get rid of anything else? I don't look too fine, do I?"

"You look perfect, love," Hunter told her, rolling up his sleeves. "You'd fit in anywhere. Come on."

Her hand felt positively flaming in his, and the heat raced through each finger up to her elbow, then seemed to scream into the very center of her chest and down to her legs. Dancing on fiery legs would be interesting, but coursing through her was also the infectious mood of the gathering, so she had no doubt she would manage well enough.

Hunter led her into the dance, seamlessly merging them into the group and joining hands with those around them. There were no steps in particular, as far as Lucy could tell, but patterns did tend to repeat like a country dance blended with a jig. It was easy enough to follow, and after a few minutes of participating, she no longer cared.

It was simply a time to dance.

The song finished and everyone clapped, with a few people whooping. Lucy turned to Hunter, more invigorated than breathless. "What's a *cèilidh* anyway?"

"It's a celebration, really. Dancing, singing, storytelling, what have you. Mostly dancing, in my experience, and it can go all night and into the dawn sometimes." He whistled in appreciation for the fiddlers and leaned closer. "Nobody celebrates quite like the Irish. Except the Scots, who are fairly matched, but don't tell either I said so. It could start a war." He grimaced dramatically, making her laugh.

Lucy patted her hair, feeling parts of it coming loose. "I don't think my hair is going to hold with all of this dancing. I'm probably scattering pins everywhere. Perhaps I should take part of the ribbon and plait it back."

Hunter surprised her by shaking his head. "No, don't. Let the pins drop, let your hair fall from its hold, and don't worry about any of it." He reached out and began to curl one of her loose tendrils around a finger. "You have magnificent hair. It deserves to flow in all its glory."

Heavens… he could have pulled her into his arms by that simple coiling of her hair. She'd have gone willingly and sunk into him without a second thought. But he only played with that lock of hair, coiling and uncoiling, and she was not pulled in any particular direction.

Not physically, at least.

She felt a rather captivating spiral of a pull somewhere in the center of her, threatening to drown her eventually.

But not yet.

The musicians struck up again, rejuvenated by another round of drinks, and more dancers joined in the ranks, forming lines on either side. Lucy joined the women, looking at the two on either side of her.

"What dance is this?" she asked them with a bright smile.

One of them paused a moment. "It's a bit like the Duke of Kent's waltz with Rural Felicity, but all in a reel." At Lucy's bewildered expression, the girl laughed heartily. "You'll catch on, dear. I love a dance, and this is me favorite. And not a bother, half of us are a wee bit toppled wi' drink, so it won' be as pretty as we'd like." She winked, and Lucy found herself far more at ease.

She could certainly manage a passable Duke of Kent's waltz and Rural Felicity without much trouble, but doing so at the pace of a reel would be complicated. But as the girl said, if the other dancers were a trifle inebriated and thus less coordinated, she might do well enough, indeed.

She looked across the way at Hunter, who was watching her with a fondness and understanding that left her feeling rather exposed. As though he knew she was trying to figure out how to manage the dance without bungling it up too much. As though he knew her thoughts would be rambling about the formations and steps in a way that could paralyze her, if she were not too careful. As though he knew everything about her, and he enjoyed what he knew.

But of course, that was silly. He couldn't know everything about her, and he certainly couldn't enjoy everything he did know. She was quite the mess of a person, and her rambling was ridiculous. But she did want to dance well, particularly when dancing with him. Not for the benefit of onlookers, as so many young ladies did in Society, but because she did not want to ruin this moment with him.

This dance with him.

Who knew if she would ever get another?

They stepped forward in lines, then backwards, then waited for the lead couple to skip jauntily down the rows of them. Then each couple stepped to each other and took hands, turning around and around before all skipping in a movement of fours. They twisted hands so Hunter's arm was across her shoulder and then walked forward, then backward, while side by side—and again, the heat of their joined hands, skin on skin, was positively inflammatory. More than that, she knew exactly how much space was between them purely by feeling.

And she wanted to be closer.

Swallowing hard, she allowed Hunter to turn her under his arm, her eyes falling to the buttons of his weskit as they turned again before separating to the line, then coming together once more for the lead couple, now back at the head, to race down the center of them beneath a tunnel of hands.

Then the formation started again.

Each and every time she touched Hunter, the same thing happened, and each time, her breath grew harder and harder to come by. For a lighthearted dance like this, she was feeling more and more like they were engaged in some intimate waltz. She was well aware of all the other couples, but it was as though each round brought them closer to each other, and yet she was quite certain they were the same distance apart. Her fingers gripped his a trifle differently. His touch felt gentler. Her toes began to grow numb. His eyes became more impossibly blue. Their movements together became so easy… so graceful… so natural…

She was getting lost in this dance and in him. Lost and spiraling, though she could see now that the spiral was not drawing her down into the earth, but into him. Towards him. He was at the center of it all, the eye of her storm, and she was growing weaker against the tide.

Blissfully weak.

Hunter was still smiling as they danced, but it was so small a smile, so gentle, it was like a touch upon her skin. Like the night before when he had traced her tears. When he'd cradled her jaw.

It was a smile that held dozens of answers for questions she didn't dare ask. And that exact curve was seared onto her heart, which beat in time with their dance and their steps.

And if the pulse in his wrist were any indication, with his heart as well.

The music ended with slight fanfare, and everyone cheered, but Lucy didn't move out of Hunter's reach. Kept her hands in his. Kept her eyes on his. Let him see how she struggled to breathe.

His brilliant blue eyes were now a dark shade that made her tingle from head to foot, and as one more breath passed her lips, he took a step closer.

Raw instinct took over, and she arched up, meeting his mouth as it crashed down on hers, one hand cupping her face while his other reached around her waist. She clung to his neck and weskit as her lips molded against his, as he tutored her in a manner of heartbeats, seconds turning to eons with every delicious taste of him. Her entire frame shook and trembled as he drank from her, as she gave herself to this moment, as she gave herself to the imaginations and dreams she had told herself could never be.

This was real, as the stubble of his skin scraped against her face, making her shiver and gasp into his lips, drawing an occasional growl and rumble from him as she reached for more of his kiss, more of his fervor, more of everything and anything, her fingers clinging to him with a need she did not—could not—comprehend.

The whistles and cheers were thunderous now, and it faintly

occurred to Lucy that they might not be for the musicians anymore. Hunter seemed to freeze at the same instant, and their lips parted just enough for air, and eventually sense.

Lucy tried to duck her chin in embarrassment, but Hunter caught it, searching her eyes quickly before giving her another gentle, soft kiss.

"Do you know how long I have wanted to do that?" he whispered, his thumb stroking her cheek. "How badly I've wished to?"

"I know," Lucy managed, "how much I've wanted it… and I couldn't believe that…"

His thumb moved to her lips to shush her, and he kissed her brow. "Believe it," he breathed against her skin. "Believe all of it." He pulled back a little, his smile returned and bright as dawn. "Now will you dance with me until our feet are in agony?"

She curled into him, smiling up into his glorious face. "I can't even feel my feet, Hunter. I don't think they'll be in agony at all tonight."

His grin grew wider still, and he shook his head. "Then I suppose we'll just be dancing until the dancing ends. And possibly beyond. I've no intention of stopping."

"Nor do I." Thrilled with her boldness, she kissed his jaw and stepped back, loving the startled, heated look he gave her as the next formation of dancers set up.

She hadn't thought the night could become even more magical than before, but here it was. Magical and real and brilliant and perfect. In these slums of London, with this group of merry strangers, she had found perfection.

Did anything else truly matter beyond that?

How much longer they danced was hard to say. Time seemed to lose all meaning, and the dances themselves grew less and less structured with every passing song. It was a celebration like no other, and the energy of the gathering did not even begin to wane until the first hints of pink began to dot the horizon.

One by one, people began to trickle away back to their homes, or stumble, in some cases, and Hunter and Lucy were eventually part of them. But they had no home to return to, and Hunter's flat was nowhere near them. So they silently walked, hand in hand, fingers entwined, until Hunter moved to the side of a building against a green. He sat down on the grass against the building and tugged Lucy into his arms, kissing her softly before covering her with his coat.

With Hunter's arms securely around her, his heart beating a lulling cadence against her back, she nestled against him and felt the drowsiness of sleep descend upon her in a mighty wave of fatigue that hadn't even been hinted at before this. Her breathing slowed and deepened, her body relaxing and growing heavy.

"Are you asleep?" Hunter breathed against her hair.

She had no energy to respond, her mind already half-filled with dreams and fog.

"I love you," he rasped hoarsely into her scalp. "I love you. I love you."

Lucy sighed deeply, wondering if her lips formed a smile as sleep finally took her.

Chapter Twenty-Two

Hunter did not sleep with Lucy in his arms. Could not. He only held her and watched the sun slowly light the eastern horizon and eventually peek over it.

He felt no joy or satisfaction at the sight of it.

Today was the day he would have to let go of Lucy.

The hollowness of the prospect had begun as soon as the first rays of the sun had hit him, draining him more and more of life even as it lit the world in greater force. What a paradox this was and what agony daylight was bestowing upon him. He'd never wanted to curse his occupation before, but now…

He couldn't abandon his work for anything, not even love. Lives were at stake, and he was in too deeply to be able to leave with ease. He couldn't straddle both worlds, not if he wanted to keep Lucy safe and be an exceptional operative. There was no choice here.

There was only duty.

Cursed, ugly, soul-decaying duty.

And God help him, he was enough of a patriot to succumb to it. He had just enough honor to keep his word to king and country.

But how he would manage to function without his heart would remain to be seen.

Lucy stirred against him, and Hunter closed his eyes at the flash of pain. She was waking up, which meant they would have to go soon. This was the end, and he would rather be shot, stabbed, or strangled than face this.

But no one was going to oblige him with the physical torment, leaving him cold and empty as Lucy pushed against him, sitting up.

He watched her blankly as she stretched and rubbed her eyes, tucking his feelings away in the deep cavern that had formed within his chest. He would not be distant if he could help it, but he had to remove what he could in order to survive, and in order to encourage her to leave.

Encourage. He wanted very much to do the opposite. He wanted to beg her to run away with him and hide from her father and the world for the rest of their lives, to hell with the consequences. They could figure something out. They were both resourceful enough to do that, and she was resilient enough to adapt to whatever life they chose.

But he wouldn't let her do that.

Couldn't.

Lucy sighed at the dawn and turned to smile at him, the sleepy bliss in her features stabbing him directly in the heart. "Good morning."

He tried to smile. "Good morning."

Her eyes darted around his features, her lips falling from their pleasant curve. "What is it?"

Hunter stared at her for a moment, then reached into his pocket and pulled out the crumpled piece of paper from the night before and handed it to her.

She took it at once and unfolded it, reading quickly. Her breathing stilled and the color from her cheeks began to fade. "You've found him."

"Yes," he managed to grunt.

Her throat bobbed. "When did you get this?"

He could lie. He could tell her it had just come. He could…

"Just before the opera," he admitted, his throat feeling raw.

She nodded once. "Thank you for letting me have last evening without this. It was very kind." She crumpled the paper again and looked away, her hair streaming in the morning breeze and making his fingers tingle with the temptation to run his hands through their locks one more time, just as he'd done all night.

But there would be no more of that.

"Should we go?" Lucy asked in a tiny voice, tears evident in every word.

If hell could have swallowed him whole, he would have felt less pain. "Yes," he said, against all inclination. "We probably should."

They rose, and Hunter took his coat from the ground, sliding his arms back into it. It still smelled of the free-flowing ale from their Irish friends the night before, bringing back with it the memories of dancing and laughing with Lucy. Of kissing her until he thought his soul would burst. Of believing his life could embrace her just as his arms did.

He forced himself to inhale the stale morning air of St. Giles as he began to walk towards Camden Town, Lucy a half step behind him. He didn't look back at her and refused to do so unless the situation called for it. Now he only had to return her home, and then she would be out of his life and his care. He would have no more responsibility for her, and he could return his focus to finding Martin and discovering what he was doing with the money he was raking in from the gaming dens.

Wasn't that more important than his own happiness?

Neither of them said a word as they passed out of St. Giles and into slightly more respectable neighborhoods. It was only two miles or so to Camden Town, and at this time of morning, it was an easy enough trip to make. But each step was weighed down, and he wondered if it was evident in his pace that he was making no haste with this part.

Every now and then, he could hear Lucy sniffle behind him.

Gads, he wanted to take her in his arms and kiss away those tears.

But his feet kept moving forward, and only when her shoulder brushed against his did he actually feel himself take a breath. She nuzzled against him very slightly as they walked, and he let his fingers graze against hers. She didn't reach for him, and he did the same. These passing touches they were stealing would be the last, and they both knew it.

"I'll miss you," he heard her whisper.

"And I you," he let himself reply, though his voice felt strained and taut. "Will you… will you let me know if there is a problem with your father?"

"How?" Lucy asked, looking across the street. "How would I even find you?"

How, indeed.

Did he dare give her this path to him? Or should he sever all things now?

"Meyer," he ground out, clinging to his last hope. "If you need me, write to Meyer. Use my code name. He'll get it to me."

"Need," Lucy repeated softly. "What about want?"

Hellfire, brimstone, and all the damnation…

His fingers brushed against hers again, and this time she gasped. He, meanwhile, only burned.

And then they were there. The house was before them, and he was stepping forward to knock, every motion feeling foreign and strange, as though his body were no longer his own.

A man answered the door who was certainly not Mr. Allred, but he recognized Lucy at once. "Miss Allred! You've… found us?"

"Pond? What are you doing as butler?" she asked with a small step forward.

Pond looked behind him, his white hair neatly combed back, before leaning closer. "Retrenchment is not going well, miss. The staff is down to me, Cook, and Betsy."

"Where is Mr. Allred?" Hunter asked with all due politeness, having a decent feeling about this man that he could not say for her father.

Pond looked at him without emotion or even suspicion. "Out, sir. Doesn't usually return home until eleven. He's been in a right state these last few days."

"Because Miss Allred was missing?" Hunter offered wryly.

Pond pursed his lips slightly. "That's just it, sir. He told us to prepare for her arrival the other day, and then said nothing when you didn't arrive, miss. He asked for messages regularly, but nothing came, which bothered him. But he never called for a magistrate or Bow Street, never said anything to any of us about where you could be or that you had changed your mind… It's all been very strange, and his late-night meetings are only making him more discouraged."

"He's not usually discouraged," Lucy muttered to Hunter. "Only motivated in one direction or the other."

Pond nodded in agreement.

Hunter didn't like it. He did not like it one bit, but what could be done?

He turned to Lucy and swallowed, bowing slightly to hide his eyes. "Welcome home, Miss Allred. It's been a pleasure."

Lucy inhaled sharply, then bobbed a curtsy he could only half see. "Thank you, Trick. For everything." She put a shaking hand on his arm, squeezing weakly.

He covered her hand with his own, just for a moment, feeling as though she were squeezing his heart one last time.

Then she was gone, moving into the house behind Pond.

Hunter ignored the screaming pain in his throat and gave Pond a serious look. "You'll keep an eye on her?"

Pond nodded firmly, his eyes far too knowing. "I will, sir. Like she was my own daughter."

"You're rather accommodating for a man who has never met me and works for a man who isn't concerned about his daughter's whereabouts," Hunter pointed out as he fought the tension in his throat.

"I'm too old to start over somewhere else," Pond said with a shrug, "and I like Miss Lucy too much to leave her alone. The way I see it, if she is being safely returned home by you, then we are on the same side."

Hunter held out a hand to him. "If you need me, Pond, here's what you do: step outside this house and whistle in three short bursts. Someone will show up, and you tell them you need Trick. Use the code word 'Dawn.' They will find me, and I will get here."

"Are you setting a watch, sir?" Pond inquired in a much lower voice as he shook his hand. "For Miss Lucy?"

"Yes," Hunter said bluntly. "I don't trust Mr. Allred, and I have a bad feeling. Do you object?"

Immediately, Pond shook his head. "No, sir. I'm relieved, as it happens. I hope I don't need you, but I am grateful for your instincts." He shook his hand one more time and turned back for the house, closing the door behind him without looking back.

Hunter stared at the door for a long moment, losing all sense of feeling for his body. There was nothing there anymore. Yet he was still alive and aware of a few things. The sounds of the high street on the next block. The smell of bread and horses and cooking poultry.

The breeze against his face.

But not his feet. Not his fingers. Not his heart.

Not even his head.

Somehow, he managed to turn and walk away, his eyes burning and dry, every step a slog as he moved back towards the darker slums of his world and away from the light that was Lucy.

He wandered down towards the old London League offices, which had been closed up and moved since the entire Martin case had taken place. Back when they'd only known him as One and thought he'd been captured. Before Mist and Mirrors had uncovered the deadly truth that One was Martin, and that Martin was a traitor.

He didn't know where the new offices were, but he stared at the old ones as though he might find some answers there. Not necessarily about Martin, though he'd been through the building at least a dozen times already for clues in that regard. No, now he was simply looking at the place for answers about Lucy. How was he supposed to help her when he didn't know what the problem was? How could he keep her safe when the danger was an unknown? How could he keep thinking about her when his place was somewhere else?

"You're fairly far afield, aren't you?"

Hunter slumped against the building behind him and looked at the approaching figure of Gent without emotion. Gent was a bit of a legend in London, both for his heroic tendencies and his network of child assets, who provided some of the best intelligence on various people and subjects to be found anywhere. He was one of the most senior members of the London League. And it had been a few years since Hunter had enjoyed contact with him.

He wished he hadn't had cause today.

"Probably," Hunter admitted as Gent joined him along the wall. "But I'm widening my sphere these days, whether I want to or not."

"That doesn't sound like you. What brought you here, of all places?"

Hunter's mouth lifted in a humorless smile. "Subconsciously looking for you, I suppose."

"Me?"

Hunter glanced over, finding satisfaction in the widening of his colleague's eyes. "You. I need to borrow a pair of your sharpest eyes."

"For…?" Gent prodded, gesturing faintly. At Hunter's hesitation, Gent's brows snapped down. "This isn't for an assignment, is it?"

Hunter shook his head. "I don't know what it's for. It's a feeling… All of it is because of feelings, but I have a particular feeling that…"

"A woman you love is in trouble, eh?"

Hunter jerked and stared at him in shock. "How the devil…?"

Gent chuckled. "I practically invented the thing. I watched mine myself, most of the time, which I do not recommend, though it worked out for me. So tell me the issue, and I'll give you some eyes."

Quickly, without excessive detail, Hunter told Gent about Lucy's situation and what he knew so far, and when Gent's expression turned calculating, he knew his instincts were not as far afield as his wandering had been. Gent was as seasoned an operative as anyone Hunter knew, and if he was seeing the trouble, it must truly be there. It was no longer something Hunter could blame on his love for Lucy.

It was a real threat.

"Dawn, eh?" Gent finally said with a smile after Hunter told him the signal. "Nice touch. Lucy means light, light and dawn… Hearing 'Dawn' means she's in trouble. I'll get you eyes, easy enough. Camden Town is a good place for hiding, there's no mistake about that. And I'll have my eyes get word right to you instead of me. No sense in getting in the middle. But if you need help, you know we're here."

Hunter nodded, grunting once. "I already had to use Trace this week. I'm going to be indebted to the League pretty soon."

"Well, you're related to Rook by marriage, so we'll give you this one out of sympathy." Gent clapped him on the arm and pushed off the wall. "I'm seeing your sister next. I'll give her your best."

Hunter's throat clenched. "Tell her, will you? Not about the trouble but tell her… tell her I got Lucy home."

Gent tapped his cap and nodded in understanding. "There's a way through, you know. If you can find it. I did." He turned away and disappeared down a side alley.

Hunter supposed that was his cue to leave, and he went in the opposite direction, content with knowing that word would now get to Hal without him having to voice it aloud. She would know what it meant to him that Lucy was gone, and she would have been sympathetic and concerned for him, which would only have broken him further. He didn't want emotion and sympathy and comfort; he wanted distraction.

He wanted to expel this torment in some way that wouldn't be destructive to himself or anyone else. A boxing session, if he could find one of his combat contacts. Some gaming would work as well, though it was so early in the day that he doubted anything would be available to him. He could go back to Ye Olde Wharf and talk to Meyer about suspicious activity there again, but going there would remind him of Lucy, and thus defeat the entire purpose.

There was always Briar. Their meeting the other night had been very useful, as they had compared notes about the usage on the docks. She was having some of the same issues on her side as he was on his, and it would probably do him some good to cross over for a few weeks and explore his options there. But with knowing Martin was spending more time on the north side of the Thames at the gaming tables than he was on the south, something kept him from making that crossover. Besides, Briar might take it personally if he interfered there. She had her own players to deal with, and her own assignment.

Martin was his, and Martin needed to be his focus.

Without anything specific to do, he wandered the streets in the direction of the Black Dolphin. He could at least get himself a drink and collect some gossip there, given his connection with the proprietor. And he might find Gus or one of his other assets who had been encouraged to continue patrolling the dens and clubs on their own while reporting back to him. He hadn't exactly been around for them to report to, but they could have found him if necessary.

That was what he'd told himself, at any rate.

Hunter tsked as he realized he'd also have to go back to Tilda and return his clothes, as well as give her an address for where to send the things she had created for Lucy. It was closer to do that before heading to the Black Dolphin, so he turned up the next block and walked with a bit more determination.

Tilda would ask no questions of him; she was used to the way of things in this world. She might make some stinging comments, but nothing he hadn't already thought himself, and she would know nothing was his fault. She might even take pity on him, but only for a few moments. Then she'd likely tell him to leave her alone so she could get back to work, and everything would return to normal.

He would like normal.

He saw Willow outside of the theatre and waved at her a little. By the slight way she cocked her head after the wave, he knew the lack of Lucy by his side had not gone unnoticed.

"Is Tilda inside?" he asked by way of greeting, choosing to completely ignore the question she hadn't asked.

"Yes," Willow replied softly, her eyes showing too much understanding. "She wants to talk to you about her seats last night."

Hunter shrugged slowly. "Not my fault, but all right." He plucked at his shirt. "Usual place for clothing drop-off?"

Willow nodded and pointed the way. "Your clothes are where you left them. Thank you for not tossing them around like some of the others do."

"I would never," Hunter assured her with a smile he did not feel. "Until next time, Willow." He nodded and moved into the building, ignoring the way the conversation made him feel.

Stiff, uncomfortable, false, secretive… None of those things were him.

Well, all right, he was secretive, but he didn't usually avoid specific topics with such a wide berth.

He moved first to the room in which he had changed the night before, pretending weakly that he had simply been there for another mission and doing his best to remove all images of Lucy from his mind and memories. Just for now. Just while he was here. He wanted to remember everything about her, just not here and not in this moment.

Once he was back in his own clothing, and he had deposited his costume for the laundress, he went in search of Tilda.

He did not have to search long.

"WHAT DO YOU MEAN BY RUINING MY SPECIAL BOX?" she bellowed the moment she caught sight of him in the corridor.

Hunter had heard Tilda yell before and knew her mood was as flexible as her fingers, so he only raised his brows at her before calmly replying, "Did I ruin something? I only remember someone coming after me for using those seats and having to run into the night."

As he'd suspected, Tilda immediately smiled and strode towards him. "Dear boy, I am dreadfully sorry for that. I've spoken with the necessary authorities, and it will not happen again."

Hunter nodded in acknowledgement. "Thank you, but I don't believe I'll have need of the box again."

Tilda's eyes narrowed, and she glanced around quickly before coming back to him. "You are alone."

"I am." He took the slip of paper with Lucy's address on it from his pocket and handed it to her. "You can send her carpet bag and anything else you have here."

Tilda took the paper without looking at it, keeping her attention on him. "Do you need a drink, dear?"

"Probably," he answered bluntly, leaning one shoulder against the corridor wall. "Might not be able to stop easily, but I won't say no to one or two glasses of gin."

Patting his arm, Tilda nodded quickly and gestured with two fingers for him to follow her. They walked three doors down and she entered, going directly for the sideboard as Hunter followed behind. She pulled out a clear bottle and two small glasses, setting them all on the top.

"I only give this to my favorites, you know," she told him as she uncorked the bottle and poured some into the glasses.

Hunter smirked a little. "Lies," he countered blandly. "You gave some to Rook not a fortnight ago."

Tilda turned to him, aghast by all appearances, then broke into a smile and shrugged a shoulder. "He brought me a new contact for silks in Paris. That is worth some gin." She set the bottle down and handed one of the glasses to him before picking up the other for herself.

"Cheers," she said, clinking their glasses and downing the entire contents in one go.

Hunter downed his in two, not wanting to give the impression that he was that desperate to forget.

"I really am sorry about the seats," Tilda murmured as she took his glass from him and filled it again. "Did she have a good time otherwise?"

He appreciated that she wasn't using Lucy's name. It was as though she knew it would sting worse to hear her name, little as that made sense. Memories of her at all would sting, but her name…

Her name would be another blade thrust into his soul.

"She did," he managed to admit. "And don't be sorry. We found ourselves in a *cèilidh* in St. Giles because of it. The O'Keefes, do you know them?"

Tilda shook her head, smiling brightly as she handed him back the glass. "I do not, but I adore a good *cèilidh*. I trust she had never seen anything like it."

Hunter shook his head. "No. It became a memorable night, and very sweet."

"In that case," Tilda mused softly, clinking her glass to his again, "*sláinte.*"

"*Sláinte,*" he replied, downing his gin in two gulps once more, taking comfort in the soothing burn down his throat and into his chest. It wasn't quite the pleasurable warmth that being with Lucy gave him, and certainly couldn't hold a candle to the fire that had engulfed him as he'd kissed her last night, but it served as a hearty preoccupation for his thoughts.

He set his glass down on the sideboard, clearing his throat. "If you happen to hear the word 'Dawn' in the next few weeks, send for me. It's probably nothing, but just in case."

Tilda gave him a scolding look, cradling her unfinished gin. "It's never nothing with you lot, and especially with you. But I will keep an ear out."

"Thank you, Tilda." He smiled with genuine gratitude, in spite of his present torment, and started for the door. "If you ever find some good tartan, I'll take you to the next *cèilidh* myself."

"Don't make me promises, Trick," she called. "I always collect."

He glanced over his shoulder and tipped the brim of his cap. "Good day, Tilda." And with that, he left the room, striding down the corridor, and soon, out into London, praying he might find some solace in the days ahead, and that, crave her though he might, Lucy would not need him.

But still want him.

Chapter Twenty-Three

Lucy had never known empty days like this.

Three of them, all in a row, filled with nothing of significance or entertainment, nothing of substance, nothing of usefulness. Just nothing. She had seen her father twice in each of those days, one of which was supper, but there had been no show of affection or concern and no real care for her presence.

Why, then, had he wanted her home? She'd told him her story, and he'd only responded that hired carriage drivers could be so unpredictable, and it would all be better when he could afford to bring Cox back.

How he planned on affording that, he did not care to share. But the signs of his poor retrenchment were everywhere. The walls of the house were bare when their gallery had always been well stocked before. The furnishings of her room were no better than what she'd had at Ye Olde Wharf, and the bed was worse. The rooms where he might have visitors were furnished, but only with what could be considered the bare essentials for respectable people. Once the family rooms were looked at, there was almost nothing. One of the parlors did not have any furniture in it at all apart from a lopsided ottoman whose legs had been removed.

She imagined that had come with the house. There was no way her father would have kept such a thing from their former residence.

What he had chosen to keep was an interesting insight. She'd gone up into the attic yesterday and found all of her mother's remaining things in trunks. Most of her gowns had been given to Lucy when she'd gotten older and made over as a way of saving money, but there were one or two still salvageable, should she wish. Some of her watercolors were there, as well as sketches of Lucy as a child, none of which would have made any money, which was probably why they remained in the family's possession. There were also a few sets of jewels, which she distinctly remembered her mother wearing. These she took from the trunks to keep her father from ever selling them.

She had no idea if he'd ever stoop that far, but she was not willing to take the chance. Of course, they could be paste, given the way her father had always been and her mother's wisdom in that regard, but Lucy wanted these pieces for her own memories.

She recognized none of the furniture in the house, but there was a small writing desk in the attic that had once sat in her mother's parlor. So her father did have some tenderness towards the memory of her mother, it seemed. Why else would he keep a decent piece of furniture that could be sold?

As for her own belongings, Lucy had held no expectations, which had served her well. He'd kept almost nothing of her remaining clothing, which meant she only had the clothes at the school and Tilda's new creations to call her own. There had been no known recovery of her trunks, but since her father had never reported her missing, there had never been an investigation.

Perhaps Trace would one day find her trunks in his corner of London. Not that he would know they were hers. It was far more likely that someone would be wearing one of her dresses at some charity event that she would see, and then she would know that someone, at least, had profited off of the crime.

She could write to Tilda, she supposed, and let her know what had happened. But she could not call upon that woman's generosity again. She refused to become a charity case, and she was not so desperate as to beg. And besides, her father had not informed her of any social events for her to attend while she was here, so what need did she have for any other gowns?

She was curious as to why he was not pushing her out the door to events here in London. It was his favorite occupation for her, making him look good by whatever means necessary, and yet he had been going out without her every evening after supper. She did not mind it, as it allowed her time to read some of the few books in the house and to enjoy a small fire and pot of tea by herself, but the change was jarring, considering she had not been gone that many months.

Tonight, however, they would be attending a small supper and card party for someone she did not know. A lovely, respectable family, her father had said, and he'd be pleased if she would look her best. It was the nicest request he had made of her in years.

Which probably indicated they had an eligible son of decent prospects.

Everything was confusing for her at the moment, and her loneliness was only compounding it.

How could three days with Hunter feel like a lifetime? She had fallen in love with him after spending practically every moment of those three days with him, and now that he was gone, her life was a void. If she had been at the school, she would at least have something to fill her time and make her feel useful—a purpose and something to distract her from thoughts and emotions, memories and dreams—but here in her father's house?

There was nothing.

She had written Hunter so many letters that would never be sent. If he thought he was needed, if he thought she was in trouble, he would come, and she couldn't take him away from whatever it was that drove his life. She couldn't pretend that her loneliness was as important as someone else's protection, or whatever it was that he was involved in. Just because she wanted him with a depth and drive that showered her pillows with tears at night did not mean she had the power to bring him to her.

So she had her letters, all filling a blank diary she had found in the bottom of one of her childhood trunks in the attic. And to keep her brain active, she had written them in cipher, just as John had taught her. Her father was absolutely the sort of man to enter her room without permission and pry through her things, and if he knew that she had fallen in love with a man she'd met on the streets of the slums of London...

That would certainly give him reason to restrict her freedoms and fob her off on some eligible bachelor of means, with no consideration of age or taste.

Lucy smiled to herself as she recalled Hunter telling her on their first day that he was in line to be a viscount. His uncle held the title, or some such. She had no idea if that was in any way true, and she did not particularly care. Without knowing Hunter's surname, she couldn't look it up in Debrett's. She also didn't know Hal's surname, though she knew her real name was Henrietta, and she was married to John, but there was no surname given for John. He worked at Bow Street, but the idea of looking through every John who worked for or was associated with Bow Street? It was laughable.

She might have a chance of marrying Hunter if she knew his exact connection to the viscountcy, should it exist, but that would only matter to her father. She didn't know Hunter the future viscount. She knew Hunter the street wanderer. She knew Hunter the virtue defender. She knew Hunter the secret-opera-box companion. She knew Hunter the *cèilidh* dancer.

She knew Hunter the delicious kisser.

Lucy sat forward in her chair with a moan, putting her face into her hands. She could not continue to torture herself like this. Day in and day out, she relived her London street adventures because she had nothing else to do with herself. She needed to get out of this darkness she was content to wrap herself in, this agony and ecstasy of her memories, and do something with herself instead of simply exist.

Christmas was in two days, and then she would ask to return to the school. Surely her father could not argue that with her. She had come home for the holidays, as he had requested, and he had not done anything that had resembled familial connection or festive celebration. Perhaps she could make the decision and inform him of it instead of asking for his thoughts.

Taking charge of her own life might be the next step to improving things. Perhaps that was what her time with Hunter could teach her and would help her to improve the quality of her life going forward. He was a man, and therefore his life was his own to control, but he associated with such independent women and respected them so highly. He did not expect them to fit into specific little boxes that had been designated for them by others.

He saw them for the women they were and the skills and talents they held. He valued them for these things and for their particular and peculiar natures. They took their lives by the reins and drove them in the direction they wished, not the other way around. There was no other driver in their lives but themselves, and Lucy hadn't tried to do anything of the sort.

Except for the one time she had taken someone else's advice and tried for the open position at Miss Masters's School for Fine Young Ladies.

She did have this power within her. She'd already tested it once with great success. All she had to do was continue to pursue this bolder, more determined version of herself. This woman who had loved every moment of the unexpected, risk-infused life in corners of London she'd never seen. This woman who had run from an opera's staff chasing her for the theatre fee. This woman who had danced all night with strangers and kissed a man for the first time in her life in their midst. This woman who had fallen asleep in his arms without fear or shame, without regret or remorse, who had asked him what she should do if she did not need him but wanted him.

There was an independent woman in Lucy. She had simply never allowed her the breathing room to do much. She hadn't known that she could allow her that sort of breathing room. Her entire life had been conformity into a particular role or figure or form, whatever her father dictated. But now her father was not invested in her or her life, and still she was allowing him to dictate how she viewed herself.

"No more," she murmured to herself as she straightened, lowering her hands to her lap and shaking her head. "No more."

She looked at the clock on the mantle, which was the only properly working item in her room and sighed. It was time to begin getting ready for their evening plans. With only Betsy in the house for a maid, it was hardly worth the effort to have her hair finely dressed. Betsy was trying to keep up with all of the household chores aside from what Cook had agreed to do in the kitchens and what Pond could do as butler, valet, and footman. There was no time for her to dress Lucy or her hair.

Besides, Lucy was more than capable of doing both fairly well.

There was a faint scratching at her door, and she turned to look at it with a hint of amusement. No one in this house usually scratched at doors. "Come in?"

The door fairly burst open on its hinges and two men entered, kerchiefs tied over their faces, gloves covering their hands. And they came directly for Lucy.

"No!" she screamed, hastily backing up, slamming into the desk chair and tumbling over. "No, please!"

But they seized her arms and legs, one of them large enough to hold her wrists with one hand while covering her mouth with another. She thrashed in his hold and attempted to bite down on his hand, but the gloves were made of a thick leather, and her teeth had no impact on them. Her legs and wrists were bound with cloth while another length was tied around her mouth before she was lifted from her place on the floor and chair. Then she was bodily flung over the shoulder of the large one and carried from her room.

Lucy screamed with all her might against her gag, but only muffled sounds came free. The house was not large, but with so few people within, there were fewer people to hear.

Instead of using the main stairs to escape, the men carried her down the servants' stairs. Far out of earshot of anyone working among the house, and given the lack of staff, they were unlikely to encounter anyone. How did they know their way around the house? The staff here had come with Lucy's father to retrench, and they had all known her for several years. They treated her with kindness and care, even with the abuses of her father upon each of them with their minimal wages and maximum workload.

But perhaps someone had been driven to this because of her father. Perhaps that was what had happened upon her arrival in London from Kent. Perhaps all of this was to try and teach her father a lesson, and she was simply the weapon that had been chosen to do so.

Unfortunately for whomever was scheming in such a way, she was not an effective weapon to use upon the man.

Whomever it was, whatever it was, this abduction was not about to be foiled, unless someone else was planning on meeting a contact in the corners of Camden Town. Evening had fallen, but surely someone would notice if she were being put into a coach against her will. She had to hope for someone to step in, just as Hunter had done. She had to keep hoping that someone would see this and help her.

To her surprise, once the men opened the servants' entrance door, they did not go towards Greenland Street, where the front door was. They moved towards the back of the house and into a small mews that barely seemed to fit them all. Lucy tried to look around her captor to see where they were heading, only to be turned and tossed roughly into the back of a wagon, her elbow and head whacking against the wood sharply.

Stars flickered in front of her eyes just as a canvas was tied down across the top of the wagon, hiding her from view. She yelled and screamed against her gag, thrust her bound hands against the canvas, and kicked her ankles mightily, but all to no avail. The canvas was strapped down so tightly that it did not give at all when she pressed against it, and she could not even push up on her hands and knees. She tried inching towards the back of the wagon, hoping there might be an opening wide enough for her to slip through in spite of the canvas, but the wagon lurched forward then, slamming her against the backboard with a sickening thud, even to her own ears.

The wagon wheels creaked, but the horses moved at a decent pace even out of the mews, and within moments they were out on a main street. The poor light made it impossible to even guess in which direction they were heading, and Lucy knew almost nothing about Camden Town to be able to guess or note any familiar sights, even if she could see them.

Weakly, she nudged her feet against the backboard of the wagon, closing her eyes in a faint prayer that it might give a little, but she could hear the telltale sounds of metal bolts and chains. She turned on her side and pressed up into the canvas again, reaching over the backboard, but only her smallest finger could get through. Everything was fastened and secured, and there was no escape for her.

Which meant she would have to wait for her absence to be noted, and for someone to do something about it. Or she would have to take matters into her own hands once she was delivered to her destination. She had no particular skills when it came to criminal activity, and she was not physically imposing or talented, but she did have a quick mind, according to John. Surely, she could find a way out of this once she was there.

She had nothing to offer anyone for herself, which meant she was not likely to come to danger. Her father had no money to raise for a ransom, but he was good at making profitable connections. There was hope to be found there, she supposed. After all, no respectable man would want it to be known that his daughter was missing, even if he was not especially fond of her.

Lucy curled into a ball in her wagon bed as it thumped and rattled along the streets of London, knowing bruises were going to form all along her body from the excursion. She needed to save her strength as much as possible if she was going to attempt an escape. Wherever they were going, whatever the plan for her was, she couldn't do anything about it now.

Tears leaked from her eyes all the same, and she clung to the image of Hunter dancing with her at the *cèilidh*, looking at her as though the stars of the heavens were dancing in her eyes.

I love you.

She hadn't imagined him saying those words as she'd fallen asleep. She couldn't have. She'd heard them, felt them against her hair, experienced the way his arms tightened around her as he'd whispered them. He loved her and had told her when he thought she wouldn't hear. She wasn't meant to know his feelings, and she knew why.

Duty was his guiding light—Hal had told her as much—and his life was dangerous. He wouldn't want to put Lucy in danger or give her reason to cling to him when it would be dangerous to do so. He had pretended at distance when they'd parted for her sake, loving her all the while. She'd known she had to return to her father's house. She'd always known that. Somehow, there had been hope in her reprieve from that life, and in dreaming that they could make something together in spite of everything.

But they had both known better, so the parting had come.

Yet he loved her. And she knew full well that she loved him. He might not know her feelings, but she knew them well. The opportunity to tell him might never come, but he deserved to know, did he not? Or would that affect his sense of duty and disrupt what made him the man he was?

None of that mattered now, she supposed. Being tossed to and fro in the back of a wagon, bound and gagged, and taken to locations unknown tended to put things into a particular perspective. She could worry about Hunter knowing of her love another time, perhaps when her safety was once more in place. She could wrap his love around her like a protective shield or a comforting quilt during this time of fear and would do so freely.

The rest of it would have to work itself out later.

The wagon continued to turn, rattle, and bounce over cobblestone, making her head ache along with the rest of her body. There was nothing in here to make her in any way comfortable, so she tried to lay her face against her arms to keep from additional injury in her neck or head. With her eyes closed, she might be able to imagine herself stretched out in a carriage, poorly sprung and in need of better cushions, but a carriage nonetheless, and the opportunity to rest within could be upon her. The waning light of evening was made even less by the tight canvas above her, so she might imagine herself better able to sleep in this darkness.

She would know more when she woke, and nothing could be done until she did. With all that in mind, surely sleep ought to come to her.

Sleep, of course, had other ideas.

She lost track of time while she hovered between sleep and waking, stopped considering the directions of turns and the implication of large bumps in the road. She ignored the sounds around her of other horses and carriages, of voices attending parties or theatres or clubs, of shouts and calls and the unmistakable sounds of the river slapping against the boats and ships in port. All of these were there, all of them meant something, and yet all of it meant nothing to her.

The sounds of the river increased, yet the wheels were bouncing and creaking over stones at the same time. A different, hollow-sounding creaking.

The bridge. They were crossing the Thames into the southern part of the city.

Lucy groaned and turned her face into her arm, exhaling without tears. She knew absolutely nothing about this side of London. Her escape would be all the more difficult, as she would now need to attempt to find one of the bridges to cross over, unless she could find a decent ferryman who would not take advantage of her. And also would not require payment, as she had no money.

At least she was wearing one of Tilda's simpler gowns at the moment. She would not appear as a fine lady to anyone, which would only work in her favor. Unless it made her an easier target for those who wished to take certain liberties.

The dangers were weighing on her; the reality of her present situation something that could not be ignored. This was the situation she would have been in last week if not for Hunter. This completely helpless feeling of being devoid of resources and help, of having to rely on one's own abilities, knowing they were limited at best for what must be faced.

"What would Tilda do?" Lucy whispered to herself.

She began to giggle at the thought. Tilda would be profoundly outraged at being strapped into the back of a wagon. She would be full of indignities about being trussed at hand and foot—such an inelegant state for a lady—and would probably have a weapon hidden somewhere on her body.

Lucy had no such weapons, she was quite certain, and even if she had, she would have no idea how to use them. Even the fan with a hidden blade Tilda had given her sat neatly on her bedside table, serving absolutely no purpose whatsoever.

Utterly useless. That was what she was at the moment. Useless as a hostage and useless as a potential escapee.

This was not going to end well.

Hope, that weak, flickering flame she had been determined to have, was wavering even more than before, winking in and out within her.

It felt as though the wagon had driven the entire night, though she knew that was not the case, when it finally pulled to a stop. Lucy lay as still as possible, making the decision to feign sleep for her captors. Perhaps they would speak more freely if they thought she could not hear them, just as Hunter had done the other night.

She heard the ropes being loosened across the top of the wagon and felt the rush of air as the canvas was thrown back. The bolts of the wagon backboard were unhooked, and she felt arms reaching under her and dragging her body towards the back of the wagon.

"Is she dead?" one of them asked, not sounding particularly concerned.

"Don't think so, she's still warm." She was hefted into arms, thankfully not thrown over a shoulder this time, and carried away from the wagon. "She don't weigh nothing, you know. Like a leaf."

"Well, she'd better be worth it. You know what happened to them that botched the first time." There was no laughter after his statement, but she thought the one who held her stiffened at the mention.

That wasn't good.

"We've got her, though. That was our task," the one carrying her pointed out. "We got her here, and no one followed."

"She's nothing," the other pointed out. "I heard Key, mate. He wants her father to pay for not arranging the first better, and she's just going to be off to the plan once the payment comes through."

They weren't holding their tongues, that was for certain, but there was some sort of code here that she wasn't following. Her father was involved, that was easy enough to pick apart, but arranging the first? Did that mean the first kidnapping? Had her father had something to do with her abduction attempt? Could that explain why he hadn't looked for her? And what did they mean that she would be "off to the plan" when payment came through? What plan? Where was it?

How could she be nothing and still be part of some plan?

And if her father was supposed to pay for something, those expecting it would be waiting a very long time, unless she was mistaken. Unless things had changed, or he had developed better skills at his gaming.

Whatever plan she was going to be forced into, it would seem that her being returned to her father was not part of it. How much did he know about this present abduction? How involved was he in the plan they were talking about?

They entered a building, and Lucy immediately caught the stench of fish, of sawdust, of alcohol, and of citrus. The only thing she could guess was that it must be some building on a wharf or dock on the river, but there were hundreds of those, and they all looked exactly the same.

Lucy forced her body to be entirely relaxed as she was laid down on a rough wooden floor with surprisingly gentle hands, and a blanket was laid over her. Footsteps faded away from her, but she could still hear the voices. Until she knew more, until she understood what part she was meant to play, and what part her father did play, she needed to remain here and take in as much as she could. And if she could appear as innocent as possible, she might not be so carefully watched.

Perhaps she could begin to adjust the linen binding her ankles and wrists, if she moved slowly enough. She cracked her eyes open just a touch to see if she was obstructed from view, and snapped them shut when she saw that, to her disappointment, she was very much out in the open, apart from one barrel near her head.

Well. How was she going to get out of this?

Chapter Twenty-Four

The picture was an extraordinary likeness. Hal had really outdone herself, and he could tell that she had put a lot of effort into the piece. Hunter hadn't been entirely certain he was pleased to have it when it arrived, but considering how often he had looked at it since, he decided he was grateful.

A picture of Lucy would be all he ever had of her, and Hal's drawings from her own memory were always exact. It was one of the quirks of her mind and memories, and one of the things that made her an exceptional asset and operative, when she was called up.

Hunter stared at the picture of Lucy now, his eyes tracing over the curve of her cheek and remembering the perfect texture of her skin against his fingertips. The gentle friction of her lips against his, and the sweet, intoxicating taste of her. The curve of her smile and the sound of her laughter.

She invaded every one of his thoughts and every single dream. How he'd been able to accomplish anything in the days since she'd been gone was incredible, but he had managed some progress, he was pleased to say. So long as he gave himself moments like these where he could allow himself to remember, reflect, and dwell on her and his time with her, he found it easier to move forward in other things.

Footsteps were approaching his table, so he folded the drawing again and shoved it inside his shirt. He'd been here too long, and he needed to move on. He reached for his coat behind him and shrugged into it, another paper falling out of the pocket.

Cursing, he reached for it, but someone else picked it up first. He straightened and smiled into the face of the proprietor, St. John, as he unfolded it and stared at the drawing.

"Friend of yours?" St. John asked as he turned it for Hunter to see.

It was one of the copies of Allred's likeness, and Hunter shrugged. "Somebody I was trying to find a few days ago."

"He was here a few weeks back."

Hunter paused in the action of straightening his coat. "Get a name?" he asked carefully.

"Smith," St. John replied with a snort, rolling his eyes. "Clearly not his real name. He was with the ginger lad who swept me of three hundred two weeks later. Intense conversation they had, asked for my best whiskey. Then they were at hazard the rest of the night, and both did well. Haven't seen Smith again, but obviously, we've seen the other."

Allred knew Martin? That wasn't at all what Hunter had expected, and certainly not what he wanted to hear.

He forced his expression to be fairly easy and nonchalant in spite of his tightening chest. "Well, I'm still looking for him, so if you see Smith back here, let me know. I presume you know how to find me."

St. John nodded and handed the picture back. "Sure do. Good night, Jones."

Hunter tapped the brim of his cap and headed for the door, pausing just outside to pull out a cigar and chat with Skips. "Seen anything good?"

"Naw," he replied, spitting to one side. "Got sommat for you though. Word just came to me. Dawn, whatever that means."

The cigar dropped to the floor and Hunter looked at Skips with wide eyes, his extremities going cold. "What did you say?"

Skips raised a brow. "Dawn. One of Gent's brats said so."

Hunter cursed and strode for the door. "Round 'em up, Skips. Send them to the old place."

"Aye, sir," he called after him, though Hunter didn't care.

Lucy was in trouble. Everything else could burn in the hedgerow, including Martin. And he was not about to run to Camden Town from where he was.

He whistled at an approaching hack, the driver seeming irritated to be called upon. "Get me to Camden Town as fast as you can, and

I'll pay you double the usual."

That brightened the driver considerably, and he snapped the reins before Hunter had even sat down.

His heart was pounding furiously against every single rib, and a burning sensation was invading his face and his legs. What sort of danger was he running into? What did Lucy need? What resources would he need to call upon?

Had he been too hasty to ask Skips to call the League up to meet him?

No, he assured himself. No, if Allred knew Martin, then even if Lucy's need was manageable, there was at least something to investigate.

But he had this horrible, sinking feeling that Pond wouldn't have called for him unless things were dire.

The driver was clearly taking Hunter at his word, for Camden Town was upon them quickly, and Hunter told him the address, arriving there only moments later. He jumped from the hack before it came to a full stop and thrust several coins at him, grateful he'd won a little at the tables that night.

Then Hunter headed directly for the door and pounded furiously. It opened at once and Pond stood there, his expression gaunt.

"What happened?" Hunter demanded.

Pond stood back. "You'd better come inside, sir."

Dread licked at Hunter's feet as he did so, walking into the threadbare sitting room just to the left. A balding man sat in a chair before the fire, his head in his hands.

Hunter looked back at Pond, who cleared his throat. "Sir, this is Trick. He helped your daughter after... he returned her home, sir."

Mr. Allred's head rose, and he turned to look at Hunter, the present lines in his face making him seem older than he really was. "So. You're the reason this plan has gone to hell."

"I beg your pardon, sir?" Hunter asked, not bothering to hide his ire.

Mr. Allred waved his hand, gesturing for him to come farther into the room. "I've sold my soul, and the devil has collected. If you hadn't intervened, it might have worked, but you're clearly a good sort, so why should you be blamed?"

Hunter stared at the man, then glanced back at Pond, who only shook his head. Curious and fighting anger, Hunter moved to sit on the chair nearest Allred. "Tell me from the beginning, sir, and tell me what has happened to Lucy."

Allred began to speak, his voice hollow and hoarse. "I have debts that cannot be easily resolved. Years worth. And I get myself deeper and deeper into it. I knew I needed to reduce expenditures, and a man approached me after a poor night at the tables. He offered me this house in Camden Town for retrenchment and said he could help me to regain my footing, for a price."

"Always for a price," Hunter muttered.

"The price," Allred went on, "was my daughter. Not in a salacious manner, I am not so villainous. If I would live in this house, if I would do what they ask, my debts would be paid by an anonymous benefactor, and my daughter would be engaged to a Mr. Bichard. Half-English, half-French, very wealthy, and looking to appear in London Society soon. It was so easy, what could be the problem?"

Hunter narrowed his eyes. "But?"

Allred closed his eyes. "But… I knew Lucy would not wish to marry a man against her will, and my reputation as a wastrel is well known. So my task was to arrange for an abduction. I would appear to pay a ransom, proving my daughter is more valuable than my gaming, and I would once more be respectable. Then Mr. Bichard would appear to be the man who had provided the assistance whereby my daughter was saved, and the marriage would make sense to all. Even to Lucy."

That wouldn't have worked for Lucy, Hunter considered with a soft snort. Just because someone did something noble did not mean…

But that was precisely how Hunter had met her. He had done something noble, and they had spent three days together and fallen in love. There was no telling if Bichard would have held any sort of sway over her, if he had any charm or redeemable qualities, but if he was part of the Faction, which was what it sounded like…

Could Lucy have loved that man the way Hunter hoped she loved him?

"So when I foiled your attempt…?" he pressed.

"Well, I did not know you had, at first," Allred admitted. "When Lucy did not arrive here, I presumed all had gone off well. But then I had no word of her from the abductors, no contact telling me to move forward with the next phase of the plan. I went out to the clubs to try and meet with my contact, but no one ever appeared, and no word of Lucy ever reached me. I dared not involve Bow Street, considering my own involvement, and with what was at stake… but then word reached me that they did not have her, and the next morning she arrived at my door."

Hunter sat back, shaking his head. "So you arranged for another go."

"No!" Allred protested loudly, his voice cracking. "No, I was told that because I had failed, they would be taking matters into their own hands. I have no idea who has taken Lucy or where they have gone. I don't know if I will be getting the prearranged instructions from the last plan or if I have been completely cut out. I don't know if my debts will be repaid in full, or only the ones they've already matched in good faith. They might ruin me as well as make off with my daughter, and I don't know what to do anymore."

"It sounds as though you didn't know what to do in the first place," Hunter suggested darkly. "To use your daughter as a pawn in your own financial redemption? You have no idea how I debated not returning Lucy to you, even without knowing that much. I knew you had no care or concern for her as a father ought, but I had no idea your disgusting indifference extended this far."

Allred shoved to his feet. "I care for my daughter!" he roared.

Hunter slowly rose, towering over the man and looking down at him coldly. "Do you? We searched for you for three days, and no one had ever heard of you. No one was looking for Lucy. She was in the worst possible parts of London, and you weren't looking."

Allred blanched. "I told you why—"

"You gave me an excuse," Hunter interrupted harshly. "A real father would have torn London apart for his daughter. But then, a real father wouldn't have put her in that position, would he?" Making a sound of disgust, Hunter strode away. "I will find your daughter, Mr. Allred, and then you and I are going to talk about her future."

"You think you can tell me what to do with my daughter?" Allred called after him.

Hunter stopped and looked over his shoulder at him. "No, sir. I think your daughter will choose her future, and you and I will decide how we make that happen." He looked at Pond and gestured for him to follow. "Tell me what we know."

Pond gave him all the details he could about Lucy's abduction, which wasn't much, other than that the men knew the house and the exits. Once Hunter stepped outside, a boy of perhaps twelve was waiting for him.

"And what did you see?" Hunter asked the boy, nodding in the direction they would be walking.

"Two men had the lady bound by hands and feet, gagged," he immediately replied. "They tossed her in the back of a wagon, strapped down the canvas might tight, and went out onto the high street. I tracked 'em as far as I could, 'til they went across the river."

Hunter nodded and handed three coins to the boy. "Many thanks."

"Once you cross the river," the boy went on, surprising him, "ask for Charlie. He watches the bridges sometimes."

"Again, thank you." Hunter winked and gestured for him to leave, which he did, scampering the way boys of the street always seemed to, no matter the time of night.

Hunter's mind spun on the details he had learned, and he forced the emotion of Allred's revelations to the back of his mind. He could not go into this rescue mission with emotion at the forefront if he wanted to do it right. His biggest consolation was that it did not seem as though the Faction would want Lucy harmed. They wanted her connection to a desperate man for whomever Bichard was, if that was his true name.

Also to their advantage, they did not know that Lucy had connections in the covert-operative world, and that one of them in particular was rather passionate about her safety and security. Not to mention her marital state.

But that was slightly beside the point.

Slightly.

Hunter rounded a corner and reached the site of the old London

League office, only to find the entire League waiting for him already. Even Cap had shown up, and he was usually more of an administrator these days.

"Skips is getting better than I thought," Hunter mused as he approached, shaking hands with all of them.

Gent grinned at him. "I may have intercepted my eyes on his way to report. Did my own gathering, spread the word, the usual."

"So, all of London knows now," Rogue assured Hunter in his usual rough manner, though his eyes glinted.

Hunter shook his head, exhaling. "Thank you. All of you. Normally, I don't call upon anyone else for anything, but this…"

"We'll fight for Dawn," Trace assured him, crooked smile in place. "Nice code, by the way."

"Why are you being the cheeky one?" Rook demanded, whacking Trace on the arm. "That is literally my one job in this group."

Cap looked heavenward, shaking his head. "Why did I pair them together?"

"We tried to warn you," Rogue and Gent said in unison.

Hunter chuckled and put his hands on his hips. "So, here's what I know." He gave them the quick rundown of Allred's part in the plot, which elicited some colorful responses from the men, and about what Gent's child spy had told him.

"I took the liberty of sending one of my contacts to Briar," Trace told him when he finished. "Gent mentioned across the river, so I thought we'd get ahead of it."

"And one of my other children is looking for Charlie," Gent added quickly. "He's not one of mine, he's in with Iris."

Hunter made a face. Iris was far more prickly than her name, which made him wonder why Iris was Iris and Briar was Briar, but he wasn't about to argue the names of the Convent agents. "Lovely. Think she'll share?"

"Damsel in distress? Oh, she'll share." Gent laughed once. "If we don't get going, she might go on in there herself. And you know Iris, she doesn't leave witnesses or take prisoners."

"Yeesh." Rook made a face. "We'd better go, then."

The group of them quietly made their way towards the river and the bridges there, and Rook sidled up to Hunter as they walked. "You know, we did something like this for Trace."

Hunter found himself smiling a little. "I heard about that. Sounded like fun."

"Oh, it was," Rook answered with a dark chuckle. "I spoke to my brother yesterday."

"Any news from his quarter?" Hunter asked with mild interest.

Rook cursed again. "I knew it. I knew they told you first."

Hunter patted his arm soothingly. "She's my twin, Rook. That trumps brothers."

"Helen will have my head for letting her hear about it through a letter, but I don't know when I'm going to get up there." He sighed, and Hunter glanced at him, seeing the strain in the usually jaunty man's face.

"Hiding not going well?" Hunter asked.

Rook made a face. "No, it's going fine. I just hate it. She hasn't been there long, but it feels like ages. And who knows how long it'll be? The sooner we secure the League and the leaks, the sooner we can all live relatively normal lives again."

Hunter thought on that a moment, then asked, "Is it worth the complication? The marriage while being an operative, I mean."

"If you do it correctly, I suppose." Rook smiled a little. "My wife is a trifle insistent on some things, and I just cannot tell her everything, but that's the only frustration we face. And there is a certain sweetness in our time together when we know that it can be snatched away at any moment. I won't pretend it isn't easier to be unattached as an operative, but once Helen crossed my path, I couldn't be the operative I was without her in my life. I wasn't the same man anymore, and the man I had become needed her."

"Incoming," Cap murmured from the back, silencing the entire group.

They were nearing the end of the bridge, and a dark figure was approaching, fully cloaked, and a few others stood at the base of the bridge, apparently waiting.

The figure drew back the hood, and a collective groan rose from the group.

"Iris," Rook whined, not bothering to hide the plaintive note in his voice. "We've got this!"

Iris, perhaps forty years of age, with wild, dark curls that never managed to be confined, skewered Rook with a superior look. "One of the Convent teachers is taken, and you think this is something for you to handle?"

Rook pointed at Hunter. "He was the one who was suspicious of her home. His claim!"

"Our school." She quirked a brow, daring another response.

Cap heaved a sigh. "We'll work together and get this done quickly and with the least amount of fuss."

Rogue snorted softly. "We're going to overrun them."

Iris grinned in a rather menacing manner. "And the problem there is?"

Hunter found himself smiling at her in response. "It's been a long time, Iris. I've always enjoyed your enthusiasm."

"Nice to see you too, Trick," she replied with a nod. "Shall we?"

They all moved to join her group of Convent agents waiting at the base of the bridge and began plotting together. From what Iris and Briar had put together, Lucy had been taken to a small warehouse on a quieter dock, and only three figures had entered since those from the wagon had arrived. According to reports, this was not a regular warehouse used by their contacts for deliveries, and thus did not contain the usual stock of brandy or weapons and the like.

Minimal items within meant not a lot of cover for them, which could be a problem if they needed to ambush the group.

"What is this dock used for if not their usual drops?" Hunter asked Briar as she crouched beside him at the next dock over.

"Normally, it ferries between Brittany and the Channel Islands," she told him with a thoughtful expression. "Next ship is due in the morning, but what in the world would they be wanting with that?"

Hunter suddenly glared at the building, something feral snarling to life within him. "They're planning on marrying her off to one of theirs who wants an entrance into Society."

"They're doing what?" at least three people asked, both men and women.

Hunter nodded. "They're going ahead with the plan and cutting Allred out of it. He was desperate enough to give them Lucy before, but he was just a complication to them, so now they've taken it into their own hands. Lucy's family name is respectable enough, but she has no fortune. Bichard apparently has plenty of money but needs a ticket into Society. Lucy's beauty and respectability provide exactly what he needs. What they need."

"They wanted my wife for her money," Gent pointed out from his place against the wall. "Now they have money and want connection. What are they playing at?"

"Why don't we analyze later and get our girl out now, eh?" Trace asked, fingering the knives at his belt.

Hunter nodded in agreement. "As soon as Fern gets back with her perimeter report."

It was only a few minutes more before Fern reappeared, her dark clothing and cape rendering her practically invisible in the night. She crouched down and dropped her hood, grinning widely.

"What?" Rook asked warily, rearing back just a touch.

"Clearly, they don't think Dawn will be missed," Fern told them, almost gushing with pride. She tucked a tendril of auburn hair behind her ear. "There is nothing resembling guards or defenses. Not a lick. No guns, no watch, nothing. Two, perhaps three guards within, but nothing without."

Rook blinked and looked at Hunter in disappointment. "This is going to be the most boring rescue I have ever been part of."

Hunter gave him a sardonic look. "Terribly sorry, old sport. Would you like to go home?"

"No, no, I'm just readjusting my expectations," he retorted. "Give me a moment." He closed his eyes as though actively rearranging some furniture in his mind.

Hunter blinked and looked beyond him to Trace, who rolled his eyes. "He does this," Trace told him in a stage whisper. "It's fine."

"Having a thought," Iris offered from Hunter's left, ignoring Rook's bizarre behavior. "What if the League takes the west door and we take the east? Trick, you're still our deepest cover, so let us be the faces. You can come in after and get Dawn, but let's keep you secret as long as possible."

That wasn't exactly what Hunter wanted to hear. He wanted to barge in and take out as many people as he possibly could. He wanted to rage and roar and show these blackguards what he was capable of for stealing his woman. It was his honor to do so, and a matter of personal duty.

But for his professional duty… and to protect Lucy even further…

Yes, it might make the most sense for others to lead the charge and for him to take care of the most precious portion of the mission.

"I can support that," Cap murmured from his place near Gent. "And I believe the Shopkeepers would appreciate that discretion."

Resigned, Hunter nodded and bit back a snarl of his own disappointment. Then he found himself looking at Rook, whose smirk was smug enough to say all that needed to be said.

"Right, then," Trace said, rubbing his hands together. "Shall we make this prompt and move in at the stroke of one?"

Iris nodded and started backing away with her crew. "Perfect. Taking prisoners?"

"Please," Cap affirmed with pristine politeness. "Any information is useful at this point."

"More's the pity, but as you wish." Iris nodded once and whistled, her small but mighty band following her into the night, heading for the eastern side of the building.

The men looked at Cap, who was eyeing the building. "Trace and Rogue, lead the charge. Rook and Gent, follow behind and take care of accessories. Trick, I'll accompany you and cover whatever is needed to get you and Dawn out of the building while they are occupied. If Iris wants to take the prisoners in, let her. If she prefers us, fine."

He looked at Hunter then, every inch the military man he had once been. "Where do you want to take Dawn after this? Her home?"

"Hell no," Hunter spat. "I need a more secure location. Hal's, I think."

All of them grinned at that. "Excellent," Rook chuckled, nodding in approval.

"We'll meet there to debrief," Cap told them. "Gent, can one of your children get word to Hal and let her know we're coming?"

Gent nodded once before whistling. A young lad appeared seemingly out of nowhere. "Charlie," Gent greeted. "Can you cross over and tell Paul to go to Sketch and make a point?"

Charlie nodded but held out a hand expectantly.

Sighing, Gent reached into his pocket and dropped two coins in his palm. "Thank you."

Charlie dashed off at once, making almost no noise as he did so.

"Oh, the inconvenience of the south side of the Thames," Rogue teased with a snort.

Gent ignored him and looked at Cap, waiting for the next orders.

Cap nodded once. "Let's go."

Chapter Twenty-Five

The burst of sound in the silent warehouse was not something that any of them within were expecting, and Lucy jolted upright from her laying position on the floor. She hadn't been pretending to sleep for some time, but there hadn't seemed any point in sitting with her hands and legs bound as they had been. No one had been speaking with her or to her since her arrival, and there were only four or five men in the building at any time.

She might as well have been part of the furnishings of the place, except it was clear she was part of something larger. It was simply not happening yet.

But this…

Whirling creatures with knives came in through the east doors while charging men exploded in from the west, taking the few men in the building completely by surprise. Two of the guards immediately started towards Lucy, but the four men had them surrounded in short order, and guns were dropped to the floor. Soon it became clear that the creatures from the east were not creatures at all, but women, who looked dangerous beyond belief and had the other two men against a wall and deprived of weapons.

No one else was left in the warehouse to resist them, which made Lucy frown.

There had definitely been five men the last time she'd looked, and the one who was not here now had been the least imposing by appearance, but the one the others had deferred to.

"So we meet again," a warm, familiar voice said close to her as the gag around her mouth was released. "I didn't even have to threaten anyone this time."

Gasping, Lucy whirled and beamed into Hunter's grinning face. "Hunter!" she cried, her voice hoarse. "But how did you…?"

He leaned in and kissed her quickly, turning her unfinished question into a hum of relief and delight. "I didn't trust your father," he said simply as he slashed through the linen at her hands and feet. "I had someone watching the house and told Pond… Anyway, when you were taken, I was notified. So here we are."

"Who's we?" she asked as she began rubbing her wrists.

"You don't recognize a few faces?" Hunter pointed at a tall, dark-haired man, who was watching them and smiled when Lucy looked at him.

"Trace," she breathed, returning his smile. Again, he had done something for Hunter on a moment's notice. That spoke to the man's honor and integrity as much as Hunter's.

"And over at the wall…" Hunter whistled and one of the women looked over, waving with a quick grin at Lucy.

Lucy sighed and shook her head, smiling still. "Briar. How in the world did you manage this?"

"To be fair," Hunter said as he leaned back, putting his arms around Lucy and lifting her up into them, "I only managed Trace's bunch. The ladies had their own ideas when they heard about you, so we decided to share the efforts. I think it worked out fairly well, don't you?" He winked and turned, starting for the nearest door. "Anything you need to say to your new friends here?"

Lucy shook her head, looping her arms around Hunter's neck and leaning into him. "No. They barely said a word to me anyway. They only spoke with the other one. He must have slipped out when they came in."

"There was another?" A man she hadn't noticed before was walking beside Hunter and now looked around him to inquire. He was tall as well, golden haired, and full of some unspoken authority even she could recognize.

"Yes," she said at once. "He was not a very intimidating a figure, but he was clearly in charge. Lanky fellow, ginger haired, and I think they called him Key."

Hunter stopped in place and stared at the other man for a long moment.

"Can you get there alone?" the man asked Hunter in a low voice.

"Yes," Hunter assured him. "Find him."

The other nodded and turned back. "Rogue, Trace, with me. You two, secure the prisoners with the agents."

Hunter began to walk away from them all, but Lucy looked over his shoulder at them, curious about the now hurried conversation in lowered tones. She ducked her head as they exited the warehouse, though it really wasn't necessary, and gave Hunter a strange look.

"You don't need to be part of what they're doing?"

He shook his head. "I do not."

"It sounds important," she pressed.

"It is," came his simple response. "Which is why they are going to take care of it."

Lucy frowned at that and laid her head against his shoulder. "You feel like you need to take me home because of our connection and leave them to do the ugly work. But really, Hunter, you could trust anyone to take me home. I know you'd rather be part of what they're doing instead of—"

Hunter stopped again, his eyes searching hers. "Let me make something very clear to you, Miss Lucy Allred," he told her, his voice no more than a growl. "The only thing I want to do right now is get you out of here and to a place of safety. I don't care what they do back there, important though it is. The most important thing to me, right now and ever, is you. So I would rather be taking you away from danger than leaving you to someone else and throwing myself into it. Is that clear?"

Lucy could only gape at him, her heart weakly bouncing off of ribs and various breathing apparatuses within her, creating a cacophony of sensations that made her head swim.

"Well?" Hunter asked, clearly expecting a response.

Steeling herself, taking that shred of hope from before in both hands, Lucy swallowed. "I love you too," she whispered.

Hunter's eyes widened, and then he was kissing her again, fiercely and with a hunger that had clawed at her ever since they had parted. "You heard me," he rasped against her mouth.

She nodded, clinging to the back of his neck, brushing her nose against his. "I was half-asleep, but I heard. And I cannot tell you how many times I've replayed it in my mind these last few days."

Hunter groaned and kissed her again, starting to walk once more. "Me too. And just for clarity, while we're both fully aware and in possession of our faculties—I love you, Lucy."

She sighed and rested her face against his neck. "It sounded even better that time."

"I hope it will sound better every time I say it." Hunter chuckled and held her closer. "Provided you wish to give me the opportunity to do so."

"You can say it whenever you like," she quipped. "No one else is, and I only want to hear it from you."

Hunter groaned a little, pressing his lips to her brow as he cradled her, starting over the bridge now. "Escorting you to safety while we have this conversation is one of the more challenging experiences of my life."

Lucy snorted into his shoulder. "I am sure we can find a way to make things easier on you eventually."

"Tell me about life at your father's house," Hunter suggested. "Tell me what I don't know."

Curious at his interest, Lucy thought back. "I've decided to tell my father that I am going back to the school right after Christmas. We have spent no time together since being reunited, and he has shown no interest in my presence whatsoever. Why should I let him continue to control my life when I am clearly in my majority, and he has no care for anyone but himself? I would appreciate the distance, if he insists on cutting me off, and there is no dowry to speak of, so what hold does he have over me anyway? The whole thing is utterly ridiculous, and I would have been better served to stay at the school for the holidays."

She was rambling again, she could hear it through her own ears this time, but Hunter was only smiling.

"What?" she asked when he seemed to be laughing to himself. "My rambling?"

"No, not at all," he answered with a chuckle. "I love your rambling. I just find it amusing that you think you would have been better served staying at the school. Had you done that, we would never have met."

Now that was a harrowing thought. Lucy stared at him, even while his attention was fixed straight ahead of them. What if she had never met Hunter? What if she had never known that this sort of love existed? What if…?

"Would it entirely inconvenience your life to marry me?" Lucy asked in a rush, suddenly terrified this could all be taken away from her yet again.

Hunter's smile was so swift and so bright, she was half convinced it was dawn. "No, not entirely," he teased. "I believe something could be arranged, if that is what you'd like."

She exhaled with so much relief, she fully sagged in his hold. "I would like," she insisted. "If you would like."

The hand at her back pressed her closer, and he kissed her again, this time long and lingering and thorough. When she was breathless and delirious, he pulled back, somehow still walking.

"I would like," he breathed, his stubble creating delicious friction against her cheek. "Thank you for asking."

Lucy snorted a laugh and covered her mouth, now leaning back in his hold. Hunter laughed as well, winking at her and striding with a touch more pride, if she did say so herself.

He was surely going to get tired of holding her, if they were walking all the way back to her father's house. He was a strong man, there was no question, but the distance with her as an added burden…

Lucy sobered a little, even as her heart soared with the prospects ahead of her. "Do you know why I was taken? The first time and this time?"

Hunter grimaced a little, then nodded. "I do. How much do you want to know?"

"Everything," she said at once. "I want to know everything."

With that, Hunter launched into the explanation of everything her father had done and been a part of. It ought to have shocked her, but, sadly, none of it did. Of course her father had used her as a pawn in his attempts to recoup his losses and regain some sort of perceived respectability, at least for himself. Lucy had only ever been some sort of tool or asset in his arsenal of life. The only real question she had was if he was in any way genuinely concerned for her during this actual abduction, or if he was more concerned about the loss of his particular benefits from the arrangement.

"I'm sorry," Hunter sighed as he finished. "I really had hoped…"

"Don't be," Lucy told him, patting his chest. "I stopped hoping where my father was concerned a long time ago. It will be a pleasure to never have to return to his house. When can we marry?"

Hunter hadn't laughed at her question, which had been her whole aim.

She gave him a cautious look. "Hunter?"

"I need to tell you something, my love," he murmured, keeping his voice very low. "The answer to the question you haven't been able to ask me yet." He inhaled a little, then released the breath in a short burst. "I'm a spy. An operative for the Crown."

Lucy blinked at the revelation. "Well… that certainly makes more sense than anything I was conjuring up in my mind."

Hunter paused a step, laughter erupting from him again. "That is all you have to say?"

"What else would you like me to say?" she retorted defensively, but grinning. "Your sister told me your life was all about duty and that it was dangerous, and you cannot imagine what I've tried to create as an explanation for that. I must say, I am quite impressed. And incredibly proud of you. So have you done this ever since you disappeared from Society? I presume you truly are the heir to a viscountcy, which my father will adore, unfortunately, but how can they let an heir to a peerage risk himself in such a way? Is that not rather reckless of them? Or do you have confidence in the next heir to—what are you laughing about now?"

Hunter had been positively shaking from laughter as they walked, and Lucy wondered if he would need to put her down.

But he only adjusted his hold on her and gave her the most adoring look that had ever been given through peals of laughter. "You, my love. I am blatantly and totally laughing about you."

There arose an immediate argument of banter between them, right up until they arrived, not at her father's residence, but at Hal and John's house. Hunter approached, and the door swung open before he could even knock.

Thad was there and said nothing as he stepped back, letting them in.

"We're expected?" Lucy murmured for Hunter alone as they moved to the nearest sitting room.

He nodded, all seriousness now. "We had word sent. I wasn't going to take you to your father's house after what you've been through there. This is much safer." He set her down on a chaise and took the seat beside her, taking her hand in his.

Hal and John entered a few moments later, both dressed simply, Hal's long hair plaited over one shoulder, and John in his dressing gown. Hal came to Lucy at once and kissed her cheek before taking a seat at the foot of the chaise.

Then a new figure entered the room, this one making Hunter stand from his chair. "Weaver."

Weaver, whomever he was, was tall, dark, and as imposing a figure as Lucy had ever seen without looking like a criminal. He bore all the regal airs of a duke, with all the energy Hunter's street persona exuded, and was clearly not a man to be trifled with.

He silently acknowledged each of them in turn, then set his eyes on Lucy. He came towards her and bowed politely. "Miss Allred, I am delighted to see you well and unharmed. I have Thad bringing you some sustenance shortly, and I recommend you have a thimble of brandy as well as some Madeira. You don't seem to need calming, but take it from me, it can be a trifle delayed."

Lucy nodded hastily, ready to accept any instruction or insight from this man that he felt necessary.

He nodded and gestured for Hunter to come with him. Hunter kissed Lucy's hand, then followed, the pair of them moving to the corner of the room.

Lucy strained to hear with all of her might, and found her efforts rewarded, but it was only a summary of what had taken place in the warehouse, along with what Hunter had told her about her father's involvement. Weaver did a great deal of nodding and not much conversing, but then he clapped Hunter on the back and left the room.

Hunter returned to his seat beside Lucy and took up her hand once more.

"Is he in charge of everything?" she whispered to him.

"Not everything, but close." Hunter smiled rather flatly. "He's also Henrietta's godfather."

Lucy looked at Hal in surprise, and Hal's smile rather resembled her brother's. "For my sins. Or his." Hal exhaled slowly, sputtering. "I hate waiting."

"Easy, Ange," John murmured, putting a hand on his wife's knee. "It will be soon enough."

"What will be?" Lucy whispered to Hunter, confused.

"Debrief," Hunter told her, rubbing her hand. "As soon as the others get here." He looked across her at his sister. "Did you send word to Lucy's father?"

Hal nodded once. "He should know by now. If it matters." She snarled softly, making Hunter chortle.

"Down, girl," he teased.

"You should talk."

"I am in control."

"Says the man who came here instead of there."

"Oh, why don't you—"

The bickering siblings went silent as the door to the house opened again, and the trickle of men from the warehouse entered one by one, including Weaver.

Thad followed with the promised tray of food for Lucy, brandy and Madeira to one side. He set it down on the table before her and nodded once before going to stand by the door, his back to it. As though he anticipated a barrage of attack in response to what had taken place.

"Prisoners secure," the blond man from before told Weaver. "Iris has them. Martin was apparently there but slipped out with our entrance. We did a search of the area and found nothing. No sign of him."

Weaver nodded once, then pursed his lips. "I think it would be best if Miss Allred went to bed."

Lucy blinked and looked around, wondering how she had been thrust into this conversation. "I what?" she asked softly.

"She stays," Hunter said firmly. "She may not know everything, but she's been put in the middle against her will for far too long. She can hear everything."

Lucy squeezed his hand hard, thanking him and confessing her love in one grip.

Weaver stared at Hunter for a long moment, then nodded before giving the entire group a shrewd look. "He was there," Weaver ground out. "He was there, and you let him slip away?" He rounded on Hunter in particular. "You had one assignment, Trick. One. We trusted you with one assignment, and the moment you have the opportunity to achieve it—"

"How was he supposed to know Martin would be there?" Trace retorted defensively. "We were just after Dawn, nobody knew he was involved!"

"You're always telling us to value innocent life," the curly-haired man added in a rougher voice. "Should we have ignored her?"

Weaver shook his head. "If you had entered with more care, if you had surveyed with caution…"

Another dark-haired man began nodding sagely. "Oh, so the man should have waited to pay any attention to Dawn until we were positive no traitors were about. Particularly the traitor that only he has even come close to nabbing? Leave the woman he loves on the floor and in danger?"

A sandy-haired man who looked a trifle like John shook his head. "Pot, kettle. Kettle, pot."

Everyone in the room looked at him in surprise. Lucy wasn't certain why anyone else was, but she was exceptionally curious as to his reference.

He returned everybody's looks with outright bewilderment. "Come on… am I the only one who read the reports on this man when he was Fox?" He pointed at Weaver, and Weaver's eyes went wide.

"That's a top-secret ledger," he said in a low voice.

The sandy-haired man sniffed once. "I know that. Now." But then he took on a daring look and remained silent.

Weaver exhaled very slowly. "Fine. I take back my recriminations. No one could have foreseen this. Trick, take care of the complications quickly, and write up a report as soon as possible. We need to try and intercede in this plan before someone else is subjected to what Dawn has endured." He rubbed a hand over his hair and turned from the room, leaving them all to mull over the events of the evening on their own.

The sandy-haired man cleared his throat. "Complications?"

Hunter rolled his eyes, surprising Lucy. "Her father, Rook. His involvement. And Dawn—sorry, Lucy's—available hand."

"Not that available," she reminded him. "You did agree."

Hal snorted a laugh, quickly clamping a hand over her mouth. Rook grinned at that and gave Lucy a rather grand nod of his chin, for whatever reason.

"That's true," Hunter mused, winking at her. "If Weaver thinks we need to make haste, perhaps a special license is in our future."

"Can Mr. Mortimer return to Society so easily?" John asked him. "Your reputation was rather in tatters when you left, even if you have, as they believe, spent time on the Continent rehabilitating yourself."

They all went quiet to think on that a moment.

"What about a duel?" the curly-haired one suggested. "Not a real one but staged. Between Mr. Allred and Mr. Mortimer. After Mr. Mortimer is slightly wounded, he agrees to the marriage. Then it gradually becomes evident that Mr. Mortimer's wife is a delightful influence on him, and he becomes rather devoted to her."

Lucy looked at Hunter with some speculation, the wild desire to grin bubbling up inside of her. "Well? Am I destined to be a delightful influence?"

Hunter's eyes were lowered in thought, and then he straightened, turning to her, his smile rather sweet. "I believe you are. The trouble will be pretending not to love you from the start, but shooting at your father will help, even if I cannot succeed."

"I can be a rather quick influence," Lucy suggested, kissing his hand. "And I don't care if you shoot my father a little successfully, so long as we can send him to the Continent afterwards."

The entire room laughed at that, and Hunter rose, coming around to kiss her soundly. "Then let it be the plan, my love. It is high time I came out of the shadows and embraced your light."

Lucy smiled rather dreamily at him. "Don't leave the shadows entirely behind. I rather like being with you in them."

Hunter quirked his brows, his smile turning almost salacious.

"Well, well, well… from Dawn to Dusk, eh?"

A few of the men groaned at the bad joke, and even Hal made some comment or other about it, but Lucy paid none of them any mind as she pulled her intended in for another kiss, just to prove to him that the girl from the *cèilidh* in the streets was very much still here, and his for the taking.

Epilogue

"I don't like it."

"You aren't supposed to like it. No one is."

"No, I mean I really don't like it."

Hunter Mortimer groaned as he dropped himself into the chair beside his wife, extending his feet towards the warm fire. "Darling, I don't have any say in this. I am only telling you what I have been told. Pearl is going to meet Bichard under a guise that will not make her a candidate for marriage."

"Pearl," Lucy spat, "is in no condition to do anything. By your own account, she isn't even active anymore. It is too risky."

Hunter rolled his head to look at his wife in his full and complete fatigue. "I shouldn't have even told you about this. I've broken so many confidences already."

Lucy gave him a dark look. "Are you more concerned about the confidences to your associates or to your wife?"

A strange tingling started at the back of Hunter's ears as well as in his shoulders and the soles of his feet. He knew this feeling, and he knew it well.

He was walking into a trap.

"Trick question," he finally said, pointing at her and narrowing his eyes. "You are trying to draw a line and make me stand on either side, but I refuse to stoop to that level."

Lucy rolled her eyes and slumped in her chair moodily, reaching her fingers towards his and linking a few. "I don't want her hurt," she said softly.

"I know." Hunter rubbed her fingers gently, just the way she liked best. "She volunteered, my love. She believes she can do it, and I think we have to let her. And the only reason I know any of this is because of my previous assignment. I wouldn't even have an inkling if I were anyone else."

"Well, thank you for being you." She looked over at him finally, as beautiful at this time of night as she was in the glorious light of morning. "How do you enjoy the new assignment, Hunter? Truly."

He exhaled rather heavily, pursing his lips. "It's been a fortnight of being in the League, and I won't deny that it has taken some adjustment. You remember, I've been working alone for years and years. Never accountable to anyone, able to call upon my own resources, do as I judged best… I did not have a private life because I was so invested in the world I had delved into."

He wouldn't tell her how many fights he'd already had, mostly because it didn't matter, and they had resolved quickly enough. He missed being on his own entirely, and desperately so, but there was enough independence and autonomy in the London League to satisfy him there, and they only worked in pairs when it was required. As yet, it had not been required of him to work with anyone. So long as he remembered to write up the reports and inform Cap of what he was doing, all was well.

And having this joyous life with Lucy to come home to every night…

It was bliss that he could not have ever imagined himself enjoying.

And it was well worth the sacrifice of his career. After all, in most respects, he was doing exactly the same thing, just in a different way. A more creative way, his sister had suggested just a few weeks ago. It had taken little convincing of any of the powers that be to make this happen, and the objections over his change in position and status were minimal and fleeting.

All in all, there had been no downside, apart from not having an operative in the same sort of deep cover in those parts of London at all times. But between himself, Trace, Gent, and Rogue, they had a decent amount of coverage, and Martin did not know Hunter, so he was the smallest risk of compromise.

Which meant he was still working on uncovering Martin's trail and towards his capture.

But now he would not have to do so alone. He could call upon his new brothers-in-arms, and they would be there. Not only that, but their desire for vengeance upon the man they had trusted for so long was particularly useful fuel for him to feed on.

It was all going to work out very well, once they were adjusted to their new positions and roles.

And once he adjusted to having an actual home to return to.

"When do you need to be back at the school?" Hunter asked his wife as he continued to stroke her fingers.

"End of the week," she replied softly. "Miss Bradford has kindly let me remain here this long because of our wedding, but much longer…" She sighed and he could hear the tears in it. "Are you certain you want me to do this?"

Hunter sat up and turned more fully towards her, reaching for her other hand as well. "That is not the question I want you to ask, my love. Do you want to teach?"

With damp tears, she nodded, but then she tilted her head until it almost touched her shoulder. "But not at the expense of leaving you," she whispered.

He groaned and tugged on her hands, pulling her out of her chair and into his lap, wrapping his arms around her tightly. She tucked her head under his chin and pressed her lips to his throat as he stroked her hair.

"You are not leaving me," he told her, letting his fingers run through her long, dark tresses soothingly. "You are choosing to do something that makes you happy. And I want you to choose what makes you happy."

"You make me happy," she insisted, gripping his shirt in her hands.

Hunter smiled and kissed her hair twice. "And you make me happy, love. The happiest I could be, happier than I ever dreamed, happier than I deserve. But the two are not mutually exclusive. Miss Bradford has said we can live in the cottage on the school's estate when I can go there and will allow you the carriage to return to London when you like. She will work with you and create a flexible schedule that suits you."

"I don't want you to resent my being away," Lucy admitted against his chest. "I want to be here when you come home every day or from a mission. I want—"

"I am not going anywhere," Hunter overrode gently. He lifted her away from him just enough to see her face. "I am yours, Lucy Mortimer. We only have a few years at most before the viscountcy is ours, and then it will be impossible for you to teach. It will be hard enough for me to continue my work, but possible. So do what you want to do now, while you can, because I don't want you to be Lady Fordham and bemoan a life that was not lived."

Lucy bit her lip as she ran her fingers over his jaw. "And we'll make this work? We'll see each other often and be husband and wife, and you won't love me less for being away?"

Hunter kissed her then, his heart aching for her insecurities and her fears, for her belief that love was fleeting and connection temporary, and that she was not worth sacrifice. Or worthy of devotion.

She would learn, though. He would teach her over the years and years that they would spend together. The children that would eventually come, if they were so fortunate. The life that they would share together. He would teach her that she was worth everything he had to offer and more. That he would give her everything he could and more. That her happiness was his sole purpose in life.

That her love was the most precious thing he had.

She would learn. And one day, he hoped, she would believe.

"I love you," Hunter vowed when his lips parted from hers. He cupped her face in his hands and touched his brow to hers. "I love you, Lucy. I will never love you less than I do right now and am certain I will only love you more. Do you not know that my life is only worth really living now that you are in it? Do you not know how much I need you? Do you not understand that I would go to the ends of the earth and back again just to make sure you smile?"

"Hunter…" she breathed, brushing at his bottom lip with her thumb.

He kissed her thumb, then her lips again, tenderly this time. "I love you enough to want you to do exactly as you dream. To make a slight complication of schedule in part of our lives. To travel distances to see you and to make up for the kisses we've missed in between."

"But I love you enough to stay," Lucy told him. "If that is what you want."

They were always going to come back to this, Hunter realized. Which meant there was only one thing to do.

"What about this?" he began, settling his head next to hers as they stared into the fire. "We do this term with you teaching and my being here, just as is set for now. If either of us is truly miserable, then we will make adjustments and find another way to do this. We don't have to commit to a lifetime of our careers at this moment. We only have to decide that we want to continue our lives together, and finding the best way to do that is going to take time."

Lucy was nodding before he even finished. "Yes. Yes, I like that. We can find a way through all of this and decide on the life we want. So long as my life is with you, though, I will be happy."

"Your life will be with me, Mrs. Mortimer," Hunter reminded her, bouncing her on his lap a little. "That is already done. This is simply deciding on which happily ever after we like best."

"The part where you kiss me senseless and I fall asleep in your arms," Lucy said at once, her eyes going dark as obsidian as she inched her fingers back to his hair. "That's my favorite."

"Is it?" Hunter purred, twisting her hair around his fingers. "What a coincidence, I rather enjoy that one as well."

He drew her closer, his lips brushing against hers slowly, temptingly, the almost maddening way that he knew would drive her wild.

Lucy's breathing deepened and she gripped his face between her hands. "I still don't like Pearl going back into the field," she rasped as she caught his bottom lip on her own.

Hunter tightened his hold on his wife, grinning against her mouth. "I'll put in a complaint on your behalf, my love."

"When?" she breathed as her fingers rubbed against his scalp.

Losing himself rather rapidly to the bliss of his favorite happily ever after, Hunter ran his lips along the curve of his wife's jaw. "Tomorrow," he promised.

And the conversation ended there.

Coming Soon

Agents of the Convent
Book Five

"All that whispers might be gold..."

by

Rebecca Connolly

About the Author

Growing up, Rebecca Connolly wanted to be Elizabeth Bennett, Mary Poppins, or British royalty, so it came as a great shock when she discovered she was an American girl from the Midwest. She started making up stories when she was young, and thanks to a rampant imagination and a fairly consistent stream of hot chocolate, ice cream, and cookie dough, she's kept at it. She loves a good love story, and a good swoon, and tries to share that with her readers. She still lives in the Midwest, has two degrees in non-writing fields, and dreams of one day having a cottage of her own in her beloved British Isles.

Rebecca is a huge fan of period dramas and currently writes in the Regency era, though she refuses to rule any other time period out. You just never know where the imagination will take you, and she'll write whatever story comes to her whenever it's set! There is always a story to tell, and she wants to tell them all!

You can find out more at www.rebeccaconnolly.com.